He stayed close to her, side of the brick building as the words tumbled out of her mouth.

"I met him when we were both only fifteen. I barely saw him after we got married—he went to Ranger School and then he went off to save the world. *Leading the way,*" she said, unable to keep the sarcasm out of her voice as she used the Ranger creed.

There was none in his. "Not easy for a military wife."

"The military would've made me a widow by the time I was twenty-six anyway." She'd gotten notice of Aaron's death from the Army four years ago—gotten his personal effects, which included a key to a safe deposit box that contained the list of names, and Aaron's final words.

I'm sorry.

In her estimation, that wasn't nearly enough.

"How long have you had my name?" he asked finally.

"I didn't open the safe deposit box until two weeks ago—I didn't know he had a list in there." Her words came out nearly a whisper, but she felt as if she'd shouted them.

"And then you had your friend at the DoD tracking me to the ends of the earth."

She tilted her head to stare up at him. "Why are you such a hard man to find?"

He ignored her question and fired back his own. "Why did you wait four years to open that box? What changed two weeks ago?"

Would he believe her? She barely believed it herself, but she'd come too far to quit now. "I got a phone call from a dead man."

TOO HOT TO HOLD

STEPHANIE TYLER

A DELL BOOK

NEW YORK

Too Hot to Hold is a work of fiction. Names, characters, places, and incidents are the products of the author's imagination or are used fictitiously. Any resemblance to actual events, locales, or persons, living or dead, is entirely coincidental.

A Dell Mass Market Original

Copyright © 2009 by Stephanie Tyler

Published in the United States by Dell, an imprint of The Random House Publishing Group, a division of Random House, Inc., New York.

DELL is a registered trademark of Random House, Inc., and the colophon is a trademark of Random House, Inc.

ISBN 978-0-440-24435-6

Cover design: Lynn Andreozzi
Cover illustration: © Alan Ayers

Printed in the United States of America

www.bantamdell.com

2 4 6 8 9 7 5 3 1

For Zoo and Lily, always

ACKNOWLEDGMENTS

Writing a book is never a solitary process, and I have many people to thank for their enthusiasm and unyielding faith in me.

First and foremost, a special thanks to my editor, Shauna Summers, for her wonderful insights and guidance through this entire process.

Thanks to everyone at Bantam Dell who helped make this the best book possible, cover to cover—from Jessica Sebor, who always goes above and beyond to help, to the art department, who rock my world with their awesome covers; and to Pam Feinstein, for being such an amazing copy editor.

Special thanks to Boone Medlock and Bryan Estell, whose military insights and personal stories were invaluable.

Thanks to authors Lynn Viehl, aka PBW, and Holly Lisle, for giving so much of their time to mentor and share their own experiences with so many writers via their blogs. I can't tell you how much this helped me.

Finally, last but never least, thanks to my fellow authors whom I'm proud to call friends: Lara Adrian, Maya Banks, Jaci Burton, Alison Kent, Amy Knupp, and especially Larissa Ione, for all their support in ways too numerous to list.

CHAPTER
1

"That which does not kill us makes us stronger."
—Friedrich Nietzsche

The car wasn't moving fast enough. Eighty miles per hour would be fine for most men, but Nick Devane wasn't most men, and never would be if he had anything to say about it.

The midnight black Porsche Turbo shook when it reached 110 and skidded onto the curved expanse of highway on two wheels. His breath came in short gasps, heart slammed in his chest, fingers curved around the steering wheel. The rush spread through him like a fever until he was no longer thinking, the possibility of danger vibrating his soul, the catch in his throat urging him to push past the brink of fear.

Some people might say he hadn't changed a damned bit

from the wild kid he'd been. Built for speed and trouble, and his pulsing drive for adrenaline seemed to feed on itself, increasing exponentially through his early years and culminating with an outlet as a member of the elite Navy SEAL Teams.

It was a job he planned on keeping until they threw him out on his ass. A job he'd gotten because of his need for speed and trouble.

Hotwiring a judge's car and taking it for a joyride ten years ago might not have been the smartest idea, but Nick had to say it was the best thing he'd ever done.

Seventeen, cocky as hell and without a care in the world, he'd pushed the borrowed Porsche Carrera to the limit on that darkened stretch of highway along the Virginia–Maryland border, pushed it so hard the gears groaned and the chassis shook and he'd been sure the car would either explode or take flight off the pavement. At that point, he wouldn't have given a shit either way. If he'd had to make an honest assessment of himself as a disowned teenager of wealth and privilege, death would've been an easy option.

But it would've made things easier still for the man he refused to call *Father* anymore, and that special brand of screw-you Nick had been born with, and continued to reserve for authority, had been too deeply ingrained in him to quit anything. Especially living.

That night, he'd slowed the car, turned off the engine and rolled the sleek silver baby up the long driveway. He'd been prepared to leave it ridden hard and put away wet where the judge had parked it, no worse for wear—save the near-empty gas tank.

He'd never expected Her Honor, Kelly Cromwell, to be

standing there as though she had all the time and patience in the world. Which, he would discover later, she did.

"End of the line," he'd muttered to himself, had gotten out of the car and swaggered over to her, because he did not run.

Not anymore.

When given the choice between jail or the military, he'd chosen wisely.

Tonight, the black Porsche was his, but there was also somebody waiting for him when he slammed into the back lot of the diner and eased into the last available space.

No, nothing had changed inside of him. But on the outside, the façade, the carefully concealed past was a tightly woven secret that he refused to let unravel.

Which was exactly why he needed to meet Kaylee Smith and do what he'd promised six years ago to the man who saved his life.

Don't get yourself into trouble, his CO had warned earlier that evening. Nick had almost said, *Too late,* but figured the wiseass remark was better kept to himself.

A brutal, three-month mission overseas and the team's combined injuries—consisting of a bullet wound, two broken ribs and a broken nose, none of which were his—added to one week stateside, and a twenty-four-hour window of R&R practically screamed for a night out.

He had expected to get into trouble that evening—hadn't expected the trouble to actually find him.

When his CO put him in charge of the team's behavior, his enthusiasm lessened considerably, but didn't change his opinion that drinking, dancing and the loudest music known to man were still the night's best options. He'd planned on heading to the Underground, a place senior officers rarely frequented and where he could be semi-assured none of his team would get into a brawl. Although with most of the team in tow, including his two adopted brothers, the odds weren't on his side.

Trouble always comes in threes, Kenny Waldron, the only man Nick called *Dad* now, would always say when Nick, Jake and Chris were together in the same place.

Nick's plans had been altered when Max, a captain in Naval Intelligence, called with an urgent message.

Hey, Devane, someone's been running your name. What the fuck is that all about?

Max was the man who brought the teams home—all the SEALs owed him a hell of a lot, and somehow the chits seemed to come up in Max's favor even when the teams were on dry, safe land. Relatively speaking.

With Nick's blessing, Max had gotten in touch with the guy from the Department of Defense who'd initiated the search on Nick, put the fear of God into him and gave Nick the name and number of the woman who'd been hunting him.

Kaylee Smith.

Nick hadn't heard of her.

She's heard of you. Find out why and shut it down had been Max's final words.

He knew why now. Shutting it down was the final step.

Kaylee Smith had come to the diner early, to have dinner and to frame out some of the stories she had on deadline— a piece on a cache of weapons found at a women's shelter, and another piece where she'd gone for a ride-along with undercover policewomen. The investigations had been exciting—the writing not as much, although if she was in the right mood, she could get that partial sensation of still being in the moment.

Tonight, she couldn't get herself to that place. She hadn't eaten, was on her third cup of coffee as she tapped her pen restlessly and stared out the window that faced the back parking lot where she hoped Nick Devane would pull in. She wanted to see him before he saw her, to assess who was coming at her. To attempt to know her target on sight, since the only way she could identify him was by his voice.

"Who is this?" The voice on the other end of the line was a rough growl, had made her start initially.

"Who is this?" she asked back, even though she suspected exactly who it was, with a more than sinking pit in her stomach. Her search for Nick Devane had triggered something in the system, especially since she'd had a friend in the DoD search for his birth certificate. Her friend had come up empty.

According to the information Kaylee had, Devane was Special Ops. Navy SEAL. That was six years earlier—he could be discharged by now. Working for the CIA or FBI was a definite possibility for a man with his background.

Either way, he was a man who didn't want to be found.

He didn't answer her question—not fully. "You've been looking for me. I need to know why."

"Your name . . . it's on Aaron's list," she said quietly. There was silence on the other end, so long that she'd checked the display screen on her phone to make sure they were still connected. The call had registered as an unknown number on her cell phone's caller ID. Untraceable.

"You want to meet me," he said finally.

"I want to meet you," she agreed. "To talk about Aaron."

"City Diner, on Maple Street. Tonight, 2300."

Military time. He was still in. "I'll be there. Don't you want to know my name . . . or how to recognize me?" she asked before he could hang up.

"That won't be a problem."

What Nick didn't realize was that anything to do with Aaron was a problem—a large one that threatened her career, her past . . . her life.

Nick had known more than her phone number—he'd known what state she lived in. And he was coming to her.

"Honey, can I get you some more coffee?" The waitress didn't bother to wait for an answer before she topped off Kaylee's cup. And when she walked away, Kaylee noted that a black Porsche had pulled into the lot during that brief interruption, and the most handsome brick wall she'd ever seen in her life was standing directly in front of her.

She'd called Aaron's entire list, man by man. Each had come willingly to meet with her. Each of them told her that Aaron had been alive when they'd left him, that her ex-husband had saved their lives.

That Aaron had refused to answer questions as to whether or not he was affiliated with the U.S. military.

Nick was the last man on Aaron's list, and he was definitely not least. If she'd been writing an article about him, she could already picture the opening paragraph:

Every bit the warrior. Tall, broad shoulders, an aristocratic face—handsome . . . and it is as though Nick Devane should be modeling menswear instead of running around the world with weaponry.

But she knew differently. Underneath the calm, cool and collected man who stood before her was a hint of the fire inside he couldn't control. The heat in his belly that drove him to hit harder, fly higher, to risk his life for the sheer need of it.

It was something she both understood and hated. And right now, with Nick standing in front of her, she was convinced that she hated him as well.

For being on Aaron's list. For being a part of the same military that had taken so much from her.

For turning her world upside down in the space of mere seconds.

So yes, Nick was the last man on the list. The last one to see Aaron alive.

And maybe the one who knew how he died.

"You must be Nick." Her voice was thankfully calmer than she'd expected. He merely nodded in response.

The men she'd met over the past days had been succinct as well, but this man was a whole different animal. Taciturn. Not the buttoned-up type who called her *Ma'am* and expressed sincere apologies for her loss.

Yet, somehow, she had little doubt that whatever came out of his mouth would be sincere.

"Thank you for agreeing to meet with me. Please, have a seat." She motioned across the table to the empty half of the booth, a booth she'd picked specifically to watch both the entrance and the lot. A place where her back could stay against the wall—the first rule of combat in the world according to Aaron.

"Not here" was all he said before he turned and strolled out.

She had no choice but to follow. Hurriedly, she threw money on the table to cover her bill, then caught up with him halfway up the street.

He didn't turn to acknowledge her presence, had assumed that she'd follow him to wherever he was going.

And he'd been right.

Yes, he was definitely proving to be the most arrogant of the bunch.

"Aaron was your husband," he said once he finally stopped at the entrance of an alleyway between two buildings at the corner where the lamppost had blown out. Then he gazed at her and corrected himself. "Ex-husband."

She was going to have to give answers to get answers from this one. "Yes. He was my ex for a long time before he died."

"You were young."

"Too young," she agreed. "Just eighteen when we married." Aaron had been a way out. She hadn't known that she'd been running into more of what she'd left behind, after being deserted by her mother and left with a grandmother who neither wanted nor had any love for Kaylee.

Her life was so much different today. She'd molded herself into a cold, ruthless undercover reporter who was both respected and feared.

No guts, no glory.

No emotions, except when it came to Aaron. Her first love. Her first everything. And most of those emotions ran between nostalgia and hatred.

"I met him in Africa," Nick said finally. His rough voice shot up her spine like a direct caress, the way it had on the phone this afternoon. But it was so much better in person.

"I know. In the DRC—the Congo," she said. If he was surprised that she had that information, he didn't show it. She hadn't expected him to anyway, but just as she wondered if there was anything that could break through the façade, he swallowed hard, then rubbed the base of his throat with two fingers as he stared at the night sky as though reliving that time in Africa.

"Aaron saved my life."

"The list of men he left for me to find—he said that he'd saved all their lives. Except for you."

Nick looked at her with eyebrows raised, waiting. So patient, but somehow impatience radiated off him in waves.

"He said you would've done fine without his help," she finished. "Is that true?"

"You want me to use twenty-twenty hindsight on something that happened six years ago?" he asked, his voice tight. "Hell, I don't know how to answer that."

He stuck his hands in his pockets, the leather jacket flaring out to the side, and she half expected to see a gun holster.

"I tried to get him to come back with me, on the helo," he said. "He refused. He said that there wasn't a way back for him. And then he gave me this—told me to give it to his girl when she came looking for me."

She felt the tears jump to her eyes, hot and too fresh as Nick took a hand out of his pocket to place a worn circle patch, a gray background with a black symbol crudely sewn in, into her palm. "You've kept it all this time?"

"I always keep my word."

That was so much more than she could say about Aaron. "When you saw him last . . . I mean . . . how was he?"

Nick nodded as he spoke. "He was all right. I was the one who'd been shot."

"He was a good Ranger." She couldn't bring herself to say *man,* even though the military seemed to think the two terms were synonymous. She knew better.

"I believe you."

"How did he look?"

"I don't know what he looked like before. I have nothing to compare it to."

She pulled a picture out of her bag, the one of a non-smiling Aaron, fresh out of Ranger School and in full uniform. The day it had been taken, the moment, actually, she'd known it had been the beginning of the end for them.

Nick took the picture from her and stared at it. "That's him. His hair was longer. He had a beard and he looked like he'd been through hell."

He stayed close to her, both of them leaning against the side of the brick building as the words tumbled out of her mouth.

"I met him when we were both only fifteen. I barely saw him after we got married—he went to Ranger School and then he went off to save the world. *Leading the way,*" she said, unable to keep the sarcasm out of her voice as she used the Ranger creed.

There was none in his. "Not easy for a military wife."

"The military would've made me a widow by the time I was twenty-six anyway." She'd gotten notice of Aaron's death from the Army four years ago—gotten his personal effects, which included a key to a safe deposit box that contained the list of names, and Aaron's final words.

I'm sorry.

In her estimation, that wasn't nearly enough.

"How long have you had my name?" he asked finally.

"I didn't open the safe deposit box until two weeks ago—I didn't know he had a list in there." Her words came out nearly a whisper, but she felt as if she'd shouted them.

"And then you had your friend at the DoD tracking me to the ends of the earth."

She tilted her head to stare up at him. "Why are you such a hard man to find?"

He ignored her question and fired back his own. "Why did you wait four years to open that box? What changed two weeks ago?"

Would he believe her? She barely believed it herself, but she'd come too far to quit now. "I got a phone call from a dead man."

CHAPTER
2

Nick was doing a piss-poor job of shutting this one down, could just imagine the shit his brothers would give him if they knew where he was and what he was doing. Thankfully, he'd managed to slip out the back of the bar when they were both too distracted to notice.

They'd notice soon enough.

"Hold on a minute—you think Aaron called you? Dead Aaron?" he asked Kaylee.

"Yes. Maybe. And you can stop speaking to me like I'm crazy."

He let his eyes flicker over her—he had the advantage, was used to working in the dark even without the benefit of night vision goggles. She thought she was hidden, didn't realize how much her body language, her expressions, gave away.

Even now, she sucked her bottom lip lightly between her teeth—something she'd done often and well in the ten minutes he'd known her. It drove him crazy every time.

She was telling the goddamned truth, for sure, and he dragged a hand through his hair and wondered why he wasn't running for the escape hatch.

"What did he say?" he heard himself asking, against his better judgment.

"He said, *Happy birthday, Kaylee*. The line was all crackled—I asked him where he was and he didn't answer. And then he said, *I'm sorry, KK*." She paused. "He was the only one who ever called me KK. Always in private."

"It's a mistake. Someone playing a trick, a horrible trick, on you."

"I never saw a body, Nick. I didn't go to the funeral—I don't even know if he had one."

"What exactly did the Army say when they notified you?"

"They told me he was KIA," she explained. "The problem was, the list of names he left me was dated . . . the dates begin a year later than the Army claimed he died."

She might not have known that Aaron had gone over the hill, but how could the Army not have known? "Aaron was AWOL when he saved me."

She shook her head in complete disbelief. "No, not Aaron. The military was his life. He loved being a Ranger. Loved it more than anything else."

"Including you?"

"Yes, including me. To be fair, I didn't do much to try to keep him from that."

The way Kaylee looked should have been enough. She was all long-legged, hot as anything, with dark auburn hair, long and wavy and kind of wild, like the woman herself. He'd noted the black leather pants and vintage AC/DC T-shirt the second he'd laid eyes on her, and yes, Kaylee Smith might just be the most dangerous thing he'd run across on a non-mission basis. Part angel, part hellcat, and shit, it was not cool when he realized that one night wouldn't be enough time with her. Not even close.

She was trouble.

"I know what happened that night, on your mission," she told him. "Aaron wrote down more than your name. He's got a whole report. He called it a Situation Report."

Damn, that couldn't be good. What had Aaron been thinking, writing up a SITREP?

This had gone from being a favor for a dead man to something much different. "If you've got the whole story, why am I here?"

"For your side of things. I want to fill in the gaps, to know what Aaron really did for you. Please."

Whether or not Aaron had deserted, a plea from a widow couldn't be ignored. Nick could tell her the story without telling her the whole story.

There are such things as false truths and honest lies, his dad would say.

He shifted away from her and began to walk slowly toward a small playground beyond the apartment buildings—mostly grass, with a swing set in the middle of the area. And he laid down, flat on his back, arms folded behind his head, and stared up at the night sky and wondered why the hell all this chose to come down on him now, after all this time.

He closed his eyes and tried to recall his memories from that night, pulling it into sharp focus.

Six years ago, he'd been Petty Officer Third-Class Devane, twenty-one years old and on his first mission with his original SEAL team. And members of the militant militia group he'd been sent to recon in the Congo were trying to kill him.

Near death had happened to him before, mainly when he was younger and was not expected to live past his first, second, third birthdays, and he'd honestly never thought he'd make it to legal age.

But still, lying there, just beyond the row of tin-roofed, pastel-colored houses in a small town on the outskirts of Kisangani, he'd been going down hard, and he remembered how badly it had pissed him off.

"That mission was supposed to take under six hours from start to finish," he said finally, more to himself than to her. In at dark, out before the dawn.

"American helo arrived in the DRC at 2200, just outside Kisangani," she said, and she was speaking from memory rather than from paper.

She'd lain down on the grass next to him, despite the fact that the air was chilled and the ground even colder. Like him, she stared up at the sky when she spoke.

He'd always made it his practice to not look backward, to keep moving forward and to try not to make the same mistakes twice. Apparently, that wasn't in Kaylee's plan.

You owe this to Aaron, he told himself, because he understood what it was like to not want to be found, even as the other half of his brain told him that he didn't owe anybody shit beyond what he'd promised. And he'd kept that promise by handing over the patch to Aaron's girl.

He didn't like thinking about Kaylee as *Aaron's girl*.

"Six men inserted into the LZ," she continued. "Blue on Red fire began immediately, forcing the group to split. Blue on Red means you took on enemy fire, right?"

He nodded in agreement. Six SEALs from his team were prepared to insert just below their intended target for recon of a potential new terrorist cell that utilized monies and resources from the militant militia. A completely classified, locked-down mission with the highest priority.

The helo had traveled up the Lualaba River toward Isangi—a small town outside Kisangani and their ultimate destination—would drop them over ten miles away along a deserted part of the river and far away from any checkpoints and towns, save for the smaller villages.

As soon as the last man, Wolf, had fast-roped down to the ground and their ride left, the team had begun taking on enemy fire.

The shadows seemed to surround them from everywhere and anywhere, their howls echoing through the jungles, to start a chain of events that would spiral quickly out of control. An ambush of goatfuck proportions.

The militia wanted nothing more than to make examples of more American soldiers, the more elite, the better.

Nick remembered Wolf radioing for a Quick Action Force, remembered Brice and Jerry and Tim going east to try to get behind the enemy.

Nick had split west behind Joe and Wolf, covering their six as the rapid fire of AK-47s rang over their head.

Divide and conquer, Wolf had said.

"Man number six caught artillery fire to the chest after killing two militia and launching a grenade to push back the enemy." Kaylee's words echoed in his ear and he could hear the sharp impact of the shots echoing in the night—the bullets that tore through his shoulder had taken him down briefly.

Joe had already gone down—a shot to the thigh that had him cursing and still firing as Wolf had been dragging him to safety, while Nick had been trying anything to buy them some time.

"Man number six is separated from his team."

When the bullets hit, Nick had been knocked backward and unconscious—woke seeing stars, but he'd still been able to feel, and move, fingers and toes and he'd known that there had to be a reason he wasn't moving. Because the sound of renewed automatic machine-gun fire in his general direction had been as real a wake-up call as he was going to get.

Fight or flight had been ingrained in him from the time he could walk—that response wouldn't desert him now without a damned good reason.

He raised his head slowly off the dusty ground, a bare-bones movement that sent a shot of pain through his skull and nearly knocked him out again. By the time he put his head back down, he had his answer.

The damned good reason was a loose wire attached to a claymore that he'd fallen on when he'd passed out. If it had been a tight wire, he wouldn't have had a shot in hell. As it was, the mine was less than twenty-five meters from him and it was live, lethal—and tangled in his gear.

So fight or flight had now become be still or die.

Fucking motherfucking clusterfuck.

His radio was long gone—smashed when he'd slammed to the ground. His only way out right now was himself.

He kept his breathing shallow, by design more than choice, given the wounds he'd sustained. They were closer to his shoulder than his chest—at least that's what he kept telling himself, but he couldn't be sure of anything. The fact that he was conscious and breathing was the best sign.

He closed his eyes and listened to the quiet surrounding him, searching out any scrap of intel.

This is the best adrenaline rush you'll get this side of legal, *his old CO had boasted during training.*

Yeah, this was a real fucking adrenaline rush. Complete with the dizziness and dry mouth, life flashing before his eyes. His body was too far gone to feel much pain—his nerve sensors were pretty much destroyed, so much so that in order to feel any physical pain, he'd have to be hit pretty damned hard.

He'd been hit pretty damned hard.

Carefully with his right hand he reached into one of the utility pockets for his Ka-Bar knife—once he had it firmly in his palm, he cut the loose wire on the right side. It probably took less than five seconds but it felt like he'd been swimming through oil to get the job done.

He transferred the knife to his left hand and prepared to cut that wire, when he realized that someone had come behind him—someone as covert as he'd been trained to be, and that was the only reason his senses went on alert.

Friend or foe might not even matter, not if he couldn't cut the other end of that loose wire. The wire was designed to be a closed loop—if he didn't cut the wire on both sides, the claymore would still be live.

"Man number six is wounded and is found lying on a loose wire attached to a live mine." Kaylee's words were soft, a relief against the harshness of the memories. His chest grew tight, the way it had been that night—from fear, from pain, from the will to get the hell out of there alive and intact.

"That's when Aaron came through the brush to help me," he told her.

Don't move, the guy said with a small smile and Nick closed his eyes and fought the urge to curse. But when the guy cut the other side of the wire and said, *"All clear,"* Nick wished he could shake the guy's hand.

Instead, he'd begun a rough crawl toward the device.

"Hey, man, what are you doing?" the guy asked, put a hand on his arm.

"I'd feel better if you'd let me disarm it completely," he muttered.

"I'd feel better if I could stop you from bleeding out first."

"That might work too. Who the fuck are you?" Nick asked as the guy quickly assessed his injuries, told him he had two exit wounds and put some pressure on them with a towel first and then a bandage.

"I'm Aaron. Aaron Smith. You and your men were ambushed," the guy finally said in answer to Nick's question.

Aaron was dressed for combat, jungle greens, but so was everyone in this godforsaken place. You couldn't tell good from bad, because it had nothing to do with color. "I saw it happen," Aaron said.

"Because you planned it?"

The guy gave a short laugh as he began to search in the black bag Nick recognized as a medic's kit and pulled out a syringe. "Wasn't me. But someone sure as hell knew you guys were coming in here."

Nick held a hand up to refuse the injection. "I'm allergic."

"To what?"

"To pretty much everything you've got in that bag." He closed his eyes when he heard the man sigh.

"So you're just going to tough it out, then?"

"No other choice."

"You'll live," Aaron said and for the first time Nick opened his eyes and realized that, yes, he would. It was just going to hurt.

Pain is just weakness leaving the body, Devane. You've always known that.

"Man number six got up on his own volition to head to the next safe area, collecting a wounded teammate along the way," Kaylee continued.

It sounded so much better than the reality had been. Different than the smoke and blood and the overall sense of fucking doom that pervaded that night.

He reached for Joe's radio—his teammate had been hit hard, had lost enough blood to keep him passing out every few minutes, and Nick wasn't going to bother to wake the guy until it was time to make a break for it.

"What are you doing?" Aaron asked.

"I've got to transmit."

Aaron put a hand over his. "That's how they got you in the first place. They've known Americans were coming in. All they had to do was tune into your frequency."

"*Our source sold us down the river,*" Nick muttered.

"*We're going to need some FM,*" Joe muttered back, and yes, *fucking magic was right.*

"I want to see your scars from that night," Kaylee said.

"That doesn't sound like official report-speak to me," he said, but he shrugged out of his jacket and began to unbutton his shirt.

She leaned over him, her hair brushing along his bare chest as she studied the two scars that were nearly side by side. He'd ended up with an infection, a delayed pneumothorax that presented late and a bruised lung, but he'd been lucky. He'd recovered quickly, was back with his team after two months.

"How much did that hurt?" Kaylee asked him quietly as she put her hands on him and he tried not to jump. But her touch was firm, not soft, and that helped moderately.

"Not much." At the time, that hadn't been a concern. Getting the hell out of Clusterfuck City was.

"*We're out of here,*" Aaron said as gunfire resumed. "*You're going to have to take the Alternate Supply Route if you want out. And you're going to have to do it soon—you're losing blood, no matter how much I've packed your wound.*"

"*You're a merc,*" Nick said as Aaron began to load up his bag and reload his own AK-47.

"*I'm nobody. I'm AWOL,*" Aaron said.

"*How long?*"

"*Long enough that there's no way back.*" Aaron smiled, but it didn't reach to his eyes. "*I've lost everything, including my girl.*"

"*Jesus, man, it's never too late.*" And for the first time in his life, Nick actually believed that.

He leaned back against the rock and loaded more ammo. Joe was passed out again and there was no sign of his other three team members. "Tell me what I can do—saving my ass is going to go a long way in front of the board if you come back with us."

"Give me your name," Aaron interrupted. "I've been keeping a list—men I've helped. I know she doesn't love me anymore, but I need her to know that I tried to get out."

"Get out of what?"

"Your name, man. That's all I want, your name."

Nick grabbed a pen from his pocket and wrote it quickly on the guy's hand, because fuck, he owed him that.

Aaron reached into his pocket and handed Nick a worn patch, pressed it into his hand. "Give it to her."

"To who? Your girl?"

"She's not my girl anymore. But yeah. When she calls you, just give this to her. That's all you've got to do."

That's all you've got to do . . .

"Helo approached area of enemy fire at 2400."

He'd turned to tell Aaron to get onto the helo and face the consequences, to get out of this godforsaken country.

But Aaron had been long gone—and what the man had left behind still made Nick's blood run cold, so much so that Nick knew he wouldn't mention it to Kaylee if Aaron hadn't. At the time, Nick had clutched the patch tightly for a second before he'd shoved it into his pocket, dragged Joe up over his shoulders and ran for the safety of the helo.

"Helo liftoff with all six men at 2404," she finished.

But it wasn't finished, not in the way he'd thought it would be when this day had finally come. There was no full circle, no closure—only more questions. And her hand was still on his chest, her palm covering the old scars, white with age and slightly raised. There were more than that, but he barely noticed the others.

These two he took note of daily. A reminder, like the one on his throat that still tingled whenever he felt danger lurking nearby.

Her warm palm on his skin was also a reminder that he was supposed to be out tonight looking for something different—an outlet. A beautiful woman who wasn't bringing up his old baggage . . . or bringing some of her own.

He sat up abruptly, and her hand fell away. "Aaron was definitely AWOL, Kaylee. He told me so himself. So I don't know why the Army reported him as KIA."

She frowned, her hands rubbing together as he lightly rubbed the old tracheotomy scar on his neck, mentally cursing the tingling that had just begun.

"I'm still getting his benefits," she said.

"What do you really want to know? What do you want from me?" he demanded. He pushed himself up off the ground and she followed suit quickly, standing right in front of him. So close. Too close, and normally he'd step backward in order to reclaim his own personal space.

This time, he didn't. He could still feel where her hand had been on him.

"I want to know why the Army has him listed as dead for a full two years before he saved you. I want to know why he went AWOL. I want to hire you to help me find all that out."

"I'm not for sale."

"I can pay you well."

"I don't need your money. I'm not a hired gun, I'm a military man. They point, I go. End of story."

"The Army won't help me. The DoD won't either."

"Neither can I. I held up my end of the bargain . . . what I promised Aaron I'd do."

"You wouldn't have to do anything, you could just take me to the last place you saw Aaron—"

"That's classified."

"—and make sure that I'm safe . . ."

"I'm nobody's bodyguard. If I protect someone, it's called PSD—Protective Service Detail—and it's ordered. Officially." Okay, that wasn't exactly true—he'd done plenty of Black and Gray Ops, things the military didn't sanction, and he'd even worked with a group of mercs in Africa as recently as last year. But he certainly wasn't telling this woman that. He barely admitted it to his brothers.

"And suppose I go to your superiors and tell them that I know where that mission took place. Exact coordinates. What then?"

A chill went up his spine as her hand figuratively wrapped around his balls and squeezed.

Shut it down, Devane. "Is that why you called me out here, to blackmail me?"

"If I have to. I need to know how he died. Where he died. You're the key to that."

"I'm not the only man who Aaron saved—you said so yourself. Try one of them instead. I paid my debt to Aaron. I'm done."

"So you came here just to shove this patch at me, pat me on the head and send me on my way? You've done what Aaron asked and now your conscience is clean?"

"My conscience has never been clean, Kaylee. It's never going to be either, so don't you worry about that."

"I need to know more—about what happened that night," she told him. "You might've been the last one to see him alive."

"I thought you said he was still alive."

"It sounded just like him. He knew it was my birthday."

"So can anyone with a computer and common sense," he pointed out.

"Except for you. No one could find you."

"Keep that in mind."

"You're here now, aren't you?" She fronted big, but when push came to shove, he had no doubt she'd back down.

He leaned in toward her. "You've got nothing, little girl. You want to run with the big dogs, you're going to have to do a hell of a lot better."

Her soft laugh echoed in his ears long after he'd left her standing on the playground.

CHAPTER
3

Kaylee waited a beat after watching Nick walk into the bar across the street before turning back toward the diner's parking lot.

She'd been wondering what kind of man survived that kind of hell on a constant basis, thought she knew and realized now that she'd never had a clue.

During their conversation, her fingers had itched to pull out a pen and take notes, but her mini-recorder would do just as well.

She smiled as she switched the recorder to the off position. She *could* run with the big dogs in her world. Whether or not she could do so in Africa remained to be seen.

For right now, she had a more immediate urge.

The Porsche—Nick's Porsche, a 911 Turbo that was more than four years old but still in prime street condition—was parked toward the back of the lot, near her car, in a less visible area. He'd backed into the space and that alone had her shifting her glance around the lot in a way that made the all-too-familiar alarms go off in her head.

What are you thinking? You can't steal his car.

I just want a ride, her inner juvenile delinquent cajoled. And yes, it was a beautiful car. It was also unlocked and there was no alarm system. The temptation roiled through her, thick and hot, and somehow this was going to make things better.

She still carried Aaron's all-purpose pocket Leatherman utility tool with her—mainly for sentimental purposes, but it would come in handy now. She strolled casually toward the back of the car, crouched down low to the engine and looked around.

She had the tool—now for the wires. Luck was on her side in the form of a 4x4 parked next to Nick's car. She eased over to it, loosened one of the lights from the roll bar and took the wires she needed.

Back at Nick's car, she jimmied the lock carefully to get to the engine. There would be no scraping paint or scratching. Not on this beauty.

From there it was simple, the directions Aaron had given her all those years ago running through her brain, her hands working overtime as though they had a charge of their own—*Run a wire from the positive side of the battery to the coil, then use the screwdriver to cross over the negative and positive leads on the coil.*

The engine cranked right over, a deceptively low purr with a backside kick that made her smile.

Less than a minute and a half and she was inside the car. Not her best time by far, but she hadn't exactly come prepared for this, hadn't expected to feel this need tonight.

As the engine rumbled, she ran her hands over the sleek dash, caressed the wheel with its smooth black leather and inhaled the scent—of car and man—felt it race through her blood the way it had when she was fifteen and stealing hot cars made her a hot commodity.

Yes, she was going to do this. In the fingerless racing gloves Nick had left on the passenger's seat.

When she shifted gears, the throttle hit her right between the legs, an unexpected charge of engine and exhaust that told her he'd dirtied up his princess with headers to run like a race car.

She went out the back entrance of the lot, past her own waiting car, and took the short route to the nearest highway, where she could really open it up, could run away from Nick, from Aaron. From everything.

The walls were closing in fast on her real life, but here, in this car, on this highway, she was just a fifteen-year-old girl with no responsibilities to anyone but herself.

You should tell Nick Devane everything.

But it wasn't in her nature to share that kind of information—thanks to her ultimate distrust of authority, law enforcement and the system in general. From childhood, she'd learned that secrets were best kept to oneself.

Why didn't you call the police, honey? When's the last time you saw your mommy? Tell us and we'll help you . . .

She hated Aaron for bringing all this on her, had no

desire to have her past slammed back in her face because of a phone call and a safe deposit box. She already dragged it behind her like some kind of heavy albatross she couldn't quite cut away.

As a reporter, she knew that the best way to blow a lead was to let too many people in on it. It was the same idea here. No, she'd deal with this herself if Nick wouldn't help her.

Halfway down the open stretch of road, the engine began to sputter—of course the man would have a fuel cutoff anti-theft device installed.

And of course he'd have installed it so it was hidden, or else she would've seen it during the wiring.

She moved the car smoothly toward the side of the road, realized that she'd have no way to get herself home now, except walk.

She'd covered at least twenty miles in the short time span, thanks to this beauty's speed. And as she put her head back against the headrest, hands in his racing gloves and still on the wheel, the driver's-side door opened swiftly.

Nick was standing there, staring down at her, and no, that couldn't be a good sign.

She was so busted, but she'd learned that the best way to handle these situations was to remain calm.

Obviously, Nick had learned that as well.

"You're just full of surprises, aren't you?" he asked as he leaned one arm against the open door and held out the other to help her from the car.

Her own car was parked behind the Porsche. Obviously, Nick believed in an eye for an eye.

She attempted to slide by him and found herself pinned

against the side of the car, Nick's arms on either side of her effectively locking her in.

She could still feel the heat, the vibration from the car's rumble somewhere deep inside of her. She could feel the heat coming off Nick as well, a mix of anger and desire, and she jutted her chin up toward him, refusing to give in to either emotion. And failing.

When he spoke, he leaned in close, nearly whispered in her ear, "First you try to blackmail me and then you steal my car."

She didn't bother to deny the first accusation. "I borrowed your car. I was planning on returning it."

"How do I know that's true?"

"If I were going to steal it, I would've ripped out the wires under the wheel."

"You don't know who you're messing with, Kaylee."

"Then tell me."

He ran a thumb over her bottom lip before he spoke. She fought the urge to do the same to him. "Aaron was AWOL—he was working in the jungles for the highest bidder. He was a mercenary. You're never going to find the information you want. The Congo's a dangerous place."

"And you're just as dangerous, aren't you?" she asked.

"You'd better believe it."

"You don't scare me," she said.

"That's because I'm not trying to."

Still, her breath came fast, her belly tightened and her throat went dry. But that reaction wasn't caused by fear. "I'm seeing someone," she heard herself say, even as he moved in closer to her, his hand dropping down to the curve of her butt. "We're almost engaged."

"Then what the hell are you doing here with me?" The low purring growl caught her between inhales, made her breath hitch audibly.

"He doesn't know anything about me."

"He doesn't know you steal cars?"

"He doesn't even know how to make me come."

Nick's mouth tugged at the corner, but he didn't smile, not fully, even as his other arm wove its way around her waist to pull her closer to his body, and God, the heat raced through her like a fever she couldn't control. "Does anyone know how to make you come?"

"No," she whispered.

"Don't be so sure of that," he said gruffly, then released her. "Go home, Kaylee. Forget you ever met me."

Forget you ever met me.

From the way her body had reacted to him, she knew that was never going to happen.

Kaylee, why do you do this to yourself?" Carl Van Patterson, her boyfriend of nearly a year, stood in the doorway, watching her rifle through the box of Aaron's personal effects a half an hour after she'd lost sight of Nick's car on the highway.

"Sorry. I know it bothers you." She shoved the top onto the lockbox quickly, but not before putting the tape of Nick's story in there and tucking the patch he'd given her inside the pocket of her shorts.

"It bothers me that you can't get past it."

"Growing up was complicated," she told him as she put the box on the upper shelf of the closet—out of sight, out of Carl's mind, hopefully. It was never far from hers. "You know that. We were much more than husband and wife."

"I know that you missed another dinner with my father and our business associates," Carl reminded her, and yes, *shit*, she'd forgotten. Or else it was another case of selective memory, something that always seemed to happen whenever she had to attend events of any kind with Carl.

"I'm sorry. I had to work."

"That damned job again."

"That damned job is one of the reasons you were initially attracted to me. Or did you forget that?"

Carl was wealthy, a lawyer and the son of an even more prominent lawyer—possibly a soon-to-be congressman, if the polls were correct. Carl himself was on the fast track to that same political world—but now he feared her being a reporter might cause too much friction, be a conflict of interest.

So I won't report on politics then, she'd told him time and time again.

He'd already tried to warn her, gently, that when they got married, she'd have to retire from reporting, and she'd told him that she had no plans to marry anyone or give up her career.

So far, he hadn't believed her.

So far, she'd never once agreed to actually consider his marriage proposal. "You know my past is going to come out, Carl. Especially when you decide to run for office."

"I told you we can bury that."

"I have no intention of doing that." She fought the urge to tell him about wiring Nick's car that evening and realized that she wasn't in the mood for a lecture. She'd been in the mood to be alone, to go over the tape of her conversation with Nick.

She hadn't expected Carl to be waiting for her at her apartment.

"Sometimes it sounds like you're almost proud of what you used to do," he continued, the frustrated look crossing his face the way it always did when this subject was broached.

She stared at Carl's face and wondered again how she could get herself involved with someone who'd been attracted to her wild side and later wanted to tamp it down. "I'm not ashamed of where I came from. I don't know why that's such a problem. It used to be a turn-on for you that I had a record."

"A sealed record, Kaylee. You were a juvenile delinquent, not a hardened criminal." Carl shook his head. "Records like that are sealed for a reason. To let you get on with your life—so your past doesn't haunt you."

"Yes, well, too late for that." With her back to Carl, she fingered the worn patch Nick had given her, the one Aaron had ripped off his clothing, judging by the frayed ends.

The notification that her ex still had her listed as the sole beneficiary in his will had been nearly as shocking as the phone call. Add to that the enormous amount of money Aaron appeared to have left behind, if the bankbook he'd put into the safe deposit box was any indication.

How a man who came from a foster-care background and went straight into the Army could have that much money, doubtfully earned by legal means, made her head spin.

She wouldn't touch it, wished she could forget about it, and Aaron himself, the way he'd forgotten about her and fucked anything that moved even when they'd still been together.

Bastard.

She hadn't told Nick that part, because some things were too personal. She was still wounded deeply from those betrayals, even though she'd had her own fantasies and flirtations with other men the years they were married. The years he was away giving the military his love.

The fact that he'd cheated on her bothered her much less than the fact that her best friend had broken her trust. Badly.

"I won't hide my past, Carl. I won't hide who I am." She slammed the closet door shut and turned to face him.

Of course, her job was more covered up than she would've liked—she was an investigative reporter, doing the down and dirty kind of work that necessitated her name and image not appear in the paper. So she wrote her articles as K. Darcy and most readers assumed she was a man.

"I don't want to have this fight anymore," he told her, in the same tone he'd say that he didn't want to stay over at her apartment any longer, that he didn't understand why she didn't want to get married. He brushed past her and headed toward her bedroom and she went in the opposite direction.

Sometimes, in the deepest part of the night, when she felt most alone, she'd do this, wrap a blanket around herself and swing the patio door open. Alone, out on the balcony, she'd stand and look at the city laid out below her and she'd wonder if there was someone out there for her.

Her body ached for him, this man she'd dreamed about from the time she became interested in boys.

Aaron had always been more of a best friend than a lover. And in the recesses of her mind, she longed for the man who would come into her world and bring her body to life.

Carl wasn't that man. And until today, when Nick Devane's voice had done more for her than any man's hands over the years, she'd thought that she was waiting for the unattainable.

Until today, when she knew she was in trouble. She could still smell the leather scent on her hair, could feel Nick's grip on her hand as he helped her out of the car, as if she had just taken it for a ride with permission.

In his eyes, she'd seen the familiar spark of someone who'd had his own brushes with the law.

She could picture them, a tangle of arms and legs in the car's tiny backseat, wondered if she'd be the first woman back there and decided she didn't want to think about that.

What if I don't want to forget that I met you?

She pulled the blanket tighter against the cool spring air and wondered if she'd hit some sort of massive spring fever, if the restlessness overtaking her body was something she'd be unable to ignore for much longer.

There was only one thing that was going to take the edge off. And it wasn't going to come from her own touch.

Meeting Nick was not supposed to be about this—it was supposed to be about getting information on Aaron, discovering the mystery surrounding his death and the money he'd left her. About leaving her past behind her and thinking only on her future.

A future that if it included Carl Van Patterson might never include her career as a journalist again.

"Kaylee, are you coming to bed?" Carl's voice drifted out onto the small balcony. And she stared at the patch and thought about Nick instead of Aaron and wasn't sure how to tell Carl that *no,* she was never going to bed with him again.

CHAPTER
4

What if I don't want to forget I met you?

Nick had been halfway into his car when he heard Kaylee call those words out to him, and the relentless energy coursing through his body had nearly won out.

The hotwire had been enough to make him forget the blackmail attempt momentarily, enough to have him nearly take her right on the hood of his car or anywhere else she'd wanted him.

And she *had* wanted him. Had believed he could pull some *fucking magic* on her body that no one else had ever been able to do.

For some reason, that made a difference to him. A big

difference, and dammit, he didn't want anything about any woman—especially this woman—to make a difference.

Just your ego talking, asshole.

He'd waited until she began to walk back toward the diner's parking lot after they'd left the park before he'd started to trail her. Just to make sure she got to her car safely, he'd told himself, but fuck it, he'd never been a Boy Scout and the tail was purely a physical pull.

She'd run her hand over the fender of his car as if soothing a beast and he'd wanted to be under that hand. And he knew in that instant what she was going to do, watched and waited as she'd torn wires from the lights on the 4x4 and lit his engine on fire like a pro.

She'd put the windows down, but hadn't used the radio.

She'd put on his racing gloves.

She'd looked sexy as hell as she stripped them off and handed them to him on the way back to her car, a Mercedes sedan that did not fit her at all.

Like you know her so damned well.

No, the problem was that he didn't know her at all. It was going to stay that way.

Roaring down the highway, he felt like he had the night of his first mission. Both times were brushes with something that changed his life forever, in ways he didn't fully comprehend.

It was so easy to get caught up in the memories, from childhood, from his years before becoming a SEAL, from the missions themselves—easy to get mentally screwed for hours or a day or however long he let them take up residence. Some days they rose up and caught him off guard, until he pushed them back down where they belonged.

Most nights, he didn't let himself sleep. He didn't expect this one to be any different.

He'd taken his jacket and shirt off on his way up the driveway to the house. The jeans came off the second he hit the door, and this wasn't anything new or unexpected for him, something done without much thought—or any, no matter if the house was empty or full of company.

He was convinced that his disdain for clothing came from so much time spent in the hospital as a kid. As a patient, he'd never worn clothes. The doctors and nurses were always stripping you down, knocking you out, and you woke up dazed, balls free and surrounded.

These days, the only part of that he dealt with well was being balls free.

Now he deposited the discarded clothing in a heap on a chair in the maze of rooms he called home, part of the first floor of the house where he'd spent his teenage years. A house Dad had left to the three of them when he moved to L.A., left to him and Chris and Jake, so they'd always have a place to come home to, no matter what else happened.

He opened the windows and the sliding glass doors that overlooked the backyard and stood in the cool night air naked. If he'd been training or on a mission, that would've overrode the need to feel something on his skin, pleasurable or painful. His throat ached where the scar was and he rubbed it again and waited for the air to calm him.

There was a danger in remembering . . . but sometimes an even bigger one in forgetting.

———

Why don't you just forget about taking these crazy bands on was something Kenny Waldron was used to hearing—a question he never answered. Instead he would just smile a secret smile and think of his three sons, who were wilder than any band he'd ever managed. Then he would sign the papers his lawyer put in front of him, committing him to manage what usually turned out to be a band on the verge of self-destruction, one that had been dumped by several managers before him, one that no one but Kenny was crazy enough to take on.

There was crazy and then there was *crazy,* and Kenny had been used to all kinds from the time he'd been a young wild boy himself growing up in the bayous of Louisiana. Married to Maggie at seventeen, they'd had their son, Chris, nine months later and had taken him on the road with them as they began a career of managing bands that would make them famous.

By this time, Kenny was used to trouble, used to having his authority questioned. Used to things coming out all right in the end. Sometimes, it took his sons, and the bands, longer to figure that out.

"We could've had a bigger deal if we hadn't listened to him," he heard the lead singer of his latest project whisper now to the other members of the group from behind the half-closed door.

Kenny would speak to the kid later, privately, after the show was finished and the post-performance adrenaline had waned. When the kid was alone in his dressing room, after the fans—and the women—left, Kenny would re-mind the singer that this was all he had, right there.

All you have is your soul.

He would tell the kid that it was never a good idea to make a deal with the devil.

Kenny had made a deal with the devil only once in his lifetime and considered it worth it to keep one of his three sons out of hell's reach.

"We did the right thing," his wife, Maggie, had told him firmly thirteen years earlier as Kenny steered the SUV down the thruway that led from New York to Virginia.

The three boys—Chris, Nick and Jake—had all been asleep in the backseat by that point, the trauma of the past days and weeks having taken its toll on each of them.

"I know we did." He'd held her hand, the way he had for all the years they'd been together, with no way of knowing she'd be dead nine months later, the cancer spreading quickly and quietly in an effort to evade both of their second sights. "I wish we could do this legally. Adopt Jake and Nick."

That wasn't possible. Jake had recently lost his stepfather—an abusive man who'd nearly killed him—and going through the proper channels would've taken too long. Sad to say, the boy was never missed in the city, his disappearance had merely lightened an overworked social worker's case file.

No, Jake would have a good home with them now. There was no guilt in what they'd done.

But things with Nick were far more complicated.

"They're still ours," she'd said. "The way it was meant to be. That's all that matters now."

That had been the truth. Although only Chris was their biological son, Kenny and Maggie had become involved in Nick's and Jake's lives quickly. They'd just moved to New

York so Kenny could work with a new producer and record label he'd been developing, and Chris had met the two boys who would soon become his brothers on his very first day of school.

The Waldron family had been there all of two weeks when Jake's stepfather had died. And things were horribly wrong for Nick too, so Kenny had to work fast to stop that boy from running away.

It had taken only a moment of concentration before Kenny's gift of second sight led him to Nick, found him on the platform of the train station, ready to go and yet unable to actually leave.

Kenny had watched as Nick let three different trains go by before he'd gone to sit next to him on the wooden bench and silently handed him the papers he'd had a lawyer draw up earlier that same day.

They weren't adoption papers, but they were the key to Nick's emancipation in so many different ways.

"Is this what you want?" he'd asked. Even at fourteen, Nick had been devastatingly handsome, an heir to a throne and part of a family so cursed Kenny knew Nick would spend a lifetime trying to escape it if he'd stayed.

"It's what I want."

"There's no going back." Kenny's stomach had lurched every time he thought of what kind of man, what kind of father could blithely agree to publicly declare his son missing, believed dead, in exchange for an inheritance.

"I don't want to go back. I'm never going back," Nick had ground out fiercely.

"Then sign. And you never have to," Kenny had told him quietly, felt Nick's green eyes pierce through his in a silent *thank you,* for the way out he'd have never been able to achieve on his own. At least not back then.

After Maggie's death, Kenny had been as inconsolable as his sons, barely remembered the first years, when Chris went quiet and refused to acknowledge his own gift of second sight, when Jake pushed a paper at him and told him he was joining the military at fifteen. When Nick and Chris had tried to take themselves so far over the edge that there'd almost been no turning back for either of them.

He'd woken up when both of them were arrested for stealing cars on the same night—what had started as a stupid hobby of hotwiring cars for joyrides had veered dangerously close to a way of life for the two boys on the verge of manhood.

His three boys had all survived in a way that made his heart swell with pride. And with that, he should be happy, content, not restless, the way he'd been all night long.

When he felt a chill shoot straight to his soul, he looked around the room until his gaze settled on the muted TV that had been turned to a twenty-four-hour news station.

He saw the devil's face—contorted in fake grief—on the big screen set up in the green room of the massive concert hall, where his latest out-of-control band was currently performing.

The hair on the back of his neck stood on end and he said a silent prayer to both God and Maggie and hoped one of them was paying attention.

Senator Winfield's wife, Deidre, died early yesterday morning at the family home in New York from complications of lung cancer. The Winfields chose to wait twenty-four hours before announcing Deidre's death so they could have time to mourn in private. Services will be held this weekend in a private memorial. The Winfields have a long history of both public and political service and an even longer history of family tragedy, beginning with the untimely death of the senator's brother, William "Billy" Winfield, and followed by the still unconfirmed death of his youngest son, Cutter Nicholas Winfield, at age fourteen...

"Cutter's not coming home, is he?"

Walter Winfield looked away from the television reports to see his eldest son standing in the doorway of his office. Eric, still looking very much like the star quarterback hedging for a tackle or routing out a kick path, leaned against the doorjamb. With his body poised in a forward motion of hunger, hair hanging over his forehead in a decidedly noncorporate length, he looked every inch the man Walter's brother had been.

Walter's throat still tightened when he thought of Billy, killed in combat one month before Cutter was born.

"He can't," Walter said finally. "He knows that."

Eric hesitated for a beat, and then muttered that his day had already been ruined. He walked farther into the office, not bothering to shut the door behind him the way he would during normal business hours. It was close to midnight, and they were the only two on the floor—and most likely in the entire building, save for a cleaning staff. "You still haven't been able to get inside the will, have you?"

"No. Not yet."

"Do you think there's going to be a problem?"

"I don't. But if there is, I'll take care of it, Eric." Walter pushed back in his chair and sighed, feeling the weight of the world on his sixty-year-old shoulders and hating it.

He glanced at the note he'd prepared, one that would be picked up shortly and hand-delivered to Cutter by morning. Simple and to the point, the way he'd always taught his children to be. The way Deidre could never have acted, even later on when talking got too hard for her. And then he ripped it in half and threw it into the fireplace.

Nick, as the man was known today, would hate him for the message, but his youngest had always found a reason to despise his father. Running away, first at twelve and again, for good, at fourteen, had proven the point.

He would only have come home for his mother. Only if and when she'd called, and she never had.

The Winfields were all about public face and private pain. This would prove to be no exception.

CHAPTER
5

I need to find someone," Nick told Max, once he'd gotten onto base and into Max's private sanctum sometime after 0500.

Max sat at a long table, rows of computer monitors in front of him and overhead. "Do I have *missing persons* stamped on my goddamned forehead?"

"Aw, come on, man." Nick slid into one of the chairs next to the captain and held his gaze steady.

"You and your entire team owe me more favors, and you'd best be sure I'm keeping track. Got a nice little list. Between you and Saint and that goddamned brother of yours—"

"Which one?"

"You know which one," Max snorted, and yeah, he was talking about Jake. Jake, who was seriously missing Izzy, as she was back working a short stint for Doctors Without Borders. At least work was keeping him busy.

Both Jake and Chris had gone straight to base from their night out—as previously planned—for an earlier-than-0-dark-hundred flight for Coronado with the team's senior chief, Mark Kendall, to participate in cross-training exercises. Nick and Saint and other teammates would remain in Virginia, as Nick was finishing up training of his own, training he'd had to put aside hurriedly when his team had gotten called away months earlier.

Now Nick waited until Max stopped grumbling under his breath and finally told him, "All right, give me a few days and I'll see what I can do."

"I don't have a few days."

"Holy fuck, Devane, crawl out from my ass!" Max roared. But Nick stayed in his seat, remained unimpressed. "I don't know where the hell you got your balls, kid."

"This guy was Kaylee Smith's husband," Nick said quietly as he slid the piece of paper with Aaron's name on it, and the request for Nick's old SITREP, toward Max.

"Why didn't you just say so to begin with?"

"I never did like doing things the easy way."

"I thought you were shutting her down," Max grumbled.

"I was. I am." Nick stood. "Can you get me Kaylee's address as long as you're searching? Maybe run her plate number for me now."

Max gave him a long stare, and then began to type the license plate number into the computer as he spoke. "You're playing with fire on this one. You know that, right? Because you're supposed to get this woman off your tail, not get involved in her life."

"I'm not getting involved in her life," Nick insisted, even as his mind flashed back to last night, the way she'd have easily wrapped herself around him if he'd pushed.

It felt like it had happened ten minutes ago, as if no time had passed, and the sensation of hard needles of cold water hitting his skin in the shower earlier had made him bare his teeth and hiss—it had done little for his hard-on, only served to make him think of the woman who had gotten him this aroused.

He needed something to fill up the silence. He wanted the loud, pounding sounds of music, of combat—of sex. Tonight, none of that would do, at least not with a stranger, not that he hadn't considered that possibility.

Finding out that Deidre had died via a news report had thrown him. But losing himself in grief for a mother who'd never wanted him wouldn't do shit for him anyway. Losing himself in Kaylee . . . that was a much different story.

He left Max's lair and headed to his own office, was down the hall moving toward his cubicle in the quiet area the SEALs often used to strategize, when he suddenly knew someone was on his six and far too close for comfort.

He turned before the man could lay a hand on him, had his own palm poised to strike directly at the throat of whoever was stupid enough to attempt to sneak up on a military man just home from combat. Christ, they were all jumpy as hell when they got back, but with his aversion to being touched, he was the worst one of all.

He just hid that last part better than most.

It was his CO. Saint had his own palm raised and he was smiling. "Making sure you're on your toes," he drawled as he sauntered past Nick toward his own office.

Nick flipped him the internal middle finger. "I put in for three days of leave, starting tomorrow," he called after him.

"Everything all right?"

"Just something I need to take care of. No big deal."

"Take a week."

"I don't need a week."

"Don't fuck with me when I'm feeling generous," Saint admonished. "You come back here with any part of your body in a cast and I'll kill you."

"I'll keep that in mind."

It was well after eleven P.M. by the time Kaylee put her current story to bed and headed home. She'd been in the office from five that morning with no sleep under her belt, having fought and talked with Carl all last night and into the early morning hours. He'd finally gotten dressed and out of her apartment, without saying good-bye. He'd slammed the door behind him in frustration and all of her strain had faded away.

Free. She was free, until the thought of Aaron and his phone call weighed her down again.

She'd spent those first early hours while the newspaper office was relatively quiet following up on the symbol on the patch Nick had handed her.

The crudely stitched patch was still in her pocket now—its symbol, whose top half looked like a backward half moon, or a rhino's horn if turned on its side, was the Ako-ben. After some quick research, she was able to determine its West African origins. It was also referred to as the war horn, a call to arms, a willingness to take action when necessary.

It sounded like Aaron.

She hadn't told Nick that all the men Aaron had saved had been in Africa—the Congo, Zimbabwe. The Ivory Coast. West Africa. Maybe she should have—or maybe it held no significance whatsoever.

And she didn't owe Nick anything more than what she'd told him. Except the mere thought of his name made her heart race as if she was a sixteen-year-old with a massive crush, and she muttered to herself disgustedly as she headed down the hall toward her apartment.

For the first time in a long time, she wished someone was waiting there for her.

Sometimes that pain hit her like a physical blow. Somehow she always found herself surrounded by more people than someone could possibly ask for and yet she could never find the comfort she sought. Aaron had been her main source of both pain and pleasure, and when he'd broken her trust, he'd shattered her for what she figured to be the final time. Irreparable.

She juggled takeout and her bags and worked the key in her lock. She lightly kicked the door open, cursing as some of the bags slipped, and she froze when she heard a low, rough laugh.

Nick was waiting for her. Inside her apartment, which had been locked and alarmed.

She really had to be careful about what she wished for,

even as her belly twinged with a secret thrill at the sight of him there.

The door had still been locked, the alarm was still armed. Her place was on the fifteenth floor, and she wondered if he'd climbed up the side of the building and gotten in through a window she'd forgotten to close.

The alarm buzz continued as she stared at him.

"Are you going to turn that off?" he asked.

"How—"

He pushed past her and punched in a code—*her* code—and the buzzing stopped. He also closed the door behind her and slid the lock into place. "You curse worse than a sailor."

"What the hell is going on here?" she finally demanded, giving up the fight and dropping her bags on the floor.

"You wanted me."

"I wanted your help, not you breaking into my apartment."

He hadn't moved, and was tall, so much taller than she was. "You're going to have to be more specific about things next time."

"How did you know where I live?"

"I ran your plates through the DMV."

"That can't be legal," she said. He didn't answer, gave a small smile. "I don't understand—are you here to help me, then, with Aaron?"

"*This* has nothing to do with Aaron," he told her before he brought his mouth down on hers, swept her into his arms—and the surge of desire was enough to make her knees buckle.

The man tasted like sin, something she shouldn't need

or crave or want. Something she couldn't resist. Her hands fisted in his hair as he brought his mouth down on hers, and the fire between them lit the same way it had when she'd borrowed his car.

He'd take her here, right against the door, and it was all too fitting for what she suspected would be a quick escape route for him once the sex was over.

She broke the kiss, yanked away from him and stared into the incredible green eyes that continued to watch her intently.

"You want to go for a ride?" he asked.

"You're going to let me drive your car again?"

"I wasn't talking about cars." His thumb brushed her cheek, moved down to trace her jaw.

His touch was like a truth serum. "I told you that I was seeing someone."

"Yeah, you mentioned that. Do you want me to go, Kaylee? Because you should tell me that now. Right now."

"I'm not seeing him anymore."

"That was fast."

"Things have been happening that way for me lately."

"That's not always a bad thing."

Her hands were on his chest. "Happened after I met you. Time for a new start."

"Sounds impulsive. Like stealing my car."

Yes, it was. She hadn't managed her personal life that way for a very long time. Not since she'd married Aaron on the spur of the moment. She'd gone for a much different kind of man after him. Non-military. Law-abiding. No troubled past.

She hadn't wanted another military man in her life, but

here he was, in her apartment. Breaking and entering in order to see her. Kissing her.

She could feel the sheer strength in his body, pulsing in waves while still giving a sense that he could stay like this, silent, steady, powerful, for hours.

His training would have added to that skill, but this was a man cut out for the job since forever, rough and ready enough to make her heart pound crazily from the second she'd opened the door to find him there, sitting in her favorite chair, in the dark. As if he belonged.

She wanted him to belong here, while at the same time she wondered if Nick could or would ever allow himself to belong to anyone.

Could she? She'd always told herself that she'd do anything in order to find the right man.

There was no reason to play coy—she knew what he wanted. More so, she knew what she wanted. The fact that he was here told her what she needed, and she didn't want him here for Aaron, would've been disappointed if he'd been here for anything but her.

"I wanted to kiss you last night," she murmured, feeling incredibly bold. "Wanted to lay you back on the hood and take off your clothes and just take you, right there . . ."

"Why didn't you?"

Good question. As she mused, he began unbuttoning her shirt, easing the fabric aside as he worked. He pushed it off her shoulders and undid the front clasp of her bra with one finger—and oh, God, what a skill that was. Her nipples, already hard from his touch, grew taut when the air hit them, and as he worked down her pants and thong, Nick studied her, a small smile of appreciation breaking across his typically reserved features as he gazed at her body.

She expected him to say something, to give her some kind of compliment, but he didn't. Not with words anyway, but he held her hips and put his mouth down on one nipple and it was all over.

Before she knew it, her clothes were in a puddle on the floor and she was naked in his arms, her bare body rubbing his fully clothed one while he kissed her again. It felt so dirty, so right, with her nipples taut from the delicious friction of his leather jacket and cotton T-shirt.

She responded by kissing him back, then losing herself in the way his mouth took possession of her taut nub, his tongue stroking and sucking, and God, she wanted that tongue everywhere.

She clawed at his shoulders, managed to yank off his jacket and began to pull his shirt up as well. He took his mouth off her nipple only long enough to let her pull the shirt over his head before he was teasing her again. In that brief space of time, she'd taken careful note of the bruises and scratches that ran along his chest—they hadn't been there last night. And although they didn't appear to bother him, she still tread more lightly as she stroked her hands over his broad shoulders.

He pulled away from her touch almost immediately.

"What's wrong?" she asked.

"I want to feel you, Kaylee. Really feel you. It's not going to happen like that."

"I don't want to hurt you."

"Hurt me. Or at least try to," he rasped. "Dig your fingers in . . . yeah, like that. So I know you're touching me."

Her hands gripped him tightly on his shoulders, yanked him toward her, and he responded by kissing her again, hard, fast, taking her down to the floor in a quick and surprisingly gentle movement. The carpet tickled her back as his weight pressed her, his jean-covered thigh working between her legs in a firm back-and-forth motion until her hips rocked to his rhythm.

"Do you like that, Kaylee?"

She could barely talk, just gripped him harder, which in turn made his thigh work her faster. "I ... like ..."

"Good. Then come for me. Right now."

She opened her mouth to tell him that she wasn't ready, but his fingers had joined his thigh, strummed her clit lightly and then with a long, circular stroke that made her belly tighten and her sex contract. A long moan escaped, and she closed her eyes and held on to him as her orgasm crested.

"I told you I could make you come. That's all I've been thinking about—making you come, over and over."

"More. Please," she murmured against his neck.

"I thought you said you didn't like military men."

"I don't—I didn't," she sputtered, realized she had no leg to stand on while her body was still rocked from her orgasm, while he continued to stroke between her legs and she was responding again.

"But you like what I'm doing."

"Yes." Oh, God, yes. If he stopped ... she didn't want him to stop at all. "I like *you,* Nick ... don't you dare stop now."

Judging by the heat coming off his body, the way his

erection pressed, rock hard against her belly, he wasn't planning on it. His eyes had gone hot with desire, the way they had last night.

He chuckled softly as he picked her up off the floor and walked with her into the bedroom.

Kaylee Smith was more dangerous than any claymore he'd come upon, and yeah, Nick had just found her trip wire.

She lay on the bed below him, her hair splayed out on the pillow, her body open and inviting, a sex flush across her chest and breasts. He could lose it by looking at her, and so he'd stripped himself down in seconds and she was holding him the way she had before—hard, her fingers rubbing his biceps, his chest. Yanking his head down so she could kiss him, and *oh, fuck yeah,* this was good. Better than good.

She tasted tart and sweet, like black cherries and sugar, and he wanted nothing more than to explore her body fully, to take the time to go inch by inch.

He did, studying her as he would a map—licking her contours, memorizing freckles that mapped a scattered path down her stomach to the small soft triangle between her thighs. And when he pushed her legs apart, her body bowed instinctively toward his. His mouth met her sex and she cried out, tightened her fingers in his hair and held him there as he took her with his tongue, stroking her in the hot, intimate place that made her shudder with orgasm.

And as much as he got off on giving her pleasure—because there was nothing better than hearing a woman, especially this woman, calling out his name like she couldn't get enough—he needed more. His own skin pulled tight, blood rushing to every stimulated muscle and nerve ending as he climbed back up her body. He wanted in—slid his cock into her slowly at first, until he was sheathed to the hilt, her body accepting him with a hot throb.

"Feels so good, Nick," she murmured, her arms thrown above her head in sweet surrender. He captured her wrists, held them there as his body shuddered and he plunged into her again, letting himself go over the edge, losing himself inside of her for just a few seconds. Letting his guard down.

Fuck, it felt good. Better than good, better than any sex he'd had in a long, long time.

Her orgasm seemed to spread outward to encompass her entire body—every muscle shook and shivered and grabbed him where he needed to be grabbed, and he held her and went along for the ride. Her body arched up powerfully into his, her thighs locked tightly and she contracted around his cock as one orgasm rolled into another. And for a second, he was merely an observer, watching her beautiful face contort with pleasure, realizing that it was partially him that was causing this and partially some kind of intense chemistry that the two of them had, something he'd felt the second he'd met her.

Which was crazy, since she wasn't *his* girl. He didn't have a girl, but now he had a bucking, gorgeous woman who pulled him toward one of the hardest, most satisfying orgasms of his entire life. And she wasn't done yet. Not nearly done.

CHAPTER
6

A few hours later, Nick lay on his stomach, his cheek buried in Kaylee's pillow, his face turned toward her. She had one arm up over her head, the sheet only partially covering her, and there wasn't a hint of self-consciousness about that.

"So, do you do this a lot?" she asked.

"Have sex?"

"Break into women's apartments."

"Not usually."

"I'm glad you did. I couldn't stop thinking about you last night."

"Look, I don't do things like this—I'm not into relationships or the long haul."

"Oh. Okay." Now she moved to pull the sheet up over her, the mood broken.

He reached out for her hand, stopping her. "That didn't come out exactly right." Not that it ever did, really. But for some reason, this time, his usual bullshit one-night-stand speech didn't feel right. "Women make things...complicated, and I don't have time for any kind of personal life." Or the clearance. Sex was easier. No need for high priority classification. Just one night of pleasure and no explanations necessary.

Besides, marriage, any long-term relationship, was out of the question for him. How the hell was he supposed to commit to someone he could only share half his life with? He could never reveal his past to them—could never get beyond that trust issue. And so he'd always be hiding a part of himself that, as much as he tried to brush it off and pretend otherwise, was very real. Very persistently a part of him.

He couldn't pull that kind of deceit on someone he was supposed to love. So it was always much easier not to get involved, to play the field, to pretend that he didn't want anything more than a roll in the hay. And most days, he believed his own bullshit, which helped a lot.

Fuck, he came with a lot of baggage, even without his family background. His medical shit alone—the touching thing could really make women look at him like he was a complete freak if he spent a lot of time with them.

He was used to being touched by now, at least the normal, everyday touches like the pats on the back. Fortunately, there wasn't too much hugging in his profession on a day-to-day basis.

With sex, it was different. He was never sure if it was because it was the ultimate intimacy, but when a woman touched him, he craved more—wanted it harder, rougher.

He didn't want to think about the fact that Kaylee hadn't blinked an eye when he'd asked her to touch him hard. Of course, the longer he stayed, the more she'd question it. Women always had a lot of questions.

"I'm guessing you've got a lot of women after you for more than one night," she said finally, without guile. "There's something about a man in uniform."

"I usually don't tell women what I do for a living," he admitted. There were too many SEAL groupies out there—and many of those women wanted to try to trap him into marriage by having his baby. Of course, he never bothered to tell them that would never work—years of childhood illness, coupled with radiation, had rendered him sterile.

Kaylee already knew he was a SEAL—in fact, his military career seemed more of a detriment than anything to her.

"I don't like to lie. I tell women the truth. Normally, before things get too far." He'd tell them straight up that he'd be with them for a few hours or the whole night—if they were able to keep up with him. But he didn't do sleepovers, mainly because he didn't sleep or cuddle. He'd figured that the lack of sweet talk—all the *honey, baby* bullshit—would make things easier on him. Instead, it always seemed to backfire and he ended up with women convinced they were the ones who could bring him to his knees.

And Kaylee was still lying next to him, her head cocked to the side as if she could see straight through to the wheels working in his brain.

He really didn't like that at all. "I usually don't spend the night," he said finally. "I mean, I didn't plan on it."

He waited for her to get upset or pissed or have any of the typical reactions he'd gotten over the years. But none came. Instead, she simply said, "I'd like you to."

And then her hand went to the back of his neck, fingers working in a strong rub that shot straight through to his dick. "I mean, it's almost morning anyway," she continued, and yeah, it was already close to three A.M. "And I don't think we'll be doing too much sleeping."

He rolled off his stomach and pulled her body against his. When he noted the flash of ink, he turned her quickly to study the intricate black tattoo of a tiger along her lower back. "No, definitely no sleeping," he murmured as his fingers traced the design, the way he was going to do with his tongue in seconds, and contented himself with that deception—that this didn't really count as spending the night—and wondered why it was so easy to accept.

He leaned down and grabbed his discarded T-shirt from the floor before he turned Kaylee over in his arms, trapped her underneath him once again.

She looked surprised when he used the shirt to tie her wrists to the bedpost. It wasn't a hard tie, but it still left her comfortably immobile. It was what he'd wanted to do before, but she'd touched him so well he hadn't allowed himself the luxury. But now, now he could take his time, and she smiled and relaxed even as her cheeks flushed.

It was her first time being bound like this during sex— he could tell by the way her body attempted to anticipate where and when he'd touch her, the way she jerked her wrists occasionally in response, forgetting momentarily that she was held open to him.

His hands slid down the length of her body, capturing the curve of her hips in his palms and dragging her pelvis into his. Within minutes, he'd rolled on a condom and was buried deep inside of her, his cock vibrating inside her wet heat. He wanted to go slow with her, but they had all night long—hours and hours that he didn't want to spend thinking about tomorrow or the next day or the next.

He closed his eyes for a second, opened them to find her watching him intently, a wide smile of pleasure on her face as she came. "Yes, Nick, please."

Yes, he could please her, but there was no promise here. He ached at the thought, made him realize that he'd been right to push away the possibility of relationships all those years.

And still he forgot about all of that when he came hard enough that his dick ached and his body relaxed into hers.

"I liked that," she sighed.

"I noticed." He forced himself onto his knees, rubbed her arms for a few minutes as she looked on him with sleepy, satiated eyes.

"Not yet," she murmured as he went to untie her.

No, not yet, his body agreed instantly.

Hours longer than he'd planned on staying, Nick was still in Kaylee's bed.

He blamed the tattoo.

"I got it a few years ago," Kaylee explained. She was on her stomach; he was on his side next to her, unable to stop tracing the delicate but bold design, complete with tribal markings. "I wanted to do something different, something just for me."

"It's nice."

"Not everyone thinks so."

"Yeah, well, fuck everybody else. You're the one who counts, right?"

She laughed, a low throaty sound. "I like the way you think. Sometimes I worry that I'm too much in the moment—I see, I want, I do, you know? I guess I don't see the point in wasting time. I'm a first-instincts kind of girl."

He understood, was driven by his compulsion, a need to kick it faster, harder, to top himself every time. To take risks.

To take everything to the extreme.

Kaylee was one of those extremes. She had the same revved-up drive. But being here with her, his need for anything beyond just this canceled itself out. He didn't know how that was possible, but it was. Living proof stretched out next to him, and no, they hadn't done any sleeping. Their sex was hot and rough and perfect—at this point, he shouldn't be lying here in the bed with her, just before dawn. He should be up and out, moving on.

Her index finger reached out to touch the scar he'd shown her the other night, but more hesitantly, and he grabbed her wrist to stop the touch.

"Sorry, I didn't mean to—"

"It's all right. Not a big deal—it's just numb," he lied.

"You said the other night that it didn't hurt badly," she said finally.

"Not at first. At first, you don't even realize it, especially if you're knee deep in the action. Your adrenaline's going, your mind is on other things and your brain shuts down to the possibility of pain." He wondered why the hell he was telling her this, and then realized he'd already shared more of himself with her than he had with most people who'd known him since he entered the military.

"Auto-pilot."

"You're so intent, so focused on what's right in front of you that you don't have time to look down. And then you start to feel these warning tingles. You ignore them. Tell yourself, *This isn't really happening.*" He paused, locked onto her eyes, the deepest shade of blue he'd ever seen, next to the water at high tide, and just as beautiful. "By the time you admit to yourself that it has happened, it's too late to do anything but curse."

She smiled. "Which I'm sure you did."

"Especially because I'm not exactly the best patient."

"I can't imagine you being forced to sit around for any length of time without taking some kind of action."

"I can do it if that's what the job demands." He shifted reluctantly away from her body. "I've got to go."

He dressed quickly, grabbing his clothing where he'd tossed it the night before. Phone and beeper had been quiet over the past hours and he double-checked them to be sure while Kaylee walked past him, still naked, and rifled in her closet until she pulled out a short white robe.

He thought about staying longer, putting off what he'd promised himself he'd do, because he was much more about pleasure than punishment. But he wouldn't be able to live with himself if he didn't keep his promise.

While he washed up in her bathroom, he noted a large diamond engagement ring sitting casually by the sink, mainly because he'd almost knocked it to the floor when he'd grabbed a towel. He walked out with it in his hand. "You probably should keep this in a safer spot."

"What are you—*oh*." She took the ring from him and shoved it in the pocket of her robe. "Carl gave it to me— he's the guy I broke up with last night. I'm going to give it back to him."

"He wanted to marry you."

"Yes. When he asked me again last night, it was more of an ultimatum than a proposal."

But it was a proposal just the same. That really pissed him off, and he wasn't exactly sure why.

Fuck. Just *fuck.* "That's an expensive ring."

"Carl's from a wealthy family. Lots of parties and dinners. I would've had to quit my job, especially when he ran for office. I didn't want that kind of life."

Deidre Winfield hadn't either, but her family wouldn't let her turn down a chance at being a Winfield. Every girl's dream. Until she had to give up her dream career on order.

Deidre had planned on studying to be a teacher. He'd always wondered if her unhappiness had to do with the fact that she'd had to give up so much of herself just to be a Winfield. And where had that gotten her beyond a spot on the society pages, beyond the constant glare of media attention that demanded perfection?

Of course, he also wondered if the rumors were true—if Deidre had really loved his Uncle Billy instead of Walter. From the few times he'd observed her with Walter, he hadn't noticed any affection there. Just coldness—it was always so cold between them.

"You're better off without him," he said shortly, wondered

why in the hell he'd come here in the first place. Outside, the nor'easter the weathermen had been promising for days raged on, rain sheeting against the windows, wind banging against the side of the building as if it wanted in. His kind of weather. "I've got to go."

He wanted to ask her things, like what she did for a living. Why exactly she'd broken up with her boyfriend last night, but he didn't do discussions well. Yet with Kaylee, he wanted to let it all hang out, spill his guts to her, let her actually hold him while he explained the whole story to her, while he sorted it out in his mind.

Yes, this woman was more dangerous than he thought. Getting the hell out of her apartment was maybe his best idea ever. He could go straight to base, work out, take a nice, long swim in the freezing cold ocean.

Except that wasn't in the cards for him this morning— no, he had something important to do, something that needed to be done.

"Will I . . ." she started when they got to the front door of her apartment, then stopped, shook her head. "Sorry, I guess I'd forgotten about what you said last night."

He paused for a second, and then, going against his better judgment for the nine millionth time since he'd met her, he grabbed her cell phone from the hall table and programmed his name, address and number into its memory before handing it back. "If you need anything."

"Anything?" she asked softly.

He wasn't sure how to answer that, so he went out the door instead and closed it behind him with a soft thud.

———

Kaylee stayed in her robe, staring out the window for at least an hour after Nick left. Normally, she'd be racing to work, especially on a day like today, when the rain clouds moved like dark ink across the sky, the gloominess invading her soul, making her feel more alone than ever and craving human contact. This morning, she merely felt content.

She could still smell the scent of his skin on hers and was reluctant to wash that away just yet. She thought she could still feel his fingers tracing her tattoo. And so she moved to the kitchen table, listening to the rain on the windows and looking through the morning editions of several newspapers she read for work—some her competitors and some, like the one whose headline caught her eye, merely tabloids she read to see what rumors they were printing.

The story was on Cutter Winfield, and the reporter claimed to have a reliable source feeding him information about the missing heir.

She flipped the pages to read the copy.

Cutter Winfield has been a mystery for years. Now, with the death of his mother, an independent source close to the Winfield family claims that Cutter is indeed alive and well, and purported to be readying to take on the title of Winfield yet again.

Cutter found his outlet in being part of an elite group of the military . . . and a chance to keep his true identity hidden from the media. Amidst rumors of his true paternity and increasing troubles with the law, he left his family and has never looked back.

The picture this reporter painted of the lost Winfield heir would've made a great movie.

She'd been on the Winfield story herself for as long as

she'd been reporting. It had always fascinated her, the way Cutter disappeared from a seeming fairy tale life. With Deidre's death, everything about him was stirred up again, and put a kink in her plans to take some time off to figure out what was happening with Aaron.

Aaron. God, what a mess.

Her past with him was exploding in a way that threatened to quickly spiral toward something she had no control over.

Sure, she'd tried, had methodically gone through Aaron's list of men, searching for some semblance of power over the situation. The patch provided a small clue, but it wasn't enough.

She could choose to let herself be haunted by Aaron or she could do her job. She'd finish up her current story on the death of Deidre Winfield and then she'd figure out a way to convince Nick to help her unfold the mystery of Aaron's phone calls.

Thanks to the relentless, driving rain, Nick blended easily into the background of the cemetery, away from the media frenzy of the press, who were pretending to be respectful and give the Winfields their privacy in grief.

Nick knew the Winfield family—Walter, in particular— didn't really want the private time. *Life without the press to see it, record it and send it out to the voting public isn't worth living,* Walter used to say.

Even hidden as Nick was, this was dangerous, made his heart pound and throat tighten, which was exactly why he forced himself to stay put, feet planted to the muddied earth until his mother's coffin was lowered to the ground.

He'd made the drive from Kaylee's apartment in Maryland to New York for the burial for so many different reasons—for an unshakable need to show respect for the woman who'd given him life, a sense of honor and pride in proving that he could give all of this up and because he'd never, ever had a feeling of closure with the Winfields.

After today, he still didn't. Probably never would, and that made his ulcer—the one he'd had since he was a child—burn.

After he'd left home, he'd seen Deidre in person only once. He'd been in New York with Kenny and Chris—it had been two years after Maggie passed and Kenny had hauled the two boys with him on a business trip in an attempt to keep them out of trouble.

Nick hadn't wanted to be that close to his home territory, but it had been the middle of August, and the Winfields traditionally shut down their Manhattan home and spent most of their time in the summer house.

And he saw her—slim and regal in a simple white suit, no sunglasses to shield her.

She saw him too, looked at him for a moment with no real expression on her face, and he remembered thinking, *If she calls to me, I'll walk over to her,* despite the cameras that followed her relentlessly, flashbulbs popping like small firecrackers echoing in his ears.

She'd simply brushed by him as if he was invisible and continued walking. And he cursed himself for being weak, for letting himself get pulled in again. For letting himself feel.

He'd rented a car using a fake ID and driven back to

Virginia without telling Chris or Dad where he was going or why. Didn't give a shit about anything but the feel of the road under him and the hours-long drive that put space between him and his old life.

He hadn't been back to New York since, until today.

Now he brushed the wet hair out of his eyes and scanned the crowd. The extended Winfield clan was all there, but he honed in on his immediate family.

His sister looked suitably classy. Eric looked the same. The familiar chill started at the base of his spine, worked its way up as it always did when he caught a glimpse of these people who were supposed to be his family, whether it be on TV or in the newspaper. But this, this was the first time in eleven years that he'd actually seen any of them in the flesh, that he'd been this close to the blood ties that he would've done anything as a kid to cut.

He was supposed to be a part of them, should feel something, any kind of connection, kinship.

But there was nothing, the same disconnect from childhood. He knew it didn't matter, that he was better off.

The front page of the paper Nick had torn away and held on to tightly throughout the graveside ceremony was now crumpled in his fist, the page with the headline that read *Cutter Winfield—a Special Forces Soldier. Hidden by the US Military?*

Nick wasn't prone to panic; early life experiences coupled with his training taught him that knee-jerk reactions did no good. The report claimed to have a legitimate source, but Nick knew that his family would rather die than admit him into it.

None of these so-called reports ever panned out. It

helped that Nick had been reclusive, that he looked like his mother's side of the family and not like a Winfield. He'd never been tagged by anyone in that regard, although he was stopped frequently to ask if he was some kind of movie star or model.

The advent of video enhancement made things slightly more interesting for him. He'd been helped only because the picture the press claimed was him was really one of his nurse's sons. If the Winfields knew the difference, they weren't saying. But if that was all about to change, he needed to play defense harder and faster.

He turned from the scene at the cemetery and started to walk away, his head pounding. And when his cell phone vibrated in his pocket, he knew exactly who it was. He'd ignored his dad's numerous phone calls, sent them all to voice mail and responded with a brief *I'm fine* text message. But Dad wouldn't be deterred for much longer.

He flipped open his ringing cell and Dad was speaking before Nick got the *Hello* out.

"What are you doing?"

"Walking."

"That smart mouth never got you into anything good."

Nick shook his head, the mood dissipated momentarily and he wondered why this man could call him out every single time with a minimal amount of chafing on Nick's part. Only Dad and a handful of superiors. "I went to the funeral."

There was silence on the other end, and then, "I'm coming home."

"You don't have to do that."

"You're alone. Your brothers aren't there."

How Dad always knew that was beyond him, because yes, Nick was alone. Really alone. And it was the first time that had happened since he'd been eight years old and Jake had barged into the special education classroom where they'd stuck Nick.

Jake had stared at Nick's face and then at his throat where the trach was still in place. "That must feel weird."

I'm used to it, Nick had signed, because at the time, his teachers, his family, everyone thought that he didn't know how to speak, that he actually couldn't speak. But he could, because he'd practiced in private every single chance he got, covering the trach and hearing the comfort of his own rough voice, biding his time until the plastic tube came out for good.

"I have no idea what the fuck you're telling me," Jake had responded, in that demanding, blunt and somehow charming way he'd had even way back when. "Teach me."

And so, after school, behind the auditorium where the teachers would come out during their breaks to smoke, Nick taught Jake the sign language he'd learned. Jake, of course, insisted they modify it so no one could understand what the hell the two of them were talking about.

When Nick spoke his first words, he waited for Jake's reaction.

"I always knew you could speak," Jake told him.

Just like Nick had always known his past would come back to haunt him.

"This will go away." Dad's voice was calm and quiet. "Now that Deidre's buried, the press will find something else to focus on besides looking for Cutter."

"I hope that happens fast."

"I'm sorry about Deidre."

Nick opened his mouth to say that he wasn't sorry, but nothing came out. He didn't want to feel anything for the woman. Shouldn't. And he closed his eyes and pictured Maggie's face, her warm smile, and let himself remember the woman he'd always think of as Mom.

Maggie was there when he'd developed bronchitis, when he'd bucked at going to the hospital. She'd stayed with him non-stop, got him through the worst of the illness. She spun him stories, read him poetry and sang songs she'd written. He still remembered that comfort, wondered if Deidre had ever done that for Eric or for Cass.

Maggie, cremated, ashes spread—*So you can come visit me anywhere and everywhere,* she'd told her sons. And yes, that had been a terrible day, a terrible time.

Still, to know the love of a good mother for nine months was better than never knowing it.

"It's okay to be upset over this. I'd be worried if you weren't." Kenny paused. "I've seen the reports, the papers."

"They're bullshit," Nick retorted, threw the now sodden paper he'd still been holding in his palm in the nearest trash bin and headed toward his car. He was soaked to the skin. "I'm not worried."

"And you're sure you don't want me to fly in?"

"I'll be fine, Dad. I've got some things I've got to take care of anyway."

Being all alone gave him that powerless feeling he remembered all too clearly.

He did not do alone well, not off the job. Jake and Chris got along just fine with solitude but Nick needed something to fill up the silence.

Going back to Kaylee's place wasn't an option, no matter how easy it would be to put himself into her care for another night or two or more, to drown his grief inside of her.

He already knew more about her than he wanted to. Her apartment was clean and sleek and modern, but it wasn't a home. There were no pictures that he saw and nothing looked lived in. The furniture still appeared to be new. Maybe she'd just moved in recently, maybe she'd come from California or Seattle and had ten brothers and sisters and went home to visit every Christmas and Thanksgiving.

Maybe he had to stop thinking about her before he got himself into some real trouble.

Six shots of the local pombay did nothing to her, and yet Sarah Cameron had to practically carry one of the male doctors back to his tent after he'd had half that amount. He'd been attempting to win the bet forged around the open area of the refugee camp as midnight approached.

"You could join me, you know," he murmured against her now, his skin damp from the humidity, his body hard against her own.

And yes, joining him would be easy—would help them both to forget that they were in the middle of a refugee camp in the DRC, and it would mean nothing to her but a release of the relentless, restless energy that had pervaded her since the man she loved had disappeared.

"You'll be passed out before you get your pants off," she told him. "By the way, you owe me. Ten dollars. American money."

She'd never see that money, was only a guest here and

would be gone long before this man was able to drag himself out of the bed. Vince, the American reporter she'd been working with for the past week, would want to stay here through the night and be on the road by dawn. She hadn't been able to sleep and spent most of the evening trading stories with the locals and the doctors.

They'd begun telling ghost stories around the campfire, fueled by the locals' tales of the living dead—zombies—that they swore were true. The superstition went that once you heard the story, you needed to tell it to another person to rid yourself of the bad karma that went with it.

Sarah understood superstitions, understood karma and Africa and its many facets as well as she understood her own soul. She'd grown up here and when she was little—maybe five or six or seven—she'd loved ghost stories. She and her sister would sit under the old porch on the family's farm in Zimbabwe in the dark, only a thin beam of an old flashlight between them, and with the whisper of the tobacco leaves as a soundstage they'd try to scare each other silly.

Sometimes, they used classic stories from books they'd gotten out of the school library—others were from local traditions, like the tales of walking zombies, thanks to local voodoo legends.

But those ghosts were always smoke and mirrors, never flesh and blood. They were never real, and Sarah and her sister would end up laughing until their sides hurt and Mom would call them back inside the house.

Her sister and her parents had been dead for years, since Sarah was sixteen, and she had no idea if the old porch was still standing. Today, she hated ghost stories and she'd been about to leave the circle of people around the fire when the liquor came out and the young doctor who'd been flirting with her had challenged her to a shot contest.

He was so young and yet she had to remind herself that he was years older than she was. But sixteen and the family porch were another lifetime ago and these days the years faded like the sunsets.

Now she lowered the man onto his cot and pulled the blanket over him before leaving the tent. She took advantage of the outside shower available by the doctor's quarters of this French-run refugee camp. As one A.M. approached, the air was still warm, the water almost more so, but good enough to wash the long day of traveling away. She stepped out of the small enclosure holding a small towel against her body.

She dressed quickly, skin still slightly damp as she pulled the black tank top on and scrambled into cargoes. She walked back to her car, where she planned to spend the night, mapping out tomorrow's route for Vince. Going over the pictures she'd taken for him.

She grabbed her camera from her bag and watched through the backlit viewfinder as she thumbed through the day's pictures.

She didn't remember walking through the frantic refugees who'd gathered for food and shelter and medical attention. Looking back at the photos she'd taken, she vaguely recalled the afternoon spent there while Vince interviewed survivors of the most recent violence in the DRC. She'd walked through so many—as a guide and a photographer—and she didn't like to think of herself as immune to the heartache that was all too apparent to an outsider.

But when she photographed the atrocities, it was as if all her pent-up emotion, her anger and shame and wish to help came through the lens.

She'd captured a few children running, laughing. A mother nursed her infant in some sparse shade and she could almost fool herself that the scene was serene.

But the reminders of where these had been taken came quickly—the image of a young man missing both legs below the knees, an old man who kept repeating *Karibu* at the top of his lungs to no one in particular.

He'd lost the worst thing of all, although some would say it was better to be stripped of your senses if you lived here.

Lately, her pictures had been getting better—more focused. Tighter.

These days, photography was all she had to concentrate on and she was grateful for the distraction.

Vince walked up next to her and she silently handed him the camera. This trip, he'd been her biggest supporter and she'd sold more pictures to his paper than she ever had during a single job.

She didn't need the money, but for now work was about *her* survival, putting one foot in front of the other.

"Why don't you work outside of Africa? You're good— really good," he asked finally.

"I like it here."

"My paper wants to hire you full time. You just have to say the word. You'd get to take pictures, have health benefits. Security."

Right now, her jobs consisted of meeting the American reporters who traveled in country, taking them around, giving them protection and getting them in and out of where they needed to be. They came too few and far between.

She'd be a fool to refuse, and yet, for her, there was no other answer. "This is the place I know. That's what makes me such an asset."

"Your talent is what makes you an asset." He was still looking at the pictures. "You're wasting yourself with this part-time guide crap."

If he only knew what she was really capable of—what she'd learned over the years. Then again, he was aware she traveled with automatic weapons, so maybe he did know. Maybe he wanted to save her from herself. "What do you care?"

Vince was mid-forties. Fit and handsome. He'd never married.

Married to the job, she'd expected him to joke, but he hadn't. Hadn't hit on her, hadn't made stupid comments about her country... hadn't done anything she'd expected.

"What are you so scared of, Sarah?"

She wanted to say that nothing scared her... and she wanted it to be true.

These days, there was so much that frightened her. She was invested in things in a way she'd hadn't been before. She hated that. Or at least she wished she could. But hating that would mean she was still denying her feelings for a man who'd wanted her more than any man ever had. And that was something—someplace—she never wanted to go back to.

It had been nearly three months since Clutch left her

behind in the hotel room in Uganda. Three months since he'd held her in his arms and promised not to leave.

Three months since he'd saved her life by doing so. He was into something so deep that she'd begun to fear he'd never get out of it.

"I love it here—this is my country. I grew up here."

"It's all you know. You could learn to love other places too. Or else you've got to do more with your gift, Sarah. You've got to get serious, not just dabble."

He'd looked through her portfolio, the one she'd put together last year. She'd updated it recently, found herself wishing she'd been able to sneak some pictures of Clutch. She wanted nothing more than to set Clutch down in a field and just snap away, map his body, every single part, with film. Black and white, she'd decided, for the shades and shadows. It would work with his blond hair and eyes, would work with who he was—light fighting to stay in the shadows and never succeeding. At least not when he was with her.

She'd met Clutch two years earlier, when she'd been trying to get a picture of the famed mercenary. At the time, she had no idea that she would become his lover for a year.

The first time they'd made love had been fast—hot—up against the door of the office.

She'd been attempting to capture him on film, had been lucky he didn't break her camera. Instead, he'd lowered them to the ground and took her like a man possessed.

"Long time for me, Sarah," he'd said fiercely. "Tired of my own hand."

She'd been tired of hers as well.

They'd broken up when Clutch refused to train her as a

mercenary—reunited when Clutch helped to save her life when she'd gotten herself involved with another mercenary, who'd meant to kill her.

But Clutch had gotten called back into service by his government nearly three months ago and was involved in something really bad, over which he had no control. Since he'd left her in the hotel, she'd done nothing—barely surviving. Crying. She'd gotten sick of that, sick of herself, had finally pulled herself together, even if it was only a temporary patch job, and she'd gone back on the road.

She still looked over her shoulder, around every corner, waiting to feel Clutch's presence, but there had been nothing. Only stone-cold silence. Loneliness. And most of the time, she hated him for forcing her to feel again, only to take himself away from her, leaving her right back where she'd been.

You're not the same person.

She looked the same as she did last month—last year, even—her hair was still short, her tattoos still there, ink bright against her tanned skin. Yes, flesh and bone were the same, but the insides, the hot blood through her veins, that was changed.

"Think about the offer, Sarah. From here, I go to Nepal for three months to live with an indigenous tribe. You'd be perfect for the assignment." Vince pushed away from her car, leaving her by the abandoned fire and all alone in the hot night.

As much as she didn't want to think about her past and her future, both were right there in front of her, their paths too divergent to ever cross and the choice between the two inextricably bound.

CHAPTER
7

When he was young and handsome and had visions of taking over the world, Walter Winfield had women of all ages after him. And at eighteen, nineteen and twenty, his life had been a string of formal parties, college studies and secret affairs with women, all of whom expected to be the next Winfield wife.

Deidre hadn't wanted to be a Winfield at all. And certainly, she'd never wanted to be attached to him or the legacy of fame, fortune and pain that abounded.

No, she'd wanted Walter's brother, Billy, instead. At that time, when Walter turned twenty-five and became serious about being a Winfield and all that entailed, Billy was the black sheep of the family, only eighteen when he'd been sent to the military to get himself straightened out.

Billy had served a tour, was visiting the family estate in Nantucket on leave when Deidre came to the house for the first time. She'd been escorted by her mother and father. Walter had been struck from the first moment the blond beauty had walked through the door.

Billy had been mesmerized as well. And as they lunched on the patio in the spring warmth, Deidre's attention was subtly pulled in his brother's direction. They talked books and art with a passion Walter remembered well—his own hobbies were not in that area, varying instead from golf to polo, his reading mainly history and politics.

Deidre was going to be a teacher. She would head to school in the fall. Later, Walter's father told him that Deidre's parents disapproved of that career for their daughter. They were of the mind-set that she should be focused on settling down and starting a family.

They said she'd always been too absorbed with the needs of others.

Billy wasn't even close to marrying anyone, not even a girl like Deidre, who came with a large fortune, class and political power in the form of her very Republican family—all of which would help to bring more stature to the Winfield name. And so when Billy was away on his second tour of duty, Walter asked for Deidre's hand in marriage.

Pressured by her family, told that Billy was already engaged to another woman, a heartbroken Deidre gave up her career and the idea of marrying Billy.

She would be the perfect wife of a potential president. She was perfect—beautiful, fashionable, kind. She was also well read, passionate about children's rights and the American public adored her. The press couldn't get enough of her, and although she never complained once about life in the fishbowl, it took its toll on her.

Walter's own father had told him early on, *You're never going to find true love, Walter. It doesn't exist for people with the money and background we have. The best you can hope for is a companion who'll support your political career and give you children.*

Walter had convinced himself that Deidre was shy. Demure. That once they married, things would be different. That she was merely nervous about the responsibilities she was about to take on.

He'd been very, very wrong.

Deidre had spent their wedding night in bed, alone, sobbing in her sleep. Walter sat in the chair until the sun came up, the weight of the Winfield legacy planted firmly and irrevocably on his chest.

Deidre had only enough love in her heart for one man. She'd finally consummated that love, had ended up in Billy's bed time and time again, until Walter finally confronted his brother. Threatened him.

Billy, who'd been planning on leaving the service and then New York, and taking Deidre with him, had re-enlisted.

A month before Cutter's birth, Billy was killed in combat. The press reported it as friendly fire, but Walter and the Winfield family knew the truth—Billy had been targeted by the foreign militia, kidnapped and killed before he could be rescued by Special Forces. Deidre had never forgiven Walter.

Walter had never forgiven himself for driving his brother away and into that final tour of duty. And now that decision weighed heavily on his mind in light of what Deidre had done.

Immediately after her death, Walter was given a private letter penned by his wife before her death. He'd burned it in the fireplace in his office at the family estate, but not before he'd committed the contents to memory, elegant handwriting that told him Cutter was his son and not Billy's as Walter had always been led to believe by Deidre herself.

Walter remembered that every time he had looked at Cutter while the boy was still living as a Winfield, Deidre's betrayal had stung. He'd assumed the same held true for her, given she couldn't bear to be near the preemie after she'd given birth, much too early.

He was ashamed to admit that there were many nights he himself prayed the tiny infant wouldn't make it through until morning. But against all odds, Cutter Winfield did.

Walter used to try to force himself to see his brother in Cutter. In truth, the boy looked far more like Deidre's side of the family than anyone else.

All those years, Walter had let his pride and guilt get in the way of so many things. It was time to set things right.

Nick stepped on the SITREP Max had slipped underneath the back door as he came in from the garage. He'd spent hours on the highways from New York back home, letting the radio and the road distract him.

Now, well into the evening, he'd finally relaxed enough

to come home. And still, he wanted to kick the file aside and not deal with it.

But that had never been his style.

He scooped up the folder and scanned the familiar report as he headed to the shower to wash the chill of the dank day off him. What he found—or didn't find—in that report, written six years earlier, and two days after he'd met Aaron Smith, stopped him dead in his tracks, shirt dangling from his right arm and pants unbuttoned.

This SITREP had most definitely been altered. Not to the naked eye—nothing had been blacked out. No, the changes were more sophisticated. The report had been retyped so as not to include a single mention of Aaron Smith.

The report had Nick being a hero and completely saving himself, just the way Aaron had reported it back to Kaylee.

And yes, his own signature remained intact and on the bottom of the page.

Shit.

He stared at the report until the words blurred, until his memories got clearer and he could see what he hadn't told Kaylee about—saw the dead men lying on the ground behind Aaron and the lifeless look in Aaron's eyes.

Maybe none of this was a big deal, maybe it was all magnified because of Deidre's death and the great, ongoing search for Cutter.

And maybe this was something worth looking into further. He'd need to get the list of the other men from Kaylee, contact them. Ask Kaylee exactly what they'd told her about their time with Aaron, the exact locations. Everything.

The knock on the door, two sharp raps, made him jump first and then curse as he yanked his clothes back on and shoved the papers aside. Letting his guard down when he was home with his brothers was fine—home alone, he needed to be more on guard.

From what, he wasn't exactly sure, until he looked out the window and caught sight of the big black car with the New York license plates in the driveway. His breath caught and for a brief second, he thought about not answering the door.

Instead, without bothering to look through the peephole, he opened the front door and planted himself firmly in place.

The man Nick had vowed never to call *Father* again stood on the other side of the door. Alone. Not even a chauffeur in the car, as evidenced by the half-rolled-down driver's-side window.

"May I come in, Cutter?"

Nick stepped aside and let the man into the house that had sheltered him from harm for all these years, watched as Walter moved stiffly across the threshold as if he knew what an invasion his presence was.

Nick shut the door behind them and cleared his throat before he spoke. "I'm sorry about Deidre."

"She didn't ask for you before she died," Walter told him and for a second Nick felt the familiar one-two punch that came with his biological family. But when Walter continued, the blow softened slightly. "I wish she had, for both our sakes."

"Why's that?" This time, he was unable to keep the bitterness from his tone.

"I understand your anger. But it should be directed at your mother, not at me. She lied to both of us."

"I know I'm Billy's son. I knew that before I left your house for good." It was the first time he'd ever said the words out loud to anyone, although they'd been in his mind for as long as he could remember.

There was a pause as he waited for confirmation from Walter. "No, you're not my brother's son, Cutter. You're mine. My biological son."

For a moment, it was as if someone held his windpipe closed. When he was finally able to take a breath, it came out in a long, whistling wheeze.

All this time . . . all this time he'd thought he understood why neither parent wanted him—he was an embarrassment, a reminder of an indiscretion. A real live bastard.

To hear that he was legitimate broke his heart more than he ever thought it could. "You're lying."

"If I had known . . ." Walter trailed off.

None of it made sense anymore. It had always been nothing more than a slight comfort as to why Deidre had hated him—he'd figured that she saw him as a living, breathing reminder of her affair. "I don't understand . . . when did she find this out?"

Walter hesitated, and Nick saw a pity in his eyes that he never, ever wanted to see from anyone. "She knew the whole time, Cutter."

"I'm not Cutter. Stop calling me that."

"I know this can't be easy to understand."

Understand? He closed his eyes and sagged against the wall and wondered how the hell anyone was supposed to understand that their own mother couldn't bear the sight of them.

"By the time Billy reenlisted, it was too late to think about repairing our marriage," Walter admitted.

"She hated you, that much I know. I might not have spoken much, but I sure as hell was never as stupid as you thought."

"Your mother and I grew apart for many different reasons."

"She loved Billy. So why the hell didn't she just save everyone the trouble and divorce you?"

"We're a public family, Cutter. The world expects different things from us. Our own happiness can't come first."

Nick's chest felt tight and he fought for breath. His ulcer burned. "What kind of way is that to live?"

Walter's face told the strain of the past days. Although Deidre hadn't loved Walter, it was apparent that Walter had never been able to stop loving his wife. "I don't have the strength for a philosophical discussion with you."

"Then why, after all this time, are you here? I'm dead, remember? So you've said what you had to say—I hope it made you feel better, because it sure as shit didn't do anything for me."

Walter looked pained at Nick's words. "I lost my brother before I had a chance to make peace with him. I won't let that happen again."

Nick ran both hands through his hair, muttered to himself that he needed to stay calm and focused, and *fuck,* he wished his brothers were with him now. "You can't walk in here and expect me to give up my life."

"I don't expect that."

"If I'd turned out to be Billy's son, then what? I'm assuming you wouldn't be at my doorstep."

"I don't know," Walter answered honestly. "Finding out you are my son was a wake-up call for me. You were a child and I punished you for no reason. A father should never do that to his own flesh and blood."

Nick felt the lump rise in his throat, pushed it down with a hard, silent swallow and told himself that this was all bullshit. He fought the urge to tell Walter that no, he wasn't his father. And then he thought about Kenny, how he'd pounded it into him to always be respectful. How sometimes it was better not to argue, especially if you knew the truth inside your own heart. "I really don't know what you expect now . . . why you suddenly care."

"Your job is dangerous. Like your uncle's was. I couldn't live with myself if I didn't reach out to you. But I can't expect your forgiveness."

"No, you can't," Nick said firmly.

Walter nodded in his direction and moved toward the front door. He stopped before he exited. "I've followed your career. I know you're a hero."

Nick didn't bother to ask him why, didn't want to know any more than he already did. His mind couldn't process this information—not now with Walter standing in front of him. "I do my job."

"Better than most. One of your most recent missions to stop an assasination saved an African country from potential economic ruin."

"Details of that mission are classified."

"Not to a senator." With those words, Walter was gone, shutting the door softly behind him.

How much of Nick's life Walter Winfield knew about or cared to know was something Nick had never really stopped to consider. The man had written him off as dead, discarded him—Nick never thought further contact would be an issue. But Kenny Waldron wasn't a hard man to find and Nick still lived at the house that Kenny had signed over to his boys, the one Nick and Jake and Chris spent the better part of their teenage years in. The one he and Jake had continued to live in while their teams were stationed in Virginia. The one Chris recently moved back into when he'd been transferred back East from a West Coast team.

Nick had never felt so exposed in his life. He'd let a piece of paper his father signed put him at ease, when he'd always known to be far more suspicious than that.

He also knew it was impossible to live on high alert all the time.

For a few seconds, he sat still and let the old house comfort him—if he closed his eyes and listened, really listened, he swore he could hear Maggie calling for *her boys* through the maze of hallways he and Jake and Chris used to get lost in.

He waited for a few moments after he heard Walter's car pull out of the gravel driveway and then he grabbed his jacket and his phone and his keys—the SITREP too.

Tonight, there was no comfort to be found alone.

There could be so many reasons why a senator was visiting a SEAL at eleven o'clock at night.

While Kaylee sat outside of Nick's house trying to catch her breath as she watched Walter Winfield's retreating car, another set of headlights came up from the long driveway. She was blinded momentarily as the car jerked out of the driveway and turned the opposite way Walter's car had gone.

A sleek, black Porsche. Virginia plates.

Nick's car.

Nick's car. Nick's house.

At that moment, her ambition crashed headlong into desire and she knew she'd crossed a major threshold. Nothing would ever be the same.

There was no way this was really happening.

The entire ride down, she'd practiced what she'd say to him—that she really, really needed him to go to Africa with her to possibly find Aaron. To figure out what was going on.

He'd refused her once before, but maybe now . . .

If you need anything . . .

She needed, and she wasn't giving up until she got more from him. He'd been right when he'd told her that his visit wasn't about Aaron—in so many ways, hers now wasn't either.

But when she'd arrived, Nick's front door had been open and someone was there, his silhouette illuminated by the porch lights.

She'd spotted Nick easily, he'd been standing there as well . . . next to a man she swore was Senator Walter Winfield.

There was a car in the driveway—black. Expensive. The way it was angled in the circular drive didn't allow her to see the plates and she'd hurriedly pulled her mini-binoculars out of the glove compartment. When the man had opened the door of his car, the interior light illuminated his face quite clearly.

It had most definitely been Walter Winfield.

As he pulled out of the driveway, she caught a quick glimpse of New York plates, but no numbers. When she looked back at the door, it was closed and Nick was nowhere to be seen, until now, when his car raced past hers.

Could Nick be Cutter Winfield?

What did she really know about Nick Devane? He was in the right age range. Military. And Walter Winfield was making a secret, late-night visit to him.

There were so few pictures of Cutter, none had a clear view of his face save for a black-and-white baby photo. Sketch artists had compiled their takes over the years, but none of them had ever seemed to fit, in Kaylee's estimation, although she wasn't quite sure why. Those generated images told her nothing—the face was too cold, too fake.

Pieces from an article she'd written on Cutter years earlier came into sudden, sharp focus.

She shoved the binoculars aside, looking over her shoulder in complete paranoid fashion until she had the key in the ignition and was safely on the road back to Maryland.

The drive home was a blur. Her hands gripped the wheel tightly and even though driving always soothed her, tonight the low, hard thrum of the sleek engine was merely a reminder of Nick.

He'd sat in this seat. The leather held his scent the way her skin had that morning. She didn't turn on the radio, just let the scene replay itself in her mind and tried to forget that he'd programmed his phone number into her cell.

She could still feel Nick's palms on her, his body warm in the cool night air, the rumble of his car beneath her.

Once she pulled into the safety of her own parking garage, she became aware that her breathing had turned harsh. It had been months since her last asthma attack, and she took a hit from her inhaler, forcing the air into her lungs, and waited in the dark car in the dimly lit garage.

So many secrets. In some ways, Nick was just like Aaron, holding back from her—although that was hardly a fair assessment after knowing him all of forty-eight hours.

God, if this was true, if he was Cutter, he'd probably never been able to get close to anyone because of it. A part of his life blocked off from any woman he chose to get close to.

He'd already told her he didn't let women in. And now she knew why. She could possibly have his secret life in her hands.

What was she supposed to do now?

CHAPTER

8

The elevator moved too slowly. Kaylee paced the small area, not exactly sure why she was in such a rush—it was as if she was the one in hiding now.

Shit. Just *shit.*

She rounded the corner out of the elevator and stopped dead when she saw Nick standing in front of her apartment door. Clad in his black leather jacket, he leaned casually with his back to the wall as his eyes caught hers.

For a second, she couldn't breathe again, had to remember to draw air and not stand stupidly, staring at him.

"Are you all right?" he asked and in that instant she knew that he hadn't seen her at his house, that he was here for an entirely different reason.

She wasn't sure if she was relieved or not.

You have to tell him what you know.

She hadn't even told him what she did for a living. In all fairness, he'd never asked, but she'd learned that most people who wanted to stay out of the public eye didn't much appreciate her profession. She hadn't wanted to see that kind of suspicion from Nick, not when she'd approached him as Aaron's widow and nothing more.

"I'm okay—just surprised to see you," she answered honestly. She stared at him, the possible missing Winfield heir, and tried to see any similarity between the proud, handsome man in front of her and the pictures of the Winfields she'd studied over the years.

"It was a last minute decision on my part. Rough night," he admitted and then looked as if he wished he could take that last statement back.

She took a deep breath. "Why don't you come inside? There's something I need to talk to you about. It's important."

"You're not okay." His warm hands covered hers, his body behind her as he took the keys from her shaking fingers and opened the door for her.

"Asthma attack. It's the medicine—I'm always shaky after I take it," she explained, and yes, that was a partial truth. He closed the door behind them, unarming her alarm at the same time she dropped her bag to the floor. "Did you let yourself in here before I got home?"

"I waited outside this time. Why?"

"Someone's been here." Her coat closet was slightly open. If that had been the only thing out of place, she wouldn't have thought anything of it, but she also noticed that a few things on her table had been shifted around. The papers were still neatly piled but the laptop was slightly farther to the right than she'd left it. Her Internet Explorer browser had been closed as well and the machine hadn't rebooted.

Nothing obvious, but someone had been in her apartment, in her things.

"I've been outside your door for about half an hour. I didn't see anyone—or hear anything." He was checking the windows. "They're all still locked."

A knock at the door made them both go still. He put a finger to his lips and walked quietly toward the door to look through the peephole. In seconds, he was urging her to do the same.

She saw two men dressed in dark suits, waiting patiently. They looked to be federal agents and she thought back over her last few stories and wondered if she'd gotten into anyplace she really wasn't supposed to.

"Do you know them?" he mouthed when she pulled away. She shook her head and he pulled his gun and urged her to open the door halfway—he was right there, close enough to touch. In fact, he did brush his fingers against hers, which were wrapped around the door frame tightly.

She ordered herself to hold it together and she did, calmly facing the men with an inquisitive frown.

They'd already pulled out identification, badges and FBI ID cards with their pictures—Agents Simms and Ferone.

"Kaylee Smith?" the taller of the two men asked, and continued before she could respond, "I'm Agent Simms, FBI. We need to talk about your ex-husband, Aaron Smith."

She swallowed hard and was half-grateful that he at least confirmed that something was going on with Aaron.

"Ms. Smith, can we please come inside to talk?" Agent Simms was asking.

"I'm more comfortable with talking right here." She didn't want these men in her apartment—her safe zone. Anything they had to tell her about Aaron, they could say right here. "Just tell me what's going on."

Agent Simms nodded. "We have reason to suspect that Aaron Smith is alive."

She didn't say anything, just let her eyes go slightly wider, as though this was actually news to her. She'd learned a long time ago that talking got you in trouble, but listening helped you learn exactly what your battle was.

Agent Ferone cleared his throat and Simms continued, his voice low and soothing. "We know this is hard for you to hear, but we received some information last week that leads us to believe he faked his death. Our intelligence has placed him close to the DRC—Democratic Republic of the Congo."

"Why isn't the military here?"

"They've turned the case over to us—we'll hand it over to the CIA once we receive more information on Aaron," Agent Simms said, although that didn't ring true to her ears. From what she knew of the military, they didn't hand over their AWOL soldiers, if that's what Aaron truly was, so easily.

"You're coming to me because Aaron has no other family."

"We'd like to speak to Aaron."

"I don't know how to get in touch with him. I didn't even know he was alive," she lied, the old protective instincts coming out despite her anger toward Aaron. Another lesson learned early—protect your own. You never knew when you would need the favor returned.

"You'll want to cooperate with us." Agent Simms's tone had lost the kind edge it had earlier.

"I've told you everything I know. If I hear from him, I'll get in touch with you. Please leave me your card and go."

Agent Ferone smiled, but it didn't reach his eyes. "I'm afraid that's not the way this works, Kaylee. You're going to have to come with us."

"I'm not going anywhere with you—not right now. I'll be happy to meet you at the FBI offices in the morning," she said.

"That's not going to work for us." Agent Simms kept his tone reasonable. "This is time-sensitive information. I'm sure you don't want any more harm to come to your ex-husband than necessary."

Something was very, very wrong. Nick squeezed her hand, as if he agreed.

She pretended to look at the floor for a second so she could catch Nick's face from her periphery. He was motioning for her to invite them inside.

"Okay, fine. I just need to grab my bag." She opened the door wider and walked away, feeling the two men following her inside the apartment.

She turned around again only when she heard the door slam shut, feeling the sick plunge of her stomach as she saw the gun Agent Ferone had pulled on her. "What are you doing?"

"We're going to need whatever Aaron Smith left you in that safe-deposit box," he said.

How did they know about the safety deposit box? She fought panic, asked, "And then what?"

He ignored her question, which told her more than if he'd threatened her outright. "Hand over your bag."

She held it out to him, feet rooted to the floor, right before Nick took him down from behind with a pinch of his fingers on the man's neck.

"Leave, Kaylee—go now," he instructed even as Agent Simms lunged for him.

But she didn't leave—instead, she watched Nick wrestle the taller man, waiting to see if there was anything she could do to help. Every instinct she had fought running away from any situation—this was no different.

The men appeared well matched for a fight, but without any apparent effort on Nick's part, he had the dark-haired agent headlocked and unconscious within seconds.

When the knife clattered from the agent's limp hand, it was then she noticed it was covered in blood. As was Nick's arm.

He appeared unconcerned, was rifling first through one agent's pockets and then the other's while telling her to collect her things fast.

She did so: computer, passport, Aaron's envelope and some clothing were stuffed into an oversize bag, which Nick took from her.

"Where did the men go?" she asked. Her apartment door was slightly ajar.

"Janitor's closet. We don't have much time before they wake up. Lock the door behind you," he told her as he slipped her bag onto his shoulder and grabbed her hand.

In what seemed like an eternity, they were on the street and in Nick's car, careening away from the curb and her apartment and the life she'd known since Aaron died.

Nick was yanking his jacket off as he drove and she saw the wound he'd received during the fight. She looked around, found a towel in the backseat and pressed it to his arm without thinking.

"Stop, Kaylee. Just let me drive." He pushed her hand away.

"You're bleeding everywhere," she pointed out, her calm demeanor returning before she glanced behind them.

"They didn't follow us."

Momentarily placated, she returned to putting pressure on his arm. "Where are we going?"

"My house. We'll make a plan from there."

"Your house?" she asked with just enough of a catch in her voice to make him glance her way.

"Problem?"

"No, no problem. Those men weren't FBI agents."

He shook his head. "I don't know," he admitted. "But the FBI doesn't typically try to kill people like that and I wasn't willing to take the chance."

She was glad he hadn't. "What would they have done if you hadn't been there?" she asked quietly.

"I *was* there. That's all that matters."

They drove in silence for a while. Kaylee felt her body relax with every mile they put between them and her apartment, but it jolted when her cell phone rang. She grabbed it, praying that it wouldn't be her Winfield source. *Not now, not now.*

"Do you recognize the number?" he asked.

No. "No." She held out the phone to him and he stared at the small screen.

"Out of the country area code," he said slowly. "Africa exchange."

Her mouth dried.

"Answer it—put it on speaker. Tell whoever it is that you're alone if they ask," he told her.

"Hello?" No answer, just the familiar crackle, the faint hum and pause of an overseas line.

"KK."

Aaron. "What's going on? The FBI were here asking me questions about you."

"What did you tell them?"

"Nothing. I told them nothing. But they know you're alive—said you faked your death."

There was a long break, and she thought for sure she'd lost the call. And then she heard his voice crackle across the line. "Don't tell them anything. Don't trust them."

She didn't say anything, stared up at Nick while he listened intently.

"KK, are you there?"

"I'm here. I don't know what to do. I don't know what you want from me."

"I need you to pull the money from my account and bring it to me, to Africa, or else I'm a dead man for sure."

"What do you mean?"

"The less you know for now, the better."

"Where am I going with the money? I can't just show up in the middle of Africa."

But he wasn't listening, was giving her a string of numbers, repeating them over and over. They sounded like latitude and longitude.

"Please, just meet me, bring me the money—I'll need it within forty-eight hours."

"Aaron, I can't—"

"Please. It has to be you who brings it. I would never

hurt you, KK. You know that. Please just come to Africa now." A long pause and then, "If it wasn't so important, I'd never ask you to do something like this."

The line went dead and for a few minutes she closed her eyes and let the motion of the car transport her to someplace else—anyplace else—until Nick jerked the car off the road at a secluded spot along the thruway and slammed it into park.

When she finally opened her eyes, Nick was staring at her, waiting, and her words came out in a rush. "He left me money—a lot of money, too much for him to have gotten legitimately."

"Did you check with the bank?"

God, why was he so calm? "Right after that first call from Aaron when I opened the safe-deposit box and found the list and a bankbook. Do you think those men know about the money?"

He drummed the top of the steering wheel with his fingertips, like he was sending out some kind of code. "They seemed to know a whole hell of a lot."

Yes, they knew too much, and she far too little. That needed to change. "What kind of game is this, Nick?"

This situation was far from a game. Nick had wanted to pull over, grab the phone and demand that whoever the fuck was pretending to be Aaron cut the bullshit immediately, but Nick was well aware that his emotions were far too close to the edge. The past forty-eight hours had been a whirlwind—the past twenty-four alone had drained nearly all of his reserves.

So he'd listened instead. Listened to the man begging Kaylee for help, giving her the coordinates of where he wanted to meet her. Aaron wanted Kaylee to walk into the middle of the DRC and deliver money.

"You met him, you spoke to him—it sounds just like him." There was an urgency in her voice that was hard to ignore, and he wondered why in the hell it was so important to her that it be Aaron.

"It could've been anyone. It was a long time ago." He turned on the overhead light and handed her the file from Max.

"What's this?"

"The SITREP I wrote after meeting Aaron," he said.

"Oh." She placed it on her lap but didn't make a move to open it. "I know what it says."

He slid a sideways glance at her before he pulled the car back on the thruway and gunned it to make up for lost time. When it approached ninety, he told her, "You don't know everything it said. The report you're holding has been sanitized. I wrote about Aaron in my report—what he did, and how he saved my life. But that information is missing. And there's something else I didn't tell you, something that, at the time, I didn't think you needed to know."

"What?"

He gripped the wheel hard and floored the accelerator, raised his voice slightly to be heard above the noise. "I didn't want to ruin your memories of Aaron. I had a promise to keep, and that didn't involve spilling the man's secrets."

"Why the change of heart?"

Because someone wants you dead. "I have a feeling all of

this somehow ties back to what I saw the night Aaron saved my life."

He didn't even have to try hard to memorize the numbers Aaron—or whoever it was pretending to be the former soldier—had rattled off. They were the coordinate points of the mission in the Congo, the exact place where everything happened, which didn't make it into his report.

Latitude: 0.516667

0° 31' 0" N

0 degrees, 31 minutes, 0 seconds North

Longitude: 25.2

25° 12' 0" E

25 degrees, 12 minutes, 0 seconds East

DRC, Africa. Aka, hell on earth.

With Aaron's help, Nick half dragged, half carried himself and Joe to the shelter Aaron promised them for the time being. Judging by the way the enemy fire was bouncing through the sky like fucking Fourth of July, the QAF wasn't coming through anytime soon.

On the way into the enclosure, he turned slightly to the left to make sure he wasn't going to trip on anything while walking backward, and noted the bodies. The bodies that had to be the reason Aaron had blood all over his hands, his neck . . . covering the front of his cammies. At first, Nick convinced himself that the blood was his, even though his mind told him that Aaron had come to him covered in the stuff.

Looking at the bodies in real time, Nick understood why there had been so much blood. The men had endured torture. They'd possibly been soldiers or mercs—Nick didn't have the time to find out, as he was letting off as many rounds of ammo as he could to keep the rebels at bay and away from his wounded teammate.

And Aaron was on his flank, helping him. The AWOL soldier had saved his life, continued to do so, and Nick didn't have time or energy to wrap his mind around the fact that the same man could be a murderer.

"I had my reasons," Aaron said. "I had my orders."

"You're AWOL. You don't take orders once you're AWOL."

"You're still really green, son. Maybe one day you'll understand." Aaron paused. "Then again, I hope not . . . I hope you never understand this."

Nick shook his head to get the picture out of his mind. "There were bodies."

"Bodies," she repeated slowly. "As in . . ."

"He'd killed them. Aaron had killed the men I saw."

"How do you know that?"

He hesitated. "I could tell the way the men were taken down, the look in Aaron's eyes when he saw me notice them. Aaron had blood on his face and neck. I can't explain it to someone who's never been in a combat situation—I just knew, Kaylee."

"But you don't think Aaron killed them in a combat situation, do you? You think he murdered them."

"That's the way it looked. The men weren't rebel soldiers. But I don't know if they'd threatened him. I don't know what the hell I walked in on. All I know is that, for whatever reason, Aaron let me walk away."

She was completely overwhelmed. He thought about pulling the car over again but figured that might make her fall apart completely. No, she needed the motion and he needed her functioning.

After a long minute, she spoke. "I wish I didn't know that. I wish I didn't have to know about any of this. This changes everything for me. Aaron was a killer. He was AWOL and he was a killer. And maybe he still is."

"You don't know all the circumstances. No matter what else, he saved my life. And the lives of the other men you met."

"Does that balance out the other things you said he did?"

"I don't know how to answer that. We're paid to do things—things that most civilians don't want to know . . . or think about." He threw a quick glance her way.

"You think he was paid by the military to kill those men?"

"I think there's a hell of a lot we need to figure out. What do you want to do?"

"I have to bring the money to him. I don't have a choice."

"There's always a choice—you just might not like it much." He pushed his hand through his hair. "Someone could take it for you."

"No, he said that it had to be me."

"And that didn't raise any red flags?"

"He didn't want anyone else involved."

"So he'll involve the love of his life? A woman he'd do anything for? Think about that—it doesn't make sense."

"No, it doesn't. Aaron was many things, but he'd never willingly put me in danger."

"Yet he has."

"I guess I shouldn't be surprised that Aaron turned into a killer for hire. You probably all lend yourselves out like that. Just like you're doing now."

"Don't lump me in the same category as Aaron."

"I'm sorry. I never got a chance to take it out on him. Do you know what it's like never being able to speak your peace to the most significant person in your life? Someone who hurt you so badly you feel permanently scarred inside?"

"Yeah, actually, I do. Contrary to popular belief, not all of us are machines. But there comes a time when you've got to let it go, before it breaks you. When are you going to let it go, Kaylee?"

Who the hell was he kidding to give this kind of advice—*any* advice, for that matter? Granted, it was advice Nick had tried his best to follow. Told himself that it would make him stronger.

But when was he ever going to be strong enough? Any stronger and he would be a fucking machine—and he'd seen his share of guys like that. He was almost one of them. And he didn't want to end up some random merc pining for a lost love, with death and murder behind his eyes.

The fact that Kaylee tugged at him meant he hadn't gone all the way, that he could climb back slowly from the lonely place he'd found himself in these past years when he'd been all about work and random sex and more work and more sex.

Kaylee, who sat quietly next to him wearing a pair of hot faded jeans—she'd looked long and lean as she'd strode toward him in the hallway outside her apartment tonight—paired with a tight black shirt that made her hair look like it was under klieg lights, Nick could almost forget that they were here together for a very serious reason.

How he'd gotten so close to this woman in such a short amount of time was beyond him.

"If I can get to the bottom of things, I'll have closure,"

she told him now, as if she was trying to convince herself as well.

If he closed his eyes, he could see the bodies, two men, mutilated. Tortured before they'd been killed.

More than likely, they'd prayed for death. Begged for it. If there was closure for them, it wasn't anything he wanted a part of.

He cursed himself, wondered how he'd gotten pulled into all of this from merely doing his job all those years ago.

The universe gives us what we need when we need it, Dad always said. Nick had never been one to believe in that superstition bullshit, had a hard time believing his dad and Chris, even though they were always spot on with their Cajun gypsy shit. Nick believed in intuition. Dad. His brothers. His team. Beyond that, the world was a crapshoot and he played the game accordingly.

"First order of business is to figure out if he's alive or not," he said.

"The only way to do that is to go to Africa."

"I know."

"You'll come with me?" she asked.

He would. Under normal circumstances, it would be the kind of mystery that intrigued him to the point of taking on the danger single-handedly. Now that he might actually be involved, he realized he had little choice.

"After tonight, I'm in this as deeply as you are. And you're in danger." From the authorities perhaps, which was sometimes worse than being in danger from common criminals. "I can't walk away now."

"And if I don't go, if I don't do something, I'm going to be haunted for the rest of my life." She swallowed hard before she spoke again. "Do you think that the people who broke into my place would just stop?"

No, they wouldn't. None of this would just stop—not without interference, and fuck, just how much did he owe Aaron? When did the favor end?

And still, the altered SITREP didn't sit right in his gut.

He understood government interference. Confidentiality. The need to keep certain mission details—or even certain missions—completely off the record. He'd been on some of those himself. That, coupled with what was happening with Kaylee right now, told him this was bigger than just a single man who'd gone AWOL.

"I don't understand . . . I don't know what happened to him." She paused, rubbed her hands together as if praying. "I feel like I never really knew him."

"You did, Kaylee." He kept his eyes on the road as the world sped by through the tinted windows of the car. "You knew a big part of him. You have to trust what you knew."

"So there's a part of you that whoever you're with will never know?"

He pushed the accelerator further to the floor before he answered, hanging on to the wheel as hard as he could. "There's a part of all of us no one will ever know."

Bobby Juniper, aka Clutch, aka someone no one really knew, was a thirty-year-old white man working as a mercenary in one of the most dangerous places on earth. The DRC. Congo. A place that most people tried to get the fuck out of. Clutch and the men—and the one woman—he worked with under the name GOST would head for the hills too, if they could.

Unfortunately, the U.S. government had them completely by the balls.

But the air was heavy with change, so strong he swore he could taste it, imbibe it the way he did the strong local pombay when he wanted to forget who he was now—a man without a country. Africa had never felt like home to him. No place ever had, except maybe lying in Sarah's arms.

He tried his best not to think about her—it had gone from every minute to every hour and now he was sometimes able to go half a day without feeling the ache.

Settled into the bar in Ubundu, he took a swig of the beer and called for another shot of the local brew to pass the time as he listened to the tourists who'd climbed the Nyiragongo volcano near Goma and who were headed out of the Kisangani Airport come evening.

There was a Congolese woman giving palm readings to the tourists in the corner of the bar. Now she sidled up to him, asking, "Why don't you let me read your future?"

"I'm not paying you."

He'd spoken to her in her native language, and she gave a soft smile. "For you, no charge."

"I'm not—" But she'd taken his free hand in hers, didn't realize that a move like that could buy her a pass to death in three seconds flat.

She stared at him, big brown eyes growing hard within seconds. "You don't have much of a soul left, boy. Better hurry and get out before the *masuka* get you."

Masuka was the African word for ghost. He jerked his hand away, her words burning him like a brand.

"There's a way back for you," she told him.

He regained his composure easily, forcing his heart rate to normalize and his breathing to ease. "I'll bet you say that to all the soldiers," he told her, even as he cursed himself for getting taken, had lived here long enough to know you didn't accept anyone or anything at face value.

No, Africa never felt like home, but he'd tried, kept house staff like he'd been expected to, housekeepers and cooks who did his chores and laundry and made him food and cajoled him into eating, even when he didn't feel like it. He'd adopted their culture and traditions, given in to the rhythm of the day and night by throwing out his watch and letting his body tell him when it was time to do things—to eat and sleep and play . . . and work.

When GOST set him free, he'd had time. Nothing but. And so he'd set up house and he'd grabbed a radio and bought books from the local vendors and he'd read. Never thought about finding anyone special.

Women looked—they'd always looked. But he'd never had interest in casual rolls—they would only serve to remind him of what he couldn't have, a relationship where he could tell all. It was always need-to-know, thanks to many years in Witness Protection and then under the cloak of secrecy that came with being a Delta Force operator, and he'd never found anyone who'd been able to breach his walls.

Sarah had. And so much for not thinking about her. It was a losing battle.

She'd let him take her that first time against the outside wall of his office, in the dark with her naked and him still fully clothed. He remembered her rubbing against him like a cat in heat, her hips undulating as he drove into her, her sex sheathing him like a tight, soft glove.

The last time he'd taken her had been on a bed in a hotel in Uganda with sheets as pretty as any he'd ever seen and Sarah looking even more so as she told him she loved him. That and every other time he'd held her naked body to his had burned itself onto his brain until the memories were more tortured than sweet, until he wondered if he ever had any control over himself at all.

When it came to Sarah, he knew the answer was no. And that's why he'd put his plan in motion to get himself free for the second time from GOST—for good. He'd long since left Witness Protection and Delta Force and if he only had himself to worry about, he could remain doing what he was doing now—killing at the government's mercy—and it wouldn't have mattered.

But it did matter—*she* mattered.

He wondered if she'd lost faith in him, if she was angry. If he'd ever be able to win her back.

But failure wasn't an option. The palm reader had been correct—his soul was almost gone and he held on to the last of it with a death grip.

If Kaylee Smith had taken the bait, her plane would land soon. She was a reporter, smart enough to know that there was no fooling around when it came to kidnappings.

Smart enough to know better too, but that never seemed to stop anyone these days.

He wondered if Aaron would even forgive him for what he was about to do, and realized that it was too late to stop it, no matter what the answer would've been.

CHAPTER

9

Chris Waldron hitched a ride on a helo from Coronado—the proverbial red-eye, although he really couldn't remember the last time he'd slept through a night—and was back on base in Virginia by 0500.

Dammit, he needed sleep, didn't function as well as Nick did on short naps.

The thought of his brother made him walk faster toward his office. He pushed through the door and found it all quiet, which was as rare an occurrence as any.

He'd fielded calls from Dad and Jake all day yesterday—with one out of state and the other called suddenly OUT-CONUS and not within reach of a face-to-face with Nick, both were understandably worried.

No wonder Nick had turned his phone off completely. Which Chris would kill him for when he got *him* face-to-face.

"Look, I'm sure he's all right. This is the way he operates," he told his dad now, cell phone balanced between ear and shoulder while he quickly went through the shit that had piled up on his desk in his absence.

"He went to the funeral," Kenny said. "Something's going on with Walter."

Shit. He shoved the mess into a drawer for the time being.

"He is *not* all right," his father continued. "You go find him, right now. And Christopher Waldron, you call me the second you find your brother."

There was no saying *no* to that tone. "Yeah, I promise, Dad."

Chris already had car keys in hand from the second Dad mentioned the funeral. Now, bag slung over his shoulder, he headed for the back door.

"Why is there a female FBI agent in my office asking about your brother?" His CO's drawl was thick, the way it always got right before he threatened bodily harm on one of the men under his charge.

Escape thwarted momentarily, Chris turned away from the door to face Saint. "Jake's off the market."

"Wrong brother."

"Oh. Well, Nick's available."

"Special Agent Jamie Michaels isn't interested in his dick."

Chris snorted. "She'd be one of the first."

"Listen up, Waldron, I don't have time for this crap. I'm

leaving for Coronado and I'm turning this problem over to you. I don't want to hear another word about Nick and the FBI, understood?"

Chris pocketed his keys, figured the best way to help Nick at present was to keep this new problem as far away as possible. "Consider it done."

Special Agent Jamie Michaels waited in the CO's office for Chris Waldron for ten minutes before getting more than mildly impatient. In seconds, she was out of the office, prepared to stalk the still quiet halls in search of any SEAL she could get her hands on. She stopped short when she saw Juliana Sinclair, former model turned actress and new Hollywood hottie, the *it* girl of the moment. She was strutting her stuff all over the large TV screen framed in the doorway of the conference room down the hall from Captain John St. James's office.

In all fairness, it was the man standing and watching the screen that stopped her in her tracks. She followed his focus to the glamazon while he continued to talk on his cell phone.

"You look fine, Jules," he was saying, his drawl barely there but still noticeable—Southern, Cajun, actually. "Christ, no, I'm not—how many times do I have to tell you . . . Fine. Whatever."

She looked between the man and the TV, where Juliana was wearing a pink dress and holding up her left hand to show off a huge engagement ring. The reporter was saying something about how Juliana was planning to do a cameo guest spot on a reality show called *Can You Survive It Island* or some such idiocy, and Jamie determined instantly that Juliana probably couldn't survive a hangnail.

Jamie felt a small twinge of guilt when she heard the reporter say that Juliana was doing it for charity in a friend's name.

The man hung up and stared Jamie down for a second before he spoke. "She's my ex." He nodded at the TV, and then continued to watch the screen.

"Oh. Oh," she stuttered, and caught herself. "I guess the news of her engagement is upsetting."

"It's bullshit."

"Obviously, you two still have some issues to work out."

He turned back to her with a slow shake of his head. "The engagement's bullshit. As in, not real, complete fake Hollywood bullshit," he explained. "Good for PR on her new movie, though."

"You're serious."

"I just spoke with her. She's nervous about doing the show—wanted me to come with her and be her consultant so I could give her some tips, like how to make a bomb from a coconut shell."

"Can you really do that?"

"I can, but it's not information I give out readily."

"So you want her to fail on the island?"

"It's not my problem, now, is it?" His voice was slow and measured, but she'd never mistake that for laziness. The energy was positively vibrating off his body and it shot straight through her when he extended his hand and introduced himself as Chris Waldron.

He was tall. As in, she could wear her tallest heels with her five-foot-eleven-inch frame and she'd still come up shorter by quite a bit. And if they'd met in a bar or on a blind date or under any circumstances other than this, Jamie would have no problem feeling almost petite.

So the CO had gotten rid of her by sending in the distraction. And Chris was distracting, so much so that she wanted to freeze time and just stare at the way one of his eyes was a deep cerulean blue and the other an intense green—eyes that made him look slightly unbalanced but somehow handsome in a crazy, rock star kind of fashion.

The bandanna wrapped around his head, along with the tie-dyed shirt and the green cammies, would've looked ridiculous on anyone else. On him, it looked completely right, imposing, even, in a *Don't fuck with me unless you want to fuck me* way.

She ignored every instinct that wanted to take him up on his unspoken invitation.

"It's a little early in the morning for the FBI to be poking around, isn't it? I thought feds didn't like to get to work before 0900."

"You heard wrong, Chief Petty Officer Waldron."

"You're looking for Devane," he said finally.

"Yes."

He shrugged. "He could be anywhere—he's on leave and I'm not his mother or his keeper."

Yeah, she could've seen that answer coming from a mile away. And there was no way she was letting it suffice—this meant far too much to put up with bullshit.

She was still on leave from the FBI and her visit was unofficial, but Chris Waldron didn't have to know that.

She had no reason to explain to him that it was the most important case of her life, a way to finally help her sister,

Sophie. A culmination of months of secret investigation that involved members of Witness Protection who'd disappeared off the face of the earth, just like her sister had, and had been tied into a secret government group of mercenaries. Nick Devane had worked with one of those men. Nick Devane could give her the last known location of Bobby Juniper, aka Clutch, could get her closer to Sophie.

It had been more than eight months since Jamie had seen her sister. Even with her own resources at the FBI, Jamie had been unable to get any help.

There was no way Sophie had gone willingly, not when she'd known Jamie had been hurt. One week before Sophie disappeared, Jamie had been shot twice in the thigh by a drug lord's right-hand man—an American liaison turned fugitive who she and her partner were attempting to apprehend in Mexico, after an exhaustive investigation and a two-month tail. After extensive rehab and psych testing, she was field ready once again. Alone. She'd requested it that way. She wouldn't be ready for a partner again for quite some time.

Mike's death—Mike's murder at the hands of the same man who'd shot her—had hit her hard. The department thought that was normal; the death of a partner was always difficult for any agent to deal with.

Her thigh still ached, especially when she overdid it on a run or in the training room, but she was ready to get back physically. And the only other person besides her who'd known that Mike was not only her partner but her lover was her personal shrink, the private one she'd seen on her own, under an assumed name, not the FBI-appointed one.

The psychiatrist had told her over and over again that it

wasn't her fault Mike was dead, that she had to stop blaming herself or she'd never be very good at her job.

She'd given herself back over to work but refused to think about dating again. Or sex. Or any combination of the two in the near future.

But this man who stood so arrogantly in front of her made her belly clench in that really good way—she wanted to pull her jacket off and let him buy her dinner and drinks, wanted to flirt her ass off and then take him to bed.

She took two steps back and turned on her heel in order to regain some inner control, to remind herself that she was close to finding out what happened to her sister. "I'm assuming he's got to check in sometime?" She held her card out to Chris, who was busy typing something into his phone.

"What? Yeah, I guess. I'll tell him to get in touch."

"You're going to have to do better than that, Chief."

"Could you please call me Chris? And what, you gonna put a tail on me, sugar?"

"Could *you* call *me* Agent Michaels? And if I have to, yes."

He seemed to like that answer, enough to scribble something on the back of her card and hand it back to her. "I'll meet you later—I'll find him and bring him along. How's that?"

"You do that, Chief," she called over her shoulder, with absolutely no intention of sitting around waiting for it to happen. She was under the gun—and according to the rumblings she'd heard, so was the future of the group called GOST. There wasn't a moment to waste. "I'll see you tonight."

He merely nodded at her before turning his attention back to the TV screen.

Nick knew the back roads leading to his house better than anyone—mainly because he and his brothers had cut some of them out themselves, then covered them so to the naked eye they didn't look like there was any passage. And as he wound his car under the branches through the dark, the radio blasted away the silence between himself and Kaylee.

The house was on a quiet block, on a corner facing the woods. Originally, the location had afforded privacy to the more famous musicians Kenny and Maggie worked with— Nick remembered, in those first months, the house often teeming with people and music and parties, until Maggie had gotten sick. But even then, there had always been music playing, although the soundproofed recording studio downstairs had been silent for years.

He slid the car smoothly into the garage and waited for the door to close behind them. When he saw it had armed, he cut the engine.

"We should go inside," he started, but she shook her head.

"I'm not ready to go inside yet—I like being here, inside this car with you. Inside means serious business, more talking and what-ifs. But here, against the leather, sitting close to you, nothing's a problem." Her fingers stroked the soft upholstery on the seat on either side of her thighs—her hair was loose around her shoulders and her cheeks slightly flushed. She looked vulnerable and hot at the same time and when she tugged at his arm he knew what she wanted. What he wanted.

Yeah, the headers in this car tended to do that easily enough thanks to the vibrations they created.

He closed the small space between them in seconds, kicked his shoes off as he went over the gear shift and ended up on top of her.

She didn't appear to have any problems with being in the small car, in the dark, inside the closed garage. No problems at all, judging by the way her body rocked easily under his, her breathing quick from lust, not fear.

Her hands were still on either side of the seat, bracing herself in the small space, the seat all the way back . . . and this long, slow grind was going to kill him. It was like being a teenager and dry-humping in the backseat all over again, although for Nick the dry-humping usually moved quickly to skin on skin. But as much as he wanted Kaylee's skin, he wanted the warmth of her breath against his neck more, liked the way the windows fogged and the Porsche rocked with them. He had the willpower, the ability to take things slow when necessary. This seemed like one of those times, especially with his brain already doing the *What the fuck do you think you're doing* dance.

He knew, though—the recent danger was more of an aphrodisiac than anything, and this slow, rough make-out session was life-affirming. Neither of them knew what was going to happen next, and the attraction between them was something he wasn't about to deny.

"God, I could come like this," she murmured against his ear and he pressed his cock, straining against denim, between her legs. She arched up into him as he did that again and again, until he knew she'd come by the small, soft noises she made, the way her body went rigid for a few seconds and then relaxed back against the seat.

He wanted that too, the mother of all releases, but he had to get things back on track. He reminded himself that he was dealing with two crises threatening to break down life as he knew it and reluctantly pulled away from her. He helped her climb out of the car, their limbs tangled, clothing wrinkled and askew.

Kaylee suddenly looked shy and uncertain, almost vulnerable, the sex flush still staining her cheeks.

"Come on." He urged her gently through the doorway, which led into the large kitchen. "Have a seat. Try to relax."

Once she was comfortably seated at the table, which had been the scene of more late night discussions and eating sessions than he could remember, he passed her a glass of water and put some coffee on for her.

"What happens now?" she asked finally.

"There's someone I can call. He might be able to help, if I can get in touch with him."

He'd met Clutch through a network of retired Special Forces men, many of whom had turned to mercenary and private contracting work after they'd gotten out of the service.

Nick had heard the rumors of a government-funded military group—stories had abounded beginning about a year after his incident with Aaron. The only person he'd ever asked about it was Clutch, an ex-Delta turned merc Nick had done some work for in Africa last year.

"You lost track of him?"

"The connection I had in Africa hasn't been seen in a

while—he helped my brother out of a jam about three months ago. I've worked with him before too."

"He's a mercenary."

"Yes."

She crossed her arms and shook her head. "I won't be able to trust him."

"You shouldn't trust him. You shouldn't trust anyone, not in a situation like this."

"I trust you. And I don't want to be wrong about that. I can't afford to be wrong," she told him.

"You're not," was all he said before he put the cell phone to his ear.

CHAPTER
10

Nick walked away from Kaylee, left her in the kitchen and moved toward the office for greater privacy. He needed space, mainly because he was still turned on, despite—and because of—the danger that surrounded them both. He pulled the door nearly closed behind him, leaving it open just enough so he could see if Kaylee decided to leave the kitchen and wander.

But before he could try to wrangle Clutch's new phone number from a guy who knew a guy, his cell began to buzz. It was Max, who didn't even wait for Nick to acknowledge him before he spoke. "You're not going to be happy."

Max didn't sound happy himself at all as he continued. "I did a little more research. Called that asshole back at the

DoD who owed me a favor and got him to spill a little on Kaylee Smith."

"And?"

"And she's K. Darcy."

A journalist. He recognized the name as one who'd been working the Cutter-Winfield-is-alive angle for years.

"What the hell does this undercover reporter want with you?" Max asked.

She was investigating him and he'd just committed to helping to save her life. He'd invited her inside. And he couldn't totally blame his dick for it either.

Not totally, but a little.

Fuck. Me. "It doesn't matter what she wants. She's not getting it. What did you find on Aaron Smith?"

"He's not in the system."

"He's AWOL. Deceased."

"Doesn't matter, that would've shown up in my search. He's erased. Which means back off. I'm not raising any more red flags on this one. I'll be lucky if no one notices these searches." Max paused. "We'll see just how well my track-covering skills are."

Someone didn't want anything about Aaron getting out. It was too late now—too late to worry about it too.

"I assume you got the file."

"Yeah, thanks." He didn't bother with the usual *I owe you.* "I just needed to check a point of fact."

"*Point of fact*—hanging out with a reporter is never a good idea."

"Point taken." There were too many things running through his mind that he needed to sort through, and getting Max—or anyone else—more involved would only trigger more governmental red flags.

Max pulling this particular SITREP had most likely done so already.

Kaylee definitely had more she needed to share with him about this situation—he was sure of it. Last night he hadn't cared much. Right now he cared.

He'd figured she had the DoD connection because of Aaron. He'd been really off his game with this one. Normally, he'd be able to sniff out a reporter a mile away. This time he'd been distracted by the Winfields and Kaylee's hair and the way her perfume stayed on his shirt long after she touched him.

Finding out she'd lied to him—even by omission— didn't dampen his want for her. The tattoo along her back was firmly etched in his mind, and even the warning tingle of the scar at the base of his throat wouldn't be enough of a deterrent. And that pissed him off even more.

It was time to have a nice chat with K. Darcy.

Nick had disappeared to make his calls, and half an hour later, Kaylee continued to drink the strong coffee he'd made and drum her fingers nervously on the scarred oak table to break up the silence of the large old house.

Her life had changed dramatically in a matter of days. It had happened that way when she was younger—being left behind by her mother, meeting Aaron. But things had settled down for her in recent years, and as much as she thought she enjoyed the stability, the status quo, the subjects she picked to investigate told her otherwise—she was always pushing limits. Her fear sometimes got the better of her, of course, but never like today when those men came to her door.

Whoever they were, they'd tracked her. She was in so deep that there would be no getting out until she got to the bottom of all of this. And so she waited impatiently for Patrick, her assistant, to call her back with the name of someone who could help her get around in Africa, in case Nick's resource didn't pan out.

Her phone vibrated: a text message from Patrick with the name of a woman—a photographer and a guide.

Kaylee would have Nick with her for protection—but if this woman was half as good as her reputation, they'd be guided through the DRC with minimal hassle.

She dialed the phone quickly. A woman answered on the third ring, giving a soft hello with a British accent.

"Is this Sarah Cameron?"

"Who's asking?"

She turned toward the door Nick had left through before responding in a low voice, "I'm a reporter—K. Darcy for the *Ledger*."

A pause, and then, "I've heard of you."

"I got your name from a colleague of mine, he worked with you last year—Richard Kent. He said you really know your way around the area."

"Do you want me as a photographer or as a guide?"

"I need to get to an area in the DRC safely. I'm going to be arriving in Africa by ten in the morning tomorrow—my time—I'm going to need a guide."

"The DRC's a dangerous place."

"I can pay you well," Kaylee assured her.

"The DRC's six hours ahead—you'll land at four in the afternoon here."

"Can you help me?"

"Where exactly do you need to go?"

Kaylee read the coordinates to her—Nick hadn't mapped them yet, but he'd told her it was along the Lualaba River.

"That's Ubundu," Sarah told her after a few seconds of silence. "I can help. Call me with the exact time you're landing. I'll meet the plane. Fly into Kisangani—it's the closest to where you need to go."

"Are you sure?"

"Are you going to trust me or not?" Sarah asked her, and before Kaylee had a chance to answer, she continued, "Are you working on a story? Because if you need a photographer, I'd be happy to help."

"This isn't for a story—it's personal," Kaylee told her.

"I understand personal. I'll wait to hear from you." Sarah disconnected the line and Kaylee stared at the phone for a second before shutting it and placing it on the table.

It took her a moment before she realized that she was no longer alone in the room. There was a well-over-six-foot-tall man, dressed in some crazy mismatch of camouflage and tie-dye, at the back door, and he was staring at her in a way that she wasn't sure was friendly.

The rifle he wore casually around his neck did little to shake that feeling. She wondered just how much of her conversation he'd heard.

"Chris, what the fuck?" Nick barreled through the door and came up behind her. She sighed in relief that at least they knew each other.

"So what, now you've got a thing for reporters?" the man drawled, but still he didn't move from his position, nor did he take his eyes off Kaylee, and yes, the man called Chris had heard enough.

She took a physical hit from those words but Nick didn't seem surprised at all. In fact, the only one who was surprised was her, and that was never a good thing.

They know who you are, but they don't know what you know.

She could do this. "It's true—I wasn't trying to hide it. I was about to tell you, back at the apartment before we got, um, interrupted."

Chris raised a brow and looked at Nick, who told him, "It's not what you're thinking, asshole."

"You have no idea what I'm thinking, trust me," Chris retorted, still calm, and after that brief exchange, all eyes were back on her.

She turned her full attention to Nick, stood up and held out her hands as if in surrender. "I didn't tell you because I didn't think it mattered. We weren't going to see each other again—you said so yourself."

"And then I came back." Nick's teeth were gritted.

"But you told me..." She faltered, not wanting to reveal more than she had to in front of Chris, although he seemed to have gotten the gist well enough already.

"Chris, I need to speak with Kaylee alone." Nick's voice was tight and oh-so-angry. She wrapped her arms around herself for only a second and then let them fall to her sides, hands fisted.

She'd dealt with angry military men before, she'd do it again.

Chris didn't argue. She watched him move, silent as a shadow, out a side door to God knows where. Nick didn't say anything until she turned back to him.

"Look, I'm sorry that you had to find out about me from someone else," she started.

Nick didn't acknowledge the apology, barely blinked as he stood, unmoving, in front of her. The large kitchen seemed smaller with his presence and far less comforting than it had just a mere hour earlier.

She wondered if he'd always given off that air of control and decided yes—his demeanor was something that couldn't be faked or learned. He'd been born with that easy grace, that rough prowl that defined him as a man who was a lot to handle. Tonight, he looked ready for combat. Ready for anything.

She hoped she was as well. "Are you going to stand there and stare at me all morning?"

"You're something else, aren't you? Now you're pissed at me?" He shook his head. "I wasn't listening at the door, but obviously you somehow gave yourself away to my brother."

"Then how did you find out about K. Darcy?" she asked. "Did you run some kind of background check on me?"

"I was trying to get some intel on Aaron. And I also know you ran one on me."

"I tried."

"Of course you did." He turned away from her and laughed, but all too soon he was facing her again, holding her tight by the shoulders. "Are you screwing me, Kaylee? Are you and Aaron in on some kind of sick scheme together?"

"What? No!" She struggled to get away from him but he held her fast, even pulled her closer so that his body pressed against hers as intimately as it had last night.

"How do I know? Maybe you fucked all the other men on Aaron's list in order to do a story on this."

Tears sprang to her eyes as she wrenched away from him and slapped him hard across the face. He didn't even flinch but the crack of her palm meeting skin made her feel better. Her voice shook with a barely restrained anger when she told him, "You basically told me you were a bastard—I should've listened to you."

It was his turn to jerk away. He swallowed hard, and a sudden show of emotion filled his eyes all too briefly before it was replaced by a cool gaze. "You should have."

"You were the one who came back, not me. Why the hell did you come back?"

That stopped him cold for a second. When he spoke again, his words were unexpected. "I don't like thinking about you with anyone else." His voice was quiet, rough, and he'd moved closer to her, although he didn't touch her. "I didn't like seeing that other guy's ring at your apartment. And I sure as hell don't like not being able to stop thinking about you."

"Well, look at that, the big bad warrior is afraid of something. Well, here's a tip, Nick—I'm scared too. I didn't want this, didn't expect to feel anything for you. The last thing I wanted was to get involved with another military man."

"Well, good thing we're not involved, then."

"You left me your phone number. You came back to find out more information on Aaron. You were worried about me," she continued. "I'm not writing a story about this. I'm trying to get out of this alive. I'm..." She broke down then, unable to hold back the frustration and the anger, and she turned away from him completely so he wouldn't see the tears. His words bit at her, crude and harsh, but knowing what she knew about Nick, about his past, a small part of her understood.

If he was truly Cutter Winfield, he'd have spent his entire life avoiding reporters. She supposed she would lash out too. And so she drew on her own strength, because that was what had gotten her through all the tough times in her life. "It's hard for me to trust you too, Nick, because of what you do for a living. I think you can understand that, based on what's happening around me. Please believe me— I'm not planning on doing a story about you or about this. I just want to figure out what's really going on."

"And I'm supposed to trust that?" His laugh was short. "Sorry, Kaylee, but I'm not that fucking naïve. What's to stop you from writing about what happened between me and Aaron?"

"My word. I understand undercover. My job depends on it. And sometimes, even, my life."

"Why is that?" he asked.

"Don't you get it? I get threatened almost every time one of my stories is published. The threats that aren't discounted immediately are forwarded to a special branch of the police. They don't do much except file them away, in case..." She drew a deep breath. "I stopped asking about what the notes said after my third month on the job. It's been easier not knowing."

He hadn't thought about it like that, not at all, and

every protective instinct in his body came to life more strongly than ever. "Why didn't you say that before?"

"Because it's not something I like to admit. Saying it out loud makes it real."

He rubbed the small scar on his neck as he stared at her. "This is as real as it gets, Kaylee."

"I'm not afraid of real, Nick," she told him. "Right now, there's just one thing that scares me."

"What's that?"

"I don't want to lose you when I've just found you."

CHAPTER
11

I don't want to lose you when I've just found you.

Kaylee would fight to keep him—Nick was sure of it. Liked it, even, and a strange pride swelled inside him at the thought. "I can't make any promises. Especially now. Not with all this shit coming down around our ears."

"I understand. I just...wanted you to know where I stand." She moved closer, went to touch his arm softly but he jerked back.

"You barely know me."

"I know enough."

She knew nothing. He planned on keeping it that way, no matter how hard his cock got. "I've got to talk to my brother. I'll be back. Don't answer your phone without me here."

"I have to tell you about the call I made," she said quickly. "I found us a guide through the DRC."

He exhaled. Tried to stay calm. "Do you know this person? Can you trust him?"

"I didn't say anything, just that it was a personal matter. She's a photographer who lives in the area—she's worked with colleagues of mine. She's good."

She. Jesus, he was in real trouble here.

"She said to fly into Kisangani, said the coordinates were in Ubundu—"

"You gave her the coordinates?"

"I had to. Is that the right place?"

It was—he'd mapped it out quickly while he'd attempted to get in touch with Clutch. "Yes, that's the right place."

"Did your source come through?"

Clutch hadn't. The man had fallen off the face of the earth. "No. And we don't have time to wait on him. I'll book the flight."

He had friends he could call, could probably get use of a private plane in order to bypass security and allow him to bring weapons. Anything else would leave them too little time. They were pushing it as it was, according to Aaron's forty-eight-hour timetable.

And so he left her in the kitchen before he did something even more stupid—not that *admitting* he couldn't stop thinking about her wasn't stupid enough—and went to find his brother.

Better to face Chris alone than to let Kaylee fall under his scrutiny.

There'd be plenty of time for that later, with an extra brother who wasn't nearly as forgiving as Chris could be.

Chris sat behind the desk in what was once Dad's office, legs propped up on its corner, waiting patiently. His iPod was on and his eyes were closed as he belted out a version of Nazareth's "Hair of the Dog," but they opened the second Nick walked into the room.

I just sense things, Chris would say with a dismissive shrug when questioned. His gift, like Dad's, was both amazing and unnerving, and Nick wasn't particularly grateful for it, not when Chris's eyes bore through him like a laser.

"Chris, before you start in on me—"

"Seriously, what the fuck? Like you need this now, with everything else going on?" Chris asked and then stopped. "Shit. You like her."

Nick couldn't put voice to it, just nodded. For a second, the two men sat there in silence and Nick prayed Chris wouldn't push him on this.

But Chris, being Chris, didn't say another word about it, knew how significant it was that Nick had admitted as much as he had. Instead, he asked, "Do you know that the FBI is asking questions about you? Any idea what the hell that's about?"

Nick didn't answer, just dumped out the contents of the envelope he'd gotten from Kaylee—everything Aaron had left her in the safe-deposit box—onto the desk between him and his brother.

"It's amazing that a man's entire life can boil down to this," Nick murmured as he sifted through the contents. He pushed the patch aside and opened the folded legal-size paper that contained the list of men. It was ten sheets, meticulously written out and stapled together, and worn, as if Kaylee had read the reports Aaron had written out dozens of times.

He handed them to Chris and then turned his attention to the bankbook. He thumbed through it quickly, whistled when he saw the numbers involved.

Chris was moving Aaron's dog tags between his fingers as he read, flipping them back and forth, the steady soft clink of the metal the only sound between them for several minutes.

When Chris finished the last page—the report that talked about Nick—he put down both the papers and the tags and began to rub the fingertips on his left hand together, an unconscious signal Nick knew all too well. "That's why she came to you," he said finally.

Chris knew about the mission and the patch—Nick had told both him and Jake about it and where to find the patch in case they needed to be the ones to hand it over to Kaylee.

"Aaron's been . . . calling her. At least he could be. Shit, Chris, I heard one of the calls. Something's going on, and it's not good. I already committed to going with her to Africa," Nick said, felt the heat of his brother's unlikely anger shoot across the room.

Chris was typically slow to burn—it showed just how on edge he was, how much they all were because of the Winfield situation. "So you uncommit. You did what Aaron Smith asked of you, you met with her."

"Someone wants her dead. Two men tried to take her out of her apartment tonight—they said they were FBI but I don't think they were. I hope they weren't anyway."

"What the hell did you do? If she's in danger, she needs

to go to the police or someone higher up the food chain. You're not going to fucking Africa with her—you don't know what the hell you're getting into." Chris slammed a palm down on the table while Nick tried to remain unimpressed at his brother's show of temper.

"Are you going to stop me? Because I'd really like to see that."

"Fuck you, Nick. You know that jones for danger you've got is going to get you in some major trouble one of these days."

Chris was right—Nick always had to hit it harder and faster, to up the bar. But that wasn't what this was all about.

"Speaking of jones for danger, I seem to remember you sitting next to me in that jail cell. And this is my mountain," he said tightly.

Dad's favorite expression made Chris's face soften, but only for a second. "You barely know this woman."

"I know she's not making up being in trouble."

"I'm going with you for backup. I've got the time. *Shit.*" Chris rubbed his fingers together. "You're going to have to give me the whole story."

Nick did so, quickly and quietly. When he finished, Chris sighed, scrubbed his face with his palms. "Christ, Nick, if those men were FBI . . ." He trailed off, shook his head.

"You're going to need to stay here, deal with the fallout."

"You want me to run interference while you run off to Africa to figure all this out? Send you there with no backup?"

"I tried to get in touch with Clutch, but no dice. Kaylee's got someone to help."

Both his brothers—especially Chris—had shit a brick when they'd discovered he'd worked with Clutch off the books and off the radar last year.

Chris continued to stare at him. "When were you going to tell me that Walter came to visit you?"

"How the hell—" He sat back in his chair. "Dad," they both said simultaneously.

And then Nick spoke the words out loud, the ones that had been echoing inside his mind since earlier that night. "He came looking for forgiveness. He told me . . . Fuck, he told me that I'm his son, not Billy's."

Chris shot forward on his elbows, nearly jumping across the desk. "Ah, shit, Nick."

"Yeah." He closed his eyes and then opened them to look into his brother's.

"Do you think Kaylee suspects anything?" Chris asked him. "I recognize her pen name . . . She's been writing about Cutter for a while now."

Nick shrugged, like it didn't matter, but Chris's sentiments echoed his own worries. "None of those reporters are that good—you know that."

"She's major, all right? Big-time. Comes off as unassuming, Nick, but K. Darcy can take you down at the knees. She's got a hell of a lot of clout in her industry. Has a reputation of not being afraid to take on anything."

"Yeah, I have the same one in mine."

Chris grew impatient, turned the laptop that had been facing him toward Nick, an article written by Kaylee on the screen. "She's broken some big stories, unearthed corruption in the government and the military, opened her mouth when she was bribed—and threatened—to try to keep it shut. Took some big personal and professional risks. And that's not including the times when she delved into people's private lives too—do you remember this story she did?"

Nick scanned the piece and recalled reading it last year. Kaylee had been the first to break the news of a very married presidential candidate's affair with a very married U.S. congresswoman, despite pleas from the candidate's family.

The anger swelled inside of him again. What if she was lying to him? What if all of this was a ruse to get close to him? "She's good, okay. But she'd have no reason to suspect me, and the angrier I get at her, the more suspicious she's going to be, right? Besides, she's here because of Aaron. That's all." He was well aware that he sounded like he was trying to convince himself.

Chris nodded slowly as he peered past Nick toward the kitchen. "Let's keep it that way."

"Yeah, you know me, spilling my guts to every woman I meet."

His brother snorted.

"You heard from Jake?"

"No."

Nick stared down at some faint scratches on the surface of the desk. If Jake was just in training in Coronado, they'd have heard from him by now. Another thing to worry about. "I don't want to talk about Kaylee and her motives now." Or ever, preferably.

Chris nodded, grabbed the bankbook. "How do you know the money's still in the bank?"

"I don't. But I'm betting that if I try to access it, the system will trigger."

"If it hasn't already. You're not bringing this much cash

with you. And look, if you transfer it—if you and Kaylee both have half the code, that could be your insurance policy if something bad goes down."

Nick nodded. "Do what you have to do with it."

Chris leaned forward on his elbows. "I got rid of the FBI agent for a while. If you haul ass, you can avoid her."

"I need to get a flight."

"I'll take care of that. I've got a pilot who owes me a favor. A big one."

"Thanks." Nick stood and bypassed the kitchen for his room.

Before he began to pack, he rooted through his dresser for the old St. Jude medal inscribed with the initials *CNW*—Cutter Nicholas Winfield—that he still kept, hidden away for safekeeping.

He held it in his palm, the cool metal leaving its brand thanks to his tightened fist.

He'd never been able to stand to wear the medal around his neck, and he didn't believe in talismans or juju—bad for the teams to put your faith in an outside source. Still, beyond the clothing on his back, the medal was the only thing Nick took with him the night he'd left the Winfield estate for good.

Deidre had given it to him—her only gift, supposedly left next to his crib for his first birthday, although his first clear memory of the medal on the chain wasn't until he was five and her visits had dropped off completely.

When he was old enough to know that St. Jude was often referred to as the patron saint of lost causes, Nick thought it an appropriate enough reminder of where he'd come from. Where he was headed.

And now Deidre Winfield was dead. He'd seen reports over the last few months that she was sick, knew she was dying, and still the ending he'd been anticipating hit him like a fresh wound.

After all this time, he hadn't thought it would affect him. Why it did was more of a mystery than anything.

Within seconds, it had gone from the present day to ten years ago, twelve, even twenty-seven years earlier when it appeared that no one was happy to see him born, put him right back where he was before he'd walked away.

Nick shook off the memories. He shoved the medal into the drawer, back where it belonged, and rubbed his palm hard.

These days, he didn't have to pretend to be someone else—in his mind, he already was, and he wasn't about to get sucked back in. He could be ruthless about stripping things from his mind when he wanted to; today would be no exception.

Kaylee caught sight of Nick as she passed the open bedroom door, pausing without realizing it.

He was stripped bare to the waist. If he noticed her, he didn't let on.

There were several guns spread on the king-size bed in front of him—she also saw the unmistakable glint of metal from knives and other assorted weaponry. He chose methodically, unfolded and refolded each blade and then strapped them to various places on his body—around his biceps, his thighs, as he wore only a pair of black boxer briefs. He strapped a pistol to one calf as well and then pulled on a pair of well-worn jeans, yanking on the leg to cover the weapon.

They must be taking a private plane to Africa—there was no way he'd get all that past security. And yet, despite the weaponry before her, she knew it wouldn't be enough.

"I'll have more firepower waiting for me," he said, without looking up from the gun he was studying. "We leave in half an hour."

"I don't think I have the right clothes for this trip," she said.

"I've got some things for you." He pointed to a bag on the corner of the bed. "You're going to have to contact your job."

She nodded. "That won't be a problem."

"What about family—you'd better think of something to tell them so you don't sound any alarms on their end," he continued.

She longed to wrap her arms around herself, or better yet, to put herself into Nick's arms and make him forget about weapons and Africa and everything else but her. Instead, she said bluntly, "No one will be worried. I don't have any family."

"There's no one else those men can contact about you?"

"Other than my co-workers? No. No family," she reiterated.

God, she hated this feeling, as if she was nine years old again, alone and scared because she'd admitted to the nice social worker at school that her mom had been gone for a week and showed no signs of coming back home. In return, that nice woman who'd promised her everything was going to be all right had called the police.

Kaylee had moved in with her grandmother that same evening, had hated that cramped apartment—the way it smelled like chicken soup especially, because that smell was supposed to bring comfort, but there was no comfort with her grandmother. There was only talk of sin and following rules so no one went to hell.

I'm already there, she'd wanted to tell her grandmother. But she couldn't bring herself to outright disrespect the woman who took her in and saved her from a life of foster homes. The woman who referred to Kaylee as the child of sin.

Red hair is a sign of the devil, her grandmother always used to murmur with a disapproving look at Kaylee's wild locks, which tumbled down past her shoulders. *You and your mother—there was no hope for either of you.*

Aaron had been her escape, her way out. He'd always been so self-assured and protective.

They were friends—best friends—probably should've stayed that way instead of trying to pretend it was something more. Things would've been better, although in the end, she still would've lost him completely.

Nick was watching her carefully. "You like being alone."

"I got used to it," she clarified. "There's a big difference. I've been on my own for a long time. Even when I was with Aaron—although I kidded myself into thinking I'd be less lonely, that I'd have the family I wanted."

He nodded, didn't press her any further.

"What about you? I'm sure your brother will worry."

"Don't worry about me."

"It's too late for that," she shot back.

He stopped what he'd been doing with the knives. "My

brothers are both military, both SEALs. They know I can take care of myself. Speaking of which, do you know how to shoot that gun you've got?"

She didn't bother to ask how he knew about it. "It's registered."

"I know—that's not what I asked you."

She should've expected nothing less. "I can shoot. I go to the range once a month."

"You didn't have the gun on you when you met with me."

She hadn't. "I didn't think I'd need it with you."

"You always need it, especially with someone like me."

"You don't have to try to scare me. I know what you're capable of." She couldn't take her eyes off the weapons still free on the bed, and knew that his hands were just as deadly. But they could also keep her safe. "What's it like, having the ability to save someone?"

"It's just something I do."

"But it must be an incredible feeling to know that if you had to, you could save someone you cared about who was in trouble."

He didn't answer at first, instead closed the distance between them and put his hands on both sides of her face. "I've saved a lot of people. Doing it for someone you care about isn't any different. Can't be, or you risk fucking it up. So you do your job, revert to your training. And then you try not to think back on what you've done, because that can really fuck you up."

He pulled his hands off her, but she grabbed his wrists, held them in her hands.

He stared at her for a long moment. "Who couldn't you save, Kaylee?"

"I wasn't speaking in the literal sense. When I was with Aaron, I'd thought love would be enough to save us both."

"Love doesn't save people."

"For someone who doesn't believe in love, you sure know a lot on the subject."

"I didn't say I didn't believe in it. I just don't expect it to happen for me. I'm not built for it."

"Sounds more like you're afraid of it," she muttered.

"Smart, not scared."

"I don't know how you can say you're not built for love. You can't just say that, can't stop it with your mind. When it happens, it happens."

She released his hands but he caught her around the waist, pulled her in close and kissed her—hard and fast enough to curl her toes, even as the weapons he'd strapped onto himself dug into her.

He kissed her like he couldn't stop himself. She attempted to wrap herself around him but he caught her wrists and held them behind her back with one hand, and still her body responded. His hand traveled to her breast, over her shirt first and then swiftly under the fabric, under her bra, fingers tweaking an already taut nipple until she gasped against his mouth.

That made him pull back, look at her like he'd taken things too far. She hung on, not willing to let it go that easily. "Don't stop now, Nick."

"I have to. Don't you understand, to keep you safe, I have to keep my guard up. That's necessary for both of our safety."

"You meant what you said before . . . that you can't stop thinking about me?"

"Yeah, I meant it."

"I know you think you can't trust me...but you can. Please, you have to believe me." She thought about telling him everything, right then and there, spilling that she knew who he was. Proving herself.

But before she could say anything, he pressed his forehead to hers. "I don't trust easily or well, Kaylee. And I'm someone you don't want to fuck with."

He had reason not to trust her. If he'd kept up with the media over the last years, he knew she'd written extensively on the Winfields. And dammit, she wanted him to tell her who he was—not for any other reason but because he loved her. She knew this was the man for her as surely as she'd known Carl wasn't.

She knew it was far too soon for her to think about any of this—about love and Nick in the same sentence.

So no, now wasn't the time to reveal what she knew about Nick. She'd figure out a way to help keep Nick's identity under wraps for good, and then if he still didn't trust her enough to tell her who he was, she'd tell him what she knew.

There was a firm knock on the front door. Chris unfolded himself from the couch where he'd been thinking about what the hell he was going to tell both Jake and Dad, plus calling in for emergency leave and practically selling his left ball to get it, to peer outside from one of the side windows. "Shit."

Nick rounded the corner from his bedroom, bag in hand, dressed and ready to go. Earlier, Kaylee had emerged from Nick's room and was now waiting in the kitchen, and although he didn't think it was a good idea for her to be left alone with her cell phone, he didn't push things. His brother was already on edge—no need to shove him over it.

Who's there? Nick motioned.

"FBI woman," Chris mouthed.

"I thought you said you got rid of her for a while."

"I thought I did."

"Does she know she's a mirage?"

Chris growled low under his breath. "Get the hell out of here. I'll distract her."

"Can you do a better job this time?"

Chris bared his teeth at his brother, who suddenly seemed oddly calm. "Go. Keep your damned phone on, Nick."

They touched fists in the familiar way they always did before heading out on a mission and then Nick disappeared into the kitchen.

Chris cranked up the music in order to hide the sound of the garage door opening and Nick's car blasting out along the back roads. With any luck, Nick would make it to the airport and take off before he had to give any intel to this agent. And then he opened the front door and put on his best *What the hell are you doing here* face.

"Surprised to see me, Chief?" she asked.

"You are keeping tabs on me, Agent Michaels. I guess you couldn't wait until tonight to see me again?"

"Your guess would be wrong. And imagine my surprise on discovering that your address is the same as Ensign Devane's."

"That's classified information."

She didn't deny that as she pushed past him into the house. "Can you turn down this music, please?"

Damn, she was pretty. She'd be prettier without the black suit crap, and the thought of helping her take it off made him smile. She was wearing a wedding ring, a simple platinum band, but it was on her right hand, not her left. He hadn't noticed that before, had been distracted with Nick and by Jules.

He noticed now.

He'd been with Jules long before she became Juliana Sinclair, since he was fourteen and she was sixteen. Then they'd dated off and on from the time he'd enlisted and she'd moved, first to New York and then to L.A.

They'd always been a volatile couple—if they weren't fighting, they were fucking. Jules was complicated, and although Jamie appeared completely straightforward, his instincts told him that wasn't the case. She was guarded, closed off—it was in the way she kept her hands fisted at her sides or crossed across her chest even as she looked him in the eye.

There was something brewing under the surface, something she was trying her best to keep concealed, but she wouldn't be able to hide it from him for too much longer— people were never able to. He wasn't ever sure if it was his second sight that drew people to him like true confessions or something, but it was inevitable that she'd spill her secrets to him.

He rubbed the fingers on his left hand together, the ones that always itched when he knew something. He was sensitive—not like Dad or Momma was. No, his gift was more of a sixth sense, a freaky intuition that his teammates admired, counted on, even as they freely admitted to being slightly spooked by it. To his brothers, it was more of that *psychic Cajun bullshit,* as Jake so charmingly named it years earlier.

But there was a darker side to the crazy Cajun bullshit, one Chris hated, and so he'd refused that part of the gift—pushed it away and had so far been successful.

She was hiding more than one something. Like he'd thought—complicated as hell. "You don't like loud music, Jamie?"

She frowned a little, scrunched up her nose, and she looked fucking *cute.* He fought the urge to just reach over and kiss her, and then he wondered where the hell this was all coming from. One brother losing his ever-loving mind was quite enough.

"When it's appropriate." Her voice was loud and clear over the driving beat.

In his world, loud was always appropriate, but Nick was long gone by this point so he complied and lowered the volume. "Better?"

"I don't think you understand the seriousness of this situation," she said.

"Why don't you tell me, then?"

"It's not your business."

"It is when the feds come knocking on my door."

"You don't trust the FBI much, do you?"

The FBI—well, any kind of law enforcement—always made him uneasy. He'd had way too much contact with them growing up and enough in his time in the military to know that his mind-set and theirs just didn't mesh.

He and Nick had gotten themselves in a damned good amount of trouble, had a lot of fun doing so in the years after Jake pulled out of their merry band of men and headed for the Navy at fifteen.

It had been one of the only times he'd seen Nick really pissed at Jake, had seen Jake's move as a betrayal rather than a way for Jake to save himself. Something Nick hadn't even admitted to himself until that memorable night when he and Chris got caught boosting cars and everything changed.

That particular evening, they'd been delivering the cars to a dock, driving them into a container where the vintage vehicles would be shipped overseas to waiting buyers. There had been a bust, and although the two of them were merely on the periphery of the operation, they were still arrested, hauled in and booked.

It had been Chris's first arrest—the first time he'd been caught—but Nick was particularly vulnerable, having been brought home a night earlier by Federal Court Judge Kelly Cromwell, whose car Nick had taken for a joyride, and the judge's husband, who was a recently retired four-star Navy admiral.

Obviously, she hadn't expected Nick to go right back out and do it again while they were waiting for Kenny to fly in from California the following evening to discuss Nick's options for punishment.

Chris and Nick managed to look appropriately chastised and solemn as the couple had spoken with them and with Kenny, who'd refused to post bail. The two boys would stay overnight in a cell before appearing in front of the judge the following morning.

Kenny had known that the chastised shit was merely an act. So had Kelly Cromwell's husband, apparently, since he'd gotten the paperwork for Navy boot camp for both of them in order.

It's your choice, Kenny had told them, shoved the papers across the table as the lawyers looked on.

Chris had signed immediately. Nick had been a tougher sell, refusing to sign until the last possible minute. Nothing Chris or Kenny—or even Jake, who'd flown in from Coronado especially to see his two brothers—said could convince him.

Chris had a pretty solid feeling what finally did was the realization that sitting in jail would be proving Walter and Deidre Winfield's view of Nick right.

And Walter was now visiting Nick—fuck, no good could come from that. Or from this.

"I like the FBI just fine—we're all on the same side, aren't we?" He motioned for her to follow him, first into the kitchen and then to sit, and at first he thought she'd refuse, but she finally did take a seat on the opposite side of the table from where he stood.

She looked nice there, at the old scarred oak table.

He moved so he could sit next to her. "We do a lot of classified shit, Jamie. We get blamed for a lot that's not our fault, so we've learned to stay tight. If you want to know where Devane is—and he's currently on leave, so he's not AWOL, just to clarify that—you're going to have to give me a little more intel."

"Your brother worked for a mercenary in Africa last year," she said, and fuck, Chris had known that was going to come back to bite Nick in the ass.

You can't be a SEAL and a merc at the same time, Chris had told his brother when he'd discovered that Nick had done a job for a mercenary named Clutch when he was on a month's leave.

"Do you know anything about it?"

"No, ma'am."

"Look, I'm not trying to—" She stopped. "You're sure?"

He wasn't sure of anything anymore, but he was too superstitious to tell the same lie two times in a row. "Is Nick under investigation for something?"

"I can't disclose that at present. Can you tell me where he is so I can speak with him?"

He snorted, drummed his fingers on the table in time with an invisible beat as he kept eye contact with her. But he wasn't so much looking at her as looking through her, keeping an eye on her as he weighed the possibilities in his mind. "I don't know where he is."

"Fine, if you want to keep playing this game—"

"Do you know two agents named Simms and Ferone?"

"Why?"

"They threatened a friend of mine tonight. Said they were FBI."

"What friend?"

He decided to take the risk. "Kaylee Smith."

She cocked her head to the side as if trying to process that name. "Is Nick with this Kaylee Smith now?"

"You answer my question first."

"Chief Waldron, you tell Ensign Devane that he's got four hours to voluntarily surrender himself to me."

"Where's he supposed to meet you?"

She handed him her business card and he let his fingertips brush hers. When she pulled away, hard, he knew she'd felt the jolt of energy too.

"Nick can call to get that information."

"What happens when the four hours are up?"

"He doesn't want to find that out." She got up without a second glance in his direction and let herself out of the house.

It didn't take him more than three seconds to grab his bag, which was always at the ready, and follow her.

His fingers continued to itch—he rubbed them along the steering wheel as he followed Jamie's basic FBI black Town Car at a safe enough distance all the way to the airport, to the section that housed the private corporate jets and the ones that the FBI and CIA used.

He waited to see if she'd leave her car, search the airport for Nick and Kaylee—and *shit,* he just hoped they'd already gotten off the ground. Nick wasn't answering his phone, a good sign.

But no, Jamie didn't leave her car. And so he settled in for a long four hours of surveillance. It was a lot like sniping . . . except here he didn't have to remain belly-down on the ground and stock-still. He had the radio, could sing while he kept a watch on Jamie inside her car.

She just sat there expressionless, didn't talk on the phone or read. Maybe she had the radio on, but if she did she never once sang along.

Music was in his blood, something that had always brought out a smile in him—albeit sometimes a wistful one. So he sat back and he watched and he waited for a smile that never came while he planned his next move.

CHAPTER 12

Kaylee jerked awake as the plane jolted hard from turbulence and felt the unease settle into her body. She was completely spooked—tried to remember if she'd dreamed about something specific and told herself it had to be the tension from the situation. Calls from beyond the grave, someone trying to kill her and the missing Winfield heir sitting next to her on a private jet heading toward Africa.

Yes, that would certainly do it.

The airport in Virginia had been teeming with people— some milling around, some rushing to their destinations— and the cacophony of noise had made her already pounding head throb even harder.

Nick had ushered her as though she was a celebrity, his

arm firmly around her, his large body shielding hers as he'd eased her through the throngs of people, bypassing security in order to head to the entrance of the private jet.

She hadn't asked why or how he pulled this one off. She had her new, fake passport tucked into her pocket, her gun was still in her bag and she'd felt some of Nick's weapons press her since he held her so closely.

"Keep your eyes down," he'd said, and she guessed it was so they wouldn't get picked up by the security cameras. She'd almost told him he was being too paranoid, and then she recalled the scene at her apartment and she'd bitten her lip instead.

By the time they'd taken off, she'd been exhausted and she'd let herself try to fall asleep.

She checked her watch and realized she'd slept—albeit an uneasy, toss-and-turn sleep—for nearly the entirety of the flight.

Nick was staring out the window into the mass of white clouds, newspaper tossed aside. "We're almost there. You'll need to change soon."

He hadn't broken his gaze from the window when he spoke and she didn't bother to answer, merely pulled the blanket tighter around her to ward off the creepy feeling that still invaded her and noted that he'd left a pair of jungle fatigues next to her, plus a hat and boots.

"You're not going to freak out on me, are you?"

She'd been staring off into space, hadn't realized he'd dragged his gaze to her. "No. No freak-outs."

"Good."

How much did she really know about this man? Decorated Navy SEAL. Adopted. Two brothers, and a father who lived cross-country. And now she was taking him deeper into a web that Aaron's past had woven for both of them.

And yet, she knew more about Nick than she had about Aaron when they first began hanging out. It wasn't until after they'd run across the state line and gotten married that he'd revealed his juvenile record to her—that he'd been taken out of his parents' house because both parents were drug abusers and Aaron had been caught stealing at school. She knew he'd done so for survival, and even knew that the stealing cars was more about thrills than money, despite his needs.

When she'd gotten arrested, she'd never been so scared in her entire life. The police hadn't been nice, the way they were when they found her home alone after her mom took off. No, this time, there were only short, clipped voices, the reading of her rights and the sensation of handcuffs being roughly clicked onto her wrists.

She hadn't been with Aaron that night, had gotten into a fight with her grandmother about her grades, which had been slipping since she'd started hanging out with Aaron. It was only a matter of time before she'd begun cutting classes and living up to her mother's reputation.

She'd stormed out of the house and down the block and she'd walked and walked until she'd seen it—the beautiful black Ferrari parked in front an apartment building.

She had it coasting down the street in less than thirty seconds—her best time yet. Wind in her hair, the car turning her on as they took each other for a ride down the highway; she was never going back. She'd call Aaron when she got farther out.

That was how a sixteen-year-old brain functioned—act first, questions later.

She'd gotten somewhat better at that—tried to ask the questions first now, but impulse still reigned supreme.

"Why don't you like to be touched?" she asked before she could stop herself. Around Nick, she didn't want to stop herself from anything.

He closed his eyes, like the question pained him. "I like being touched just fine. I let you touch me the other night."

"You start to, and then you stop. Hold my hands away from you, distract me."

"It's not a big deal. I wasn't held a lot as a baby. Wasn't touched. Doc at the base says that could account for a lot of my aversion." He ran his hands through his hair before he continued. "I get this fight-or-flight response. Great in the field, not so great in bed. I can usually bite it back for sex . . . especially because all my relationships have lasted approximately five hours or less."

She'd passed that mark—granted, not in the way she'd have liked to. "Have you tried to let someone help you with it?"

"I've tried," he admitted as he stared at the ceiling. "It didn't work."

"Maybe one day it will. Things change," she said. "Then again, so do people. Not always for the better."

"What happened to your parents?" he asked suddenly, as if he'd been mulling it over since they'd spoken back at the house. Fair was fair—she'd brought up a topic he hated talking about, now it was his turn.

She shrugged, like it didn't matter. But it did. "I never

knew my dad. My mom left when I was nine." Kaylee remembered waking up one morning with the realization that she was all alone in the small apartment. *She'll come back tomorrow,* she'd told herself. And she told herself that every day for a week, until the food ran out and the cafeteria at school wouldn't serve her without paying anymore. "I was raised by my grandmother. It didn't go well."

"Why? I thought grandmothers were supposed to be all nurturing and shit."

That made her laugh softly, but only for a second. "I was too much like my mom. It was a problem."

"I was nothing like my family at all—that was a problem too."

She wanted to ask him so much more about that, but she didn't. "My mom had a juvie record by the time she was fourteen. My grandfather died when my mom was young and my grandmother was raising her on her own. She was so embarrassed—their daughter from a good, God-fearing home hanging out with hoodlums." She laughed again, because it was better than crying.

Sometimes, she felt as if she was still in mourning for the life she could've had if her mom had cleaned up her act, if she'd risen above her rebellion and just grown up. "I became a journalist because of my mother. I found her diaries hidden in the attic—that's all she wrote about, what she wanted to be when she grew up. She must've forgotten about them when she ran away, and I found them and read them over and over again when I was ten. They were my lifeline."

"Does your grandmother know what a success you are?"

"She died a few years ago. She knew about my job but

that didn't much matter to her—not after Aaron and the divorce." She paused. "My grandmother worked for the church, believed in God, ran a household. She collected money for the poor, was at Mass every day of her life. And she was the meanest person I knew."

"She hit you?" Nick asked, his voice almost a growl.

"She didn't hit me. Not physically. But I swear sometimes her words hurt more than a blow ever could."

"Great to have family," he muttered, more to himself than to her.

"I'd like to think so," she said sharply. "It's something I want. I'm really looking forward to having a family, to starting from scratch. I know they say you can't choose your family—"

"They're wrong. Love trumps biology every time."

She thought about his brother, about the fact that Nick had been adopted into a family at fourteen—and wondered how that had happened, if they knew who he really was.

She had a feeling they did, that they'd go far to protect him. If they'd ever accept her was the question.

For Nick, love had trumped biology and for that she managed a real smile as she thought about her own future. "I hope you're right."

The plane was slowing in preparation for landing. He looked out the window, then asked, "You've never tried to find your mom?"

"No. In my gut, I know she's dead, but sometimes I wonder if she's out there somewhere . . . if she got clean and sober and has another family and she's just too ashamed to reach out. I mean, I represent her past."

As she said that, the jet touched down. As they taxied

down the runway, she threw the blanket off and grabbed the clothes.

The bathroom was small—too small to move around in—so she merely pulled the curtain that separated the cabin from the food prep area and changed.

When she finally did go into the bathroom, she looked in the small mirror, the camouflage close to her face, the hat pulled on so her hair didn't show, and she almost didn't recognize herself.

The fatigues were big on her but she rolled the sleeves a bit and then nearly tripped on the bottoms as she walked back toward Nick.

He was sitting on the floor, having dressed in similar clothing. He'd pulled on his shirt and was currently holstering a weapon, and he stopped to assess her as she walked toward him.

Without saying a word, he closed the distance between them and began to work on the sleeves, unrolling and rerolling them expertly so they weren't flopping around uselessly. And then he moved to button the jacket she'd left open over the T-shirt.

"It's going to be hot, I know, but you need to keep this closed." His hands brushed down the front of her body, even as his gaze held hers.

"We won't stand out in these clothes?"

"Trust me." He knelt down and helped her ease into the boots he'd brought for her—tucked the pants into them and laced them for her, and she resisted the urge to bend down and run her fingers through his hair, to join him on the floor.

When she was finally properly attired, he stood. "I'm sorry your family's all fucked-up."

She wanted to hug him, but she didn't. The guilt of not having told him the truth ate away at her, especially after his sincere words. "Thanks. Your brother . . . he seems nice. Will you tell me about your family sometime?"

"Sometime. All set?"

"Yes. Sarah will meet us on the tarmac."

"Keep your head down and stick close to me. No matter what happens, we don't separate. Just hold on, Kaylee. Do you understand?"

The heat and humidity hit his face like a heavy cloak the second the door of the private plane opened, and immediately Nick thought about Kaylee's breathing, at the same time he scanned the throngs of people, looking for anything out of the ordinary.

There were people dragging boxes—in Africa, boxes taped together and luggage were interchangeable; 9/11 hadn't changed much about the way this country managed their airports.

He went down the small flight of metal steps first, Kaylee close enough on his six to nearly trip him.

She *was* freaked. He didn't blame her, but he'd need to keep a much tighter watch on her.

The story about her family hit him harder than he'd thought, and he almost wished he hadn't asked, hadn't wanted to even consider getting closer to her.

But who the hell was he kidding—it had been too late for that from the second he'd seen her.

She'd looked so damned earnest, innocent, even, and although he knew better, he could still get a glimpse of the little girl with freckles sprinkled lightly across the bridge of her nose who wanted to be a reporter when she grew up.

He tried to reconcile that picture with the car-stealing young girl and the beautiful woman in front of him who was in more freakin' trouble than she could possibly understand, and he quickly gave up. She was complicated—maybe more so than he was—layered and willing to be peeled. That was the big difference between the two of them—and now was not the fucking time to think about any of this, it was time to think about how to stay alive.

His gut clenched as if something wasn't right, but it did so every time he set down in this country—most of the time, things weren't right here, and they certainly weren't right in his world.

Still, he pushed past the people dragging their own checked luggage from the bellies of the overcrowded planes toward the airport, past soldiers with machine guns who were everywhere, despite the fact that security didn't seem to be a priority.

The car was waiting on the south side, just off the edge of the tarmac, near the back road leading toward the underbelly of Uganda. It was just where Sarah had promised it would be, a white bandanna tied around the antenna.

But the car appeared empty, and he looked around for signs of anyone as he pulled his Sig stealthily and kept it down at his side.

Empty or not, the damned car would be his. Whoever this Sarah person was could catch up later.

But as they got closer, a woman came around from the

other side of the car—she had a rifle around her neck, a sleeve of tattoos down one arm. She wore a tank top and camouflage pants and looked like she could handle herself.

Kaylee extended her hand. "Sarah, hi, I'm—"

"You're K. Darcy. Aka Kaylee Smith. And I hear you need a ride to the DRC."

But it wasn't Sarah speaking those words. Kaylee froze at the sound of the familiar voice as he stared down the barrel of a large rifle.

Fuck.

"You don't look happy to see me again, Kaylee. Then again, the man you're traveling with isn't one of my favorite people either." The man who'd called himself Agent Simms still had a large bruise across his throat and another on his cheek and Nick wanted nothing more than to put his own hand around that neck again.

He didn't need to turn around to know that Ferone was behind them—the click of a rifle at the ready was enough of a hello.

"Where's your badge now?" Nick kept his voice calm, didn't attempt to bring up his weapon. Instead, he held Kaylee tight against his side with an arm around her waist—*shit,* she was shaking—and shifted them slightly so he could see both men surrounding them.

Simms sneered, his teeth nearly bared. "Don't worry about that—all I need is Aaron's bankbook and after that you two can rest in peace."

And then he turned to Sarah, "You get out of here now. You saw nothing."

Sarah nodded and backed up, following the man's directions. Nick ran through two possible plans in his mind—

both of which consisted of literally pushing Kaylee to the ground and out of the way, but before he could react, Sarah brought the butt of her rifle down hard against the back of Simms's head.

Nick immediately slammed Agent Ferone hard, in the gut, used his elbow to angle Ferone's gun in the air. It went off, the shot ringing through the chaos outside the airport, and Sarah was yelling, "Get in the car!"

They all heard the screech of tires and turned to see a vehicle careen around the corner heading directly toward them.

"Soldiers," Nick told Kaylee, and yeah, if it was a choice between soldiers and Sarah, he knew who he'd rather be with.

Simms was up, though, moved toward Nick even as the soldiers came closer in their own car.

Nick didn't hesitate, pushed Kaylee into the backseat and turned to slam Simms to the ground with a well-placed foot to the man's knee. It was fighting dirty, but Nick wasn't in the mood for fair play—not when he and Kaylee were in the crosshairs.

When Simms didn't get up immediately, Nick followed Kaylee into the backseat, closing the door even as Sarah peeled the car away from the tarmac and toward a strip of red road.

"Those men knew you," Sarah said.

"I didn't know they'd follow me here," Kaylee told her.

Sarah glanced in the rearview mirror. "They're not following us now—only the soldiers."

Nick had already grabbed one of the automatic rifles

from the back of the ancient Land Rover as Sarah sped along the back paths like she owned them.

"I can lose them, but it's not going to be pretty." Sarah looked over her shoulder. "Don't shoot first."

"Like that would matter," Nick muttered.

"You're going to have to trust me, considering I just saved your damned life," Sarah answered him. "You should've killed those men."

Yes, he probably should have, but killing possible FBI agents wasn't on his list of career goals. Because when this was all over, he'd like a career to go back to.

"How did they know we'd be here? How did they beat us here?" Kaylee asked him as she watched the soldiers out the back window.

He had no fucking idea—although his guess was that the agents were CIA, not FBI. In his experience, the CIA was more likely to take care of a problem by getting rid of it. "Get down, Kaylee."

"We've got more company," Sarah called.

Nick turned to see two more cars join the first and put a hand on Kaylee's shoulder. "Get down, stay down and hold on. And cover your ears."

She nodded, even as she lowered herself to the floor. He ducked when bullets hit the car, heard her cry out and then watched as she covered her ears as he'd asked.

Sarah was somehow driving and shooting, and damn, it was like being in the car with Jake, but at least he was used to it—ended up balanced on the seat and went out the sunroof, alternately ducking and shooting for the tires. A risky fucking proposition, but better than sticking his head out the back.

After a few wild minutes—which included the sound of glass breaking and Sarah yelling to him and bullets flying—things calmed. Not Sarah's driving, however, as the car zigged and zagged and he hung on until a sickening slam shoved Kaylee against the door hard.

He dropped down onto the seat, dragged her up into his arms to steady them both until the car made a sudden, sharp right turn that yanked at his neck.

And just as suddenly as the sounds of gunfire had started, they stopped, the silence in the car punctuated only by the tinkling sounds of African drum and percussion music playing on the radio and Sarah's own soft mutterings.

Kaylee felt like rubber, as if she'd lived a thousand lives in those fifteen minutes of car chase, and she resisted the urge to look down at herself and check for wounds as the ride straightened out but continued pace.

She did, however, check Nick. His forehead had a small gash that bled, but otherwise, he seemed in one piece. Breathing.

She noted that he was doing the same thing to her—checking her over, assessing her, feeling for a pulse even as the car continued to careen at a speed that forced her to hold on to him tightly.

"I'm okay," she told him.

He nodded, touched her cheek for a brief second and then looked toward the front seat as Sarah asked calmly, "Would one of you like to explain what that was all about? Because if you're going to put me in harm's way, I'd like to be prepared."

Kaylee wanted to ask Sarah how much more prepared she could be, since the woman hadn't blinked in the face of danger. She was one hell of a cool customer, although with growing up in this environment, Kaylee supposed she had to be. Kaylee had always assumed that the stories her colleagues told about working with the photographer-slash-guide had been exaggerated—fish stories, so to speak, with each man and woman trying to show how much they were willing to put their own lives on the line for a story.

But the quiet confidence . . . the way she'd taken that man down back at the airport. Kaylee wondered what Sarah Cameron's deal was, and then reminded herself that she had enough of a story of her own to unravel. "I'm sorry, Sarah. I should have warned you that I didn't know what I was walking into when I came here."

"Those men followed you from the States?" Sarah asked, and Nick nodded in confirmation. "We've lost them for now, but if they're hell-bent on finding you two, we're going to need a much better plan. They mentioned money."

"Yes. I was bringing money to my ex-husband. He might've been kidnapped."

"Might have been?"

"I don't know if he's really alive," Kaylee admitted. "I don't know what's going on anymore."

Sarah kept her eyes on the road. While the airport had been loud and dusty, where Sarah drove them was scenic—almost serene. It was beautiful, with lush green surrounding them on both sides, even as it was cut by a swath of unpaved road that contained craters the size of cars. So much beauty and so much danger in one place.

"You're not carrying cash, are you?" Sarah asked.

"Just enough to get us past the border guards if we're stopped," Nick told her.

"We'll have to stake out the area first. When are you expected?" Sarah asked, and none of this seemed out of the ordinary to her.

"Tomorrow morning."

"Then we'll have to get there first. We've got the weather on our side for the next twenty-four hours. After that, I can't promise we can move fast," Sarah told them. "We'll have to drive in the dark. It's risky—parts of this country are under curfew and night's the worst time for travel, but I should be able to cover enough ground to get us there between ten and eleven. Minimal stops."

"I can switch off driving with you," Nick told her.

"If we come upon those men again, do you need me to kill them?" Sarah asked Nick. "I'm assuming you're American military. I'm assuming that killing American agents wouldn't be good for your career."

"I wouldn't put that on you," Nick told her quietly.

"If you'd prefer to work with a male guide—"

"No, that's not it. You saved our asses. I don't discriminate when it comes to that," he told her.

"Nick, do you really think..." Kaylee trailed off, not sure how much to say in front of Sarah.

"Yeah, I think they'll keep trying," he said. "We'll be cutting it damned close."

Kaylee turned around to stare at the road behind them. It was all clear, and much easier to deal with right now than the road that lay ahead.

CHAPTER
13

Chris Waldron didn't show himself until four hours into the flight, when they were well over water and there was no way to get him the hell off, except by parachute. Which he probably wouldn't mind at all.

"Glad I didn't miss wheels-up, Agent Michaels" was all he said when he strolled down the aisle, ducking slightly to avoid smacking his head on the ceiling.

Jamie had underestimated him—stupidly, perhaps. But in her defense, typically, most military men wanted nothing whatsoever to do with the feds or any kind of investigation. "You are not authorized to be on either this plane or this mission."

"I'm willing to bet you're not either. This isn't an FBI plane," he countered.

It wasn't—she'd paid money for a private charter to Kisangani . . . and she didn't want to know how he'd found that out. She opened her mouth to protest but in the end the need to go find her sister was stronger. She wouldn't let him—or anyone else—screw this up for her.

In this case, she let her weapon do the talking and she pulled and held her gun steadily on him. "You're going to back off, Chief Petty Officer Waldron. You're going to sit down and shut up, and you're going to deplane at the very first opportunity."

"And if I don't you're going to kill me?"

She didn't answer.

"Put the fucking gun down, Jamie."

She didn't—he was faster, much faster than she was with a weapon. Just because his wasn't drawn right now didn't mean anything—he still had a better chance of taking her out. "You're interfering with my investigation."

"I'm starting to lose my patience, and that doesn't happen all that often. Lower your weapon and tell me what the hell's going on."

"You're unauthorized. I want you to sit down and let me restrain you properly."

He laughed. It was a low snort at first, turned to full-blown laughter fast, his head thrown back as if it was the best joke he'd ever heard.

It was enough to distract her.

Within seconds, despite her years of training, Chris was behind her, his arm slung across her chest in a diagonal hold, her arm with the gun forced down to the floor. "If you looked in my file," he murmured, his lips close to her ear, "you would know that I'm a very dangerous man. A man you'd want next to you in a combat situation, if your life needs saving. A man you wouldn't want next to you if you're not on my side."

With that warning delivered, he yanked the gun out of her hand and held her there, her back pressed to his chest—it was like being trapped against a solid brick wall. An angry one.

Calm, Jamie, just stay calm. "I don't have the clearance to look in your file. Nor the desire." A total lie, since she'd found the necessary clearance to get a basic rundown on the man's skills after their first meeting.

"I don't give a shit about that. I want to know what you know about Aaron Smith. Because Nick's in big trouble and there's no way you're holding me back from this."

"I understand worrying about your teammate—"

Chris cut her off. "Nick's more than a teammate. He's my brother."

"I know, the brotherhood of the SEALs—"

"I mean, he's my brother. As in, raised in the same family," he clarified.

His brother. God, she wished he hadn't said that. "When we land, you're free to go where you'd like."

"Make no mistake about it, I'm going with you." He released her. "Over the years, my team and I have made friends with a lot of people. We help each other when it's necessary."

"I didn't ask for your help."

"I'm willing to give it anyway." He held his gaze steady,

as if searching her face for any signs that she would give up her intel.

"What if I don't tell you? What if I can't?"

"Then it's going to be a hell of a ride into the motherland."

She turned from him, wished there was someplace else to go to move away from his gaze. The little voice inside of her told her to trust him—the same voice that had always told her to never, ever trust anyone fully, and she didn't understand what kind of magic Chris had in him to do that to her.

She sat and bowed her head in her hands, elbows on the small table where she'd been studying the map of Ubundu earlier, trying to figure out the best routes to get to the warehouse—the last known rumored address of the GOST group, which she'd gotten from searching through confidential files.

I would know if my sister was dead—I would feel it.

Jamie just had to get there in time to warn Sophie, to pull her away from this group and face the consequences later. There was no other choice.

"Why are you so sad, Jamie?"

Chris's voice was like a long caress across the back of her neck. For a second, she'd forgotten she wasn't alone. Unconsciously, she put her own palm there and attempted to rub some of the tension away.

She hadn't heard him walk toward her, but suddenly his own hand eased over hers and she let it. His palm was rough, calloused—hands that worked for a living, and it felt wonderful against her smooth skin, hot to her cool.

She should've shoved him away, stood up, demanded

that he stop—stop touching her, stop being so nice . . . stop everything.

But she didn't. "I'm not sad—my head hurts." Half truth, half lie.

"Migraine."

"Yes. I get them sometimes."

"What do you take?"

"Nothing."

"So what, you just will them away?"

"Something like that." She shouldn't be doing this, letting his hands roam on her. She needed to focus, to figure out her plan once the plane landed.

But his hands, so good—she could sleep right now. Sleep with her head against his chest. "You're good at that. Good hands."

"Runs in my family on my momma's side."

"She was a sniper like you?"

"She was a midwife when I was growing up."

"Do you deliver babies too?"

"Sometimes. I'm also the team's corpsman."

"Sniper and a corpsman. Seems like an odd combination. Do you feel the need to bring people back from the dead or something?"

His hands jerked away from her, fast, like he'd received an electric shock from her body.

"What's wrong?" she asked, turned to him. His discomfort was more than evident, if only for a few seconds before it faded.

"Nothing. I just don't like talking about my job."

She wondered if that was a superstition common among

snipers or if it was only Chris's, and she didn't question him further. Her own hand was palm down on her right thigh, covering the healed wounds. She often did that—touched them as if they were some kind of strange talisman. A reminder of where she'd been and where she was going—what she had to do to survive. So yes, she understood superstition.

There was still so much time left before the flight landed, and already her body felt heavy from under-use. The past few days had taken their toll on her emotionally and she was a bundle of nerves. Frayed at the edges. And about to get into more trouble than she'd ever been in.

She could lose her job for this, but for the first time in her life, she didn't care. His touch had, at least, cleared her head. "Does your offer of help still stand?"

"Yes." Chris was in front of her, on his knees, his palms over hers. "It's you and me—Jamie and Chris. Fuck the agent shit, tell me."

"I don't even know you."

"You know my brother's in trouble."

Yes, she knew.

And by letting him in, she was breaking all the rules and risking his life in the bargain. "I have to know how far you're willing to go."

"For my family? All the way, Jamie."

She nodded, had suspected as much, but needed to hear that confirmation. "I'm looking for a group called *GOST*. It was started by a few high-ranking government officials—senators and congressmen, although their names haven't ever been revealed—with the help of the FBI and CIA. And for a while, GOST served a necessary purpose." She glanced toward the cockpit door. "It was created to get around Executive Order 11905."

"Prohibition on Assassination," Chris said slowly. " 'No employee of the United States Government shall engage in, or conspire to engage in, political assassination.' "

"Right. It was an experiment," Jamie continued quietly. "A group of supersecret and highly trained men and women to do the kinds of jobs nobody wanted to know about and everybody wanted done. The dirty work. The kind of work that keeps the economy and our world safe. But things went wrong."

"I imagine they would. How were they recruited?"

"Mostly they were culled from the military—which they went to from Witness Protection. GOST threatened them . . . with their own safety."

"That wouldn't be enough to force me into something." His voice was low and steady. Calm, even, but his body still vibrated with that invisible energy, more so now than before.

"It wasn't," she agreed. "So the CIA came up with something different to keep them. Threatening their loved ones."

"That would do it. Motherfucker."

"Chris, if anyone knew I was telling you this—"

"They won't," he interrupted. "How the hell do you know about it? Are you part of the team that created them?"

"No, I had no part in it. I'd heard the rumors about it for years—and when I began to dig, I found things I didn't want to. And you're right, this whole investigation is unofficial."

"How the hell did you get involved in all of this?"

Her voice was hoarse when she spoke, like she'd been choking back tears. "I have reason to believe they recruited my sister."

He grasped her hand and swore under his breath.

She liked that Chris was holding her hand. Comfort flooded her. "Sophie was in the Air Force, a pilot. There was an accident—a crash—and after that, she wasn't herself. The Air Force cleared her of any blame, but still, she resigned her commission. And then she was approached by the CIA—she told me it was her second chance."

"How long has it been since you've heard from her?"

"She's been missing for almost nine months. The CIA said she stopped showing up for training—no one could find her and no one could help me. No one wanted to help me. They said she was a grown woman and she'd probably gone off on her own. But while I was searching for her, I began researching others who'd been in Witness Protection who've disappeared without a trace—fallen off the ends of the earth," she told him.

"Isn't that the point of Witness Protection?"

"Even the marshals, their only contact points, don't know where they went." She didn't tell him that her foster father was a U.S. marshal and he'd reluctantly shown her the database in the interest of helping Sophie. "I saw the reports. They were released from the program and allowed to join the military. And then they disappeared. Some were discharged, like Sophie. And some just never showed up for work again," she explained.

"You think they were the ones recruited for GOST?"

"It's a perfect plan—sick, but perfect. They couldn't go

against GOST and risk being exposed to the people who'd wanted them dead to begin with—the people who'd forced them to go into hiding in the first place. Comply or die."

"Your sister was in Witness Protection before she was commissioned?" he asked.

"From the time she was twelve," she said, braced for his next question about her own Witness Protection status, but he didn't ask.

That was good—she wasn't ready to tell.

Instead, he got up off his knees. "We've got to figure out how fucked my brother and your sister are."

She could barely look him in the eye when she delivered her next words, the ones she'd been dreading saying out loud. "Based on the intel I've got, it might be too late for both of them." She'd spent more time around computers than humans, knew how to get what she needed. When it was her against the computers, she could always win. "I found a CIA directive from a man named John Caspar to Agents Simms and Ferone—an order to eradicate GOST and its members ASAP. Africa was the test ground. If things went the way they planned—if their operatives did what they were supposed to—they were going to train a new group and take it global. Obviously, it hadn't gone well."

"Who is this John Caspar guy?"

"That's the problem—he doesn't exist. I've been trying to get a handle on him for months. He's virtually untraceable. And since I can't get a picture or address or even a job description, I can't follow him on foot." She sighed, pushed some stray hairs off her face.

"How does this tie to Nick?"

"Your brother did some work for a mercenary named Bobby Juniper, aka Clutch."

Chris nodded slowly. "You think Clutch is part of that group."

"He fits the profile."

"Nick was trying to make contact with Clutch before he left but couldn't. He left him messages. The location that he and Kaylee were headed toward. They're about five hours ahead of us—landing in Ubundu."

"You have coordinate points? From who?"

"Look, this is going to sound crazy... but based on what you're telling me, maybe not so much. Kaylee Smith's husband was an Army Ranger—the Army claimed he was KIA and then, a couple of weeks ago, Aaron called her. And then some FBI agents came to her and said he'd gone AWOL. And then Aaron called again, told her to go to Africa. Gave her coordinate points."

"I ran Kaylee Smith's name earlier—she's not in the system." She yanked her computer closer. "What's her ex's name?"

"Aaron Smith. I tried to run a line on him but came up empty."

"You would. I won't," she said without thinking. But when she looked up, he didn't seem offended or put off. Instead, he smiled, like he enjoyed the one-up and sat next to her as she began to work the system again in an attempt to beat the clock.

S arah was the most efficient guide Nick had ever had through this country—she knew the roadways and the detours and she hadn't consulted a map once during the ten-hour drive from hell.

Kaylee looked rattled still—a lot of that had to do with the condition of the roads. If you weren't used to it, the bone-deep jostling could unnerve you completely.

But she'd had no complaints at all. Just coped—even slept a little, albeit it was most likely a stress-induced nap, and what the hell had she been through in her life that she took all of this in and bucked up under the pressure? Her home life must've been far worse than she'd made it out to be. He knew from experience that it was usually easier to gloss over a bad childhood than to talk about it. Easier to remain stoic, which was exactly what she'd been over the past hours.

He'd wanted to reach out, massage her shoulders, maybe even hold her hand to reassure her—but none of that would keep his head on straight. Not with Chris's voice mail still echoing in his head.

Hey, man—the agent's looking for Clutch. I'll explain more when I can. I'm headed your way . . .

It seemed a lot of people were looking for the merc, and no one was having any success in finding him. What the hell had Clutch gotten himself—and Nick, by default—involved in?

If Chris were here, he'd remind Nick about synchronicity. Dad always said that nothing was a coincidence—not the places you ended up or the people you met—that in some way everything would end up circling back to you, to either help or harm. It was up to you to figure out which.

Nick had always been able to tell good from bad—easy enough when someone with a weapon was coming after you. But in this situation, it felt as if good and bad were mixing, and he couldn't tell yet what end was up.

He'd have to trust his gut to get him through. That's what Chris would tell him to do. Dad would tell him to look for the signposts.

Jake would tell him he was out of his motherfucking mind to go on this mission without authorization and to back away from Kaylee as quickly as possible. But it was far too late for that now. Even more, he didn't want to back away from her.

But that couldn't be Nick's concern, not when Sarah had them parked about half a mile outside the coordinates.

When she'd pulled the car over, Kaylee had woken up and Nick had discovered that he had put his hands on her, had been stroking her hair while she'd been curled up next to him along the seat.

He pulled away fast and climbed out of the car.

"No one's been through this way for days," Sarah told him now as she traced the ground with the thin beam of light from the flashlight. "It's the only way into where you want to go. The other route is blocked right now, thanks to the rains."

He walked the path she'd motioned to—because of the recent rains, it would've been easy enough to see tire tracks or footprints along the only strip of land able to be called a road. Sarah was right, there was no need for him to leave her and Kaylee behind and go searching any farther in. They'd be smarter—and safer—waiting here, hidden just off the path to see who went by.

"I'll keep watch, stay outside," Sarah told him.

"We'll rotate. You need sleep."

"You don't?"

"No."

She gave a short laugh. "American soldiers—you're all the same."

You've met a lot of American soldiers?" Kaylee asked Sarah as Nick moved off with the flashlight, muttering something about checking the perimeters and ignoring Sarah's last comment.

"Usually they come to this country when their career is over and they're looking for more action. Quick money."

"Private contractors," Kaylee said and that made Sarah smile.

"We still prefer to call them mercenaries here—there's no shame in the word. I was training to be one myself."

Kaylee studied Sarah from the light afforded them by the open driver's-side door. She was pretty—Scandinavian features played heavily across her tanned face, the wide eyes, the full lips, features just odd enough to make her deviate from the standard ideals of beauty. Even the heavily tattooed left arm added to the picture instead of making her appear hard. She just looked sexy, with her torn shirt and her cargos that hung low on her hips. "Really? You wanted to be a mercenary?"

"At first no man would train me, so I learned as much as I could on my own, and then one man finally agreed to." Sarah pressed a finger to her lips before continuing, as if thinking of the right way to explain things. "I wanted freedom. I wanted to be able to protect myself—to take care of myself. I wanted people to fear me. It's hard being a woman in this country, especially a woman alone."

"It's hard being a woman alone anywhere."

"I imagine it is." Sarah was studying her now. "Is he your boyfriend?"

Kaylee glanced over at Nick, who stood alone and silent on the edge of the clearing—broad-shouldered and stock-still—and she wondered if her stomach would always flip a little when she saw him. "Nick? He's, um . . . a friend," she finished lamely and Sarah smiled as she yanked a rifle from the backseat.

"Pretty good friend to escort you into the jungle. I'll take first watch so you can spend some time with your friend," she told Kaylee. She stopped halfway out of the car. "You're prepared that it might not be your ex-husband who wants you here, aren't you? Because most of these kidnappings . . ."

She trailed off and shrugged and Kaylee felt the quick jolt of panic run through her again. Nothing Sarah said was new—Nick had warned her, over and over—and still, here she was in the middle of nowhere, fighting her better instincts, which told her to verify her source much more thoroughly than she had for this one. "I'm aware of that. I wouldn't have been able to forgive myself if I didn't do this, though. I loved him once."

Sarah nodded. "I just want you to be prepared."

Kaylee wanted to tell her that she could never have been prepared for this, but even as she thought it, she realized it was a lie. So all she said was, "Thank you," before Sarah closed the door quietly behind her.

She shifted in her seat to watch Sarah and Nick talking.

Earlier, when she'd been unable to fight her exhaustion, she'd slept—a feat in itself in the fast-moving vehicle that tore over the bumpy roads. Sleep had been uneven and she'd sworn Nick was touching her, caressing her outer thigh, brushing some stray hairs off her cheek ... even settling a palm on her shoulder with a touch that was at once protective and seductive. Before that, he hadn't so much as looked in her direction since they'd escaped from the soldiers' bullets earlier—had pretty much ordered her here and there, and she'd listened because she knew he would protect her.

As she'd stirred, opened her eyes, she'd seen him jerk a hand away from her.

He *had* been touching her. And it had been nice. Comforting. For a man who didn't trust well, he was putting an awful lot on the line for her.

When he was a boy of maybe six or seven, Clutch vividly remembered playing hide-and-seek with the neighborhood kids every summer evening at dusk, when the fireflies began to blink in the humid air of Northern California.

If picked to be the seeker, he always found the kids easily—so much so that they quickly learned it was more fun to search for him than to be searched out by him.

No one ever found him. He was so quiet, so still. He loved it—watched as other kids came so close to him that he could feel the tensing of their bodies as they struggled to stalk quietly through the familiar backyards. As big and broad as he was, even as a child, he managed to remain hidden in plain sight. Part instinct, part too many hours reading books on spooks and spies.

In his life, these skills had continued to serve him well. He could almost smell an intruder in his space, could feel the change in air pressure. Hairs on the back of his neck would stand now that his skills were finely honed, and here in this jungle, nearly a mile outside of the coordinate points where he was set to meet Kaylee Smith tomorrow morning, he knew something was very, very wrong.

Someone was there, sitting on a cluster of boulders that would give them enough height to see over the brush if it were daylight. But in the dark it just made them more of a target to anyone wearing NVs, like he was. He soon realized that whoever it was sitting there wasn't the danger he sensed.

He moved closer and closer still, so he could get a look at the person's face, saw the slim back and the arm covered with tattoos and realized quickly that it was a woman who waited there.

It was Sarah.

He tore off the NVs. Had she tracked him, he wondered—had she found the other members of GOST and been sent to find him?

No, they wouldn't have helped her, not without calling him first to verify. None of them knew about her—no one spoke of their lives before GOST . . . they cried out for those missing pieces of themselves only in their sleep.

His hands began to sweat and he forced himself to keep a tight grip on his weapon as he locked eyes with the man standing behind her.

That man presented less of a problem, however, than the one standing next to him.

Clutch opened and closed his hands as he watched the man prepare his rifle silently. Sarah sensed something, began to raise up from her sitting position, and Clutch had no time to waste. He moved behind the man, killing him with one sharp, swift movement, so he fell softly to the ground as Clutch grabbed the rifle out of his hands.

He'd go back for the man's identification later—right now, the other man near Sarah, who'd seen him, needed to be taken out and fast.

The quiet seeped into the night around her—it had been a while since Sarah sat watch like this, alone without the welcoming sounds of her country.

Except tonight, her instincts burned. She tried to blame the incident with the men at the airport, but knew it went beyond that.

Whatever Kaylee Smith was dealing with in her personal life was proving to make this trip more than a simple guided tour to the DRC. The man she was with—American, military and Kaylee's lover. In Sarah's experience, that combination always brought trouble.

And someone else was out here in this jungle besides the three of them.

Slowly, she pushed off the rock she'd been sitting on, weapon by her side, scanning the rapidly fading darkness for movement.

She wasn't sure if dawn was her friend at this moment, but Nick was close too . . . he'd hear her if she yelled.

She turned left, saw nothing. Turned right—and froze.
Clutch.

He was in the shadows, looked so angry and so hand-some at the same time. She held her breath while he stood not more than five feet from her, gun drawn, appraising her as if she was a total stranger. Looking through her.

She did not like the look in his eyes. A flash of panic hit her, too late to do any good.

He might not be the same man you knew—who knows what going back to GOST did to him.

She hadn't wanted to consider that possibility. He'd never given up on her, even when she'd pushed him away brutally. She at least owed him the same.

"Bobby." The name hung between them, her voice barely above a whisper. And still, he said nothing, cocked his head to the side, an almost indiscernible motion.

Her stomach lurched when he pulled his rifle. She smelled the fear—wasn't sure if it was all hers or if some of it came off his skin.

His shot seemed aimed directly at her. She mouthed the word *no,* but no sound came with it. And just as suddenly, she felt a sharp blow to the back of her head and her world went black as the shot echoed in her ears.

When she woke, not more than a few seconds later, she was lying on the soft jungle floor with Clutch hovering over her.

He'd been stroking her cheek lightly, waiting for her to wake up.

"You pulled your gun," she whispered. "At first I thought..."

"I know. He was behind you, hit you before I got a clear shot."

Sarah sat up, looked over at the man he'd taken down—the one who'd called himself Simms at the airport.

"He had his rifle trained on you. He was going to kill you," Clutch said.

"He followed me from the airport—he wasn't alone."

"I already took down another man. He's over there." Clutch pointed and Sarah shifted, and recognized the lighter-haired man immediately. "Why were these men following you, Sarah?"

She realized she was shaking, but it wasn't from fear. "Not me—the couple I'm driving through. They're meeting someone here; they have account numbers to transfer the ransom money." She paused and then jerked her chin toward where Simms's body lay. "You knew him, didn't you? Is he . . . one of them?"

He nodded in confirmation. "Both of them work for GOST."

She grew cold at the thought of how close GOST had gotten to her. "Are you free? Please, tell me you're free and all of this is over."

But even as she spoke, she knew it wasn't so, couldn't be that easy.

"I'm not free, Sarah. Not yet. But I have a plan."

She put her palms against his cheeks for a moment, then ran her fingertips along his brow bone, down along his jaw, reassuring herself that Clutch was really, truly there—living, breathing and not some figment of her dreams, dreams so vivid that she'd often wake up with aching hands from fisting the covers.

But now she was holding him, and she wasn't letting go this time. "You left me," she told him, her voice fierce.

"I just saved your life and you're angry with me?"

"Yes, so angry." But she was kissing him even as she breathed those words against his mouth, her cheeks wet with tears—hers and his running together.

Together.

CHAPTER
14

The shot—a single one that pierced the night—was close. Kaylee watched Nick survey the area calmly, rifle cradled in his arm.

He looked back at her as if debating something, and finally he mouthed the word *quiet* and handed her a pistol. Then he took her hand and placed it on the waistband of his BDUs so she could follow him in the dark.

He didn't call out for Sarah, but they'd only needed to walk a bit longer before they'd come upon her, lying on the ground, a man kneeling over her.

It had only taken them a moment to see the dead body—another to realize that Sarah wasn't in danger from the man she was currently kissing, although the couple quickly pulled apart when Nick called Sarah's name.

"Both of the men from the airport are dead," she told them. "This is—"

Nick stared at the man. "Clutch? Shit, I tried getting a message to you through the usual contact. He'd said you'd disappeared."

"I did."

"You obviously know her."

Clutch glanced over at Sarah—even in the thin beam of the flashlight, Kaylee could see the softness in her eyes now as she looked at the man with the nearly white blond hair. "I never expected to find her here, with Kaylee."

"You're looking for me?" Kaylee asked, heard the uncertainty in her own voice even as Nick pulled her tighter to him.

"I brought you here," Clutch told her.

"I came for Aaron—I don't even know you."

"I served next to Aaron for three years."

Kaylee had been holding on to Nick's free arm tightly, had taken a step toward Clutch without even realizing it. "Do you know where he is? The Army told me he was KIA—and then those agents from the airport said he went AWOL."

Clutch paused again. "He was KIA, Kaylee. He just wasn't a part of the Army when it happened."

"But he's been calling me."

"I've been calling you, KK." Clutch's voice was oddly hoarse.

"How did you know he called me that?" she demanded. "How do you know so damned much about me?"

Nick knew—one look in Clutch's eyes and he knew.

"I was with him that night—we'd taken fire, there was no way to get him to a hospital. He talked about you before he died," Clutch said, his voice halting. Nick lowered his weapon at the sound of the big man in front of him nearly breaking down, and part of him wanted to sink to his knees himself.

"He died here, in Africa?" she asked.

Clutch nodded.

Gunfire shattered the surrounding quiet. Kaylee jumped and Clutch and Sarah both stilled. Nick had too—the shots were far enough away and scattered, random fire . . . more soldiers.

Instinctively, the group pulled together a bit more closely, although Kaylee noticed that everyone's weapons were at the ready. "I don't understand any of this—you're going to have to explain why I had to come here, and what was so important that these men were trying to kill me."

Clutch nodded. "What I'm going to tell you, where I'm going to take you . . . let's just say you'll need to decide how deep you're willing to go."

"I'm not going anywhere until I know more," she told him, the feeling of dread growing in her stomach. If Aaron had worked with—died next to—this man, she had to know everything.

"We need to wait out the soldiers anyway," Sarah said as she stared off into the distance—the sounds of sharp gunfire permeated the air, distant but still close enough. "Not safe to push on right now."

Nick pulled Kaylee gently to his side as he held the

semi-automatic pointed at Sarah and Clutch. "The question is, is it safe to stay here with you two?"

Nick would kill both Clutch and Sarah if he had to. As he pressed his anger back—anger mostly aimed at himself for trusting anyone beyond his brothers—the mercenary held up both his hands as a show of peace.

"Nick, just give me a chance to explain," Clutch said. "You've got nothing to fear from me or from Sarah."

Nick didn't move, kept the rifle trained on Clutch. Sarah had, so far, kept her own hands down at her sides.

That meant nothing.

Clutch looked at Sarah, who nodded. "Tell them, Clutch. Tell them everything you told me earlier," she implored.

"And start from the beginning," Nick said.

Clutch drew a deep breath and Nick swore he saw a shudder go through the man, even in the darkness. "I was in Witness Protection before I went into the Army. I was given another new name then, a new identity, and Witness Protection cut me free. But it wasn't that simple. Years later, the government came back, wanted more from me. They killed the woman I was engaged to just to prove their point and threatened to turn my mother and me over to the men who we were hiding from in the first place. They forced me out of Delta Force and into this government-funded group of mercenaries. They call us GOST."

"I don't understand—I first worked with you a year ago," Nick said slowly.

"When you worked with me, and then again when I

helped you and Jake a few months ago, I was out. I got called back immediately afterward—something I'd never wanted to happen."

"What about Aaron—you said he served with you?" Kaylee asked. "Was he part of this group?"

"Yes, he was one of us, was killed during a GOST mission."

"But Aaron wasn't in Witness Protection—I would've known that," Kaylee protested.

"He wasn't in Witness Protection," Clutch agreed. "He'd ordered his team to fire on a caravan of UN peacekeepers in the Sudan—he was following a direct order, but Aaron's CO let him take the blame for all the deaths, in order to save his own ass."

"He chose GOST over jail."

"Not exactly." Clutch glanced at Kaylee. "They didn't threaten him with Leavenworth—they used something worse."

"I can't imagine what would be worse than being imprisoned for the rest of your life." Kaylee was still holding Nick's free arm with a death grip.

"They threatened him with *you*, Kaylee. His best friend. The only woman he ever loved. Using the people we love against us is the most effective way to keep us in line."

Her voice was halting, like she was having trouble breathing again, when she asked, "Who the hell are the people in charge?" Nick noted that her hands shook, and *fuck*, he wished she didn't have to hear all this.

"You met two of them."

"Were Simms and Ferone really FBI?" Nick asked.

Clutch shook his head. "They were CIA when I knew them."

"CIA posing as FBI—probably the closest the two agencies will ever come to working together," Nick muttered. "They followed us here from Virginia. How did they know when we'd be landing? How did they even know we'd be coming here?"

"I don't know. I didn't set Kaylee up—I need her alive. I want her help."

"You want her money, Aaron's money."

Clutch shook his head impatiently. "I don't have any use for that money, but it was the best way to get Kaylee here— I didn't think she'd come here just for my story."

"Your story?" Kaylee looked between Nick and Clutch. "You brought me here to write a story about GOST?"

"One that could possibly save my life, Sarah's life—as well as the lives of the other people pressed into service," Clutch told her.

"What did I get you involved in?" she muttered to Nick, who held her around the waist tightly. She held the pistol loosely at her side.

"You called Kaylee—did they tap your line? Could they have found out about this through you?" Nick demanded of Clutch.

"They can do a lot of things. But I'd never have called if I'd known they'd follow you, Kaylee. You have to believe that. Aaron was a good man—I would never do that to a member of his family."

Nick didn't know what Kaylee believed...he wasn't sure himself what the hell to believe anymore. "Which members of GOST know your plan?"

"All of them," Clutch admitted. "It was too risky not to let all the members know what I was going to do. In order for Simms and Ferone to know your location, one of the people I work with had to tell them—one of them has to be a plant."

"That's the only way they would've known when we might be flying in and to where. Simms and Ferone got here ahead of us, just in time." Too close for fucking comfort.

"And we need to get the hell out of here. Find someplace where we can circle the wagons and decide our next move," Clutch said. "It's got to be one of the two newer members. I'm not alerting them of anything yet. It'll keep them guessing if they don't hear from me or from Simms and Ferone."

"So what do we do now?"

Clutch stared at Kaylee. "If Kaylee agrees to write the article, she writes it here. We get it transmitted and then I have to go back to the warehouse and find the leak."

Nick shook his head. "Once they figure out that those men are dead, we're all in big trouble."

Clutch stared up at the sky. "They won't know tonight. Big rains are coming in. We're going to have to get to higher ground once the soldiers move."

"When will that be?" Kaylee asked.

"Borders are closed, can't go anywhere for at least a few hours—they'll have their fun and then we can go," Sarah told them.

"Who else is involved in all of this?"

Clutch hesitated and then, "There aren't many. As far as

I know, GOST consists of five men, including me, and a single woman. And then the two former agents—"

Nick was beyond patience. "Who else? There's got to be another person out there that's making you all run. Because if the two agents were it, you wouldn't need Kaylee to write your story."

"That's true. There's the one man out there—the one you need to worry about the most." Clutch paused. "We know him as John Caspar. He gives us our orders, knows all our secrets."

"He's the one who'll hunt you until you're gone," Nick said finally.

"We believe so," Clutch said quietly.

"Is he CIA too?"

"Once he'd been placed in charge of GOST, he wasn't officially assigned anywhere, not under CIA, FBI or any other agency that might be located at Liberty Crossing in DC. He's stealthy and lethal. He has no conscience and no soul. We don't know if he works alone or not—I've only met him twice. And I'm sorry, Kaylee. You have no idea how sorry I am." Clutch's voice broke slightly and Nick watched Sarah put a hand on the man's shoulder.

He still hadn't moved his own weapon.

"You don't know what these men have been through. They've had everything taken from them." Sarah spoke when Clutch couldn't. "The article could be their way out—their only shot at living. I won't even say a normal life, because it's never going to be that way for us again."

"Us? You're part of the group too?" Kaylee asked, but Sarah shook her head.

"No. But I'm not going anywhere without Clutch.

GOST used me to get him back in. I won't let that happen again." Her voice was fierce as she held on to Clutch, and Nick had to admire Sarah's loyalty.

Still, Kaylee was his priority. "Kaylee needs some time—I won't let her make this decision right now," Nick told them. Any other time, he knew Kaylee would no doubt chafe under the *I won't let her* comment, but for right now, she seemed grateful. He couldn't tell if she realized that the article was the best chance at saving her own life as well.

"I understand." Clutch shuffled the ground with his feet. "No matter what, we'll make sure you have safe passage— whether it's back to the airport or with us to write the article and then back home again. We mean no harm."

Reiteration aside, Nick could still feel Kaylee shake next to him—part fear, part emotional exhaustion; there was a huge decision looming in front of her and the past she'd thought Aaron had was blown wide open.

She had to understand the full implications of what had happened the second they'd touched down on African soil—probably from the second she'd opened Aaron's safe-deposit box.

There was no real way out for her now that the man who ran GOST had her firmly in his crosshairs.

Nick was used to impossible situations—he'd lived one for the better part of his life, in one way or another. Maggie used to read his palm and tell him that everything would work out. As much as he'd wanted to believe her, he never had. And telling Kaylee Maggie's theory wasn't going to do either of them any good.

He'd have to figure out what would.

Clutch and Sarah had gone to set up what they'd called a perimeter—Kaylee remained by Nick's side, trying to process all of it. Trying to stay on her feet.

Nick handed her water, ordered her to drink it. She drained the bottle, played with the top as she stared at the red dust beneath her feet. "My God, Nick—their story... is it true?"

"I've heard rumors about a group like this—there are always rumors, though. But I've worked with Clutch before—and he helped my brother out a few months ago."

"So you still trust him?"

"He's in trouble, Kaylee. People in trouble don't always act the way you'd expect."

That didn't make her feel any better. The air had cooled, made her breathing slightly easier than it had been before, but the stress coupled with the dust wasn't a good combination for her asthma. "I don't understand any of this... what these people do. I don't get how they can just kill. And don't give me any of that *They didn't have a choice* bullshit. You're the one who told me that we've always got a choice."

"They chose to stay alive any way they could," Nick said. "This is why people have secrets, Kaylee. It's easier that way." He looked around to see where Clutch and Sarah were. "Get into the car—backseat."

Clutch had already pulled his own car close to Sarah's, circling the wagons as he'd mentioned earlier, and now Kaylee climbed into the backseat of Sarah's car, with Nick right behind her. He shut the door, and even though the windows by the front seats were open, she felt safe and private. Finally.

"You can let it go, Kaylee. You're allowed to have a freak-out now."

The way he said it made her laugh, like he could command her freak-outs—and so she laughed and she laughed and then, just as suddenly, the tears were rolling down her face.

He simply held her, told her that it would all be okay.

In his arms, she believed him. And they remained that way for long minutes, until he pulled back. "I have to make a quick call."

He quickly spoke in numbers—she guessed longitude and latitude, and then gave a condensed version of what they themselves had just found out. "That was for Chris—the brother you met," he told her when he'd hung up.

"You're sure he's coming here?"

"Yeah, he left me a message earlier. He shouldn't be, but I can't stop him."

"Nick, Clutch told us a lot of things...how do we know he's telling the truth?"

"You want to try to fact-check his intel? Because I'm thinking having the CIA try to kill you is pretty good evidence that you're on to something dangerous."

She pressed her hands to her cheeks for a second and then let them fall to her lap in loose fists. "I'm on to something dangerous and Aaron's really dead. I don't know why this feels like mourning him all over again."

"You really wanted to see him. You counted on it. Maybe even thought you had a second chance."

"I wanted a chance to end things the right way. A

chance to part friends instead of holding on to unnecessary anger."

"You loved Aaron, didn't you?"

"I did."

"What was that like?"

"You're serious?"

"Yeah, I am. I want to know what it felt like."

She frowned a little, as she tried to figure out how to explain it. "At first it was wonderful. I couldn't be with him enough, you know? Then...I told you that he loved the military more than me—and that was true. But he also loved other women too. Lots of them," she said softly. "That betrayal nearly killed me. I knew we weren't compatible, that the passion wasn't there between us the way it should've been. But maybe our friendship could've been salvaged if he'd been honest with me. By the time I found out about the cheating, it was too late for me to forgive him."

"Relationships take a lot of commitment," he said.

"Yes. They also take a lot of trust. And after Aaron, I didn't trust anyone. I didn't think I ever would."

He didn't say anything to that. At some point, he'd wrapped his head in a green bandanna—it made his eyes stand out even more, made his cheekbones look sharper, made him look deadlier.

"What's going to happen to me if I don't do this article? I know you're trying to protect me, that you don't want me to know the full reality of this situation...but I need to know."

"Kaylee, fuck...let's just get out of this jungle first."

"Please."

He shook his head slowly, like her knowing was a bad idea, and he didn't take his eyes off the road. "You know about Aaron. About GOST. And the men behind GOST know about you," he said bluntly.

Yes, she'd known that from the moment Clutch informed her about GOST—but she'd needed to hear it spoken out loud, because knowing and hearing it said out loud were two different things entirely. She could quite possibly lose everything, depending on how this shook out. And while she'd told Nick that there was no one who would worry about her . . . that just served to make her chest ache even more. "I have no one."

"You have me, Kaylee. I told you before, we're in this together. I'm not going to let anything happen to you."

She willed herself to believe him. She also knew they were working on borrowed time—she had to make her decision fast. Her heart already told her what she needed to do, she just had to make sure her head was ready to follow. And in order for that to happen, she needed answers. "I need to speak with Clutch—the sooner I get this started, the better off we'll all be."

Her decision was made.

"Let's go, then—we don't have a lot of time." He opened the door and helped her back outside.

Nick called Clutch over—he and Sarah came toward the car as Kaylee pulled herself up onto the hood and pulled a pad out of her bag to take notes on. Nick leaned against the side of the car, far enough away to give her space, close enough to make her feel comfortable.

Sarah, however, stayed close to Clutch, like she refused to let him out of her sight. Still, both of them looked like they were guarding against some invisible but all too real threat.

Clutch was Nick's height, maybe a little broader, and his eyes . . . even in the dim light, she could tell he'd seen far too much.

"You have questions."

"Was the military involved in any of this, beyond what happened to Aaron on that mission with his CO?" she asked.

Clutch shook his head. "As far as the military is concerned, we simply disappeared. Most of us were listed as AWOL for a while and then dead—we assumed that the men who ran GOST took care of all of that. But people searched for us, I know that. The military doesn't take kindly to its elite soldiers just disappearing. They put a lot of money and training into me. I was the best of the best."

Nick's voice floated quietly over them. "Still are."

Clutch didn't say anything, just ducked his head and stared at the ground for a few minutes.

Kaylee waited until he looked back up. "So what happened to you . . . you don't blame the military?"

Clutch shook his head. "Not in my case. The military— the Army—saved me, took me in and trained me to protect myself. I was finally able to stop looking over my shoulder in fear, I had confidence that I could handle anything anyone threw at me. And I can. So no, this wasn't the military's fault—this is a government plan gone bad. Because while I understand their theory, I wouldn't have done this to my worst enemy."

She nodded. "Normally, I'd have to meet the rest of the group. Interview them."

"That's not possible now, not until I figure out which member is setting us up," Clutch said.

"I need some kind of proof, my paper's going to ask for it. You've got to give me something else," she told him.

"I'd expect nothing less." His eyes took on the green color of his camouflage jacket, and he stared at her as if he was weighing something heavily in his mind. And then he pulled out his phone and dialed. "Here's the last order I received."

She put the phone to her ear and listened—the voice was deep and dark, the kind she supposed could be sexy under other circumstances, but since it spoke of killing, it definitely sent chills down her spine in a not-so-good way. "I don't understand all of it, but I think...if I'm hearing right, this is an assassination order."

Nick took the phone out of her hand and replayed the message so he could listen. He nodded in confirmation to her words and tossed the phone back to Clutch.

"The order isn't sanctioned by our government," Clutch said. "John Caspar started selling us out to the highest bidders. The last order from the U.S. government was to get rid of a head of state who refused to shut down a known terrorist cell. This order's much different—and it could cause political unrest in an already unstable country."

She stared down at her hands, rubbed the third finger of her left hand where she'd worn Aaron's ring for so long—even after the marriage dissolved, because she couldn't let go of the loss of what she'd considered to be her family.

Clutch spoke quietly. "Aaron wasn't perfect, but he did love you."

"Aaron loved me the best way he knew how, that's what

I believe. He gave up his life for me. I have to make sure that he gets what he deserves. I want to stop whatever dishonor the government's trying to put on his record. He would've wanted that," she said, with another glance over at Nick, and then she turned to Sarah. "Sarah will be in danger now that she's with you again, won't she?"

"Yes. The men who wanted me for GOST have used my love for two different women against me. They killed Fay—raped and killed her and told me all about it. I refused to take the same chance with Sarah; I complied with John Caspar's orders. I know now that was a mistake, but I haven't stopped thinking of a way to get her back for a single second since I left her."

Her head ached at the thought of the sacrifice this man had made, of the one Aaron had made as well.

"You have no idea what it's been like, living like this." Clutch was speaking to her, but it was almost as if he was talking about someone else. "I haven't been *me* for so long, I don't know who I am. Or I didn't until last year."

"I can't imagine," she said softly, the image of Nick as Cutter still enough in the forefront of her mind to understand.

K aylee needed space to process everything—Nick could see that easily as she remained seated on the hood of the car, sounds of gunfire occasionally marring the quiet.

She'd stopped reacting to those. He knew that wasn't a good sign. She was off in her own head—her own world—dealing with everything she'd learned and trying to make sense of it all. For the article . . . for herself.

"Why don't you try to get some sleep? You've got a big job ahead of you," he said quietly.

"I could try, but I'm sure I'd end up just tossing and turning," she said, her fingers playing along the bottoms of her rolled-up BDUs.

"Did you get what you were looking for from Clutch?"

"It helps to know that whatever Aaron did in the end wasn't his choice. It's horrifying to know, though, that there are groups out there like this one, forced to do things they don't want to do," she told him, and he understood what she meant.

Aaron had made the choice to keep Kaylee safe at the cost of his own life, and Nick would be forever grateful for that.

"The men you saw with Aaron, the ones he'd..." She stopped, couldn't bring herself to say the word *killed*. "Do you think that was part of his job with GOST?"

He nodded, had been trying to not think about that or how badly Aaron had probably wanted to get on that helo with him. Aaron had wanted a way back but knew there was none.

There was nothing Nick could've done for him then. What he could do right now was a different story.

"This must be hard for you to hear too," she murmured. "All these good men, forced into something like this."

"I meant what I told Clutch. They *were* good men, still are."

To have that kind of control taken from him would've been unbearable. How Clutch stood it for so long was a testament to how strong he was. How much he loved his mother—and Sarah.

And then Kaylee asked, "How do you do this? Day after day, not knowing what's coming, where you're going to be . . . whether you're going to live or die?"

He shrugged, but knew she wouldn't take that for an answer. "I do it because I don't know any other way. I do it because it's my job. It's not like you don't take risks."

"None as big as this one," she said.

"You don't have to do this, Kaylee. I mean that. Clutch will find another way. He's resourceful. And he's got Sarah by his side now."

"They look like they can do anything together," she murmured, and yeah, they did. "I made a promise. I'm going to do the article. I've got to get in touch with my boss."

"Service is going to be spotty out here—I'll walk you to more of a clearing," he said and she slid off the car and walked with him, holding her cell phone in front of her until she got a decent number of bars.

Roger answered on the third ring, sounding sleepy. "This better be good, Smith—do you know what time it is?"

She didn't—not back home anyway—and she didn't care. "I've got the story of a lifetime for you, Roger."

CHAPTER
15

"Y ou're sure this is safe?" Jamie asked him for the billionth time as the small plane started with a rumble, nearly shaking her off the seat.

The pilot was a former SAS agent who'd relocated to Africa under circumstances beyond his control, or at least that's what he'd told Chris. The guy was nearing sixty, wore an eye patch and he'd had his plane up and running the fastest.

No, Chris wasn't sure of safety at all, but their options were few and far between. "We'll be fine."

He'd checked his cell the second their plane landed, had been relieved to hear Nick's message that he was all right and that Chris should stay on track and head to the coordinates. That he'd met up with Clutch.

Chris didn't think that was a very good thing at all—Jamie had reserved judgment when he'd told her, but the frown on her face said otherwise. If Clutch was a member of this group, he was on his own side—or whatever—and that made Chris's gut churn.

He'd tried to speak with Nick directly, but service had been for shit. Still was, but that didn't stop him from trying as the plane taxied down the small runway.

When he still couldn't get through, he fought the urge to throw the phone on the floor. It would be the fifth one he'd broken that year. He and electronics never did mix all that well—everything from phones to computers to cars seemed to break down around him. But motorcycles—well, he did just fine with those.

There hadn't been any Harleys to be seen, though. And so he'd paid through the nose to get them on this plane so they could reach Nick's last destination fast.

"Is that noise normal?" Jamie had a vice grip on his arm. He could feel the tension bouncing off her.

It had taken three hours for them to find this pilot, another hour to get the clearance to take off, and still, this would save them more time than driving.

And no, that sound wasn't normal. But the plane shuddered into the air and leveled out and so he told her, "Totally normal."

She shot him a sideways glance. "Yeah, sure."

He settled in as best he could—he'd practically had to fold himself in half to get on this damned thing. After watching her white-knuckle it for a while, her face practically glued to the window, he went for a distraction. "What's your deal?"

She turned from the window reluctantly, her hand still gripping the armrest. "My *deal?*"

He could see underneath her shield so clearly. He wasn't sure if it was *the sight,* as Dad called it, but when he looked at Jamie, he didn't see the buttoned-down suit or the sleek, sophisticated ponytail. No, he saw her running in a field of flowers, hair down, wearing a flowing dress. He saw her smiling.

And he saw himself wanting more. That hadn't happened to him in forever, beyond a few purely physical bump and grinds.

All right, more than a few. He had needs—lots of them—and there were always women who were willing to spend time helping him fulfill them. But unlike Nick, he'd always been wide open and ready for a relationship.

Chris believed fully in fate. Destiny. Jamie was now tangled up in his life—and in Nick's—and no matter what, he had no choice but to follow her and see where that led him.

"Yeah, your deal. Have you been with the FBI long?"

"I don't want to talk about me, Chris."

He leaned in close, put a hand on her arm and felt the soft zing again, the way he'd felt it back at the house and again on the flight in. She felt it too—he was sure of it. "I'm not asking you about your past, I just want to know more about *you.* Do you understand?"

She got it, because she finally answered, "I've been with the FBI for eight years."

"I've been in the Navy for nine."

"I was recruited right after college."

"I enlisted to avoid jail," he said.

"You're kidding."

"Why would I do that?"

"What did you do?"

"Borrowed some cars. Which escalated into more than borrowing."

"If you're trying to distract me from being nervous about this plane, it's not going to work."

"That's not why I'm doing it. I like you," he said simply.

"You like me."

"Yes. As in, I'd like to take you on a date. Like to watch you let your hair down, get drunk and dance on a table or two."

"I don't do those things," she interjected quickly.

"Maybe you should."

"That's what you like in a date?"

"No. I'd like you naked in bed with me too. Before or after the table dancing."

Her mouth opened and he wanted to chuckle at this woman who carried as much firepower as he did blushing at the thought of someone wanting to bed her.

He needed to find out the story behind the wedding band.

"You can't just say things like that," she told him finally, a slight blush still staining her cheeks.

"Why not?"

"It's not... appropriate. Didn't your mother teach you about polite conversation?"

He gave her a long, cool stare. "My momma taught me a lot of things, sugar."

"I think we should forget about getting personal."

He snorted. "You just let me in on a huge secret and you don't want to get personal? Sugar, you need to check your definition of *personal*."

"I told you everything because of your brother. I'm just as worried as you are and I'm not prepared to let Sophie down." She paused, and yeah, so much for professional. There was something about Chris that made her want to spill her guts, and that never happened. Not even with Mike, and they'd been together for five years. That was long enough to trust anyone completely and she'd still never let herself go. "Sophie was always pushing my help away even when she gave me anything I needed. When she finally came to me and confided, I felt like we'd finally broken through some invisible barrier. Our relationship has always been complicated."

He didn't say anything, just waited for her to continue. When she did so, it was with a great reluctance. "I don't like talking about myself—I've always had to hold back because of Witness Protection."

"But there's more to you than what you went through to put you into protection."

She shook her head. "You'd think, wouldn't you?"

Chris wouldn't let her get away with that, wouldn't let her shut down the way she normally would have—the way she'd learned to deal with things throughout the years. The only way she knew how to live.

He took her face in his hands—God, those hands—and stroked her cheeks lightly. "I know there's more to you. I can see it in your eyes."

"My life is my job. The way it needs to be."

There had never been much outside the lines for her. As a young girl, she hadn't really understood that her family had been keeping secrets—not until her parents had been killed and her world changed forever.

Later, the structure was something she'd learned to embrace. Sophie, on the other hand, chose an environment that was as by the book as you could get with the Navy; she'd balanced it by learning to fly F-14s and Tomcats. She'd told Jamie that being aboveground made her feel completely safe, like no one could get to her. And while Jamie envied that approach, she stayed closer to what she knew—the FBI and its own by-the-book approach.

And still, neither woman had been able to successfully escape their worries of the past. "Have you and Nick always been close?"

"Very. I've got another brother too."

"Another SEAL?"

"Actually, yes. He went in first—willingly. We followed in his footsteps." He ran a hand through his hair—it was longer than most of the military cuts she'd seen, long enough that he could blend in most places without looking particularly military.

He was also visibly upset and didn't bother to try to hide it. "Nick's vulnerable," Chris admitted.

"He's a SEAL."

"He's falling in love with Kaylee. Love makes you vulnerable."

It did—she knew that. Even though she hadn't been madly, passionately in love with Mike, she did love him. She'd always told herself that working with him wasn't a problem, that their outside relationship didn't affect their professional one.

For her, it hadn't. For Mike, it had been a different story. The night he'd been shot, he'd been so busy covering her he'd forgotten to watch his own back.

The guilt welled up inside of her, the way it always did when she thought about the circumstances surrounding that night. "He'll protect her. Make sure nothing happens to her."

"Yes, he will." Chris stared off into space. "Nick's good, no doubt about it. Nick against those men trying to get him, well, they don't stand a chance—especially if they try to get to Kaylee—but man, I want to call in backup."

"You can't."

"If I have to, I will, and there won't be a thing you can do to stop me."

"Try me, Chief."

"Ah, back to that. Guarding yourself against me again, against anything personal. Have it your way." He put his head back against the seat, hands dangling between his long legs. Then he took his iPod from his pocket and shoved the earbuds in and almost immediately his feet tapped to a beat only he could hear. He began to hum, a deep, melodious sound from the back of his throat.

After a moment, he began to sing. Loud enough to be heard clearly over the engine, which was no mean feat. In tune. Like, if there were a stage around, he would be a rock star.

He was good, really good. He sang like he didn't have a care in the world. She wished she could be that free . . . although she knew that, inside, this man wasn't free at all.

He reminded her of Sophie in that way.

She leaned over and tugged on the wires of the iPod, causing the earbuds to pop out of his ears. He continued singing for a few seconds, as though he hadn't realized that the music had stopped, and then he turned his gaze to her and the singing ceased.

"I'm guarded, yes. I just can't hide it as well as you can." Her eyes met his, held them in a steady grip, and for the first time in his life, he felt as if he was the one who'd been locked and loaded, target on. "You're so free—I envy that part of you—I know it's not an act but I also know it covers something. I'm betting a lot of people don't get that about you, at least not right away. Maybe never."

"Yet you think you know." His voice sounded oddly hoarse but he didn't give any other indication that her words bothered him. And no, he wouldn't.

But they did. And she opened her mouth to tell him that yes, she did know, but just then, the plane jerked hard and banked right.

"I thought you said this pilot knew what he was doing?" she asked.

"He does. Planes don't always want to cooperate."

"What's happening?"

"Whatever it is doesn't sound good. What the fuck's going on?" he yelled to the man piloting the Cessna.

"Engine cut out. I can get us down, but it won't be pretty."

"Fuck," Chris muttered. Jamie was trying to get up but he shoved her back down into her seat, buckled her in even while she attempted to push him away. She knew that's what panicked people did, knew she was slightly claustrophobic to begin with—and the thought of being strapped down now was making her fight.

But Chris spoke calmly. "Jamie, listen to me, we're going to crash land. You've got to be prepared." He showed her the position, waited until she did what he wanted, and then he strapped himself into his seat in the same fashion.

"You both ready?" the pilot called.

"Get us on the ground, my man," Chris called back, right before he started to pray.

After hanging up with Roger, Kaylee went back to the car with Nick. Roger had agreed immediately to run the story—front page. He'd been concerned for her too, she could hear it in his gruff voice even as she assured him she'd be okay.

And then Sarah had insisted that they eat—even though Kaylee's stomach was in knots, it was also growling, an odd combination. Sarah had packed fried chicken pieces and hard-boiled eggs, plantains and bread she had called *kwanga*. Kaylee had nibbled enough to keep her strength up and drank water to stay hydrated. She'd felt better.

Now, a couple of hours later, she sat in the backseat of Sarah's Land Rover and wrote out the facts about GOST that Clutch had revealed, to get them straight in her head. To make sure she hadn't missed anything along the way.

She didn't want to kill the laptop's battery with her note-taking—she'd type it all out once she had the skeleton of the story.

Skeleton was such a perfect term for this story—so many

of them pushing out into the open, insisting on it. And yet, she still had so many unanswered questions running through her mind.

If she broke the story open, would the government or whoever was responsible for Aaron's death still come after her and Nick and Clutch and Sarah? Or would she take the wind out of their sails?

She had to figure out what going public with this piece would actually mean, had to figure out exactly what the end goal was.

She'd broken some stories concerning governmental abuses before, but none as big or far-reaching as this. Typically, she discovered that whatever government agency was responsible for the problem would quickly disavow any involvement and drop the project immediately, which typically corrected any abuses.

Would this work the same way? The trump card was the order she'd heard on Clutch's phone—if she had the balls to publish that, she had a feeling the government would disavow any involvement and it would stop the assassination. Furthermore, it would effectively out John Caspar.

If only she could figure out who he was.

She put the paper aside and stretched. The heat was relentless, brutal even—and it was still dark. The air was heavy, an impending storm on the horizon, and she'd stripped down to a tank top and yanked the pants legs up over her calves. She'd pulled her hair off her neck, was barefoot and still had the urge to stick herself in a freezer somewhere for a good, long time.

Being in such close proximity to Nick didn't help. She felt like her blood was on fire around him.

She pressed her thighs together to ease the ache, but that only served to intensify the need. Staring at Nick's broad back as he stood outside the car as if to guard her didn't help—naked or clothed, he still got to her on a level she hadn't known existed but had always hoped did.

She let herself out of the car, found Nick in the process of pouring water over his head, letting it drip down his face and neck without bothering to wipe it from his eyes before he yanked his shirt off and tucked it partially into his back pocket. They were both full of dust and dirt.

"You didn't sleep at all," he said.

"I couldn't—I had to work," she said. "Where are Clutch and Sarah?"

"They're in his car, mapping out a route."

"What Clutch said, about not knowing who he was . . . it's like he hasn't had a real identity since he was young. How does he keep it all straight, pretending to be someone else?"

She'd asked it in order to gauge Nick's reaction. The small shrug and the way he gazed at her told her what she needed to know. His words told her even more.

"He's strong. You don't ever lose that."

He wasn't going to tell her—not now, maybe not ever. And as much as she understood why on one level, it still bothered her.

Could she live with a man with so many secrets? If she hadn't stumbled onto them, she never would have known. Eventually, there would be a wall up between them—an invisible one she would hardly even know she needed to penetrate.

But she did know.

"Today's my birthday," he said suddenly, stared off into the distance beyond the trees, toward something she couldn't see in the dark, bringing her back to the dilemma she wished she could forget.

"Oh, I thought—" Thankfully, she stopped herself short. She knew the sparse details of Cutter Winfield's life like the back of her hand, knew his birthday was in February. But they were well past that date, and she wondered if he ever thought about that birthday at all, or if he'd acclimated to his new life so much that all of the Winfield past was a distant memory.

She wanted to know how he was able to put that behind him so well, wanted to ask him to teach her how he did so. Wanted to tell him that she knew his biggest secret, and that it—and he—were safe with her.

"What did you think, Kaylee?" His voice cut into her thoughts, deep and rough and oh-so-close, his warm breath fanning her ear. While she'd been lost in thought, he'd moved behind her, his arms wrapped around her waist. Maybe he was just lonely, looking for the feeling of two bodies rubbing together, or maybe it was because of all that had happened, but the way he looked at her . . . she never wanted that to end.

Instinctively, she covered his hands with hers, even as he dragged them over her belly. "Nothing. I'm just . . . glad you're not alone on your birthday."

"Would you have called me if this hadn't happened, would you have used my number?" he asked.

"Yes."

He believed her. "When I'm with you, nothing else

seems to fucking matter—not your job or this fucked-up situation."

"Then maybe it shouldn't."

She realized just how close she was standing to him, how he was half-naked and they were alone again in the middle of nowhere and she was so damned attracted to him it hurt. And the rational side of her brain knew this was neither the time nor the place, that maybe it could never be the right time or place between them, but she quickly went with the other side, which liked stroking his hard biceps, feeling the flex of that muscle. The steam rose, the sounds and smells of the jungle echoed inside of her and every part of her felt raw. On edge.

And somehow, in the dark, she was in his arms and against his bare chest and she was kissing him, or he was kissing her; however it had happened, she didn't care because it was a hot and brutal kiss, one that threatened to take her past the point of no return in seconds flat.

It would have too if she hadn't pulled back. Here, in the jungle, where everything was already intensified, it was time to reveal it all. "There's something I have to tell you. I hate to do it now—God, I wish I didn't have to—but we've got another problem."

He gave a short laugh and looked up at the sky. "Well, hit me with it."

"I saw the meeting at your house," she blurted out, and he stared at her like he was attempting to process what she'd said and coming up blank.

"What meeting? What are you talking about, Kaylee?"

She took a deep breath to compose herself and started

over. "Walter Winfield was at your house—I saw him there. I think I know who you really are, Nick."

He didn't say anything for a long moment, surveyed her almost casually, the mask of the man she'd met that first night firmly back in place. And then, "What do you know, beyond the fact that I know how to make you come?"

She wasn't sure of what to do, but it was either stand there, gaping openmouthed at him, or lunge at him.

She chose the latter, but he was on her before she had a chance to get very far. Within seconds, he had her pinned under him, her back flat on the jungle floor. The weight of his body rested on her hips and thighs, and his knees held her arms pinned.

"You think it's fun to fuck with other people's lives?" His voice was low, with barely couched anger. "You think you're going to make a name for yourself by screwing me over?"

With that, she had her answer. Nick Devane was really Cutter Winfield, and both their worlds had just changed forever.

She didn't bother struggling. It wouldn't have done her any good. "That's not what I was planning to do, not after I found out it was you."

"But you would've done it to someone else. Fucked with his life."

She couldn't deny it—she would have, in the name of her job. She had done it before. "Nick, look . . ."

But he was beyond listening. Instead, he was intent on bringing up her ruthless edge. "What about that piece you did on the presidential candidate last year? You know, when you ruined his entire life thanks to your source. Who the hell gave you that information?"

"I can't tell you that."

"But you mentioned that the man's wife begged you not to run the piece, his daughter too—but you refused to comply because of your journalistic integrity. You couldn't hold back the truth about the man's morality from the American public. They have a right to know—public figures can't be public when they choose to be and private when they choose." He repeated her own words back to her as if he'd memorized them recently. He'd done his research on her before they'd left for this country.

"That's different." It had made her sit up nights with a bottle of Tums, wondering if she could really handle the business.

"No, it's not."

"You didn't choose your life as a Winfield."

"I chose to walk away from it—and you know all about it now. But if you're expecting me to beg you not to run the story, don't bother."

"You don't have to do anything, I'm not running it."

"You haven't run it *yet*. Maybe you're waiting for just the right time. Getting closer to me for maximum impact. A blow when I least expect it, once I save your ass. And what's to stop me from revealing your secrets, Kaylee? Putting your picture on the front page—show all those people you exposed where they can find you? How would you feel?"

He leaned over her, his face inches from hers, daring her to do anything, to say anything. She was helpless under him and a small sob escaped her.

His demeanor changed instantly—he lowered his head

to her breasts, she felt his warm breath spread along the fabric of her tank top. "I'd never hurt you. Never. And I'd never expose you like that." He raised his head after he spoke, his green eyes glowing with hurt and truth. His voice sounded rougher than it usually did, like he was having trouble pulling air.

She took a deep breath. "Nick—"

"Not another word about it, Kaylee. Not a single word."

"I'm not going to do anything with the story—I haven't and I won't. I owe you. After what you've agreed to do, the way you saved me . . . after what's happening between us."

"There's nothing more between us than danger—that's what's been making you so hot for me, nothing more."

"If you can make yourself believe that, then you've definitely got some great magic tricks."

"I haven't been able to make you disappear yet," he told her as he rolled off her, moved to help her up off the ground.

She refused his hand, could only mumble, "I'm sorry," didn't know what she should do next.

She ran. Barely able to see, she kept her legs moving as she stumbled along, eyes blinded by tears until she couldn't run anymore, until she collapsed on the ground.

And he was there, right there.

"Kaylee, stop—you have no idea where you are, where you're going . . ."

"You're right, I don't have any idea about a lot of things." She tried to control her breathing, but nausea and dizziness overtook her. She knelt where she'd fallen, her lungs pulling tight enough to make her eyes water, her breath coming in ragged gasps.

Nick tugged at her pants—she realized he was searching for her inhaler. He found it and she took a hit and prayed it would work quickly.

He rubbed her back, spoke to her in a low, controlled voice that made her somehow feel more in control of herself as well.

"S'okay. Relax." His voice was comforting in her ear. His strong hand rested on her thigh. "Please, Kaylee, relax. We'll talk about it later. I'm not going to yell at you—I'll listen. Please, just fucking *breathe*."

It took ten dreadful minutes for things to ease up. Nick knew, because Kaylee counted all the seconds softly and out loud to distract herself.

"Are you guys all right?" Clutch called softly through the trees.

"We're fine. Leave us," Nick told him.

Kaylee's breaths eventually grew softer. At some point, she'd actually crawled onto him. Her arms were around him, her face partially buried against his neck.

"I didn't want to know this, Nick," she whispered finally, her voice slightly hoarse from crying, and then it was, *"I'm sorry, I'm sorry,"* over and over again, murmured against his skin.

And his worry turned to anger again, molten and red hot, and he was so conflicted. She knew. Everything. The first woman he actually cared about—as much as he liked being naked physically, he was more exposed now than he'd ever been in his life.

The betrayal—however unintentional—kicked him in the chest and he didn't know what the hell to say to her.

He started when she kissed his neck—a soft touch of her lips that made him suck in a breath—and then the kisses grew harder, until she was nipping at his skin and he was yanking the tank top from her pants.

This was all out of control—*he* was out of control, and while he hated every second of that feeling, Kaylee's body against his felt nothing if not right at this moment.

She arched against him, hard, her fingers digging into him as he pushed his hand inside her pants, found her wet and willing for him.

"What are you sorry for, Kaylee?" he murmured. "Sorry you met me?"

"No." She shook her head wildly on the ground as he took her with his fingers—one then two sliding deep inside of her. "I could never . . . be sorry . . . about that."

"What were you planning, Kaylee? Going to tell the world that you'd found Cutter, that you slept with him? Were you going to tell them that I made you feel good?"

She tried to grab at his wrist, to stop him from stroking her, but he wasn't having it. "I would never have betrayed you. I didn't betray you."

She hadn't. Not that he knew of anyway, and he figured that if she'd turned the story in he'd have heard about it by now. In the space when he stopped to consider that, she managed to get her hand between their bodies and began to stroke him through his pants.

"Kaylee, Christ . . ."

"I didn't betray you. I wouldn't. I won't." She timed her strokes to match his until he couldn't stand it any longer.

He flipped them, so she didn't have to lie exposed on the jungle floor, pulled down his pants so she could straddle him.

He steeled himself against her touch, was ready when her hand hit his skin. The jolt was palpable and he clenched his jaw to keep from groaning, from taking her hand and pushing it down between his legs again . . . from asking her to put her mouth on him until he couldn't stand it anymore. Right now, he needed to feel—the harder, the better.

Her sex rubbed his cock—she was so wet for him, *so fucking wet*—and he grabbed her hips and pushed her down without finesse.

For that moment, when she was first sheathed around him, there was total silence, almost reverence as she looked into his eyes. And she was making love to him as Nick and Cutter and all at once the two worlds melded and for just that moment, the burden lifted.

All that was left to do was give up and give in. This wasn't about power anymore. This was about them, that undeniable heat that rose up between them every single time they were together.

"Go, Kaylee," he murmured, and she did, rocked back and forth, her palms flat against his chest, eyes never leaving his. Her breasts rose and fell with the exertion and he wanted them in his mouth, wanted his face between her legs. Wanted to come deep inside of her. Mark her.

The primal urge rose up inside him in a hot rush as he grabbed her hips and thrust up into her so hard all she could do was hold on to him.

All he could do was breathe and pretend nothing else mattered.

Are you sure they're okay?" Sarah asked when Clutch came back to the car. She'd opened the back where they'd been sitting together—both had wanted to talk, but had been unable to do more than simply kiss.

It was only Nick yelling for Kaylee to stop that had broken them apart.

Now Clutch slid next to her, gathered her into his arms. "They're safe. I don't know if they're okay."

She nodded, pushed herself more tightly against him.

She and Clutch didn't even have the safe part and she hated having to think about that now. She just wanted to tangle her body around his until neither of them could stand straight.

"I didn't want to leave you behind. It nearly killed me," he whispered into her neck. His warm breath fanned her skin as she sat with her back to his chest, one of his hands between hers. She ran a thumb inside his palm, felt the calluses that she knew came from firing a weapon and thought about that last night they'd been together.

"I got a job offer," she said finally. "For an American newspaper. Full time."

She felt his body tense, but he didn't say anything, and so she continued. "They wanted me to leave Africa, wanted to send me all over the world so I can take pictures for them."

Still, nothing. She moved from his grasp and turned so she could look at him.

His expression was hard—the one she remembered all

too well from the first time they'd met. "Why didn't you take it?"

"How can you ask that?"

"The whole time we were apart...one of my biggest fears was that, when I was finally able to be with you again, you'd be gone." He paused. "It was also something I was hoping would happen—for your sake. I knew it would've broken me, but I wanted it for you as badly as I wanted you for myself."

It took so much for him to tell her that—even more for him to actually mean it, to wish that freedom for her, and she wondered why the anger still ran so deeply inside of her. "You should've taken me with you."

"You know I couldn't do that. And look, I'm in the same exact place I was anyway—putting your life in danger again."

"If you try to leave me—"

"I'm not going anywhere." His voice was equally fierce. "Do you understand? We're in it together now. You've always told me how tough you are—you've shown me too. Now it's time to stick together."

It was okay for him to say it now, okay to talk about what they wished and wanted because they'd found their way back to each other. Whatever happened, she wasn't letting go.

"I wanted to take the job, Bobby. And I felt like I was betraying you because of that."

"You weren't."

She didn't say anything for a long moment and then her cell phone was ringing, disrupting the quiet. She stared at the number that came up on the screen before clicking the button to send it to voice mail.

"Who is it?" Clutch asked.

"It's just Vince. He's the man—the reporter I was working for on the last job."

Clutch tried to look uninterested and failed miserably. "The one you want to work for. He obviously won't take no for an answer."

"Bobby, please, there's nothing going on between us."

"He wants you—"

"For his paper."

"Don't be naïve, Sarah—you never were before this and I can't believe you'd start now."

"So you're saying I couldn't get the job because of my talent?" She pushed away from him.

"No, I'm not..." He ran a hand across his mouth in frustration, held it there for a second, as if gaining patience by doing so. When he pulled it away, he reached for her hand. "You know I think you're an amazing photographer. It's just that you have no idea how badly I wanted to be there for you these past months. How much I fucking worried that they wouldn't keep their promise and leave you alone..."

"But they did. And I'm here. And we have to put all of this behind us—we start doing that now."

Vince's offer was the road less traveled, the path she would've taken if Clutch hadn't been around to screw things up for her.

But Clutch—no, Bobby, they were so close to him being Bobby again—pulled her close to him again. "I'm sorry—after all that's happened I have no right to be a jealous bastard."

"But you are."

"Yeah, I am." He wrapped his arms around her protectively, even as her phone began to ring again. "Are you going to get that now?"

Vince. Again. She switched the phone off. "No. There's no reason to answer."

Her future was right here, where it had always been. In Africa and in Bobby's arms.

K aylee lay on top of Nick—both of them half-naked out in the open, the need still pulsing between them even though they were spent.

She moved her cheek so she could rest it on his heart-beat—steady and strong against her skin. One of them would have to speak soon, to figure out where they went from here.

It would have to be her. "I'm going to keep you safe, Nick. I know that sounds ridiculous, considering where we are. But I will."

When he finally spoke, his voice sounded rough and weary. "I don't want you to know this, Kaylee."

She lifted her head to look into his eyes, into the perfect, handsome face that held so much pain. She was responsible for some of it. "If I hadn't brought Aaron's secrets into your life—"

"My burden would still be exactly the same." He shifted to free himself from under her and he stood. It was so quiet out here—made the energy vibrating off Nick even more intense. "What the hell were you thinking? Why did you wait to tell me?"

Her own anger was there, deep, dark and unresolved, and pushing Nick Devane was the stupidest thing she could do. But she was through being rational, done with being poor Kaylee the juvenile delinquent or K. Darcy the journalist. All she wanted was to figure out who Kaylee Smith really was, deep down. What that woman wanted.

The problem was, she knew what—who—she wanted. He stood right in front of her. But every second had him slipping through her fingers.

"I was waiting for you to tell me," she said honestly. "I wanted you to tell me, I wanted to be the first woman you ever shared that secret with."

He didn't say anything right away, a Herculean effort, she was sure. When he finally did speak, they were words she hadn't wanted to hear. "I wouldn't have told you. Ever. If it wasn't for our connection with Aaron, I wouldn't have been with you for longer than a night."

And then he walked away from her.

"I don't believe you," she whispered to his back.

If he heard her, he didn't turn around. She had no choice but to follow him out of the brush and into the car.

CHAPTER
16

Chris had remained conscious during the crash—Jamie hadn't, but she was coming around quickly.

Both seats—all the seats—had been ripped away from the sides of the plane, and they'd both been ripped out of their seats. Chris had ended up shoved in a corner and Jamie was stretched out on the other side of the plane, seemingly unharmed—he'd carefully threaded his legs around the debris in the dark to get to her and now remained over her, checking her pulse and gently stroking her cheek to facilitate waking her.

All the while, her last words to him echoed in his head. *You're so free—I envy that part of you—but I know it covers something. I'm betting a lot of people don't get that about you, at least not right away. Maybe never.*

She saw right fucking through him, and here he thought he was the one with all the insight.

As much as he didn't like it, he knew he wanted that—needed it. He'd learned a long time ago that letting people inside wasn't always the easiest thing for him. But fuck it, he sure as hell wasn't going to help her climb inside. If she wanted that, she'd have to fight for it.

Jamie opened her eyes and saw Chris's face hovering above hers. She wanted to move but the heaviness of her body told her that wasn't a good idea.

"What happened?" she asked.

"We crashed."

"Yeah, thanks—I got that."

"Are your ears ringing?"

"No."

"All right, that's good. Stay still—let me check you out first." He moved so he hovered over her, beginning with her legs, asking her to move her toes and limbs, and finally he touched the knot on her head lightly.

"That hurts."

"It should—but I don't think you've got a concussion." He helped her sit up. She winced when she got completely vertical and let her back rest on the side of a broken seat. "The pilot?"

"He's dead, ejected on impact. His body's on the ground below."

"The plane?"

"Same."

"Shit."

"Yeah."

She checked her watch. "We're late."

"No one's ever late in this country. Besides, we're not going anywhere fast now," he said.

"Maybe we landed in a populated area?"

"No such luck."

"Check again. Wait, I'll go check." She found herself actually trying to claw her way off the plane.

Chris was easing her back down to the floor. "Jamie, listen to me—we're not leaving until this rain stops, understand?"

"By then it might be too late to get out of here."

"Walking around here with no visibility isn't a good idea—you and I both know that. For now, we stay put, we're safe."

It looked like midnight out, thanks to the rain and the jungle they'd landed in the middle of, which blocked out any source of light in the hot metal box of a plane. "But I can't stop now—don't you understand?" She pushed at him, knowing he was one hundred percent right and still seeing her chances of finding Sophie slip through her hands like tiny sand grains.

"You're damned straight I understand. I've got as much at stake as you do. And we're still staying put."

"You're not in charge here, Chief Petty Officer."

She'd reverted back to the familiar form of comfort and she waited for him to buck that order—to push back, to tell her that she couldn't be in charge all the time.

Instead, he stood there watching her, that same quiet

strength emanating from him. "I hate being helpless too. I don't do it well."

Shit. Maybe she could be less selfish about all of this. "You're doing a much better job of hiding it than I am."

"Smoke, mirrors and years of training." He turned and was rummaging around in the ruined back of the plane.

She looked out the window and saw nothing—it was as pitch black outside as it was in here, save for the thin beam of Chris's penlight. Rain sleeted hard against the small windows and it was still hot as anything. She hoped the inside of this crushed tin can would cool down soon. "What are you doing back there?"

He emerged, holding a bottle in his hands, looking victorious. "Here we go."

"What's that?"

"Our bottle of patience." He shined the light so she could read the label.

"I'm sure bourbon's not what you use for patience when you're sniping."

He snorted. "That's just plain old willpower."

The man never stopped moving—even trapped in this stupid tin can, his body seemed to vibrate through the darkness. She tried to picture him lying facedown on the ground for hours without moving and failed. "This is probably nothing for you, right? I'm sure you've had lots of narrow escapes."

"A few. I try to avoid the plane crashes, though. Typically, I just bail before it happens."

"I forgot that you could do almost anything. Including building bombs from coconuts, right?"

"Now she gets a sense of humor," he muttered.

"Well, not everyone gets to be a consultant on a reality show for a major movie star."

He snorted. "I'm not doing the man-versus-wild thing for Jules, no matter how many times she asks."

"It sounded like she really wanted you to."

"Yeah, she wants a lot of things. We have some unfinished business—but all of that's on her end, not mine."

Jamie understood unfinished business. Sometimes she felt as if her entire life had been one long string of unfinished—memories, experiences. Childhood.

At college and at work, she'd liked completing things. Even the simple act of actually filing a folder away after finishing a case was pleasing to her.

She wondered if having things messy and complicated would ever actually satisfy her, the way it seemed to for so many people around her.

Things here—in this country, on this personal mission—were far too tangled, becoming more so by the second. Her worry merged with Chris's until it bubbled over into this—sitting next to him in the dark.

Or at least that's what she wanted to believe.

Over the years, she'd met her share of men—all of them, including Mike, seemed to want to crack her open, figure her out, try to loosen up the serious act. But it wasn't an act, and Chris seemed to understand that. Didn't seem to mind it either.

He'd settled in next to her, handed her the bottle. "Are you all right in the dark?"

Why wouldn't I be? nearly shot from her mouth before she reined it in. "Not always, but I'm okay for now."

Yet even as she spoke the words, the familiar panic

spread inside of her, hot and fast, and she was drawing her knees to her chest, her brain working overtime because she couldn't think of what she was supposed to say, didn't remember her made-up story. She could only think of the truth, and she'd sworn she'd never tell anyone that.

Before her parents had been killed, life in Witness Protection had consisted of a home in Minnesota. But Jamie had been born in Brooklyn, where her mother, an ADA, had successfully prosecuted the wrong man, a high-ranking member of the Russian mafia. The man's son swore revenge on her and her entire family, no matter how long it took.

After her parents were murdered, Kevin Morgan, the U.S. marshal who'd followed their case and counseled them, had taken them in with him. His wife, Grace, had reluctantly agreed and Jamie and Sophie lived there under Witness Protection until Sophie turned eighteen and enlisted. Jamie remained until she was eighteen as well, then left for college.

It wasn't surprising that both women ended up in law enforcement, that both of them carried weapons. They'd been looking over their shoulders their entire lives anyway.

Now Chris was rubbing her neck and shoulders again. "Your pain's back."

"Yes," she lied, because really, it had never left. When the headaches got really bad, she swore she could hear Sophie's screams—screams that had woken her up from a dead sleep when she'd been eight years old and had her running to find her sister.

It had been the night the man who'd hunted her parents since they'd all gone into Witness Protection, had found them. That night, there had been so much blood—it covered the ground, it was all over Sophie's feet and her hands, but somehow... somehow Sophie managed to calm down and tell Jamie, *Go downstairs*.

And in between the screams, Jamie remembered the sirens; the only thing that had saved her and her sister that night had been Sophie's quick thinking—even in her panic, the fourteen-year-old had remembered her training from the marshals and the drills their parents had run them through regularly.

When Sophie heard the man murdering their parents, she'd called the police. And then she'd started screaming.

Jamie fought the urge to put her hands over her own ears to block out the yells now only she could hear. "Did your iPod survive the crash?"

"I think so. Do you want to listen to it?"

"No. I'd like...would you...would you sing for me again?" she asked, wanted to take back the "for me" part, because he'd been singing for himself earlier.

Then again, maybe he hadn't, because he answered her question by turning on his iPod—she saw the quick flash of light—and then his singing filled the interior of the plane, bouncing off the enclosed space. The song—Pink Floyd's "Wish You Were Here"—washed over her like instant comfort, his voice filling up the spaces in her mind until she was able to push all other thoughts away for the moment.

Clutch called out to them as Nick walked slowly back to the car, Kaylee at his heels, the anger between them as thick as the sudden humidity that had sprung up with the rumble of distant thunder. This was going to be some storm.

"What's up?" he asked Clutch.

"We've got to take off. Rains are coming—we've got to try for higher ground," Clutch said.

"What about pushing through to a hotel?" Nick asked.

Clutch shook his head. "I just checked with a source. Soldiers still have the borders closed in all directions—we can only get so far, if we're lucky, without attracting attention. You two ride with Sarah, I'll follow right behind."

The rains would come in another hour or so. Nick knew from firsthand experience, as no doubt Sarah and Clutch did too, that the torrential rains would bring flooding that could take the cars if they didn't find high enough ground.

Sarah was already in the car. Thunder rumbled overhead, an ominous sound as night refused to let the day through. Kaylee looked up at the lightning flash; Nick noted she looked tired, worried too, and still so fucking beautiful it made his heart hurt in a way he hadn't known was possible.

I think I know who you really are . . .

She *did* know. All these years, he'd been so careful—all ties cut, no traces of Cutter Winfield's trail left uncovered, and now, because of Walter's guilty conscience, Nick was found out.

By an investigative reporter. One he was falling for.

He could've denied it—she had no real proof other than seeing Walter at the house—but he hadn't. Hadn't wanted to. He'd meant it when he'd told her he was tired of the burden. He just hadn't realized how much of a burden the secret had become until he'd met Kaylee.

Kaylee, who had already pushed past him into the car. He shut the door behind her and walked toward Clutch. "You haven't been declared dead—you're still known. Or you were. How does that figure into GOST? It goes against what you're telling me."

"They let me have an honorable discharge for a family emergency. I was one of the first men recruited. After what happened with Aaron, the men who did the recruiting decided it was better to figuratively kill off the men and their military pasts—less ties, less chance of anyone missing you." Clutch paused. "I guess I'm one of the lucky ones."

Clutch really meant that—Nick could hear it in the man's tone.

"You sure everything's all right with Kaylee?" Clutch asked him. "Sounded like she was really upset."

"She is."

"Dammit. I didn't want to involve her, Nick. You have to believe me. If I'd known you were involved with her—"

"I'm not."

Clutch stared at him for a second. "Brother, you need to check your definition of *involved,* then, because from where I'm sitting, you're in deep."

Nick wanted to tell him that he had no fucking idea just how deep he was into all of this. Instead, he got into the car, next to Kaylee, listening to the thunder rumble overhead as Sarah crashed the car through the brush to get to higher ground.

After initially refusing, Jamie found that a few good swigs from the bottle of bourbon, as hard as it was going down, did wonders.

Now, sitting against what was left of a cushioned seat in

the darkness of the plane's interior, she still felt the slight panic whenever she thought about Sophie.

"Talking helps." Chris's voice rose up out of the darkness.

"How do you know what I'm thinking about?"

"I'd worry if it wasn't about your sister."

"You must think I'm so unprofessional."

"We've got to protect our own," he said quietly.

"I told myself I wouldn't tell another living soul, and here I am, spilling my guts to you." She shoved the near-empty bottle away from her.

"I'm that kind of person. People tell me things. Do you think I'm going to sell you out?"

"How does this liquor not affect you?" she demanded instead of answering his question.

"I haven't been given the bottle in a while."

"Oh." She did nothing to rectify that, took another swig and watched his outline—he appeared to be lying flat on his back on the floor, arms under his head, his body taking up nearly all the space. "It's still hot."

She heard the rustle of a body rising up from the floor and then he was right next to her—so close she could see the half smile tugging at his mouth. "Yeah, hot."

"You need to stop doing that."

"Making you blush?"

"You can't tell that in the dark."

But one of his palms brushed her face softly. "I can tell a hell of a lot in the dark."

Maybe he was drunk after all. But she didn't move his hand, not even when it began rubbing the back of her neck, the way he'd done before.

God, she felt lazy. Hot and bothered, but strangely

relaxed, and she began to unbutton her shirt, stripped it off, leaving just the white tank she'd worn underneath.

His hands moved to her shoulders, down her arms, and she shivered at the touch, especially when he shifted so he could cup her breasts.

"Chris, this isn't going to happen. This is the worst time for something to happen."

"That's usually when it does."

"I feel like you've got some kind of voodoo...some kind of crazy love potion, like a drug."

"It's the Cajun-gypsy mix."

"I don't like it—it makes me feel out of control."

"Try to go with it, Jamie. Sometimes it's easier than you think."

"I can't."

"You're all hard edges and buttoned-up, a hard-ass with a badge and a gun," he murmured, his body pressing hers. With what appeared to be utter ease, he'd gotten her splayed on the floor under him, and more helpless than she would've liked. "But you'd turn so sweet with my cock inside of you—wouldn't you?"

She wanted to tell him to fuck off, pull her knee up to shove his balls into his throat. But the tiny catch in her breath came too fast for her to stop it, the heat flooded between her legs and he knew.

He'd known before he'd lain on top of her. And she hated him for that.

He knew that too.

"Maybe that line works on other women, but it doesn't work on me," she said.

"Good one."

And still, he hadn't moved, not a muscle, and his erection dug into her, rock hard.

The ache inside her intensified and she struggled to keep the needy moan from escaping as she spoke. "Get off me."

"No."

"You're an asshole."

"No, I'm not." He shifted slightly so his arousal brushed her in just the right place.

"No, you're not," she agreed, right before he brought his mouth down on hers. His tongue stroked hers in a kiss so hot she thought she'd combust on the spot. Her hands wound into his hair to keep him there, to pull him closer. The heaviness of his body covering hers was wonderful, despite the heat and the close quarters—this could be the best cure for claustrophobia yet.

When he pulled away for a second, she heard her own breath, harsh in the darkness.

"Do you still want me to stop?" he asked.

"Would you?"

"That's not the question."

She heard herself say, "I don't want you to stop," and knew she was telling the truth.

"Put your arms up over your head . . . yeah, that's it, Jamie. Just give yourself to me, don't worry about control—you'll have your turn, but now, this is all about you . . ."

She obeyed, extended her arms over her head and he pushed her tank up over her breasts. "Nothing we can do now, Jamie. No guilt. Just pure and simple, life-affirming sex."

His mouth covered a nipple and she moaned at the contact, his hot mouth playing with her taut nub as she fisted the metal of the broken seat to keep herself from grabbing him and holding him there.

God, the man was good. Better than good. Life-affirmingly, bourbon-drinking or not—spectacular, especially as his hand traveled between her legs, and oh, my God, just *oh . . . my . . . God.*

He chuckled against her neck and she realized she'd been saying all of that out loud.

"You're killing me," she murmured.

"Just wrap yourself around me, baby. I'll take care of everything." His voice was like a shot of pure adrenaline rushing through her, causing her to shake and shiver and open herself up to his hand.

"I like taking care of things too," she whispered.

From there, it became more like a desperate fight than any kind of gentle lovemaking . . . they rolled, together, with Jamie ending up on top.

She tugged at his shirt, managed to help him yank it over his head. Her palms roamed miles of hard muscle and scar tissue and everything she associated with the purely male animal Chris was. She worked his pants next, pulled them past his hips, and her hands circled his arousal—big and thick and strong like the rest of him, and so ready for her.

There was no condom, no barrier, but at the moment, she didn't care. In the humid, broken body of the plane, in the midst of the crash they'd miraculously survived, she let Chris Waldron take her . . . and in return, she took him too, made him cry out with a sharp groan that vibrated in the small space until that was all she could hear.

CHAPTER
17

T his is a good spot." Sarah had pulled her car up a slight incline along the side of a large rock formation—Clutch did the same on the opposite side. Kaylee could barely see the top of his car—could barely see the boulder, it was still so ominously dark outside. It didn't feel like daytime, felt as if the night before continued on in a neverending stretch. "Besides, my tire's shot and I don't have a spare."

"I'll check with Clutch." Nick was out of the car in seconds, leaving the two women alone.

"The rains get pretty bad, but we'll be all right up here. We'll just sleep in the cars," Sarah explained. She switched around in her seat in order to face Kaylee and turned on the overhead light. "Are you okay?"

God, no, she wasn't okay. "He's so angry with me."

Sarah tucked her legs under her. "I've found that the angrier they can get at you is usually a sign that they love you."

Kaylee jerked her head toward her. Sarah was smiling a little. "You can't tell me you haven't felt it. I can see it happening between you two."

Kaylee couldn't disagree. "There are just . . . things between us. Insurmountable things."

"I used to feel that way too."

She thought about what Clutch had said earlier, about not letting Sarah go again, no matter the cost. "Did you know Aaron too?"

Sarah shook her head. "I only met Clutch last year. He never talked much about what was going on with him and GOST, even after I found out."

"I can imagine he'd want to forget all about it."

"Forgetting about things always comes back to haunt you. Trust me, I know all about that."

"Do you have family here?" Kaylee asked.

Sarah shook her head slowly. "No. They were all killed in the riots in Zimbabwe years ago."

"I'm so sorry."

Sarah didn't acknowledge the apology. "I shouldn't try to talk you out of writing the article, shouldn't tell you how risky it will be for you," Sarah said. "But I'm going to. Maybe you should just go somewhere, lay low. They might forget about you."

She and Sarah both knew how complicated that would

be. "Aaron and I wouldn't have been together—GOST or no GOST. But he went in because they threatened me. All that time and I didn't realize how close I came to getting hurt." She stared down at her hands. "Writing this story is the very least I can do."

The article would free these people and somehow she felt it would also free Aaron's soul.

The car door opened and Nick climbed into the back-seat. "Car's fixed."

"If it's all right with you, I'm going to stay with Clutch," Sarah said, even as she began to get out of the car. "We won't be able to do anything for hours—not until the rain stops and the ground dries a bit. The good news is no one's able to get to us here."

Yes, that was good news.

"Go for it," Nick said, and Sarah shut the door behind her, leaving Kaylee with Nick . . . and total and complete silence between them.

"I know you don't want to be here with me," she said when she couldn't stand the quiet any longer. Which had only taken about three minutes but felt like forever.

He didn't answer, glanced at her and then back at the rain lightly flicking the window. He kicked the car door open and climbed out.

Of course, she followed him. She had to get this settled before she could move on and write the article. "Are you ever going to speak to me again?"

He whirled around on her. "When I first found out who you were, I should've figured it all out. I'm so fucking stupid—I should've known when you didn't ask questions

about my family. You didn't because you knew everything...
or else, you think you do."

"Nick, please, I didn't—"

His eyes coldly appraised her. "But you did. You've been
looking for me since you started your career."

"Yes."

"Searched down every lead, looked for me behind every
corner. Followed the frenzy."

"Yes, but not for the reasons you think."

He snorted, went to move away from her. She attempted to stop him with a touch, but true to form, he
pulled away. "Shit, sorry. I'm sorry—I'm trying to get used
to that," she said.

"Don't bother."

But she ignored the sting she felt and continued, "So
many people assume that Cutter was the crazy one for leaving that family—the wealth and the fame and the family
connections. And sure, maybe he was, but I'm the last one
to fault someone for getting out of what looks like a wonderful situation. People want to believe in the mystique the
Winfields have built around them."

"But you don't, right?"

"I don't believe in fairy tales. I want to—you have no
idea how badly I want to—but I can't. Not the way I grew
up. And not after knowing you—you're nothing like
they've made Cutter out to be. You're strong and brave, a
good man."

He didn't say anything for a long while, just leaned
against the car and stared at the bit of sky they could see
through the overhang of trees.

"You're so fucking brave," he told her finally. "The job

you do...I grew up hating journalists. And now you're ready to risk your own life to save these people—not because it's good for you, but because you say it's the right thing to do."

"And here I thought you hated me."

"I want to hate you, you have no idea how badly I want that. It would make all of this so much easier."

"I wish I didn't know."

"But you do. There's no taking it back. And if you're staying with me because my past fascinates you—"

"You fascinate me—not Cutter, not the SEAL—you, Nick. The guy who came to me when I needed help. The one whose car I stole. The one who, for the first time in my life, makes me feel alive."

"I told you that I'd be here for you, no matter what decision you made. I'll be here while you write the article, I'll help you get it to your boss and I'll make sure you get home safely."

"That's not what I want—I don't want a bodyguard, Nick. I could hire one if that's all I wanted."

"That's all you wanted from me when we first met, remember?"

"Now I want more."

"I can't give you more, especially with what you know—stop pushing me." It came out fiercer than he'd intended, a warning growl that made her flinch. She stepped away from him and then stopped herself.

"I can't take back what I know!" She shouted that—above the wind and into the dark sky, her frustration rising right along with his.

The sex had done nothing to take the edge off what was

happening between them—the anger ran deep inside and it had already come bubbling to the surface, so when it exploded instead into that raw roll on the ground, passionate sex, he hadn't been surprised.

He wished she could take it all back, wished he was still just Nick to her. Wished there wasn't so much shit coming down around their ears that he could barely think. "What do you want from me, Kaylee? Want to save me from the big, bad Winfields?"

She moved toward him and this time *he* fought the ridiculous urge to back up away from her, didn't want to think about or talk about Walter right now.

Didn't want to think at all. Not with the rain coming down on them, plastering the T-shirt to her body, and fuck, why did she have to be so pretty—why did she have to look at him like that, like he was the only fucking thing in the world she wanted?

She was on him now, pushing his body against the car as the rain slicked her touch. "I want to save you from a lot of things—saving you from yourself is the place I'd start."

Nick could push her away so easily right now, but he remained with his back against the car even as she worked the zipper on his BDUs. Out there, in the rain, they remained in private thanks to the rocks that lay between the two cars. Kaylee circled him, stroked him—once, twice—and his breath hitched, enough to give him away. If his erection hadn't already. She ran a finger over the broad head, swirling the drop of moisture, and he groaned. He was nearly beyond protesting and she knew it.

Yet his green eyes flashed like the lightning and his clenched fists signaled meltdown. But she was done running.

"Don't do this." That voice again, a warning couched inside the rough tones, and she ignored it.

He was so impossibly hard. For her.

His face showed desire and anger fighting each other, and she planned on forcing his hand, on suspending time and place as long as she possibly could.

"Don't shut down on me—not here and not now," she told him. God, he hadn't kissed her, not since before they'd left for Africa and she wanted that—his mouth on hers—wanted all this to be more than just sex.

But the kiss wasn't going to happen now, not when he grabbed under her arms to lift her off her feet and place her on the car.

"This is how much I still want you," he whispered fiercely, put her hand back between his legs. "This is what you do to me."

She loved hearing that.

He lifted her ass off the car to drag her BDUs off and place them underneath her before setting her back down again in one swift motion, her pants shielding her from the cold metal hood.

She spread her legs, wrapped them around his waist, and he took her right there, on the hood of the car, entered her slow and smooth, the night air dancing on her bare wet skin. The sex was hard and fast and she wasn't going to last at all.

She clutched his shoulders, buried her face in his neck. "Harder, Nick . . . please."

"Yes, ma'am," he breathed against her ear, and complied, pulling himself almost completely out of her and then driving into her again and again, until she was utterly at his mercy. The world turned upside down as her belly clenched and she sank her teeth into his shoulder through his shirt to keep from screaming as she came in a shattered, shuddering rush.

Clutch wanted Sarah so badly, enough to put away fears about his own situation and the danger they were all in. But he couldn't let himself do that.

Sarah groaned softly as he pulled back—she'd been half sitting on him, kissing him non-stop as the rain slammed the car.

"Sorry—I can't settle in," he said.

"No one's coming out in this weather, Bobby. We've got our plan in place—we're out of here and headed to the nearest hotel as soon as the rains stop. Kaylee will transmit the article and then we wait." She stroked his hair. "Maybe you need some sleep?"

"Have we been apart so long that you've forgotten?" he asked. She knew he hadn't slept a full night—more than half an hour at a time—for the past six years.

"I haven't forgotten anything." She pulled away from him, but before he could apologize, his cell phone began to vibrate in his pocket—he pulled it out and stared at the number, put his poker face on even as he knew it wouldn't matter. Sarah would know who was on the other end of the phone as soon as he answered.

He thought about not answering, wasn't sure if that would make things better or worse, and took the risk.

Caspar's voice echoed on the other end of the phone. "I know you have Kaylee Smith."

Clutch thought about telling him he was full of shit, that he didn't know what he was talking about, but he was through playing games. "What does it matter to you? I'll still get our orders completed."

"I know your plans, Clutch. Why do you think you can sneak anything by me?"

"Who spilled? Who's the rat you've got planted in my group?"

Caspar chuckled, an ominous sound. "It's not your group—especially not now. You bring me Kaylee Smith. Bring her to the warehouse."

"And then what?"

"And then you kill her and make sure the story she's writing never sees the light of day. It's either Kaylee Smith's life or Sarah Cameron's."

Asking him to choose between Sarah and his freedom was the cruelest thing imaginable, and yet, he wasn't surprised. He'd lived this life for too damned long to be surprised by anything.

That didn't mean the thought of what Caspar proposed didn't make him sick to his stomach. And so he didn't say a word, tried to keep his breathing steady and tuck all the worry inside of him instead of letting it spill out in the spaces between himself and Sarah. And he was nearly successful too, until Caspar said, "I know Sarah's with you."

Clutch choked and put a hand over his mouth for a

second to muffle the sound. And then, "Yeah, prove it..." before mouthing to Sarah, "He says he knows where you are."

"That's impossible, Bobby. One man can't follow all of you and track me at the same time," she mouthed back, even as her phone began to ring.

They both stared at it as Caspar laughed again on his end. "I hear her phone ringing—isn't she going to answer it?"

Clutch tried to grab the phone from Sarah but he was too late—she had it to her ear, trying not to let the fear show in her face. "Sarah Cameron, we know where you are..."

Caspar's words echoed into both their ears—and he rattled off their exact coordinates before he hung up.

Clutch and Sarah did the same with their own phones. "They know, Clutch—how do they know?"

He didn't answer, was already half out of the car. He dropped to the ground and crawled beneath the undercarriage. They had to have bugged it before he left.

He found the tracer wedged behind the tailpipe. And he left it there for the moment, because the rain was still coming down like crazy and the roads were a flood, covering his ankles. No one was going to be able to get to them anytime soon, but he had no way of knowing exactly how close they were.

"Who could it be?" Sarah asked him as he got back into the car. She toweled him off and he didn't stop her or tell her not to fuss over him.

There were two newer members, both of whom made him uneasy. Smoke and PJ, one of only three women GOST had ever recruited, and he hadn't wanted to give his trust away so easily. But if they were to throw off GOST's rule, they had to do it together. They'd all wanted this. "I can't worry about that now—we've got to get out of here."

"We can make it if we have to—push along the main road, it's our best shot."

"We'll leave my car here with the tracer," he said. "They have to know that you have your own car, that escape might be an option."

"The bridge will most likely be gone. We could back-track—"

"We can't," he interrupted her. "We have to press forward. There's got to be another way—we can figure it out when we get to the hotel."

When the rain got harder, Nick helped her off the car and held the door open for her.

"Come on, Kaylee, get in."

The BDUs she'd been sitting on were soaked and dirty. "My pants . . ."

"Leave them off for now—we've got dry clothes inside the car."

She did what he asked, climbed into the backseat. "Are you coming in too?"

He stripped off his own pants completely—he'd never put his shirt back on from earlier. "Yeah, I'm coming in."

He got in next to her, naked.

"Your shirt—take it off and let it dry. Never know when the next access to laundry will be." He rummaged through his bag and pulled out a towel for her. And he watched her while she peeled the shirt off and hung it over the front seat. They'd wring it out later.

His look made her feel powerful and made her blush all at the same time. And then, because she wasn't doing it, he leaned forward and wrapped the towel around her.

"You're cold."

"Where do we go from here?" she asked quietly.

"We go forward. We get out of this danger and then . . ."

And then . . .

"And then, if you want, I'll go home and try to forget you—the man I know. Not Cutter Winfield. I don't know him and I never will, because that's not who you are."

"Do you understand that no one knows who I am?"

"Is this why you said you don't feel like you're built for love? Because of your past?"

"You've researched the Winfields—have you stumbled on any happy marriages in that family?"

"That doesn't mean anything."

"Yeah, nature versus nurture. I've heard it before."

"If we can't move beyond this—"

"We might not be moving anywhere for a long while." He peered out the window, but there was no seeing past the driving rain that hit the window at a diagonal. "Why were you at my house that night—the night you saw Walter."

"I was coming to see you, Nick."

"To ask for my help."

"That was part of it. But if you'd refused, I still would've wanted to see you." She wrapped the towel more tightly around herself, a sudden chill going through her despite the humidity. "Why did Walter come to see you? Does he do that a lot?"

Even in the dark, she saw his jaw clench, and then, "He never did before this. Not once since I left home."

"But when your mother—"

"Deidre. When Deidre died, he decided to seek me out. I had only one woman in my life that I called *Mom,* and Maggie died when I was fourteen."

"Before—you said it was your birthday."

"Yeah. Thirteen years ago, I went to live with Kenny and Maggie Waldron—Chris's biological parents. I consider that my birthday now; it was the night that changed everything for me. Without them, I don't know where I'd be today."

"Will you tell me about Maggie?" she asked.

"Why?"

"Because you smile whenever you say her name."

She didn't think he would continue—he rummaged around one of the bags they'd brought. He handed her a new shirt and pants. "You need to get dressed—we don't know what's going to happen. We need to be prepared."

That reminder jolted her back into the reality of the situation. She yanked the T-shirt on quickly and pulled the pants on in the small space.

As he rolled up the bottoms of her BDUs, he answered her question. "Maggie—Mom—was protective of us. Always took our side, even if we were wrong. Of course, in private, she'd whip our tails—figuratively, but we needed it. She and Dad taught me to be respectful. She taught me so much, even though she died only nine months after I started living with them. Cancer—it all happened really quickly. But I wouldn't give up that time for anything."

"She wouldn't have liked me very much," she said. "She

probably wouldn't forgive me for hurting you the way I have." She fought to keep the sob out of her throat— couldn't at the thought of a scared, hurt, fourteen-year-old Nick with two great losses in the same year.

He slipped on his own fresh clothing as he spoke. "She taught me to trust my gut when it came to people, that I'd know if they were good or bad pretty much the second I met them."

"And I fall into the good category?" she asked softly.

Before he could answer, there was a slamming knock on the side of the car—Clutch was in the passenger side within seconds, soaked to the skin from the short walk from his own car and carrying bags and weapons. Sarah followed immediately into the driver's seat.

Nick had grabbed for his weapon, but Clutch held up his hands to stop him. "We're okay—we're alone still, but they know. John Caspar knows we've got Kaylee and he knows where we are."

"We've got to get the fuck out of here," Nick told him.

"Our thoughts exactly," Clutch said as Sarah turned the ignition gingerly and the engine turned over with a loud sputter.

"We're going to drive in this weather?" Kaylee asked them.

"Not much choice. He's on to us, knows about the article. He called—wants me to bring Kaylee to the warehouse. He says he'll let me live if I do that." The car began to move.

"We have to get the story in to my boss today so it can make the morning edition," Kaylee said. It was already two in the afternoon—they were six hours ahead of the States but there was no way to tell if they'd get to a hotel in time for her to e-mail the story.

Still, she scrambled for her computer to do a final edit on what she'd written earlier. She had some battery life—she'd have to make good use of it, despite the way the car jerked and fishtailed along the unfinished roads.

At least the rain had tamped down the dust completely—for the first time since they'd arrived in Africa, Kaylee's breathing felt clear and easy despite the complete panic that had overtaken her.

"Do what you need to do, Kaylee—let the rest of it go. Let us do what we need to," Nick told her as he held his rifle and moved into the far backseat of the car, leaving her alone on the long stretch of cracked leather.

Do what you need to do, Kaylee—let the rest of it go . . .

If only it was all that easy.

CHAPTER
18

Nick itched to take the wheel, hated sitting passively as Sarah attempted to barrel through puddles that could overwhelm the car at any given time. It was only luck of the draw and Sarah's instinct that was getting them along.

At least Kaylee was distracted, hanging on to the computer with one hand and typing with the other, biting her bottom lip in concentration.

Better she wasn't thinking about the danger bearing down on them—because Nick had the awful feeling that this John Caspar character was much closer than any of them thought. Clutch felt the same way, judging by the hand signal he'd given Nick to keep his weapons at the ready.

Nick remained in the last row of seats of the car, facing the back window for the most part, scanning what he could—although in the torrential downpour, he'd be lucky to make out even a headlight.

There was nothing, and still, he couldn't shake the feeling that they were being hunted down. Sent into a trap.

And about two hours into the trip, when they'd gone maybe twenty miles, the car jerked to a fast stop.

"The bridge is gone," Sarah told them.

"Stay with Kaylee," Clutch told her as Nick nodded at Kaylee. He got out of the car and headed over to the bridge to take a look at it for himself.

He and Clutch stood in the rain, staring at the wooden structure. Nick fisted his hand around his rifle and glanced at Clutch. Neither man said a word, but they didn't have to.

This bridge wasn't washed out—it had been blown out, most likely by dynamite.

They were trapped, caged in on three sides, and the only options were to stay put or retreat the way they'd come.

Clutch pushed the water off his face—Nick didn't bother, barely noticed the rain, was so used to being wet that this non-bone-chilling flood didn't affect him.

The gap wasn't terribly wide—maybe five feet across.

"Those trees won't hold with this rain," Clutch said, as if reading Nick's mind. "Building a bridge in this could take hours—we don't have a saw to take down the trees."

Nick pushed at one of the heavier trees. Of course, on this side of the river they were anchored tightly by the roots. "How close is the rest of your group?"

"You want me to call them?"

"If what you say is true, at least five of them are on your side. That makes two at most against all of us."

"I still don't like the odds—I've been gone for a few days, I don't know what the hell Caspar's told them." Clutch shook his head. "We could grab the trees from the other side of the river, bring them across."

"Best option, but you know as well as I do that we don't have that kind of time."

Clutch wiped the water from his eyes. "Then we've only got one choice."

Clutch opened the back of the car without warning, making Kaylee start—she couldn't see through the windows because of the rain, which seemed to have gotten worse. Sarah got out of the car to join Clutch as Nick slid in next to Kaylee, dripping wet.

"We've got to move out. Can you wrap up your computer and our phones as best you can in this sheeting, since you're still dry?"

He pointed to the plastic Clutch had thrown over the seat back in front of her.

"I can do that. But wait, we're not walking in this, are we?"

"The rain's our only cover right now, and it's not going to last much longer," Nick told her. "If we can get across the river and into hiding, we can grab a car and get to a hotel without being tracked."

It was their only choice beyond staying behind to fight. She knew Nick probably would have preferred that had she not been here—but not knowing who exactly they'd be up against made her grateful he'd chosen the path of least resistance.

Although it didn't seem like least resistance from where she stood—it looked dangerous as hell and scary and she tried to buck up for whatever lay ahead of them. And so she wrapped all four of their phones and the computer, after backing up the article on a Zip drive that she wrapped tightly as well and stuck inside the left leg pocket of her BDUs. And then she pulled the heavy camouflage jacket around her, despite the heat, and pulled her hat back on, tucking up her hair so it wouldn't drip down her neck.

The ground was slick and she was soaked to the skin the second she stepped out of the car. If Nick hadn't been guiding her, she would've fallen several times. As it was, she had a hard time pulling her feet through the mud that threatened to suck her in with every step.

What Nick had called a stream looked like a rushing white-water river to her, cold and gray and unforgiving. It wasn't a huge distance to get across but fear made her stop in her tracks.

She'd watched Clutch and Sarah cross first—Sarah had held their weapons and supplies above her head while hanging on to Clutch's back. "I can't swim," she yelled to Nick.

"We're definitely going to do something about that, but for right now, you don't have to. Hop on."

He'd turned and bent down a little, his back to her. She took a deep breath, because she trusted him to get her across, no matter how badly her legs were shaking.

She adjusted the bags so they rested on her back and climbed onto Nick's.

"I've got you, Kaylee. Just hold on, all right? No matter what happens, don't let go."

"No chance of that," she said and for a second he turned to her, and almost smiled a little before he turned back to the task at hand.

She wrapped her arms around his chest and held him tight around the waist with her legs as he waded into the river.

She felt the current dragging at him even as he fought back by pulling himself along the rope he and Clutch had wrapped around a tree across the river. The rain still pounded them, thunder and lightning, and she could barely see her hand in front of her face.

She rested her forehead between Nick's shoulders and just prayed the computer with her story on it would survive.

In this rain, nothing seemed like it would remain dry. As Nick moved, slow and steady through the water, she tried not to think of the documentaries she'd seen on crocodiles, comforting herself that they wouldn't attack in this weather. Praying they wouldn't.

No, you only need to worry about human predators, she thought with a grimace before bringing her mind back to other matters, like whether Roger would consider her article worth the risk.

When Nick slipped, she fought a scream as her legs went farther into the water, instead tightening her grip on him and felt him regain balance.

It seemed like hours but was more likely closer to twenty minutes later when Clutch was pulling Nick up onto shore and Sarah was helping her off Nick's back.

"Are you okay?" Sarah asked. "Can you walk?"

Kaylee's knees nearly buckled. She was aware of every muscle shaking, from tension, from fear and exhaustion. But she'd be damned if she was going to quit now. She looked at the concern in Nick's eyes as he came to her side, and yelled, "I'm fine," into the wind.

She was fine—until she heard the shots, automatic weapon fire that two days ago she'd never heard in person. Now she'd be able to identify it in her sleep, would most likely wake up from dreams in a cold sweat for a while because of it.

"Don't return it—they're firing blind," Clutch told Nick. "Let's just move."

Nick hoisted her quickly and ran for cover. "Hands over your ears," he told her, and she complied. It helped, as it had before, but only moderately. But as the sounds faded, she tugged at Nick and insisted she could run herself.

And she did—ran behind Sarah, with Nick on her tail, ran until she blocked the sound of gunfire from her mind.

Lying against Jamie in the dark, the worry finally broke through—an intense concern that had Chris's own head throbbing, the way hers had earlier.

He rarely got headaches—when he did, it was usually tied to something pretty bad happening to someone he loved.

Shit, he wished he could get in touch with Nick. He'd tried, but there was no cell service.

He sucked at being helpless, would've taken off into the

dark jungle if he'd been alone and damn the night. But it was a fucking monsoon out there and he couldn't justify putting Jamie in danger—still had that built-in chivalry that was always present around women. Would make it damn hard to be in combat with them.

Jamie's hands stroked the back of his neck. "It's going to be okay. It has to be."

Her legs shifted underneath his, one of them wrapping around his waist, and his cock stirred. "Let me help you forget this time," she murmured.

She guided him inside her, arching her back as he pushed in all the way and then he palmed the floor, kept his forehead against her breasts and just breathed. Her fingernails dug into his overheated skin, both of their bodies nearly trembling with anticipation, and then she bucked her hips up into his.

He heard the groan escape from his throat, a low, almost guttural sound that echoed in the empty space around them.

"That's it . . . let it go." Her own voice was huskier than it had been earlier—sexier. And just like before, she pulled him into her own need with a gentle force he hadn't expected.

He fit against her—with his body molded to hers, he waited for his psychic Cajun magic to kick in, to remind him that this was a temporary fit. But it didn't. Not when she wrapped her other leg around his waist and began to move in earnest, forcing him to give in to her.

And as they moved together in the dark, her hands tracing one of the long scars along his back, for the first time ever, he felt grounded.

At some point, Jamie had lost count of her orgasms and, she was pretty sure, of her mind as well. Now she lay on her back on the floor, spent, with Chris's long body lying next to hers.

He'd lit a cigarette and the smoke curled in lazy rings headed up to the ceiling. He hadn't bothered to dress himself yet and she'd followed suit, and for a while there was nothing but comfort between them.

She knew that would change—had to—neither of them could remain distracted for much longer. And yes, Chris had begun to tap his fingers against the floor, the familiar energy returning.

She sat up and rummaged in the dark for her clothes. The rain and wind outside had picked up and the plane shimmied slightly from side to side.

Chris had started to dress too—she heard the rustle of his clothes and the strike of a match as he lit another cigarette.

For the first time in her life, she wished she smoked.

"Those scars on your leg are pretty fresh," he said, out of the blue, as she buttoned her shirt.

"How can you tell that—I can barely see my own hand in front of me."

"I have some of my own . . . they're pretty distinctive."

She was rubbing her leg even before she spoke. "Mine are from eight months ago."

"Everything's healed up well?"

"It's fine," she lied.

Her therapist told her the problem was that Jamie said

she wanted to heal, but somewhere deep inside, she wouldn't let herself. Physically, yes. Her leg worked better now than it had before the shooting, thanks to regular physical therapy and getting back to her morning runs. But mentally, she didn't ever want to forget that moment in time when her adrenaline pumped and her reaction was too damned slow, her body caught off guard.

She wanted to remember it minute by minute so it would never happen again. "I lost my partner."

Her words sounded wistful, even to her own ears, and she cursed that weakness.

"I'm sorry, Jamie." He touched her shoulder in the dark and even though she'd seen it coming, she still jumped.

Dammit, she hated the dark. Didn't want to think about Mike or her injury right now.

Guilt washed over her for what she'd let Chris do to her—for what she'd wanted Chris to do to her.

Mike would've told her himself that it was time to move on. But Mike didn't know everything about her—she'd seen to that.

Chris had suddenly grown even more quiet—had stopped his usual constant movement, and Jamie felt herself freeze too. And then he said, "We can go now."

"I thought you said we needed to wait until the rain stopped?"

He didn't answer, had slammed the door open with his foot, was grabbing supplies and throwing them out the door as fast as he could, and suddenly, as the plane lurched hard, she knew why.

The rain was taking their shelter, and fast.

She stood, getting her bearings as the cabin rocked

viciously—he'd already gotten her bag out for her and was waiting by the open door.

"Come on, Jamie—you go now." He held his hand out to her. He was drenched already from the driving rain that was slamming into the plane and had to fight to get to the edge of the door.

The drop wasn't bad, maybe five feet straight down into the mud. She landed harder than she thought she would, had to drag her feet up as they became mired.

Chris was right behind her, literally lifting her out of the muck as it threatened to suction around his feet, and together they watched the plane drift down the muddy road.

"Come on, Jamie—up there." He pointed to a large set of boulders right in front of them—there was a flat-enough top for them to sit on semi-comfortably, more so than climbing one of the nearest trees anyway.

She scrambled up on her hands and knees, careful of her footing on the slippery rock. Chris handed her up the bags and supplies and then he was next to her.

"We've got a tent," he called above the wind. "We'll have to hold it around us, but it's better than nothing."

She helped him unwrap the sturdy canvas—he held on to it while she threaded some of the metal poles through it and then shoved the bags inside so it didn't threaten to blow away every five seconds.

"Go on, get in—work it from inside. I'll hold it from out here."

She worked as fast as she could—it seemed like hours with her dripping hair in her face and her hands shaking from the cold water, but then it was done and Chris was inside with her.

"We've got to leave the flap open—but we're against the wind," Chris said. He sat next to her and wrung out the front of his T-shirt and then opened his phone to let it dry.

"I can't believe that just happened." She looked over at him, looked down at herself, both of them drenched to the skin and the rain showing no signs of letting up.

"You should come train with us. It'll give you a whole new appreciation for wet and cold."

"I'm pretty happy with the training I've got."

"You're pretty tough, I'll give you that," he agreed with a small smile and then he grew serious again. "You sure you're okay? Nothing sprained or broken?"

"I'm fine."

"You're not fine—you're in pain," he said, even as he brought his hand to the back of her neck to knead the tender flesh. After one of her headaches, her neck and scalp were always far too sensitive to the touch—this time was no exception, although Chris's hand didn't bother her. And so, as the rain beat down around them, she didn't tell him that her pain had never really left, or that she didn't think it ever really would.

The rains slowed after they'd gotten about three miles along, Nick half dragging Kaylee as she shivered and held fast to him. She'd made it about two miles on her own steam and protested that she could make it all the way.

He didn't doubt her, and still, after a while longer, he put her onto his back again, for body warmth and so they could move faster. Clutch and Sarah led the way, Sarah scrambling as fast as Nick and Clutch through the brush.

He was definitely worried about Kaylee—she was in shape, for sure, but her asthma had been getting worse. Carrying her took any unnecessary strain off her—and helped them make time as well.

"Car," Sarah called. It was moving down the rutted road slowly, and Nick lowered Kaylee to the ground as Sarah ran into the middle of the road by herself as if she was all alone—a woman in distress.

"She's not going to kill the passenger, is she?" Kaylee whispered to him. He didn't answer, because the answer would surely be: yes, if necessary.

"Nick, please, tell me she's not going to do that."

There was no gunshot, only Clutch urging him and Kaylee to walk farther along the road, under the cover of the brush as Sarah walked away. "I'm not telling you anything, Kaylee. Don't ask, don't tell. It's better that way. We need to get you to safety."

She folded her arms tightly to her chest as she began to walk again, in front of Nick this time and out to the road from where Sarah called to them.

There was no sign of the driver and Sarah didn't say anything but "Get in" as they approached the old car.

Once in the safety of the car that seemed to move at a hundred miles an hour—a speed Nick was more than comfortable with—he grabbed his phone out of his pack and saw that he had both a signal and a message from Chris.

He called back, got his brother's voice mail and began to lay out what happened to them and where they were headed. If all went well, they could meet up and figure out the next part of the plan.

Kaylee was already thinking about that. "What about

the others—the GOST members at the warehouse who aren't traitors?" she asked Clutch.

"As soon as I get you and Nick safely to a hotel and you get the article transmitted, I'm going to the warehouse."

"Suppose John Caspar's there?"

"I doubt it—he's too busy tracking us. I'll make sure he follows me to the warehouse, keep the heat off of all of you. Once the article's out, it's a matter of staying alive to wait for the fallout." Clutch kept his eyes forward as he spoke, but Nick saw Sarah reach over and put a hand on the man's thigh briefly—a small, quick gesture of support.

Sarah would go with him to the warehouse, would put her life on the line with and for Clutch.

When Nick turned to look at Kaylee, he noted the fear in her eyes and the fact that she was shaking from being wet and cold. He was so used to it, it hadn't even registered to him that she'd need to get dry immediately, that she hadn't been built for this—hadn't trained.

And as he grabbed a blanket and placed it around her, he reminded himself that he and Kaylee had pledged their support to each other as well—what happened beyond that would remain to be seen.

Nick's phone rang—he picked it up halfway through the first ring. "Chris? Man, where are you?"

He listened carefully for a few minutes as the car sped along. "Maybe she should speak with Kaylee herself." He handed her the phone. "It's an FBI agent—she says she can help with GOST."

Clutch swung around. "How does she know about it?"

"She says her sister might be part of your group," Nick explained.

"There's one woman—PJ," Clutch said slowly.

"Did she join the group about eight months ago?" Nick asked him and Clutch nodded slowly. "That's got to be her."

Kaylee listened intently for a moment to the calm, authoritative voice on the other end that introduced herself as an agent with the FBI and then asked Kaylee to confirm who she was and what her plans were.

"This is Kaylee Smith—aka K. Darcy. I'm planning on going public about GOST—the article's written but not transmitted."

"Good. I can help you once the story hits the streets. But I'm going to need the real names of the people in GOST. Do you think you can get that information for me?"

"I can try."

"It's important. I have to be able to track those names, make sure that they're put back into Witness Protection," Jamie explained. "Once that happens, they'll be watched by marshals. That's where their real safety comes from."

"I'm going to do my best—once I have the names, I'll text them to you," Kaylee told her, and then handed the phone back to Nick. He spoke, first to Jamie and then his brother, before he closed the phone.

"Are we all set?" he asked.

"There's one thing we need." She turned to Clutch. "Do you know everyone's real name? Because Jamie—the FBI agent—she said once the article runs, she can check to make sure everyone's in the system, that everyone's back on a U.S. marshals' protection list."

"This FBI agent's going to help raise us from the dead?" Clutch shook his head slowly, as if he was having trouble comprehending all of it.

"I just need the names. Can you trust me with that?"

His eyes met hers. "I'm putting my life in your hands— mine and the rest of GOST."

"I'm only using your nicknames in the article. The names won't go any further than Jamie. I'll never, ever repeat them to anyone. I can keep a secret," she said.

"You can trust her, Clutch." Nick's voice sounded rougher than before, as if he could lose it at any moment. But his words meant more to her than anything else—and that's what she was going to hold on to.

CHAPTER
19

After getting in touch with Nick, Chris had started them hiking out of the jungle and toward the main road when the rains slowed.

They couldn't afford to spend the night in the middle of the jungle without shelter. Jamie was still in pain, but he had a feeling it was more inside her heart than her head. "I'm sorry, Jamie," he said suddenly, pausing their stride for a minute.

"For what?"

"For pushing you earlier. On the plane."

"Stop—you didn't. It's the situation, I'm not used to it being so personal."

"Yeah, I know what you mean. Usually I'm working with my brothers on the team, not racing to rescue them."

They started to hike again, with Jamie following him so he could cut away the underbrush. They were still scratched up anyway, but the machete he'd gotten off the plane was better than nothing.

"You said that you were adopted."

"My brothers were adopted by my parents when we were fourteen," he corrected her.

"That's kind of cool. Like growing up with your best friends."

"Yeah." The transition hadn't been completely smooth. He'd been used to being alone, and really, so had Nick and Jake. The two boys might've been destined to join the family, as his momma always used to say, but there were more fights inside the house than people knew about. You didn't put three adolescent alphas under the same roof without tension.

From the age of eight, there was a bond between Nick and Jake that was very cradle to grave, and soon after Chris met them, that loyalty was shared between all three of them. After Maggie died, they got even tighter. He became the confidant—the one Nick would come to when he had a problem he didn't want to upset Jake with, and Jake would do the same. Consequently, Chris knew the most secrets out of anyone in the family, and he was pretty damned good at keeping his mouth shut.

"I wish Sophie and I were closer." She stopped for a second, leaned her body against a half-broken tree and sucked some air. "Dammit, I though I was in good shape."

"You are—most people would've been done four miles ago."

"You're not even breathing hard," she pointed out. "And this . . ." She waved her arm around at the jungle surrounding them. "This is like a survival reality show gone bad." She paused, and then, "Shit, sorry."

"For what?"

"You know, the whole ex thing—I don't mean to keep bringing it up."

"It's all right. We've been over for a while."

"But she still calls you?"

"We were together from high school—sometimes it's hard to make the break."

"I'm sure it couldn't have been easy—her breaking up with you and becoming famous . . ."

"I broke up with her."

"Really?"

"Yeah, really. And it had nothing to do with her fame."

"You broke up with one of *People*'s fifty most beautiful people?"

"See, I didn't think you'd be the type to keep up with that stuff." He tugged her arm and she let go of the tree and followed him as he continued cutting a trail for them. The red-dusted roads were from hell because of the rain, and they still had a while to go. "If you want the story, all you have to do is ask."

"I . . . do not . . . want the story," she huffed. "Where's the paved road?"

"Ten miles out."

"Did you just say ten miles?"

"It's actually fifteen, but I figured I'd motivate you."

"And then what—are you going to steal a car for us?"

"Agent Michaels, I promised my dad and the law I'd only use my powers for good."

"I'm considering this good use."

"I kept my fingers crossed when I promised that anyway. You never know when that skill set's gonna come in handy." His phone began to beep—finally catching a signal again—they must be close to a road that wasn't on the map. He dialed in and first heard Jake's voice, telling him *It's all cool,* despite the sounds of a firefight in the background, and God knew where he was. For sure not in Coronado, where Chris had left him for a training exercise. No, Jake had been shipped out somewhere.

Christ, he wanted to strangle his brother sometimes. But at least Chris knew that the headache wasn't about that brother. No, there was definitely something wrong with Nick.

Nick, who in the next message told him their new location.

"Was that your brother?" Jamie asked as she busily checked her own phone. "I've got no messages on mine."

"I've got coordinates," he said, plugged them into the GPS. "We're meeting them at a hotel—it's not all that far from here." By car. Once they actually found a car. "But we've also got a big problem."

Jamie listened to the message, her brow furrowed intensely. When she handed back the phone to Chris, he asked, as gently as he could, "Is it possible that your sister is working for the CIA still—that she could be the one ordered to finish off GOST?"

"No way. She'd barely gone through the first month of training with the CIA."

"But she'd been a fighter pilot before she was recruited by the CIA—she had to have some intense training."

"Not the kind that would help her to infiltrate a group like GOST—you know that as well as I do." She'd tied one of his bandannas soaked in water around her head to keep cool, and now she put her fingers on it, kneading her temples. "But this confirms that the intel I saw was true— they're planning to take out GOST from the inside."

"Jamie, you need to be prepared, just in case. And maybe... maybe she didn't tell you everything. Maybe she couldn't. You told me you weren't close."

"I won't listen to that. Don't you dare take my words and twist them."

"Listen to me. If she's working for the CIA, you have to know she's trying to do her job—one you could be interfering with."

"If you were in my place, what would you do?" she asked.

"Exactly what you're planning on doing. I just want you to keep all the possibilities in mind. All right?"

She nodded. "When we get to the hotel and Clutch leaves to go back to the group, I want to go with him."

"That's not up to me. That's up to Clutch."

"Do you think we'll make it there in time?"

His hand clapped firmly on her shoulder. "We've got no choice. Let's haul ass."

Hours after they crossed the stream, wet, dirty and exhausted, Kaylee walked the final steps into the hotel room

Clutch had secured for them just outside of Kisangani . . . and had trouble reaching the bed.

Her lungs were heavy, and after a puff on her inhaler at Nick's urging, she felt him checking her pulse.

She was still shivering hard as Nick picked her up and carried her to the bathroom.

She protested. "Nick, the article . . ."

"There's time. You first. I had asthma as a kid—lots of breathing problems. I remembered hating how helpless I felt. How scared," he told her as he stripped her down, throwing the wet clothes into the corner before putting her into the shower.

The water was only lukewarm, but it was better than nothing. He managed to strip himself as well, even as Kaylee clung to him and he soaped them both, cleaning the river water debris and other dirt off their bodies.

"I can't imagine you being scared of anything," she murmured as her body temperature began to regulate and the tension in her chest eased as her body rubbed his.

"You'd be surprised." He shut the water off. "Come on, let's get you dry and send the article off."

She wanted to ask if they were safe yet, if Caspar hadn't been able to follow them. But if Caspar was anything like Nick and Clutch, he could no doubt get through anything.

Wrapped in a towel, she sat on the edge of the bed watching as Nick opened the bag with the computer and gingerly pulled the machine out. He turned it on and watched it power up, relief coursing through him.

"It works—we're all set."

She smiled. "I backed it up too. We wouldn't have lost it."

"This just makes things a hell of a lot easier," he told her. "There's no signal out here; you're going to have to go through the phone line. Could take a while."

He brought the computer to her and she typed fast, fingers flying across the keys as she composed an e-mail.

The Internet connection stalled out several times—but finally, twenty frustrating, breath-holding minutes later, the e-mail went through.

Once that happened, she was on the phone with her boss, confirming that the e-mail had reached him. She waited there, on the phone, mouthed, *He's reading it now,* to Nick.

She listened to Roger's praise—and his warnings. Then, "Kaylee, who are you with right now?"

"I'm with . . . I'm okay," she said. "Really. I'll be better when the story runs, though."

"This is going to shake up a hell of a lot of people in Washington. A lot of them will want to speak with K. Darcy."

"If all goes well, I'll be back home soon. I'll do what I need to do, but I stand by my story and my sources. I heard the orders myself."

Roger hesitated, like he wanted to say more. But all he told her was, "Stay well, Kaylee."

She closed the phone without answering him and looked up at Nick, who'd stood over her during the call. "He's putting it to press for the morning edition. What do we do until then?"

"I'll let Clutch know—we'll sit tight until dark and then decide if it's safer to keep moving."

"He's worried about me, Nick. He thinks...he thinks there could be real trouble because I've written this."

"There could be," he said.

"That's not exactly what I wanted to hear," she muttered.

"I told you I wouldn't lie to you," he said, then shook his head. "About this, I mean. Fuck."

They hadn't had a chance to talk about anything more that had happened before walking through the river. She knew this was neither the time nor the place, and still, she wished he would talk about it with her. Needed him to.

"Do you want to see the article?" she asked finally. "I normally don't let people read my stuff until it's copyedited, but in this case, I could really use an opinion."

He sat in silence for several moments, his eyes not leaving the screen until he was finished. "It's fantastic," he told her. "I'm not one for news articles—"

"Or journalists," she said quietly.

Nick didn't disagree. "You can understand why."

She didn't say anything more, waited until he called Clutch and told him that the article would run in the morning edition, listened to him weigh the pros and cons of staying or leaving. But in the middle of their conversation, the power cut out and the rains picked up harder than they'd been before. "I guess that answers our question."

She heard the click of the phone.

"That road we came through? Washed away," Nick told her.

"Is there another way here?"

"They'd have to get to the warehouse first, then go

around to come get us. With this weather, it won't be quick—and they didn't follow us in."

"So you think we're safe?"

"It doesn't get much safer than a monsoon and a power outage around here."

"Glad that's considered safe."

But somehow, they were—with the hotel halfway between the airport and the warehouse, a foot in both worlds. Quick escape at their fingertips, even if the hotel wasn't the best. Still, their room was clean and had a comfortable bed with simple handmade linens, a rough sisal-like rug under their bare feet and halfway warm water.

Clutch—whose room with Sarah was right next door—had gone out for food, warm vegetable samosas and beef patties and plantains from a local market, had left them in the room when they'd been in the shower. It all smelled delicious.

It was so dark, even with Nick sitting right next to her, she was still freaked.

It was so much easier asking questions in the dark, though. "When your brothers find out what I know… they're never going to forgive me, are they?"

"They'll be pissed," he said quietly. "There'll be a lot of explaining to do."

"Does anyone know beyond your brothers and your dad?"

"No. I told Jake that he could tell his fiancée, Isabelle. He said maybe, when the time was right. He trusts her. I trust her. But it's a burden that he didn't want to put on her." He shifted. "I'm sorry you have to know."

Days earlier, when she'd been at Nick's house, she'd

spent time looking at the pictures in the den, of Nick and his two brothers as they grew from good-looking teenagers into handsome men. In some of the early pictures, there was a woman there—Kaylee assumed it was the adoptive mom Nick had spoken of earlier.

Her grandmother hadn't believed in family pictures—there were some religious depictions framed throughout the small house but other than that and a few old scrapbooks Kaylee had discovered in the attic, she hadn't grown up with happy, smiling memories all around. But as she stood in his living room and then his den, the warmth surrounded her.

It was nice there—it didn't make her sad or nostalgic for all she'd missed; instead, it made her realize that what she'd wanted all along—a family, love—wasn't beyond her grasp. It was all right in front of her.

Love trumps biology every time.

Yes, she believed Nick. He was living proof of the statement. "In the car, you told Clutch he could trust me—I know you don't say things you don't mean."

"I don't have much of a choice. I have to trust you."

"God, I hate that. I hate that that's how you feel about what's happening between us."

She reached out to touch his arm, but he'd already pulled away instinctively.

"Not now, Kaylee. Not in the middle of all this. I can't."

Kaylee was the first woman who knew his secret and Nick felt the uncomfortable weight on his chest of being both burdened and unburdened at the same time.

His relief had been short-lived, though. Talking about the Winfields and the way he'd grown up had made him too pensive, less ready to take action. He had to get back into mission mode.

But sitting with her, with the new rainstorm slamming the roof of the one-story hotel, regaining mission mode seemed an impossible task. He finally lit the oil lamp the hotel had provided—it cast small shadows across the room from its place on the nightstand.

Kaylee remained wrapped in a towel and just waited. Patiently. "You haven't said one word about how tough this is—that you're hungry or you're tired," Nick said.

"You haven't either," she pointed out, then bit her bottom lip in that way he found so freakin' disarming.

From the time he'd left the Winfield house up until this point, he'd prided himself on being strong as hell—physically and, more importantly, mentally. Hadn't let anything get in the way of what he wanted—illegally, at first, and then legally, with the teams. He put his life on the line with every mission, put his soul into everything else he did, and now, to know that he could never truly escape his past was nearly too much for him to bear.

But he'd be damned if he let this break him.

There had always been a part of him that didn't believe that he *wouldn't* follow in the Winfield footsteps. As much as he'd tried to deny it, he had the nagging sense that it was deeply a part of him, like a skin he had no hope of shedding even though he wanted nothing to do with it. "Is your boss going to ask you why you're no longer working on the Winfield story?"

"Probably. I've been on it since I started at the paper.

But it doesn't matter, I'm not writing about it any longer," she told him. "You don't think that Walter would tell people who you are, do you?"

"I can't see why he would. The story would just embarrass him."

"I just assumed maybe he wanted you . . . back or something, since he came to see you after Deidre's death."

"A lot of things that happened in that family are because of Deidre, but they have nothing to do with her death." He sat down next to her on the bed, shoving the computer out of the way. He didn't look at Kaylee, but for the first time in a long while, he didn't feel like he was telling the story of someone else when he spoke of Cutter. No, this time, the memories were vivid and they were, without a doubt, all his. "Walter loved Deidre, but she broke his heart when she fell in love with Billy, his brother. But I'm sure you know that—you reported on the rumors of the long-lost love affair."

"I did," she said quietly. "There were people—staff, mostly—who came forward to talk about things they'd seen. Subtle things. A touch of hands, or a look, mostly. Nothing substantial, but enough . . ."

"Yeah, enough to go on, right?" He shook his head. "In my house, it wasn't a rumor. After Billy was killed, Deidre was devastated. She went into seclusion for months. The only time she pulled it together was for her charities."

He paused and then decided to spill it all to her. "Deidre told Walter that I was Billy's son. Up until the other night, I believed that. In a way, that made things livable for me—because Billy had bucked the Winfield thing too, had wanted to be different."

"But you're really Walter's biological son, that's what he came to tell you the other night," she said quietly, and he nodded.

"He apologized for treating me like shit, for hating me when I was little."

"I can only imagine the guilt he's feeling now."

"I don't want him to come to me because he's guilty. I don't want him to come to me at all—it would've been so much easier if he'd just stayed away. I'd never have to know all of this."

"And you might never be able to put it behind you either," she pointed out.

"It *was* behind me. Look, I get that you want to ask me questions, about growing up and—"

"I'd want to ask those whether you grew up a Winfield or not."

"I just don't want you to feel sorry for me, Kaylee. That's the last thing I'm looking for." He closed his eyes and turned away, wishing he could actually fucking sleep for once in his life. "I don't know how to do this. I'm not good at it."

"You are good at so many things. But if you want me to understand you, I've got to know where you came from, why certain things are so important to you. I need to know the things you can't share with anyone else—the things you won't."

"I've always had barriers." They were secure. Comfortable.

"You've let those barriers hold you hostage for too long."

She was probably right. Fuck, he hated this, mainly

because she already knew most of it. All those reports on the missing Winfield heir were closer to the truth than he'd have liked.

"Look, I already told you I wasn't held a lot as a baby—that's because I was really sick when I was born." He rubbed the scar on his throat unconsciously and took his hand away when he saw her looking at it. "I almost didn't live."

"But you did."

"I thought that I was defective—that I couldn't bond with other people, couldn't make connections. I thought that was my legacy." But it hadn't been true. The connection to Jake was almost instantaneous—same with Chris, and Kenny and Maggie. It was as if he'd been aching for that kind of familial contact, and once he received it, everything else fell into place.

He hated the bitter feeling that hit his throat when he mentioned the Winfields, wanted it to fade away until the memories were nothing more than a gentle scrape of a healed wound. Unpleasant, not almost unbearable. "She never came for me. None of them did. This new family— *my* family, did. They came for me, wanted me. Fought for me. Not like the Winfields—they wanted perfect. At least on the outside. By the time I left, I was already long gone from them emotionally."

"And they just let you go?"

"They just let me go," he said. "It was what I wanted. It would've happened with or without their consent. At least this way the Winfields could control it, put their own spin on the situation."

"What kind of parents do that to their own child?"

"I thought my mother hated me growing up because I was Billy's son—an accidental pregnancy because of her affair. I assumed that when I was born small and sick, she couldn't stand to be around me. Saw it as some kind of punishment for her indiscretion. She only let Walter know the truth after her death to hurt him more. I was just a pawn."

"So that's why Walter let you leave the family."

"Yeah. See, I was going to run away, but Kenny—the man I call *Dad* now—he found me at the train station and brought me back to the Winfield house with signed emancipation papers that Dad had drawn up. Dad wanted to go back inside with me, but I needed to go in alone, to hand Walter the papers myself and leave on my own steam. I'd signed away my rights, and from there it was simple. I left everything behind in my room, except for the jeans, sneakers and green sweatshirt I'd been wearing that day to school, when I pretended everything was normal. But I already knew what was going to happen." He cleared his throat. "Deidre was busy tearing up pictures of me in the kitchen, burning them. So they could say that I did it. There was nothing for me to take, nothing I wanted to take, so just after midnight, I climbed down the trellis the way I always did. Jake was waiting for me."

"Where did you go?" she asked softly.

"Walked the ten miles to Chris's house. And Cutter Winfield was never seen or heard from again."

"Until now. My God, all you've been through," she murmured. "All you've accomplished."

"I got better," he said shortly.

"You had a strong will. Wanted to survive. Lots of other people would've given up in your situation."

"That wasn't an option."

"Because you wanted to make yourself whole, better... so your biological family would accept you."

Fuck, she'd hit on something. His throat felt tight and he swallowed hard and her fingers dug into his biceps as she massaged his muscles. "I guess so. Stupid, right?"

"Not at all."

"It was, Kaylee, because it didn't work. Because even when I got better and came out of the hospital, they still didn't want me. I was wild, uncontrollable. I needed too much attention and I didn't know how to deal with a quiet, understated family. I broke all the dishes, I slid down the banisters..."

"You were a kid."

"I was a Winfield. I didn't know the rules, didn't know how to act. I craved action—attention. Pain. Anything to feel." He hung his head. "Nothing worked—not being good anyway. But doing things like stealing cars and getting into fights, that hopped up my adrenaline levels. I don't need to feel that kind of action as much today. I get it in my job, racing cars, things like that."

"And sex."

"Yeah, with sex." He realized just how much his body ached—not from exertion, but from stress and quite possibly fear.

Even his skin seemed too sensitive, the way it had earlier when he'd poured water on his body from one of the jugs Clutch had in the back of the car—and yet he wanted to be touched by Kaylee again. Craved it.

He rubbed his own arms in an effort to shake off the feeling.

He had a friend who was into the BDSM scene and Nick had tried a few things with a female dom. Let himself get tied up.

He'd had to use his fucking safe word after half an hour. The whip she'd used worked—he could go there; but the tied down, helpless feeling was intolerable.

"We'll work on desensitizing you," the woman had whispered. He'd nearly broken the wooden St. Andrew's cross he'd been strapped to.

So no, he didn't go back there. He'd just given himself another kind of cross to bear anyway. "You're the first woman I ever told this story, the first person outside of my brothers, Maggie and my dad. And I can't talk about this anymore—please, not right fucking now."

"Then tell me what I can do to make it better right now." She watched for a response, wondered if he'd shut down, the way he had before when he'd tried to tell her that there was nothing she could do to help.

Instead, he shook his head and stared at the floor for a second. And then he raised his head high—regally. Exposed. "Touch me. Any way you want to."

"Nick . . . I want to. You don't know how badly I want to, but you don't need to prove anything to me. I don't want to do anything that's going to make you uncomfortable."

He leaned back on his elbows, stretched out along the length of the bed as the rain continued to batter the windows. "We're down to the wire here, Kaylee. In deep trouble. So please, do as I say now. Just try it."

"I can't refuse you." She drew a deep breath, let her eyes rake the tanned skin on his chest, illuminated only by the small oil lamp that flickered on the nightstand. She reached out and started with a harder touch, a stroke to his biceps. And then she intermingled it with a softer one that made him start noticeably, as if he wanted to jump out of his own skin. "We can stop."

He swallowed, hard—he was breathing hard too, his face flushed from concentration. But he wasn't refusing her touch, and he was aroused.

At the sight of this strong man attempting to be even stronger, she grew intensely aroused herself.

"No, that's the thing—we can't stop."

He was right. Her finger moved toward the trach scar, stopped before she reached the familiar place he always rubbed.

"Go ahead."

Instead of a finger, she pressed her lips there, felt his pulse, his entire body react as if he'd been touched with fire.

"Just breathe, Nick."

He nodded and she saw the hard swallow, the hands fisted at his sides.

He didn't need to be put through any more hell. Instead, she hugged him hard as he remained propped on his elbows. And then she drew her nails down his back in a hard scratch and he drew in a sharp breath, as if the pressure eased.

His voice rumbled deep in his chest. "Kaylee..."

"Your lips are so soft," she murmured as she straddled his prone body. "Everything else about you is so hard— all rock solid, unyielding muscle, but your lips...I want them on me. Touch me. Go ahead—do whatever you need to."

He pulled back from her slightly, held her by the shoulders. "It might never get any easier. Would it matter if it didn't?"

She looked at his eyes, incredibly green and flecked with gold. "It wouldn't matter."

"Why? What the hell do I do for you?"

"You make me feel alive," she whispered. "Can you understand that—everything is intense when I'm with you."

She was in his lap, straddling him, her hands twined in his hair, caressing his scalp roughly. "What do I do for you?"

"Everything." His voice was a growl on that single word, vibrated through her like a shot.

"You don't always like the way I make you feel."

"Since I was little, I'm always looking for that sensation, that adrenaline rush. And sometimes . . . it's not enough to even begin to take the edge off," he admitted. "I don't know what's wrong with me, why I need that so much. What I'm looking for."

"What happens when you're with me?"

A long pause and then, "I stop looking."

She didn't say another word, just drew his body to hers and let their bodies continue the dance.

His erection pressed against her belly, her breasts rubbing his chest. The two of them were skin to skin with secrets splayed out, closet doors open and skeletons tumbling to the floor, as she lowered herself onto him and began to rock.

The lightning illuminated the room through the softly shaded windows, bold and powerful, and she took in Nick's scent, breathed into his neck. They were both slick with sweat and heat and want, and nothing was going to stop it now. Nothing.

CHAPTER
20

Chris dropped his and Jamie's packs by his feet and checked his phone for the nine thousandth time that day. No more messages from Nick. Six hours left to get to a place that was pretty much six hours away by car, miles of road with no cars and this really sucked badly.

But suddenly, Jamie, who'd walked ahead a bit, was waving her arms and yelling to him, pointing to a beat-up car—the first and only one they'd seen for miles. He shut his phone and headed over to her as she spoke with someone inside the car through an opened window.

He stopped short when he saw the passengers—an African man and woman, husband and wife.

"They speak English—they'll take us to a car only a few

miles from here, for American money." She tugged his arm as she opened the back seat of the ancient vehicle. "Why aren't you getting in?"

He was still too busy staring at the very pregnant woman in the front seat, nearly due, and he breathed a deep, internal sigh and prayed that it wouldn't happen this time.

It didn't *always* have to happen.

"Are you scared of pregnant women?" Jamie asked.

"No, it's just that it will slow us down."

"Nothing is slower than slogging through this crap on foot. Come on."

Less than half an hour later, the African woman had her legs spread, pushing against the door and one of Chris's shoulders while he began the process of delivering her baby.

It had started innocently enough: with less than a mile to go to get the car these people had promised, the woman in the front seat had yelled, so loudly that Jamie jumped and looked around for snipers or soldiers.

Chris did nothing but put his hand on the woman's shoulder and spoke softly to her, in her own language, and yes, Jamie had read in the file on Devane that his particular team spent an inordinate amount of time in this country post–9/11.

The car was pulling to the side of the road.

"We can't stop now," Jamie said to Chris, but he was halfway out the door.

He stuck his head back in briefly. "I tried to warn you that this would slow us down."

She scrambled out the other side, nearly crashing into the woman's husband in order to get to where Chris was, helping the woman out of the front seat and getting her to lay down in the back.

"Get in behind her, let her lean on you," Chris instructed the husband, who did as he was directed. "Jamie, grab the medical kit from my bag. Get me gloves and scissors and twine. And a towel and some bottled water."

"Are you really going to deliver this baby?"

Chris reassured the woman softly and placed a blanket across her legs before backing away from the car. He turned to Jamie and kept his voice low. "I told you that my momma was a midwife. And really, there's not much choice here."

"How did you know she'd go into labor?" she demanded, keeping her voice as quiet as his.

"Happens all the time." He shrugged and shook his head as he laughed softly. "I don't go into hospitals anymore—the maternity ward goes insane."

"Was it like that for your mom too?"

"Hard to say. Women who wanted to go into labor used to come to the house—I was never sure if it was me who made that happen or her. But now . . ."

"Now it's all you."

"Guess so."

"Does it always turn out all right?"

"I'm done talking about this. Can you get what I asked for? And if you can't help, you need to walk away."

She bit back a reply because of the look in his eyes, the one that told her things didn't always turn out okay. She wondered if he thought about this as a burden or a gift and realized there probably wasn't all that much difference between the two. "I'll help."

"Thanks, Jamie."

She went to the bags they'd thrown into the back and began to collect the things he asked for.

He'd turned his attention back to the woman and Jamie wondered what she was thinking now, her dress pulled up to her waist and Chris standing there, shoving rubber gloves on.

"Will it be a while?" she asked.

"She's crowning already. Push, Momma. Hard."

He counted and Jamie realized she was holding her breath as he did so. Every time he instructed the woman to breathe, she breathed as well, until Chris told her to spread a towel on the front seat, have the water and suction ready and get rubber gloves on her own hands.

"Push again, Momma," he encouraged as the woman screamed. "Last push . . . that's it . . . don't stop."

Jamie didn't breathe until Chris told her to give him the bulb syringe, and she held the breath until she heard the soft wail.

"It's a girl," he told all of them, and the woman and her husband cried and clapped. "Jamie, come here—tie the twine to the cord . . . right there, good, nice and tight. Now cut."

Her hands shook as she did so, freeing the baby. He promptly handed the impossibly tiny baby to her. "Clean her in the front, then wrap her and give her to her mama."

"Chris, I've never—"

"I have to finish here." He stopped talking to her, focused on the now nervous mom, and she did what he said, laying the baby on the towel carefully, using another one to wipe off the smooth skin until the baby was all clean and content.

The father handed her a brightly colored cloth and Jamie wrapped the infant as best she could and handed it over the seat to the mother, who was smiling again.

Jamie backed out of the car, stood a little bit away to give them some privacy. Chris had finished, was pulling down the woman's dress and taking off his gloves.

And before she could stop herself, she was walking up to him, putting herself into his arms and she was crying—for the first time this trip, for the first time in years, she was crying, and it was over a baby, a healthy, breathing baby.

She hadn't even cried at Mike's funeral, or when she'd discovered that he'd died on the OR table, because that would've been like admitting he was really gone.

She hadn't cried for her parents either.

But Mike was really gone, so were her parents—and for now, so was Sophie. Everyone was gone except for Chris, whose arms were solidly around her.

"Hey, it's okay. It's an emotional thing when you see it for the first time. Or the hundredth."

"You're really crazy, you know that?"

"I think everyone needs a little crazy in their lives. Especially you."

"I've known you for all of two days."

"My father knew my momma for one before he told her he loved her. But don't worry, I don't move that damned fast."

She laughed against his chest.

"Come on, sugar, get back in the car so we can go find your sister."

"You, Mama—you name the baby," the woman said.

"Oh, no, I couldn't possibly . . ." She paused. "She has to be named after you," she told Chris, who shook his head no.

"You have no idea how many babies are named after me. Your turn."

She looked at the baby—impossibly tiny and precious, born into a place that was half hell, and still, the infant looked happy. Innocent.

She wished it had been that easy when she'd been forced to be reborn all those years ago. And so really there wasn't any other name she could choose for the baby except the name that was her own past. "What about . . . Ana?"

He smiled at her. "I think that's beautiful. Now let's go find Nick and Sophie and bring them home."

"Yeah, that sounds like a plan. I'll put this stuff in the back—you make sure Mom and baby are all right for the rest of the ride."

"She said it'll take ten minutes to get to their house; there's an old Land Rover there we can take," he called over his shoulder as she collected the supplies he'd used that could be reused and placed them into the plastic bag.

Before she could open Chris's bag in the back of the truck, her phone began to ring. Finally. She stared at it, the information she'd been trying so hard to dig up for the past weeks suddenly right there in front of her in a text message. "Got it," she whispered to herself. "And I've got you, John Caspar. Once I tell Kaylee, it's all going to be over for you."

Kaylee was taking a hell of a chance by writing this

article, and Jamie was grateful she wasn't alone in all of this. The more people involved, the more hope she had of helping Sophie, she thought as she texted Kaylee the intel on Caspar.

Normally, Jamie wouldn't share her intel this easily, but this was anything but normal.

"Everything all right?" Chris called. "We've got to get moving."

"I'm ready." She put the phone back into her pocket and began shoving things into his bag before slamming the trunk shut.

She squeezed into the front seat next to him so the mother and her new baby could relax in the back, and as the car rolled forward she forced herself to forget everything else but their current mission.

They weren't getting power anytime soon. Nick cracked the windows but couldn't hear anything beyond a persistent wall of rushing water. Since the door opened out, there wasn't much he could secure from the inside, but he'd done a perimeter check inside and out every hour.

He was just drying off from the last one when thunder boomed overhead and Kaylee moved nearly on top of him. Jesus, she just did it for him—every time her body brushed his, he was ready for her. "Hey, it's okay."

"Sorry." She sounded embarrassed. "I know it's thunder, but I'm jumpy, I guess."

"I just checked. No one around—no new cars in the lot or on the road, which is under water."

"Here, take more towels—you're soaked." Her hands were on his chest—through the shirt, the touch wasn't bad. He'd been ready for it.

"I can't make contact with my brother," he told her as he rubbed his body down.

"Which means he'll go straight to the warehouse, right?"

"I guess. He could still make it here, though. Driving through extremes hasn't ever been a problem for him."

"But you're still worried."

In the past, he wouldn't have admitted that, would've seen it as a weakness. An admission that he wasn't up to the job. But Kaylee, she knew he wasn't weak. She knew... everything. "A little."

"He'll check in—it's the weather, he's probably just waiting it out. And he's probably just as worried about you."

"Yeah, true." He sat on the edge of the bed. "Hopefully he's already borrowed a car."

"Ah. So you and Chris have the same skills with cars." She sat next to him, cross-legged in the dark, her hair loose around her shoulders, and he leaned his elbows on the bed and told her the story.

"When I was seventeen, I was arrested for boosting cars and selling them. And I sat in that jail cell with Chris and planned to stay there as long as my sentence was. I didn't want the military, more rules and regulations. My dad tried to talk to me, and Chris, and Jake even came in to try. But I didn't listen to any of them," he told her.

"So why did you finally decide not to stay in jail?"

"It's what Walter would've wanted. And I decided, fuck

him, he'd had enough control over my life. So in a way, I should thank him for what I've become. I should thank him for my career, for my brothers, for my family—I wouldn't have had any of that if it wasn't for him. It's weird to think I actually owe that to Walter."

"Well, that's a step in the right direction, I guess—a new way of looking at things."

Yes, a new way. She was right again.

But something else wasn't right. His body stiffened, instincts screaming, and he stilled completely just before the window broke—a soft, tinkling sound.

He put a hand on her shoulder and prepared to head her out the door when he realized she was having problems breathing—and this time, she wasn't alone. His lungs were filling quickly and he noted the small grenade sending out gray smoke in the darkness. Quickly, he yanked her toward the door but it wasn't opening. He shot the lock, but still it wasn't moving. Barricaded from the outside.

"It's blocked," he choked out.

"What's happening?" she gasped.

"Some of kind of gas."

Before she could answer, strong arms pulled at him, hard. The world was going black and the last things he heard were a soft cry from Kaylee and a gunshot.

For the second time in her life, PJ was the only survivor. There had to be some kind of limit as to how many times she could get lucky, but so far her supply seemed limitless.

Lucky. She wanted to laugh as that word rolled around on her tongue until she realized she was babbling to herself in the midst of the crash. And then the words turned into a sob that wrenched the last bit of adrenaline out of her, and she found herself on her hands and knees in the dirt, breathing the smoke from the explosion.

She'd checked and rechecked the controls on the Cessna, was almost to the point of obsession about it thanks to the crash she'd endured when she was still in the Air Force.

Then, she'd landed in the freezing cold Pacific Ocean. This time, it was the jungles of Africa, maybe ten miles from the warehouse.

It must have been a bomb that wasn't timed correctly that went off and took out the wing. She'd steered the best she could to get the plane on the ground, ignoring the fact that Horse and Sway had been yanked out of the plane when the wing pulled away part of the wall. Ignored the screams of Smoke too as he yelled that it wasn't supposed to end like this for him.

It had ended for all of them quite a while ago, but she hadn't yelled that back, had concentrated on crash landing.

When she came to, her head was against the console. She'd smelled the gasoline and knew the plane was on fire.

But Smoke, he was already dead.

And now the men who run GOST will think I'm dead too.

For all intents and purposes, she was. This was her way out, her chance to escape.

But to where? She was so tired of hiding, of running. Of living by someone else's rules. So no, she was done running—this time, she'd stay and fight.

A hand on her back made her jerk up—it wasn't a comforting or a friendly touch, but one meant to shove her roughly to the ground. She let it happen, only so she could roll to her back and take down the assaulter with a strong kick to the knee.

A man howled in pain—a local, looking to rob the dead, and she must've seemed an easy target.

With her knife at his throat, he knew he'd made a mistake. Five days ago, even five hours ago, she would've slit his throat without a second chance. She didn't believe in those, didn't believe they did anyone much good. In her world now, it was react immediately, never ask questions and never have any regrets.

But this time, she merely pushed away from the man and began to stumble back through the jungled path that would lead her to the warehouse . . . and maybe to some answers.

CHAPTER
21

Sarah woke with a cough. Her head was heavy, her legs and arms like lead, and she quickly realized that she was tied and lying on a floor. She rolled from her back to her side in an attempt to sit up, opened her mouth to call for Clutch but her throat was too dry. More coughing that left her doubled up.

She remembered being inside the hotel room, remembered that Nick had called to say the article had been transmitted. Clutch had been showering while she watched the windows and the door, weapon in hand. Whoever had gotten them had moved fast—the gas grenade broke the window and worked almost immediately.

She'd tried the door right before she'd collapsed; it had been blocked from the outside.

How long between then and now was anyone's guess. It felt like days. Years. It felt like she could lay her head back down and just sleep, except Clutch...

Where was Clutch?

The figure in front of her was blurry—whoever it was leaned in and wiped her eyes with a cool cloth and then put some water to her lips. Normally, she wouldn't let herself drink like this—it could be drugged or worse—but her throat was burning and she needed to speak, to ask what was going on.

"Clutch, please, untie me."

"It's not Clutch."

She knew that voice, blinked a few times, recognized the man standing over her immediately as her most recent contact for an American paper. "Vince, what are you doing here?"

"I came for you, Sarah," Vince said, his voice lowering an octave, and for a second she just stared at him, her mouth dropping open.

It was the voice that haunted her dreams...the one that she'd heard on Clutch's phone months ago...

Bobby Juniper, we want you back.

She'd heard the same one on her phone yesterday when she was in the car with Clutch.

John Caspar's voice.

"No—no way this is happening," she said finally, but it was happening.

"I was checking up on Clutch, making sure he kept up his end of the bargain, that he wasn't sending you messages or calling you," Vince said. No, not Vince—he was really John Caspar. She'd been fooled by the man who wanted her dead. Driven him, spoken with him, shared meals with him.

She'd talked with him about her past—the first person she'd opened up to about it since she'd told Clutch, thinking it would help her heal faster.

She'd been an idiot. "How?"

He held up her cell phone and pointed to the back. "Tracking device. Very effective, and neither you nor Clutch suspected anything."

"You went through my things...You bastard." She'd brought this down on all their shoulders and she cursed herself for her stupidity—for trusting. "Where's Clutch?"

"He has some jobs to finish. Some choices to make." Vince—no, not Vince—John Caspar bent down and rubbed his hands over her arms as she tried to squirm away. "I'm just trying to keep your arms from going numb."

"Then untie me, you asshole."

He laughed. "It would take a lot to get the fight out of you, Sarah. That's why I like you so much. That's why I didn't kill you when I was supposed to."

When her family had been killed, she'd been sixteen—pampered for someone who lived in this country. And she'd been scared, so frightened of the noise and weapons that she'd done the only thing she knew at the time—she ran.

This time she knew better, knew that you could never hide from men like this. Knew that she'd never forgive herself if she didn't fight to the death for her family. For Clutch.

She brought her legs up hard—bound together, they

served nicely as a weapon—her slightly bent knees catching Caspar in the face.

He howled and backed away, his nose bleeding. "You're making a huge mistake, Sarah. Clutch isn't going to choose you. If you'd agreed to stay with me, you would've been free."

She didn't bother to tell him that what she'd done had already set her free. Now she could only hope that the same would prove true for Clutch, no matter the outcome.

Tape covered her mouth, stopped her from screaming. Instinctively, Kaylee tried to bring her hands up to pull it off, but found her wrists tied tightly together behind her back. The darkness closed in on her and her breath came through her nostrils in tight, hard puffs. Her head felt heavy and bile rose in her throat as unconsciousness threatened to take hold of her again.

The dirt floor rubbed against her exposed knee where her pants had ripped earlier. She didn't have a blindfold on, but her eyes refused to adjust to the darkness no matter how stubbornly she tried. Burning gunpowder stung her nose as she attempted to push up to a sitting position. Impossible to do the way they'd trussed her, both legs and arms, and every muscle in her body was numb.

Instinctively, she kicked her legs out straight. They hit a wall. She heard the sounds of loose dirt falling from where she'd kicked, and she tried to maneuver on her back and kicked again.

She was in the ground, in a hole that couldn't be any bigger than six by six feet. A grated opening above her provided a slight bit of light. Still, everything began to close in and her mild case of claustrophobia promised to overwhelm. She had to get out of here.

She kicked again frantically and heard a muffled groan when she made contact with something soft.

In seconds, Nick was pressed to her tightly, his voice barely there in her ear. "You're okay—I'm going to untie you."

Nick was here, she wasn't alone. She could barely stay still while he worked. Her wrists and ankles were raw but she didn't care about the burn of the ropes as he pulled them away, didn't even care about the way her face stung as she yanked the tape off her mouth.

"Easy, Kaylee—it's okay . . . just keep it quiet." His lips pressed directly to her ear, his hands on her arms, calming her. "Don't draw attention to us—I don't know how much longer we'll be alone."

"No one's up there, watching us?"

"From what I heard, there aren't enough of them to keep track of us. I heard them say they've got Clutch here too."

"We're at the warehouse?"

"I can't be sure, but I think so. You're not claustrophobic are you?"

"Never was. But this could make anyone have a panic attack." She pulled tight to him.

"Keep your breathing controlled—you'll be fine."

The only semi-comfortable position they could manage was lying on their sides, bodies pressed against each other. She took some deep breaths before she spoke again. "Is there any way out?"

"Not that I can find, not yet. But they'll be back for us."

"How do you know?"

"We're still alive."

"My God, Nick, I'll cancel the article."

"Don't you dare—you can't. First of all, that's the only thing that'll keep you alive."

He pulled away from her and lay on his back, facing the grate.

"Do you think the others are okay? Sarah and Clutch?"

"I don't know." He rolled back to her. "No matter what happens, you will not pull the article, or phone anyone to tell them you made it all up. No matter what happens, no matter what you hear."

"What will I hear? What are you saying?" she asked as the metal grate lifted with an agonizing screech of old rusted metal, and arms reached down to grab for Nick.

"No matter what you hear," he repeated softly. "It won't be as bad as you think."

She reached for him, attempted to keep him there with her, but the person pulling him was stronger. In seconds, she was alone; the grate slammed down and she twined her fingers through the squares in an attempt to pull herself as close as possible, to see and hear what was happening.

She heard the sounds of punches, Nick's rough groan and the thud of a body hitting the floor, and fought the urge to scream.

Instead, she pushed at the rough metal grate as if she could move it through force.

Dammit, he'd be peeing blood for a week, thanks to the blow across his back that took him to his knees.

Nick would have fought back if Kaylee wasn't in such

close proximity—but the two men had guns and he couldn't take a chance.

"What do you want from me? I don't know shit." Nick roughly brushed some blood away from his lip with the back of his hand before spitting more on the ground.

"You know Clutch. You know Kaylee Smith. And you know about GOST." That voice wasn't one of the men who'd roughed him up. No, it was a different man, one with cold, hard features.

"And who the fuck are you?" Nick demanded, was surprised when he got an answer.

"I'm John Caspar. I'm sure Clutch has spoken of me."

"And I'm still part of the military, asshole. Active duty. Even you don't have the kind of power it takes to make me disappear."

"Oh, I have the power all right." Caspar raised the gun to Nick's head, placed the barrel against the side of his skull.

"If you think dying scares me, you picked the wrong man."

"So brave—like a good military man. Too bad you suffered a tragic death in Africa. Happens all the time—the country demands a lot, and this time you couldn't meet her demands."

"So do it." He jerked at his chains as if trying to get at Caspar and failing—but now he knew exactly what kind of hold they had on him, and what kind of reach he had.

"First things first: you need to convince Kaylee to cancel the article."

"Too late—her boss is running it."

"Not if he knows her life is on the line." Caspar called out, "Kaylee, Nick has something to tell you."

"Kaylee, listen to me very carefully and do exactly what I say. Make sure that fucking article gets run in the morning edition, do you hear me—"

Caspar used the butt of his gun against the side of Nick's head, shoved him back to the ground.

"I'd rethink what Nick says, Miss Smith, because if you don't, you're never going to see him again."

"She's smart enough to know you'll kill her once she makes the call," Nick spat.

"Right now, neither of you are being very smart." Caspar motioned to the two men to take Nick away. "I'll take good care of Kaylee Smith."

Nick struggled against them, even threw one of them off him, but by that time, Caspar had hauled Kaylee up out of the hole roughly by the arm.

She blanched when she saw Nick's face—he felt the blood drip from his nose and mouth and reluctantly let the men grab him again.

For Kaylee. But as soon as Caspar moved her out of here, these men were in for the fight of their lives. And they had no idea who they were up against, because Nick had fought for his life more times than he'd cared to count. This time, like all the others, he wasn't prepared to lose.

Jamie shot up in her seat at the touch on her shoulder.

Chris—it's just Chris.

"Are we close?" she asked as she stared out the window, wiped sleep from her eyes.

"We're here—it's down this road." He drove like he did everything, sure and calm and yet somehow fast as hell, and she could've sworn she'd heard him singing while she slept. Sure that's what woke her up with more of a comforted feeling than the normal one of horror she had whenever she dreamed about her parents.

But she pushed that out of her mind because over the bend she saw the warehouse. "Was I talking in my sleep?"

"Sounded more like a nightmare," he said as he stopped the car and brushed some hair from her face.

God, she hadn't had one in a long time—the last one had been the night she'd been shot and had woken up in the hospital, half high and alone and not knowing if Mike had made it out of surgery. But she got herself together quickly—she didn't need to fall apart any more than she'd already done.

She moved away from his touch. "Let's go."

He was out of the car and by her side before she was even halfway out of the seat, his weapon drawn.

It made her stop and look around. "It's quiet."

"Too fucking quiet," Chris muttered, his body tensed like a bow.

She tried to do the same, hated that she found her hand shaking when she pulled her own gun.

His palm covered her hand that held the weapon for just a second, warm and reassuring. "It's personal, but you don't want to fuck up your shot."

She wanted to laugh at that, took it as a good sign that once he removed his hand, hers was steady.

"Something's really wrong." Chris paused, closed his eyes. When he opened them, she swore the colors were more intense than they'd been.

She grabbed his arm. "Whatever happens, don't let

Sophie stay here. If something happens to me, you take her back with you. Will you do that? No matter what?"

He didn't answer her, just stared for a second before turning his attention back to the warehouse.

When they heard shots fired inside, both of them took off toward the building at a dead run.

C
lutch woke and recognized the steel walls of a warehouse room instantly. Fucking sleeping gas grenade got him when he wasn't paying attention. His own trick used against him.

"Clutch? You're awake—Clutch, wake up!" Sarah's voice carried to him. He turned to his side and saw her, all trussed up against the far wall, a gun pressed to her temple by John Caspar, who cocked a finger at him like a disapproving schoolteacher while Clutch fought the urge to bite that finger off.

"You're getting complacent in your old age, Clutch—a couple of years ago you would've seen the trap I set for you a mile away. Or maybe it's just love that's got you soft."

"You bastard." Sarah tried to lunge for him and got a swift jab in the ribs for her efforts.

Clutch stood, his body still unsteady from the sleeping gas. "You leave her alone. She's got nothing to do with this."

"She's got everything to do with this."

"Where are the others?" Clutch asked.

"By now, they're probably dead. That's if they're lucky. If not, they're bleeding out someplace," Caspar told him.

"Why the hell would you kill them?"

"I was ordered to. GOST is officially over."

"Then why not let us walk away?"

Caspar laughed. "You're too much of a liability."

"It doesn't matter what you do to us," Sarah said. "The story's already been sent. You're too late."

"The only ones it's too late for are you two."

Clutch wanted him to be wrong, even got his hopes up when he heard movement behind the door. But two men he'd never seen before emerged. No doubt ex-military—*ex* in every sense of the word. Washouts, just like Caspar himself was rumored to be, from what little information Clutch had been able to collect on the man who'd ruined his life.

Rumors aside, Clutch had seen the type too many times not to recognize it immediately, had known it from the second he'd met with John Caspar all those years ago. That feeling had grown stronger when they'd met again a few months before this, when Caspar promised him that Sarah would be safe if Clutch went back into GOST willingly.

Yes, there was weakness in Caspar, and for the first time, Clutch felt his edge come back.

It was short-lived, as the two men dragged Kaylee with them. Immediately, one put a gun to her head and a knife to her throat while the other walked over and took Caspar's place, holding a gun to Sarah's head.

Caspar moved toward Clutch, motioned him to turn around to face both women at once. Clutch seethed, but did as Caspar ordered, letting the man get close until he could feel the gun pressed between his own shoulder blades.

"What a choice—if you don't kill the woman who tried to save you, we'll have to kill the woman you love."

Clutch felt calmer than he had in years, more in control,

even as his Ranger and Delta Force training kicked in. Being a merc had been different—required slightly different skills. But this . . . this he could do. "You won't let me go after I do that."

"Are you willing to take that chance? Suppose I leave you alive to mourn Sarah. Or suppose I kill you and keep Sarah for myself." Caspar whispered now, so only he and Clutch could hear. "I could've had her, so many times. She was lonely. Lost. She'd have been willing."

Clutch jerked but the barrel of the gun kept him from doing much. "Why did you kill the others and leave me alive?"

"You were always the strongest, the one I counted on the most."

Clutch snorted. "Just let me go, John. Once the article's printed—"

"It won't get printed. GOST might be ending, but its existence will never be brought to light, I can promise you that. We'll do whatever is necessary to stop it." Caspar's hand was steady as he pressed his Sig into Clutch's back, right between the shoulders, but angled so the bullets would go straight through flesh to his heart.

"You can't hurt my boss, my friends at the paper." Kaylee struggled in her bonds as she stared at Clutch and past him to Caspar.

"Haven't you figured it out already, Kaylee? I can do anything I want." Caspar laughed, a hollow sound without a shred of humor. "I'm in control here. I'm the one pulling the strings. You got yourself involved in something you shouldn't have."

"You took Aaron—you forced him into this group and

you used me against him, so yes, I'm involved the way I should be." She tried to jerk away from the man who held her but couldn't, yet didn't seem afraid of the knife or the gun. No, she was running on pure anger. "And if I find out that you've hurt Nick—"

"What will you do, Kaylee?" Caspar sneered. "Write about it? That's just words, little girl. No one's going to believe you. Or maybe they just won't care about a bunch of washed-up soldiers."

"Who are you?" she demanded as the man who'd held her tethered her to a chair. He used heavy tape around her wrists. "Are you one of them? Are you in Witness Protection too?"

Caspar didn't answer her, but Clutch felt the man hesitate, just for a second.

"I've made my decision," Clutch told him. He pressed his hands together and then fisted them, cracking his knuckles. And as he advanced and closed his fingers around her throat, Kaylee looked up at him in horror.

This wasn't happening.

Kaylee kept waiting for Nick to crash through the door, the window, anywhere to stop it even as Clutch's hands pressed her windpipe. Caspar was still behind him with a gun to his back.

Clutch meant to kill her, and yet, she couldn't believe it. Wouldn't. Looking up into his practically colorless eyes, she didn't see anything but kindness.

Don't stop now, he mouthed even as he pressed, just

enough to make her breath sound harsh—enough to make Caspar believe he'd started the job. *Witness Protection.*

Kaylee stayed as still as she could while trying desperately to free her wrists from the heavy tape. But at Clutch's words, she knew exactly what she needed to do. "You're not safe either, John Caspar. Aka James Roy. Born Alfred J. Kingston. Put into Witness Protection in 1992 after your father testified against a high-ranking member of an underground crime syndicate. You grew up as scared as the rest of the members of GOST. You were one of them until the government made you the monster you are now. How does it feel to turn against your own kind?"

Caspar froze, stared at Kaylee as Clutch's hands eased from her throat.

"I hope you don't mind, but that information's in the article too," she continued, grateful that Jamie had texted her the details on Caspar in time for Kaylee to text her boss. They would make a welcome addition to the article. "I refused to use Clutch's real name—or any of the other's—but yours seemed fair game. From what I heard, that particular crime family would be interested in knowing that you've still got all the evidence against them, and that you'd be happy to testify."

Two shots rang out in quick succession. Seconds later, she heard a loud thump from behind her, felt the weight of the man who'd tied her up initially as he fell against her. She had no way to balance herself and the chair shifted and tipped along with the man's body.

She saw stars as her head hit the ground, but remained mercifully conscious—or maybe she'd have rather not watched what was about to unfold.

The second shot had hit the man who'd been standing near Sarah—he lay half on top of the prone woman, her hands and feet tied. But Sarah kicked her way out from under him as both she and Kaylee tried to see who'd fired the shots.

"It's all falling apart, John. I'm not sure why you thought it could last this long anyway." A woman's voice—softness wrapped with a steel edge—floated across the room from a doorway in the far eastern corner.

Her back was straight and she wore her hair in a long braid that hung in a dark strip over one shoulder. She held a rifle steadily in her hands as she moved slowly but unrelentingly toward John Caspar.

"You're supposed to be dead," Caspar told her, his voice tinged with disbelief.

"I know. You did your best to make sure of that—none of the others survived the crash. None except for me." She held the gun on him. "Did you think you could train us and not expect us to turn on our owners? Especially when they turn on us?"

"You have no idea what you're up against, PJ. None of you ever did. Do you really think letting the world know about GOST will free you?"

"I'll never be free anyway," the woman answered cryptically.

Clutch still stood ramrod straight. The entire room seemed to be stuck in some kind of hazy time warp, or maybe it was just Kaylee—pain and fear and adrenaline mixing together to keep her completely off balance.

But now Caspar seemed that way too—he still held the gun on Clutch, but was so mesmerized by the woman that he didn't hear Nick come up behind him and put his hands around his throat.

The next moments were like lightning—full-on technicolor—and Kaylee could barely hear over the yelling.

Caspar bucked against Nick's hold—it wasn't enough to shake him off but all three men still went down to the ground in the struggle.

She heard one shot, and then another, and could only watch helplessly as the men rolled on the ground.

Nick heard the shots. He knew he was risking Clutch being wounded when he'd grabbed Caspar, but he'd yanked at the man hard enough that he'd hoped Caspar would lose his grip entirely.

No such luck, but he still wasn't letting go. He put enough pressure against the man's windpipe, heard the last desperate gasps for air even as Clutch managed to crawl out from underneath them on his back, blood from his shoulder smearing across the floor.

Nick wasn't sure if he wanted John Caspar dead—if the man was alive, he could talk, could maybe help to free Clutch more quickly than Kaylee's article. Kaylee, who was down on the floor, trying desperately to free herself from the chair she was tied to—it had been all he could do not to run to her when she'd fallen, but he'd remained in place, waiting for the right time to take down Caspar.

And now, even as he tried to decide the man's fate, Clutch was pulling at him. "He's mine," he said, teeth bared as he stared at Caspar. When Nick let go, Clutch's hands replaced his on the man's neck.

"Thanks for teaching me how to do this so efficiently," Clutch told Caspar. "I knew it would come in handy one of these days."

Nick was close enough to hear the snap as Clutch broke the other man's neck. Caspar's gun fell from his hand to the floor with a clatter—Clutch remained with his hands on Caspar's neck, until Nick gently pulled him away.

"You're hurt, man. Come on, it's over. He's gone," Nick told him. He eased Clutch to a sitting position, unable to do anything but help the wounded man even as he saw the woman with the dark hair move to untie Sarah and then Kaylee.

"It's not over, not yet," Clutch croaked. He was pale as shit, and Nick knew he spoke the truth. It would be days—maybe longer—before the impact of both Caspar's death and the article were truly known.

"It's better than it was," Nick assured him. "Lay on your side—I've got to stop this bleeding."

Clutch nodded, shifted his body so Nick could rip off what was left of his shredded, bloodied shirt and saw the two entrance holes through his upper shoulder.

"Kaylee, are you all right?" Nick asked as he continued to check Clutch.

"I'm fine," she told him as Sarah and the dark-haired woman helped her to sit up against the wall. "Help Clutch, please."

"Someone's coming," Clutch said, attempted to draw his weapon, until they heard someone calling Nick's name.

"It's my brother. Chris, we're okay!" he called out the opened door, heard the clatter of footsteps and then his brother was in the room, followed by a woman Nick assumed was the FBI agent.

Within seconds, Nick and Clutch were surrounded by Chris and Sarah and Jamie.

"I've got Clutch," Chris said. "You're okay?"

"Fine. Just fine." He rubbed his bloody hands on his pants.

He stood and went over to where Kaylee sat, in the corner, propped against the wall. She'd taken a good hit to her head when she'd fallen, but she managed a small smile even as he dropped to his knees in front of her. "Kaylee" was all he could manage for a second while his hands traveled over her face then to the egg-sized lump at her temple.

"I'm okay, really." She reached up to take his hands in hers.

And still, Nick's protective instincts were in overdrive. "Did he hurt you when he took you away? Did he touch you? Tell me."

"No, he didn't. I'm just shaken. But he hurt you—I heard it, saw it." Her voice broke for a second and then she swallowed, tried to remain stoic.

He didn't answer her—not with words. Instead, he simply gathered her into his arms for a few moments, holding her tight against him.

When he pulled back, her eyes were wet. "How is Clutch? There's so much blood..."

"He'll be okay." He turned to see Chris working on him. "I should go help."

"Go." Kaylee gave him a gentle push. "We didn't come this far to have GOST win."

————

Kaylee finally pulled herself up off the floor after Nick left her side to help Chris put Clutch up on a table. Jamie was going back and forth with clean towels and warm water, while Sarah remained at Clutch's side. Kaylee could clearly see the pain and worry etched on her face.

She approached the table cautiously. There was still so much blood, even as Chris put pressure on Clutch's back with a firm hand and a towel that had once been white but was now soaked with red.

"I can get the bullets out, but you need to go to a hospital," Chris was telling Clutch. "I don't have enough IV antibiotics to cover you. You'll need a full round. You'll need surgery to make sure I've gotten all the shrapnel out. You'll also need a transfusion."

"Do what you can here," Clutch told him weakly. "I'm not going to a hospital. No fucking way."

He began to cough, and she caught the look between Nick and Chris that told her things weren't good.

"I'm not losing you to an infection," Sarah told Clutch as Chris pulled out an instrument from his bag and told Clutch to hold on to something.

Clutch took Sarah's hand, the pain he was in more than evident from the way he howled as Chris worked behind him. Nick was bracing Clutch with his own body, stopping him from rolling onto his back.

"One more, man," Chris told Clutch, who nodded and held his breath. Kaylee realized she was holding hers as well. Another howl of pain that brought tears to Clutch's eyes, made him slump forward, and then it was over. Nick was helping Chris stitch up the wounds, giving Clutch whatever medicine Chris had in his bag, while Sarah spoke softly in Clutch's ear.

"We can't, Sarah—can't risk it. Suppose..." Clutch trailed off.

Suppose the article doesn't help anything. Suppose there were more men no one knew about, waiting behind the scenes to finish GOST off, once and for all.

Suppose this was all for nothing.

And Kaylee was helpless again, hated that feeling more than anything else in the world. But she suddenly knew she could do something while they waited to see the fallout from the article.

Once Clutch and Sarah broke apart, Kaylee approached the man with the nearly colorless eyes and reached for his hand. "Thank you," she said softly.

"I'm the one who needs to thank you."

"You helped Aaron—you were there for him. Maybe the only one who was, and that means so much to me, to know he wasn't alone. You let me prove that he was a good man, that he served his country well. His name will be cleared."

She reached into her pocket and pulled out the bankbook and the paper that held the codes for the new account. She opened it to the last page, the one with the total.

Clutch merely stared at it. "I meant it when I said I didn't bring you here to take your money. That was Aaron's—and now it's yours."

"No. It should go someplace where it can do some good. You deserve it. And I hope this helps give you a new start—for you and for Sarah."

"I can't—"

"Please, Clutch. Aaron would want it this way. I don't need it—I'm okay. And with this, you will be too."

Chris moved away from Clutch as Kaylee hugged him. "Go to the hospital. Please. I couldn't bear if anything happened to you when you've come this far."

She pulled back, to find Sarah smiling at her.

"I'll go," Clutch said, handed the bankbook to Sarah, who simply mouthed, *thank you*.

Jamie had watched Chris do a quick and dirty removal of the bullets from Clutch's shoulder, all the while chomping at the bit to ask about Sophie.

Kaylee touched her shoulder. "If you hadn't gotten me that information about Caspar, I don't know what would've happened," the reporter told her. "And then that woman came in . . ."

Sophie. "What woman? Where is she?"

Kaylee looked around the gray-walled room. "She had dark hair—she distracted Caspar. She was one of the GOSTs."

"She went to check for bombs," Sarah called over to the women. "She's probably on the upper floors."

Sarah was still talking even as Jamie took off through the warehouse, yelling Sophie's name.

She took the rickety metal steps two at a time up to the top floor. Her voice echoed through the broad halls, and she stopped for a second and just listened. She heard rattling coming from a room on the right, entered with her gun drawn, to find Sophie on her knees checking a floor vent.

Her sister turned and glanced up as Jamie entered—Sophie looked different, but she always managed to look so. Constantly changing, the ultimate chameleon, and Jamie was never sure if that was because of necessity or if Sophie would've been like that if they'd had a normal childhood.

Then again, Jamie had no real idea what normal was anymore. "It's really you. Thank God—I thought we were too late. I'm sorry I couldn't get here sooner."

Sophie stood, brushed her hands off. Then she moved closer, touched Jamie's shoulder, stroked her hair the way she always had when Jamie was younger and upset. "It's okay. We would have found a way on our own."

"God, that's so like you—I broke my ass, risked everything to help you, and that's all I get?"

"Okay, so you saved me. Does that finally make us even?"

"I don't want even. I just want my sister."

Sophie relented, barely, by changing the subject. She was good at that, using distraction when things got too close to her, when emotions threatened to break through the surface—hers or anyone else's. "This wasn't my choice. I'm sorry I wasn't around to help you through your rehab, or to grieve Mike."

"I knew you were—in your own way." Jamie grabbed her sister's hand. "Come on, we'll take you back. We'll talk to people at the FBI, figure things out from there." Kevin would help—their foster father would have the pull to put Sophie's name back into the U.S. marshals' system.

Sophie shook her head. "There's nothing to figure out. I'm not coming with you."

Jamie didn't know whether to laugh or cry—the laugh came first and then the sob choked her throat. "So, what, you're just going to leave? Disappear with Clutch and Sarah?"

Her sister looked at her calmly. Sophie could've been so many things—everyone who met her wanted to be her friend, wanted to be like her. Jamie included. Sophie had one of those faces, one of those bodies. Her expression was cool and haughty, and people always wanted to be like her.

"Yes. I'm going with them for now—they'll need some help, some cover. And you know as well as I do that it's not safe for me."

"Not yet. But the article Kaylee wrote about GOST will run—I can make sure your name gets back in Witness Protection, with Kevin's help. You'll be watched by U.S. marshals again. You're almost free—you can come home." Jamie heard the pleading in her voice and hated it. "Please, Soph, after all we've been through—"

"Don't bring up Mom and Dad. Not now."

"I'm not the one who's letting it get in the way."

Sophie nodded, as if Jamie was right. "Clutch understands me. He's been through Witness Protection too."

"So have I, in case you've forgotten." Jamie heard the anger in her voice and tried to quell it. "I want to be there for you, to help you, but you never let me."

"It's not the same for you. Maybe because you were so young...because you didn't see it happen. I don't know how, but you adjusted."

Jamie didn't know what to say to that.

"Stop thinking about it—please, Jamie; I can see the whole thing in your eyes," Sophie implored her and Jamie wondered what that must've been like, to see the man who'd murdered their parents. To see him coming after her, until he'd been startled by the sirens and had run off, into the night.

To have him get captured, only to escape after Sophie testified against him.

Sophie had been a fourteen-year-old, very vulnerable witness, and yet, Jamie could still see Sophie's face before she took the stand. So strong, even then.

"PJ, we have to leave now—we're taking Clutch to the hospital," Sarah's voice came up the stairs.

"I'll be right there," her sister answered. Jamie noted that a packed bag lay in the corner of this nondescript room, nearly as bare as all the others.

But that wasn't what made her blood turn cold. " 'PJ'? You're calling yourself PJ?" she breathed. Back in Minnesota, Jamie had been Ana Caldwell and Sophie had been Patricia Jane, known to everyone as PJ.

Sophie gave her a quick hug. "That's who I am, Jamie. Always was."

Sarah and Kaylee were still talking—Nick left them by the car they'd loaded Clutch into the back of and headed to talk to Chris.

"Clutch is definitely going to the hospital?" his brother asked.

"Yeah, he finally agreed—PJ's going with them." Nick stuck his hands in his pockets. "I hope this is really over."

"You and me both. By the way, you look like hell."

"Yeah, thanks."

"Come on, let's get you cleaned up."

Normally, Nick hated letting anyone fuss over him—he and Jake were very alike in that manner—but Chris pretty much insisted and so Nick sat in the back of the car and let Chris clean his face and apply Steri-Strips to his lip and eyebrow.

"Does anything hurt?" Chris asked.

"No."

"The day you say yes is the day I'll worry." Chris stepped away. "You still look like hell."

"Fuck off."

Chris snorted.

"Hey, where's Jamie?" Nick asked.

"She's talking to PJ." Chris looked over his shoulder, but Jamie was actually standing in the mowed-down field by herself. A few feet away, Sarah and PJ packed their bags into the car and drove off.

Nick and Chris watched until the car completely disappeared and they couldn't hear the rough motor cutting through the otherwise almost eerie quiet.

"Come on, let's get the hell out of here," Nick said finally.

Chris stared at him, was rubbing his fingertips together. "What did you do, Nick?"

"Nothing." And really, that was the truth. He wasn't about to spill what Kaylee had found out about his past here, in the middle of the jungle.

His brother stared at him—just stared. Nick wouldn't be as lucky when Jake got ahold of him, and he reveled in Chris's quiet disapproval as it strummed through him.

"There's a hotel close to the airport. We should be able

to catch a flight out later tonight or tomorrow, unless we can grab a ride back with Jamie." Chris glanced at the tall blond woman who stood watching the empty space the car had just passed through. "I don't know how that's going to play out."

Kaylee walked up next to Nick, was looking toward Jamie. "She looks upset."

"Shattered is more like it," Chris muttered. "I'll go talk to her."

As his brother moved off, Nick turned to Kaylee, took this quiet time to check her over again, to make sure she was really all right. "You're sure those bastards didn't do anything to you? You can tell me."

"No. I knew I would be okay, and I am." Still, she accepted his touch, fell into his arms, and then pulled away. "Sorry."

"Come here," he growled, pulled her back against him. Didn't matter that his body ached—the pain helped—and when he pressed her to him, he liked *feeling*.

She pulled slightly away a few seconds later. "Roger called—the article ran. Now we just need to hope it gets picked up by some major affiliates and other media outlets."

"No matter what happens, you did good, K. Darcy. Never forget that."

She pressed her cheek against his chest. "I don't plan on forgetting anything about what happened here."

CHAPTER
22

Jamie had brushed off Chris's concern at the warehouse, hadn't said a word during the ride from the warehouse to a hotel close to the Kisangani Airport. Instead, she chose to seat herself all the way in the rear of the car by herself, staring out the back window, as if Sophie might come bursting from the shadows.

Chris drove, Nick next to him, and Kaylee dozed on and off in the middle seat.

It had been one of the longest years of her life. Everything had changed. Things wouldn't stop changing, and there was nothing she could do about it.

God, she was tired.

"Hey, we're here." Chris had opened the door and was

staring at her. She hadn't even realized the car had stopped moving, that Nick and Kaylee had already gotten out.

"Nick and Kaylee went inside to grab a room for a couple of hours before their flight tonight. I'm guessing your plane is ready to take you back whenever you need to go. I can take you to the airport if you need me to."

She didn't want to need him for anything. "I'm going to wait here in Africa for a few days. I told Sophie where I'd be, gave her my number. I can get myself to my hotel."

"I'll drive you there. I'll wait with you."

"No thanks." She rummaged in her bags, tying them up and focusing anyplace but at him, until he took her chin into his palm and forced the issue. She fought the urge to jerk away. "Don't do this—not now."

"Jamie, please, don't shut me out."

She grabbed his wrist and pulled his hand off her. "There's nothing between us, Chris."

"You can't mean that. I don't want you to mean that. Look, I know you're upset about PJ—"

"Sophie."

"She asked to be called PJ. That's what I'm calling her."

"You don't know her. You don't know what she wants."

"Obviously, neither do you."

"I didn't mean to tell you all of it. I don't want you to know any of it—my background or the way I grew up. And I can't take it back and I'm so tired of living with regrets."

A fleeting look of pain crossed his face and she wanted to tell him that she didn't regret her time with him, that that's not what she meant. But she didn't. Because maybe if she hurt him enough, he'd forget about her.

"You didn't tell me all that damned much about how you grew up, Jamie. I can only imagine—"

"No, you can't even begin to imagine. And you let her go. I asked you not to, to stop her somehow." Irrational and unfair—she knew that accusing him was both those things.

"I don't make promises I know I can't keep. She's a grown woman. She wasn't being kidnapped—she had a weapon. She made her own choice."

"Well, fuck her and fuck you—fuck you both for making choices."

"You've got to let her come back on her own accord."

"I'm going to lose my job. I'm going to lose everything. It's easy for you to be reasonable, you've gotten your brother back. I've got nothing."

His jaw clenched. "Your sister is alive. And you've got me. I'm standing right here in front of you."

"It shouldn't have happened. This—" she motioned between them "—shouldn't have happened. I wasn't ready."

She was playing with the ring she still wore on the third finger of her right hand. She'd tried to tell herself that it was an amulet, her way of keeping Mike close and protecting her.

But he'd been gone for too long and she'd never believed in lucky charms anyway. She held up her hand while she spoke. "Mike was my partner. Five years together—on the job. And off."

She watched his eyes as he processed that information. In the sunlight, their colors should've evened out a bit, but instead, it just made the differences more noticeable.

"No one knew. No one knows a lot of things about me," she continued.

"You want to keep it that way, don't you?"

She wanted to tell him no, to throw caution to the wind, to free herself the way Sophie was attempting to do. But she knew it wouldn't work, not now. "I do want to keep it that way. I don't think we're right for each other. If circumstances hadn't pushed us together—"

"But they did. You can't change that." He reached out to her, and she let him take her hand and pull her body to his as they stood on the dirt road outside the hotel.

And then he kissed her, a long, deep kiss that made her heart sing, kissed her for what seemed like forever, so when he pulled back her lips felt swollen and bruised.

"I think you think too much," he murmured against her ear. "I think you like being out of control more than you admit. I think you need a lot of fucking crazy in your life right now, and fast."

And then he took a step back and stuffed his hands into his pockets. "I can handle a hell of a lot of things. But I can't compete with ghosts, Jamie. Can't and won't." He pulled one hand out of his pocket briefly to toss her the keys to the Land Rover.

She almost called out his name. But he was walking toward the hotel and away from her without looking back.

They had about four hours before they had to be at the airport, and so Kaylee and Nick checked into a hotel to rest and clean up.

Chris was with Jamie—what was happening there was anyone's guess, but Jamie hadn't looked happy during the ride from the warehouse to Kisangani.

While Nick checked his messages and made some phone calls regarding their flight home, Kaylee stripped and headed for the bathroom.

She showered the dirt of the last few days off her, watched the red dust of her past run down the drain. So much had happened, too much in too short of a space for her to fully process it all, but they were safe. Finally. Nick had promised that, and he hadn't lied to her yet. No, he'd even seemed to find a way to forgive her for what she'd found out.

They could forget the past.

But even as she told herself that, she knew it wasn't true . . . and she didn't want it to be. History wasn't always a bad thing—the history she and Nick had created had brought them closer. The future could only bring them closer still.

Nick watched Kaylee through the steam-misted glass door, her long, lean form outlined in a way that made him ache, and he wished he had the right words to say when the door opened and she came out holding a towel to her that did nothing to cover her.

He'd always believed in action over words—had never really seen that action from his family, from Deidre. He'd had the words, sure—in cards and letters and toys strewn everywhere so the doctors and nurses and therapists could see them. Once he'd been old enough to realize that the cards had been purchased, written and sent by personal assistants rather than his own mother, he'd begun to understand that people who said *I love you* could easily be full of shit.

The Winfields, legendary for their inability to remain faithful to any one person, were no strangers to affairs. As much as Nick tried to deny that he was anything like them, he knew that the Winfield blood ran deep, and his inability to commit could easily stem from not wanting to cheat on someone. No, it was much easier to not get involved.

Maggie and Kenny told him they loved him, and their actions matched the words. Same with Jake and Chris. Nick understood love on the deep, familial level. Sharing it with someone where sex was involved seemed more intimidating.

"You don't need the towel," he told her and she smiled, let it fall to the ground.

Her hair was wet and tied in a loose knot at the nape of her neck. Impulsively, he reached around and took the band out so the long auburn mane tumbled over her shoulders and down her back. He wanted her. Maybe, once again, for tonight that would be enough.

His hands framed both sides of her face, his tongue danced with hers, until she found herself clutching at him frantically. God, she was a walking aphrodisiac—one look, one kiss and he was ready to give up the farm and let her in more deeply.

His only comfort was that she seemed as out of control as he was.

He moved in to take a nipple into his mouth. She gasped, threaded her fingers through his hair and let herself melt into him.

Sex was far less complicated than trust. Right now, that was all he could promise.

He'd never taken the time to learn any one woman's

body so intimately and that luxury was something he enjoyed. Being able to know just the right place to make her come was one thing—knowing several that would make her alternately smile and come and moan his name was another entirely, and called to his most primal instincts.

He pulled her against him and kissed her as if it was his last breath, kissed her and then took her to the bed.

"You're so handsome," she told him as she brushed his hair off his face.

He felt his face flush—she noted it too and looked surprised. "I know you've heard that before."

"Yeah. A lot. Never means anything."

"You don't think people mean it?"

He shrugged. "I don't think it matters. It's bullshit. Skin deep."

"Is that why you don't..." She paused, sucked her bottom lip in that goddamned sexy way that got him right between his legs. "I mean, when we're together, you never..."

He'd known she'd ask eventually. "What? Whisper sweet things while I'm fucking you?"

She wasn't shocked by the words. Maybe she'd gotten used to his honesty, which he'd been told could be crushing at times.

"Yes. You never tell me I'm beautiful, or that you like my body. All things other men have said to me in the past."

He rolled over, trapping her beneath him, a thigh holding her legs apart. His erection pressing her belly. "Do you miss it?"

"No, I don't miss it," she whispered. "I'd miss you, though. Miss your body on mine."

He'd miss it too. How he'd gotten so tangled up in such

a short time was something he couldn't figure out. But with her legs scissored around his waist, her fingers digging into his shoulders, giving the right amount of pressure that made his back arch and mouth open in a guttural groan, there was nothing to miss. And if they could stay in this moment, things would be damned perfect.

"You don't have to say anything. You show me how you feel with every touch," she murmured in his ear before her orgasm took away her words.

Yes, this woman had captured a part of him he'd never anticipated. What he would do about it was something else entirely, and he couldn't bear to think about it now.

I like it here, with you, like this," Kaylee whispered a little while later from the pillow next to him. "I even like this country."

He shifted, noting how she waited for him to hold her, how she kept her hands from touching his body when they weren't having sex. He took her hand in his, threaded his fingers through hers and curled her against him. And that was all right. "After everything's that happened, you like it here in Africa?"

"I've never really belonged anywhere. I've always felt in between, never finding where I fit." Her voice drifted up through the darkness, a confessional lying naked in his arms.

"Seems like you created a pretty fit for yourself. You've got a career."

"Yes, I've got a career. That's about it."

"What else do you want?"

"You're kidding, right?" She shifted, leaned up on one

elbow to look down at him. The sheet that had been draped over her breasts fell, exposing the creamy, still sex-flushed skin, the taut light pink nipples. He hardened from watching them and wished they were done talking.

"I've let my job take over my life. I've pushed people away—kept them at arm's length because it was easier," she started. "I had boyfriends, but I never felt right with them. I used my career to pretend that I had everything I needed. A tribute to the mom who never wanted me."

He shook his head, like he was trying to tell her that she was wrong. "But you love your job."

"I love it, yes, but I'm tired of loving it because it's all I have. I want it, yes, but I want so much more."

"Family."

"Yes."

He stared at the ceiling. "Suppose that doesn't make things all better?"

"Fuck you." She shoved the sheet aside and he reached out to stop her from leaving the bed.

"Kaylee . . ."

"No, you don't get to tell me that what I've wanted won't fulfill me. You don't even know what you want."

"I know what I want. I also know what I can't have."

"What aren't you telling me?"

He wanted to tell her that this had all been too dangerous for her. That she never should've opened the safe-deposit box. Never should've gotten involved with another military man to begin with, never mind a Spec Ops one.

Instead, he simply told her, "I'm sorry."

"I'll ask you the questions you asked me the other night—what are you sorry for, Nick? Sorry you met me?

Sorry we're stuck here together? Because if that's what you're really trying to say, then have the balls to say it."

"I'm not sorry." His voice was hoarse. "But when we get back home, everything's going to change."

"Then let's not go home—not yet. Please. Can we just stay here, pretend there's nothing waiting for us?"

He shook his head slowly. "I wish we could. But it's all there—especially the press. People are going to have questions for you."

"I'm the press, not the news," she protested.

"If your article does what it's supposed to do, you're going to be both for a while. And my traveling with you isn't the smartest thing," he pointed out. "I can't be involved in this."

She hadn't thought about that. Correction, hadn't wanted to think about it. But yes, having Nick photographed coming off the plane with her in Virginia wouldn't do his career any good. "One more night."

"It's not going to change anything." He let go of her arm and lay on his back. "How many calls do you get about Cutter?"

"At least two a week," she admitted.

"And it's not going to stop," he muttered.

"No, I can't imagine it would."

"And isn't your paper—your public—going to wonder why you stopped writing about the Winfields?"

"Maybe. Probably. It doesn't matter."

"You're not going to stop writing—you're too good. Look at what you did for Clutch."

"We don't know yet what I've done for him. We don't know anything." She heard the frustration in her voice.

"What good did I do for you, if after this is all said and done, I can't be with you?"

Nick didn't answer her and she realized that staying in Africa might only prolong the inevitable. All her years of training, her ability to question, to wear down, to search and dig and find every bit of the truth, to make things better went out the window as defeat settled over her for the moment.

Clutch had stayed in the hospital a grand total of five hours. After a round of IV antibiotics, he'd insisted on pills and a shot and he'd gotten off the table.

No one would stop him—there was really no one who could, except for Sarah, and she understood his reluctance to remain strapped to anything, especially now. She'd followed behind him while he made his grand, bellowing exit and then half collapsed onto her for the remainder of the walk to the car.

She didn't say a word about that, said nothing when he lay in the backseat biting back groans as she drove them to a hotel. Instead, she dragged him out of the car and into the room, shoved him on the bed.

He slept for hours, only dimly aware of her hands with the cool washcloths for his forehead or rousing him to take medicine or drink something or to change his bandage. At one point, he heard himself asking her for his gun and her sharp reply of *No way*.

But when he finally stirred and opened his eyes for longer than five seconds, she sat next to him and waited. He knew what he wanted to ask her, but the words were a long time coming.

"A U.S. marshal left you a message on your phone, asked you to get in touch with him. He wants to know what you need," she said finally. "After that phone call, that's when PJ left."

It made sense—PJ's stepfather was a marshal. Now that PJ's sister was involved, it probably set the wheels in motion. "I've got everything I need right here." He heard the unnecessary gruffness in his voice as he rubbed a hand along her thigh. "Listen, there are still people who could find me—you know that, right?"

"I think we can take care of ourselves. I think it's time. There's an old house along the Côte d'Ivoire. Lots of rooms upstairs. It needs work . . . but I think it would be perfect," she told him.

"You bought it."

"Maybe."

Stubborn. She was still stubborn—enough to wait for him, to refuse to think he'd leave her forever.

Stubborn enough to believe that one day they'd begin rebuilding themselves together. "I know that must've been hard for you. You'd always said you didn't want a home, didn't want to be in one place."

"I was wrong," she told him. "We'll be all right, Bobby."

Bobby. The word wrapped him in a blanket of comfort, brought back memories, which was short-lived because she was off the bed and rifling his bag.

"What are you looking for?"

She lifted her head, a small frown creasing her forehead. "Did you keep that picture? The one of you in the Hawaiian shirt. You didn't destroy it, did you? Please tell me you didn't."

"I didn't. I know how much you like that picture."

"Not like. Love. Pictures are a way of making things permanent," she said. "Even when my relatives died, I was still able to page through the old albums and see them, before I lost the albums."

"Well, then, go ahead. Make it permanent," he told her. She stood uncertainly, watched him as he stripped the sheets off his body, naked except for the bandages. He wanted to be reborn, and he wanted to do it through Sarah's eyes. "Please. Take some pictures."

He thought back to their early days together, when he'd nearly killed her for trying to take his picture. He'd never allowed her to, not during all the times they'd been together. She'd attempted to sneak a few shots in, sure, when she'd thought he hadn't been looking.

But now, this was the first invitation for her to do so.

Her eyes widened and her cheeks held that special glow they always got when she was truly happy. He hadn't seen that glow in a long time; it looked good on her. And within minutes, she had her cameras out of the bag and the whir of the shutters mingled with her laugher.

The flash bathed him in warm light. He stared straight into the lens, but he didn't smile.

"Some people would say you're lucky—that you get a fresh start."

He snorted. "Some people don't know shit. I don't know who I was, who I'm supposed to be."

"It's all right to be angry about it."

"I'm tired of being angry. I just want..."

"Tell me what you want, Bobby."

"I want my life back," he said softly. "I want my teenage years to have been normal. Proms. Football games."

"I spent most of mine taking everything for granted."

"That's the way it should be." He ran his hands through his short hair, decided he would grow it again, the way it had been when he'd first met Sarah.

She moved with the grace of someone who was comfortable with her body—like a sleek cat. And even with the tattoos that adorned her arm and her belly and other places that could only be seen when she was naked in his bed, she still managed to look ultimately feminine. Despite the cargo pants and heavy black boots, and the guns she often wore slung around her body.

The look was hot, a complete turn-on. Something he'd tried to rip from his mind's eye so the ache would go away.

Tonight, she wore only a soft shirt that was nearly sheer, one that came down to mid-thigh.

"I want to take you places. Want us to get dressed up, wash the dust out of our hair and go dancing," he said. "I can picture you, on the porch . . . your legs bare and tan. A smile on your face. And you're waiting for me to come pick you up for a date."

She turned on the radio—it wafted through the room, low and sweet. And she held out her hand to him. "I can't do much about the dust and the clothing," she said quietly. "But we can still dance. We can always dance."

The ferry moved slowly up the Congo River. Raindrops patterned the murky waters and the boat rocked in a steady motion.

PJ sat toward the back, facing what she'd left behind.

Most people got seasick if they didn't face the horizon on a moving boat—the opposite had always held true for her. She supposed it was from years of looking over her shoulder, an old habit she didn't plan on breaking.

She'd waited with Sarah until Clutch had gotten the thumbs-up from the doctors in the small hospital before she'd left. He and Sarah hadn't bothered to try to stop her—they both understood, maybe more than she herself even did.

They'd take her in if she needed that, but she didn't want to need. Not anymore. She barely wanted to feel.

She took a deep breath, shifted her bag from one shoulder to the other and tried not to think about Jamie and that sad, little-girl-lost look that had never faded from her sister's face or from PJ's memory.

"How far are you going?" The man who'd been standing next to her for most of the trip sucked on his own cigar and offered one to her.

She accepted, lit it and drew the bitter smoke into her lungs like it would cleanse her soul if she tugged deeply enough before she spoke. "Anywhere but home."

He nodded, looked at the rifle she wore by a diagonal strap across the front of her body. "You know how to use that?"

"You want to find out right here?"

He shook his head and laughed, tugged on the cigar. "I can find you work anyplace but home, sister."

For now, it would do. It would have to.

CHAPTER
23

Once their plane landed, Nick and Chris had hustled Kaylee away from the crowds lining the gates and toward the parking lot where Nick had parked his car days earlier. She sat in the front next to Nick, Chris in the back, humming along with his iPod as Nick drove her back to the big white house until they could figure out what to do next.

It had been nearly thirty-six hours since the article was published. She'd been listening to the radio since they got in the car, hoping to hear anything at all mentioned about the story, since they'd gotten through the airport too quickly for her to check the newsstands.

And finally, she pulled out her phone and called Roger

to let him know she was home. "I have to know," she told Nick, who nodded.

"When are you coming home?" Roger demanded when he picked up, forgoing the usual *Hello*.

"I'm here. What's up?"

"What's up is that your piece is generating major interest. We need a follow-up."

"Why?"

"Rumor is that the president wants to convene a cabinet to investigate matters concerning GOST. If that happens, there will be members of Congress who will want to interview you. They'll need to know how you came by your information—you need to be prepared."

"That's protected information, Roger."

Her boss's voice softened. "I know. But if you want to help those people, you might have to talk."

It was her turn to pause, and then, "Some of them didn't make it. Most of them."

"But some did, right?"

"Yes."

"Then you'll need to write this article," Roger said. "Look, Smith, we've managed to keep your anonymity for now. For how much longer is anyone's guess."

After that, K. Darcy and Kaylee Smith would meld into the same person. For better or for worse.

You saved lives. You did what Aaron would've wanted.

But if Nick wouldn't stay at her side, that victory would be meaningless.

She hung up and relayed to Nick what Roger told her. "I don't know what to do."

"You'll do the right thing. Nothing you can say can hurt

Clutch and the others more than they've been hurt already." He pulled the car into the garage and turned off the engine. "Come on—you'd better get to work."

Once inside, Chris told her and Nick he'd give them some time alone. "Dad and Jake will be here soon, though," he added and Kaylee wondered what that would be like, if they'd be angry with her for all that had happened.

There was no way she could start work now—she had to resolve things between herself and Nick first.

She waited until she heard Chris leave the house and then she turned to Nick. "Look, I've been thinking—the Winfield thing . . . I could go there, to Walter's, I could talk to him."

"No." It was loud and emphatic and it made her start. "You stay out of that."

"Hey." She shoved his shoulder and he looked surprised. Good. "I want to help you, the way you helped me. I want to be the one who makes you forget all about it—and any other trouble you might have. Because that's what you do to me . . . for me."

"Shit." Nick ran a hand through his hair. "You keep doing shit like that and I'll start to think . . ."

"Start to think what?" she urged when he didn't continue.

"That you might really love me."

"But I do, Nick. I love you for who you were, who you are . . . who you'll be. Can you get that? Nothing else matters."

"But other things do matter, Kaylee. I have to finish this in my own way. Do *you* get that?"

"Yes." She tugged hard at his shirt, practically tearing it off his body as the buttons hit the floor and the walls. "I want you, Nick. I don't care about anything else. After all we've been through, I know we can get through anything. I want to get through everything with you. Do you get *that*?"

A small smile quirked the corner of his mouth. "You're manhandling me."

"Just the way you like it."

"Yeah, it is." His head bowed to her shoulder. "I can't refuse you anything, Kaylee. Why the fuck is that?"

"I don't know, but I like it," she told him. "If it makes you feel better, I can't refuse you anything either. So let me help you, even if it's only for a little while."

Finally, Nick stopped arguing, and for that moment, she was back in his arms.

An hour later, Nick left Kaylee sleeping and wandered the kitchen aimlessly, restless energy threatening to overwhelm him.

He knew, just fucking knew that he was definitely in love with her. Probably from the first goddamned moment he saw her. Anger and pain collided with that feeling, until they were all wrapped up together. He didn't have the strength to separate them.

He'd showered, let the water beat down on him until it hurt, in an attempt to soothe the ache that went far deeper than his muscles, and tried not to think about what he needed to do now.

But it wasn't working.

Instead, he went into the bathroom and he threw up.

He spat and saw the blood, and yeah, the childhood ulcer was back.

When he turned to the sink, he caught sight of Jake in the mirror. His brother was standing in the doorway. He still wore his BDUs, was probably just off the helo and had bat-out-of-helled it over here.

Just in fucking time to see him on his knees spitting blood, from the look on Jake's face. Fucking guy moved like a ghost—always had, learned from the necessities of his childhood that it was better to be neither seen nor heard.

"Walter came here to see you? Tell me that's not fucking true, Nick."

"I wish I could." Fuck, his voice was nearly gone.

He brushed his teeth and when he turned around, Jake had moved away from the doorway and into the kitchen. When Nick followed him he found his brother at the stove, watched him silently brew him the special tea that Maggie and Dad used to make whenever his voice was starting to go. Which was pretty often.

But Jake, who never went into the kitchen except to demand that someone make him food . . . well, fuck.

"Here. Drink." Jake slid the mug to him. Nick drank, let the liquid filled with herbs and honey soothe his throat and his ulcer at the same time.

Fucking Cajun magic bullshit.

Jake spoke calmly. Too calmly. "Chris told me about the reporter you're fuc—"

Nick slammed the mug down and stood so fast the chair hit the floor behind him. Jake held up his hands in silent surrender, a funny look on his face. "The reporter you like. Is that better?"

Nick nodded, sat and finished the rest of the tea in one gulp, and waited with his best friend and brother, the way they had so many times before this, bonding quietly. Not talking about the fear they both felt.

"Jesus Christ, I leave for a few days and you're with a reporter, Chris is screwing some FBI agent and you're all running off to fucking Africa." Jake slid a hand through his hair, far too long to ever pass for a military cut. "What the hell's happening, Nick?"

"I need to finish things with the Winfields," he admitted finally.

"Sometimes it's better to just leave things alone." Jake's voice didn't hold judgment, but Nick still felt the fight rise up in him, familiar and strong as though they were both fourteen again and fight or flight was the only way they operated. "Sometimes it's the best course of action."

"When you're fourteen and you don't know how to fight, maybe it is. But I'm not fourteen anymore, and I'm tired of running, of fighting it."

"Fighting didn't do me any good." Jake's eyes got that faraway look, the way they always did when he thought about his past and his abusive stepfather.

"Fighting got you the woman you love," Nick pointed out and then he told Jake what Chris hadn't: "Kaylee—she's the reporter. She knows."

Jake sat like a stone. "She knows what, Nick? Because I know you didn't keep your secret all this time so you could spill it to a reporter."

"She's not just a reporter to me. And I didn't spill it to her—she saw Walter come here."

"Fuck." Jake slammed a palm down on the table, making

the cups jump. "Do you really think she's going to keep your secret? She's probably got the whole story written already."

"She's had plenty of opportunity to do that—and she hasn't."

"Tell me what happened in Africa."

Nick told Jake everything, from the story of Aaron to what happened with Kaylee.

"Do you love her?" Jake asked finally.

"Yes. And don't worry—she's not going to expose me."

The fear and tension that ran between the two men was palpable, but slightly dissipated when Kenny Waldron walked through the back door and hugged both of the men tight. Or tried to—Jake pulled away from Kenny, his face drawn.

"Did you know about this? Why didn't you tell me?" Jake demanded of his father.

"No one interfered when you were screwing things up," Kenny said quietly, and Jake backed down, the way he did only for their father.

Kenny not only had their love, he had their respect, and it was a powerful combination, especially for Nick and Jake, who'd never been taught to respect anyone or anything.

Chris came in behind Kenny and it was the four of them, the way it had been so many times before around the old oak table. Except things were different, were changing. Soon, there would be a fifth here—Isabelle, the woman Jake was marrying.

"Where's Kaylee now?" Dad asked.

"She's sleeping. I want to be with her, Dad. It's not that

I don't trust her with what she knows. It's the rest of the free fucking world."

"I know that."

"How do you always know this shit?"

"Your heart makes the decision before your head. That's what I see, the heart," Kenny explained patiently.

"How am I going to move forward if I keep getting pulled back by the Winfields?"

"I want to help you, Nick. Stop you from getting on the train again, so to speak. But you've already got this figured out. Now you have to decide how far you're going to go to fix it."

"I've already decided. I'm talking to Walter," Nick said finally.

"No. Fucking. Way." Jake's voice was controlled but there was no mistaking the anger in his tone. "You're not asking that man for anything."

"He owes me. After all he's done, the least he can do is make an announcement to tell the fucking press that I'm dead." Nick glared at his brother as Kenny put a hand on both their arms.

"I'm not letting you two fight this one out, not this time," Kenny told them as Chris leaned back in his chair and stared up at the ceiling and sighed.

"Let them fight—better than having them act like women," he drawled.

Kenny shot Chris a look. "That's enough, all of you. We don't need any more trouble. Let me speak with Walter for you."

"What happened to it being my mountain?" Nick asked and got silence as a response. And so he pulled out his phone and he made the call he'd been itching to make since he returned home, as his brothers and Dad watched. Then he shut the phone and told them, "Walter's waiting for me. I'm making the drive to New York. When Kaylee wakes up, just tell her I'll be back as soon as I can."

"I'll go with you," Jake told him. "Or Chris or Dad, or even Kaylee. You shouldn't do this alone."

"You and I both know that alone is the only way I can do this. It's finally time." With that, Nick walked out of the house and got into his car and made the long drive to New York.

The Winfield's house was grand—grand and stifling. Nick tried to think if there were any good memories here, even one that would soften the blow. But then he remembered that he'd been allowed in the house very few times, that for the most part his home had been the Manhattan brownstone, with the various nurses and sitters who'd been paid to watch him.

"Mr. Winfield will see you now." The large security man attempted to pat him down. Shit like that did not sit well with Nick—never had—and the touch to his shoulder immediately had him putting the man to his knees with his arm twisted behind his back.

"Josh, leave him. He's fine." Walter stood in the doorway of his office. Nick vaguely remembered him doing that, when they were both younger, when Walter had cut an imposing figure standing in that doorway. When Nick had wanted nothing more than to gain access to that room, to his father and his family.

Now Nick was granted that right, stepped into the room—and by doing so, even by stepping into this house, he was entering what would've been his life.

The thing was, if he'd continued down the same path he'd been on before he left the Winfields, stealing cars and getting into trouble, he'd have no doubt received the same treatment his uncle Billy had at the time he'd been pressed into military service. Nick would've ended up in the same exact place he was now, though he'd be a much different man.

Fucking synchronicity.

Nick waited until Walter shut the door and then he turned to face his biological father. "I want you to set me free."

Walter looked pained. "I did that a long time ago. I hurt you more than a father should ever hurt a son."

"I want you to declare me dead, in public, once and for all. I don't care how you do it—you can say I was killed in Iraq, or that you found my body years ago and never said anything. Whatever it takes."

"I can't do it."

"You owe me that." His voice rose angrily for a second until he tamped it down. "Please. Do this for both of us. You know it's the only way. There's no going back for us, so let's just move forward. Make it so I don't have to look over my shoulder all the time for the press. Even your other children think I'm dead. Now's the time to let it all go. I can't give you the forgiveness you're looking for—but with this, I can move on. That's got to be enough for you."

Walter turned away from him, stared out the window. Nick watched the broad shoulders crumple for just a second and then looked away, because he didn't want to feel this, not any of it.

"I'll do it," Walter said finally, without turning around. "First thing in the morning, I'll call a press conference. I'll tell them Deidre wanted me to wait until after she'd passed to make the announcement. I'll make sure the press believe me. Now please, just go."

Nick opened his mouth to say something, to thank Walter, but he couldn't. Relief flooded him as he turned and left the room and then the house, closing the door behind him.

The path out had been different this time—the back exit and not down the trellis and across the side lawns—but the feeling was as familiar to him as the other path had been all those years ago. But the freedom was even more of a rush this time, because the fear was finally gone.

And when he walked out of the gate to the street where he'd parked, he stopped short. Because just like all those years ago, Jake was there waiting for him. Had followed his ass all the way to New York without Nick noticing.

Jake wasn't alone either. There were Chris and Kenny. And Kaylee. All waiting to bring him home.

Kaylee waited while he hugged Dad first, and then Jake and Chris. And then the men moved to the side, and finally, he put his arms around Kaylee.

"He's going to do it—hold a press conference and declare me dead."

Kaylee had tears in her eyes. "I know how hard this was for you. How hard it's all been."

"It's done now. I can move on . . . with you."

Now she smiled. "I can keep a secret, Nick. This secret.

All of your secrets. I want to keep them." She pressed her lips to the side of his neck.

"There's going to come a time when what I do compromises your job. And vice versa." Nick moved away, pressed his fists to his temples for a second. "You became a journalist because of your mother—I'm not going to let you leave that behind. I know what it's like to love your job."

"You're not *letting* me do anything." Her eyes blazed. "I make my own choices. I chose to call you that first time. And the second time. So if I tell you that, for me, finding love trumps my career ambitions, you have no right to tell me otherwise. I can opt out of stories that concern the military—I can make it work. And if I can't, I can't."

Nick could swear he felt tears rise up behind his eyes at her words. The last time he cried was at Maggie's funeral. Since then, the walls were up high enough that no one had breached them.

Kaylee had definitely climbed those walls.

"I know you thought that you weren't capable of love—that you wouldn't be able to share your full life with someone. But you did share it with me. And I'm not letting you take it back," she told him. "I love you."

"Come here." He heard the gruffness in his own voice, barely trusted it. And when she walked back into his arms and looked up at him, he told her, "I do love you, Kaylee Smith. Probably from the second you stole my damned car."

"Our car now."

He nodded. "Yeah, our car now."

Nick helped Kaylee into their car, and then he started it up, and together they followed Jake's Blazer and the rest of his family toward the best kept secret of all—home.

If you loved
TOO HOT TO HOLD,
don't miss the third and final book in
Stephanie Tyler's blazingly hot trilogy

HOLD
ON TIGHT

Coming January 2010

Read on for a sneak peek inside . . .

CHAPTER

1

So I may be tainted in my truth
When I claim I'm bullet-proof
But every half-assed assault
Has been a death by default
—Abby Ahmad, "Tri-Me"

Chief Petty Officer Chris Waldron knew he looked like hell and he felt a hell of a lot worse.

He didn't know how long he'd spent strapped to a bed staring up at a plaster ceiling in some kind of drug-induced haze while his body healed and his mind remained numb.

He floated in and out of consciousness, mainly because the doctors kept waking him up, which was really starting to get on his last fucking nerve.

He'd been a SEAL for eight years, long enough to know that complaining never did anyone much good. But inside his head—man, he was bitching up a storm and a half.

Someone had shoved his iPod earbuds in, and until the

battery died he'd been slightly contented listening to AC/DC's *Back in Black* album in a continuous loop.

He woke himself up singing the chorus of Creedence's "Green River" out loud. The nurse was staring at him as if he was crazy and normally he'd be all *Oh honey, I could give you some of this crazy if you'd just lay yourself down here.*

But not today.

Because even though she was pretty, with kind eyes, he realized on some level that his mind could take longer to heal than his body if he didn't start dealing with what had happened. Sex wasn't the answer.

Still, the nurse was so intent on staring at his eyes—the two different colors tended to do that to people—she'd forgotten about the needle she was supposed to inject into his IV tubing. Now the drug that had kept him foggy hovered in his periphery.

He was slower than normal, but still pretty damned fast. The nurse called for the doctor, but it was too late. He'd yanked the needle out and held the IV pole like a weapon, since they'd confiscated all of his.

"Son, it's all right—you're in a U.S. military-base infirmary in Djibouti. The nurse was trying to give you your pain meds, but we can talk about it first." The doctor spoke slowly while Chris stared at him, willing himself to believe that, but his body was still reacting—his hand held tight to the IV pole in a fight-or-flight response, and since flight wasn't an option, he was going to bash whoever came near him with the damn pole.

"Chris, come on, man—put that down before you fuck someone up."

It was his CO's drawl, heavy like thick syrup, which meant Saint was as tired as Chris felt.

"No more drugs," Chris told the doctor while he continued to retain possession of the *I won't take any more drugs* pole.

The doctor looked at Saint, who said, "If he needs them, he'll ask."

The doc relented, motioned to Chris for his arm, which was bleeding all over the place, and Chris reluctantly let go of the metal pole.

"Sorry, Ma'am," he told the nurse as she put a bandage on his arm.

"You've got a great singing voice, Chief," she said with a smile. Saint rolled his eyes because normally one comment like that could make Chris a one-man concert. But even though the music was still playing in his head, all he did this time was say, "Thanks."

He remained seated at the edge of the bed once he and Saint were left alone, struggling to get his equilibrium back. He stared down at his bare feet and felt a sudden urge to rip the hospital gown off his body. Which he did promptly, threw it on the ground, asking, "How long have I been here?"

"Twenty-four hours. You made it to the helo on your own steam."

He didn't remember that fully. The memories were there, the edges blurred, bleeding into the bigger, slow-moving picture like he was attempting to see clearly underwater.

Cam. His teammate's face was the last thing he remembered seeing before he surrendered to the safety of unconsciousness. "Where's Cam?"

"Already in Germany—he stopped by to see you before he left."

"I remember. Thought I was hallucinating."

"You're getting transported there yourself at 0500 for evaluation before they'll take you home."

Chris took stock of the various bruises and contusions on his body—a few stitches here and there, but nothing major. His head, however, was a different story. There was a definite aching throb behind what was left of the narcotics. "Concussion?"

Saint nodded. "No fractures. You're pretty banged up, but you should've been hurt a hell of a lot worse. They kept you here so they could run some tests."

Chris closed his eyes for a second and said a silent prayer to his momma, who he was sure was responsible for that one. "Do Jake and Nick know about this?"

"It's been all I could do to hold them back. They're calling every hour on the hour. They weren't going to tell your father but—"

"He knows." His dad always knew when things went wrong—it was next to impossible to hide anything from a parent with second sight. His brothers would've found out by the more traditional routes and were, no doubt, freaking. Not that he would've been any different had one of them been in his position.

"Are you awake enough to answer some questions for me?" Saint asked.

It wasn't really a question, since Saint had already pulled up a chair. His CO was remarkably patient, but Chris could tell it was wearing thin.

He didn't relish this conversation one bit, thought

about Jake and Nick and wished his brothers were here with him now.

He wondered if he'd make it through this without throwing up.

It wasn't everyday that you had to tell a man how his best friend had died. Their team was close, for sure, with so much history tying all of them together. This was the first tear in the fabric. "Yeah, I'm awake enough."

"What's the last thing you remember about what happened with Mark—what did he say?" Saint stared at him steadily, searching for some kind of answer before Chris even began speaking.

"He told me he was going in, against Josiah's orders. He told me to stay put. I tried to talk him out of it, but he pulled rank. I don't remember him going in, Saint. I remember every other fucking thing . . . but all I remember is Mark's hand on my shoulder and then . . ."

And *then* Josiah, the FBI member of the Joint Task Force team and the man in charge of the Op, was arguing with them, angry that Mark had gone in against Josiah's direct order to stand down. Chris and Cam insisted on going into the embassy—which was already taking heavy fire—but they were at least fifteen minutes behind Mark for the hostages. Inside was chaos—they both heard Mark yelling down the hall but they couldn't get that far without leaving the ambassador in greater jeopardy.

"We made a decision to get the ambassador and his wife out and then go back in for Mark," Chris said. "Everything was happening at once and we had a split second."

"Don't second-guess it."

Chris nodded, swallowed hard. "I was just outside the

building—Cam was maybe twenty feet ahead of me, with the ambassador and his wife and their kids close behind. I was backing him up."

"Were you alone?"

Chris thought hard. "No, Josiah was with me."

Chris and Josiah were providing cover, with Chris ready to go back in for Mark, when the explosion rocked the building. He'd been thrown hard, woke up maybe half an hour later, ears ringing and still looking for Josiah and then for Mark.

"And then they killed him," Saint spoke quietly, his voice tight with anger. "The rebels killed Mark and took him away from there so they could have an American trophy rather than leave him in the building to die in the explosion. There are already reports that have the rebels claiming they killed a U.S. Navy SEAL after they'd gotten him to give them some classified information about anti-terrorism initiatives."

"There's no way Mark would've given intel." The rebel soldiers might have killed him in the most inhumane way imaginable, but they'd never have broken him. Chris was sure of that.

"His body still hasn't been found." Saint spoke quietly, stared at the white wall of the hospital room, a tinge of disbelief in his voice that this was really happening. His jungle greens were fresh, his blond hair damp, as if he'd just showered, but there were circles under his normally bright blue eyes, his mouth pulled into a tight, grim line.

Saint and Mark had come up through BUD/S together, had served in Coronado and had come to Virginia to take charge of Team Twelve.

To leave Mark behind in this country left a knot in Chris's stomach that no amount of IV drugs could take care of. No body meant no closure, signified a failure. "I'm sorry, Saint."

"Don't give me that *sorry* bullshit, Chris. Mark died doing what he loved. You did everything you could, so fuck the guilt. He'd kill you for it." Saint's words were more than ironic, and more than true, and still Chris knew it would be a long time before he was able to let any of this go.

"They'll keep looking?"

"If they don't, I will. I already told the admiral that." Saint stood, looked toward the small open window, jaw clenched for a second before getting back to business. "You should put some clothes on. There's an FBI agent who needs to hear what you've got to say in more detail."

FBI. *Jamie.*

And he didn't bother to ask Saint if it was her coming to question him, because he could sense her, in the hall, maybe right outside the door.

He caught himself rubbing the fingertips on his left hand together lightly.

"Yeah, it's her," Saint said, catching the familiar, pensive sign that meant Chris was processing something important.

For as far back as he could remember, he'd been different, stood apart from everyone but his momma and dad, because he knew things.

Over the years, he'd attempted to convince himself that he was only dealing with a sharper, more refined instinct, that he'd merely honed something others never took the trouble to do. His brothers called it *psychic Cajun bullshit* even though they knew, the way Chris himself did, that there was much more to it than that. More than he wanted to think about right now, and so he forced his palm flat against the sheet as Saint asked, "Are you ready?"

Chris wondered how long Jamie had been here, if she'd questioned Cam before he left. She hadn't come in to see him before this—he'd have to be dead not to remember that. "You can let her in."

The Joint Task Force Chris had been a part of on this mission had consisted of himself and Mark; Josiah Miller, a hostage negotiator for the FBI; a Force Recon Marine named Rocco Martin whose specialty was languages; and a Delta operative named Cameron Moore who had extensive knowledge of the kidnappers as well as the area.

It was a relatively straightforward mission: rescue the four kidnapped UN peacekeepers, the American ambassador and his movie-star wife, who worked as an ambassador of peace in many war-torn countries, and their two adopted children. Africa was her newest project—hence, the massive publicity when she and the ambassador arrived in the Sudan.

That was never a good thing in a country like this.

As of today, the ambassador and his family were safe, the UN peacekeepers had been assassinated and all of the men on the Joint Task Force were dead except for Chris and Cam.

Chris reluctantly pulled on a pair of sweats that Saint had brought him, the pain coming on stronger now. But the pain was good—he needed to feel that after days and days of numbness. The burning hot grief was as fresh as if time had stood still while he was out cold.

Nothing was ever going to be the same, especially not when Special Agent Jamie Michaels walked into his hospital room. Her stride was confident, more than necessary, as if trying to hide her hesitancy in seeing him again.

He couldn't blame her—he'd walked away from her two months ago in the DRC and hadn't gotten in touch with her since.

To be fair, she hadn't exactly been knocking down his door either.

"You know Agent Michaels," Saint said, acknowledging the elephant in the room as he pulled his own chair closer to Chris in a show of support.

"How are you feeling, Chief Petty Officer Waldron?" She was all business, addressing him formally, although there was an edge of softness to her tone that only Chris could discern. He'd heard that same softness when her naked body had pressed against his.

"Let's get this over with." He slid back into the bed and yanked the covers roughly over his bare chest, more as a shield than for any particular modesty, and out of respect for the job she was here for.

To have to talk about this, time and time again, was hard enough. To have to share every last vulnerability in front of Jamie made every primal instinct scream.

It's not Jamie—it's Special Agent Michaels standing here watching you.

He rubbed his cheek, bruised and tender from where he landed after the embassy exploded in front of him, remembered cracking his nose back into place on his way to the helo.

She remained standing, nearer to the window than to

him. She had a pad on the sill, pen in hand, and she kept her eyes focused on his. "Can you confirm that your team could not save the UN peacekeepers?"

Chris's hands fisted the sheets tightly. "Do you think you'd be here asking me these questions if the mission had gone well?"

"Are you going to answer the question?"

"You don't want to fuck with me now—if you're not going to ask real questions, get out."

"I'm trying to make this easy on you, Chief Petty Officer."

"Well, thank you for that, Agent Michaels. I sure as shit appreciate it." His voice was guttural and Saint shot him a warning look. But he ignored it, too busy watching Jamie.

She didn't react, didn't blink. He wanted to see something from her, but she had her game face on.

It was time for him to put his on as well. If nothing else, he owed calm and collected to Mark Kendall.

It was Mark's own words that came to mind now, a speech he'd given to the new BUD/S recruits during their first Evade and Escape session.

Mark, who'd been captured twice before and escaped, had used his own experiences to pound the recruits under his charge. *Capture comes when you least expect it. Sometimes it's because you lost focus momentarily. Sometimes it's because you let your guard down when you shouldn't have.*

In real life, letting your guard down happens. In combat, it should never happen.

When anyone would ask Mark if he felt like he had nine lives, he would always answer, *No one's that lucky.*

"I'm going to cut the title crap, call everyone by their first names. I know that's not how you like to operate—"

"I can live with that," she told him, and at least she was focusing on him and not Saint. Progress.

He fought an urge to drop his head into his hands and rub his temples. "You know the mission was to rescue a group of UN peacekeepers who'd been kidnapped outside Khartoum along the road to the British Embassy. They were with an American ambassador and his wife, who were traveling to a meeting with the Sudanese government because they're trying to adopt a child from the country."

"And they had their children with them," she added.

"Yes." Losing an American ambassador would be bad enough—losing an internationally beloved movie star and her two small children would've put an international spotlight on both the kidnapping and the failure of the United States to protect their own. It would lead to copycat kidnappings and a breakdown in communications at a time when Homeland Security needed to gain much more cooperation from the Sudanese government. "That trip was a nightmare from the beginning—way too much publicity and not nearly enough protection. They didn't even bring a bodyguard with them to the embassy—a show of good faith."

"I guess they thought that the publicity would protect them," Jamie mused. "That and the peacekeepers."

He didn't answer that, still couldn't get over what the ambassador had done in leaving his family wide open like that.

Jamie pressed on. "From what I've read, your instructions

were specific—you were given an exact time and place to meet the rebel soldiers and make the trade."

Except there wasn't going to be a trade. The United States didn't play that way. The trade was supposed to have been a surprise takeout of the rebels. Nothing Chris and his team hadn't done before. Working with the Joint Task Force was new, but all of the men were more than qualified to pull the mission off.

"We arrived hours earlier than the meeting," he explained. "We were on the ground waiting by 0200, and we knew something was off." In fact, all of them had gotten an instant sense of goatfuck.

That was the problem with covert missions—they were so classified, so secret that sometimes getting help to the correct areas was difficult, if not near impossible.

"But you didn't leave—didn't radio anyone for clarification, correct?" she asked.

"No, we didn't. We made the decision as a group to move forward. We had the cover of night on our side."

"And by going in early, weren't you afraid of compromising the lives of the peacekeepers?"

He forced his voice to be dispassionate. "Those men had been dead for a long time—probably since the night they'd been kidnapped."

The mud-and-brick makeshift structure where the trade was to have taken place was still hot from the warmth of the day, the stench of death overpowering from the second they'd opened the door. Without even closing his eyes, he could still see the faces of the four men who'd been hanged, the blood pulled from their faces. It had taken him several long moments before he'd been able to force himself to look away.

Jamie paused for a second, the rat-tat-tat of muffled machine-gun fire echoing around the building—a near-constant, most familiar sound in this part of the world. "The ambassador and his wife weren't among the dead."

"No. There wasn't anyone else there—I searched the area myself, with Cam. Mark, Rocco and Josiah cut the bodies down and prepared to carry them back to the beach to the LZ."

But the blast of mortar fire rocked the structure, already precariously built into the mountainside, and the men scattered, looking for cover.

"Rocco was killed instantly," he said bluntly. "The fire-fight cut off comms on our end. When we got the bodies to the beach, we were given intel that the ambassador and his family were being held at the Sudanese Embassy, which was surrounded by Darfur rebels."

"Were you wounded?" she interrupted.

"Most of my injuries occurred after the explosion."

By the time they'd arrived at the embassy—close to dawn—the place was getting rocked. There was as near to a riot as Chris had ever seen, and he and his remaining team members waited quietly by the back wall, assessing the situation.

The carnage was everywhere, victims splayed all along the main area—men, women and children indiscriminately murdered.

But there were signs of life—signs that none of them wanted to see or hear. More rebel soldiers than their group of four could effectively deal with.

Of course, that didn't matter—each of them was more than willing to go in, despite their injuries from the earlier skirmish.

But Josiah refused that plan. "We're not going in. It's suicide."

Mark hadn't argued at that time, but Cam had, the pain in his face evident.

Seven hours later, even as Cam and Chris escorted the ambassador and his wife onto the helo, that pain was still there, as if etched forever in the man's features.

It was the screams that had gotten to them, had most likely been what forced Mark into the building against Josiah's orders. Chris had always thought he could get lost inside his own mind, the way he did during capture training exercises. But nothing could've prepared him for the gut-wrenching sounds of the ambassador's wife's cries.

"So Mark Kendall disobeyed a direct order from Josiah."

"Mark sacrificed himself so we could get the ambassador and his family out of there," Chris shot back.

"Did everyone agree with his decision?"

"I was the only one he told, until Josiah realized he'd gone. At that point, the three of us took a vote—Josiah still said no to going in but Cam and I disagreed. Josiah wasn't happy about that—he advised we stay put and refused to come into the embassy with me and Cam. But when I came out the back door, Josiah was there, waiting for me. Ready to give cover."

"How did things escalate from the rescue to the explosion to what happened afterward?"

What happened afterward... What a nice way to put it.

Made it sound like he sat down and had tea after the entire embassy exploded instead of waking up facedown in the dirt, head pounding and ears ringing.

Even now, he still smelled the burning fire, the aftermath of the explosion, as if it was embedded in his senses. "I saw the rebel soldiers carrying Mark's body out of the embassy. The next thing I knew, the building exploded. When I woke up, most of the building was down—I couldn't find any of my team members. I circled what was left of the building, looking for signs of life. Still saw none of my team and ascertained that my best course of action was heading to the LZ for backup.

"Who was at the helo when you arrived?"

"Cam."

"So he'd left everyone behind."

He let his gaze flick over her coolly for a few seconds, wondering if he could make her squirm at all.

Nothing. Fuck. "His job was to get the ambassador and his wife and children to safety. That was his charge—his order from Josiah."

"And what's the last thing you remember about Josiah—the last order he gave you?"

"One minute he was next to me. The next, there was no sign of him." Chris heard the small break in his voice, blamed the dizzying combination of exhaustion, pain and grief.

"What is the last order you received from Josiah?" she persisted.

He practically shot up in bed, which startled her. "There was none, Jamie. At that point, there were no more orders."